Henry Samuel Baynes

Horæ Lucanæ

a biography of Saint Luke, descriptive and literary

Henry Samuel Baynes

Horæ Lucanæ
a biography of Saint Luke, descriptive and literary

ISBN/EAN: 9783337343552

Printed in Europe, USA, Canada, Australia, Japan

Cover: Foto ©Andreas Hilbeck / pixelio.de

More available books at **www.hansebooks.com**

HORÆ LUCANÆ:

A BIOGRAPHY OF SAINT LUKE,

DESCRIPTIVE AND LITERARY.

BY

HENRY SAMUEL BAYNES,

AUTHOR OF THE "LIFE OF CLAUDE BROUSSON, DOCTOR OF LAWS AND ADVOCATE OF
PARLIAMENT, AFTERWARDS EVANGELIST OF THE DESERT, AND MARTYR."

" What thanks sufficient, or what recompense
Equal have I to render thee, divine
Historian, who thus largely hast allay'd
The thirst I had of knowledge, and vouchsafed
This friendly condescension to relate
Things else by me unsearchable."
Paradise Lost, vii. 5-10.

LONDON:
LONGMANS, GREEN, READER, & DYER.
1870.

PREFACE.

In the books of Holy Scripture are treasures inexhaustible by the most diligent research. Already are treatises on biblical topics so numerous, that no catalogues do or can comprise all their titles. And when as many more shall have been published, there will still remain incitements for the exercise of every mind disposed towards the study of such topics, capable of prosecuting reflection intent and persevering; and also room for every intelligent exposition of the student's gains. In the province of Revelation, as of nature, the works of the Lord are great, and invite the study of all them that take pleasure therein.

The subject chosen for investigation in the following pages is one of profound interest. Next to the life and epistles of St Paul, the life and literature of St Luke afford the most ample scope for the historian's pen of any New Testament subject, excepting the supreme subject of all. A writer of the fourth portion of the New Testament; the chief of the companions of St Paul, and the most fruitful of all his fellow-labourers in planting Christianity in Asia Minor and Europe, the first historian of the Churches of Christ, who himself occupied a large share in their history; and whose writings seem to us, on reading them, like listening to the voice of a familiar friend; that of this benefactor there exists no separately-issued biography appears remarkable; all that is to be found concerning him being notices contained in the notes of expositors, in the several lives of the Apostles and Evangelists, in dictionaries of the Bible, and in occasional articles published in periodicals. And how vague and contradictory are these in their statements, is too well known to the student.

A resolve to examine carefully the question of Luke's identity was undertaken by the writer as a biblical exercise, and from the conclusion acquired by that argument, it was resolved to pursue it in its biographical sequences. Henceforward, therefore, various intervals of his leisure, extending over twelve years, were devoted to an investigation of particulars calculated to accomplish his object.

It was a lament of a celebrated author, that there was " a deficiency of demonstrative writing." And it is still a grief that many are the essays and expositions issued, which, through defect or design, serve more for guides to doubt than aids to persuasion.

The only attempt that has been made (known to the present writer) to treat Luke's biography by deductions and arguments of a uniformly *definite* character consists of a series of five papers comprised in a volume entitled " *Fragments*," forming a supplement to an edition of Calmet's " Dictionary of the Bible," edited and published by Charles Taylor in the year 1800. In that volume those papers seem to have lain as buried until recognised by Dr Edward Robinson, the explorer of Palestine, who incorporated the essence of them into an edition of Calmet's Dictionary edited by him, and published at Boston in America in 1838. Charles Taylor was a pioneer of the host of biblical critics of the present century in this country. He died in 1821. He was elder brother of the Rev. Isaac Taylor of Ongar, and therefore uncle of Jane and Anne, and of the late Isaac Taylor, author of several important works.

In the following chapters consistency of design and execution is maintained at least. Proceeding in an unfrequented path, and often upon disputed grounds, controversies intercept the progress, and several are the encounters that are required to be made with parties holding adverse positions. At the first few steps, it was thought that the contests would have been with few others, save some of the ghosts of tradition. But the case proved otherwise, and there has been found more to oppose in the opinions of recent and contemporary than in older authors, some of the latter proving the writer's potent allies. These contests have been unavoidable. If the writer had succumbed before adverse parties, his conduct had appeared courteous to them; but by evading the dispute he would have failed in loyalty to truth. Concerning this peril of authorship Bengel has said, " If the student's attention respect the *things* to be advanced, so that he will not suffer himself to be influenced by respect of *persons*, it will be impossible for him to avoid giving offence in one way or another " (" Life of Bengel," p. 260).

And here all kindred is disowned with that purely speculative ingenuity which, exercised upon sacred subjects, is technically called ' *advanced criticism ;* ' and which seems to signify with those who use the term an advance into the region of graduated unbelief concerning the authenticity of the books of Holy Scripture, and the integrity of the several penmen thereof, and concerning the essential divinity of Jesus Christ.

Christians were first called *disciples* and *believers,*

persons, as the terms declare, widely distinct from *sceptics*, by whom Christian believers are taunted with being "*Religious Conservatives*, who in all ages cling to the letter without comprehending the spirit of the Bible" (*Westminster Review*, July 1866, p. 85). Than the conservation of the *literal* Bible there cannot be a more sacred trust; and for understanding it there is no more undeniable canon than that " the Bible is its own best interpreter." Much has been done to illustrate the *letter* of the Bible by the collation of early copies, by philology, by history, by chronology, by geography, by a study of the Eastern manners and mind, and by biography. By the added light of these, the student possesses in the Bible a perennial fountain of divine intelligence. But to comprehend the *spirit* of the Bible belongs to simplicity, and to share its benefits belongs to faith.

In sympathy with the principles revived by the reverend confessors and martyrs in the sixteenth century, and maintained by the cloud of witnesses who, in the seventeenth century, were despoiled of their estates, immured in dungeons, or doomed to the galleys, or murdered, or driven from their homes into exile, the writer makes no other allusion than this to his ecclesiastical fellowship. Occupied with the history of the Primitive Churches, he here shuts himself up to those with which their first historian was interested by personal or other relations.

Repudiating the dark dogma that refuses to whomsoever the right of private judgment upon divinely-revealed topics, and as being adapted to the aim of his present undertaking, he may say, in the words of an Evangelist whose Life he wrote several years ago, " I think I have a right to labour as my conscience dictates, and according to the measure of faith granted to me. I acknowledge that my natural infirmities cannot fail to appear ; nevertheless, it is my constant aim that all that I can do, and all that I can write, may be conformable to the Word of God—my only rule" ("Claude Brousson," p. 91).

Speaking of sustained endeavours, Baron Denon has said, " He who is in constant pursuit of any object, acquires from thence an ability to attain his aim." Whatever may be the judgment that shall be passed respecting the execution of the present work, the writer is persuaded that he has so far accomplished his purpose, that his pages present for the first time a reasonable arrangement of the facts of Luke's history, and afford for the first time, a correction of several venerable inaccuracies concerning it.

For the literary illustration of this Biography the writer has possessed a peculiar advantage. Pursuing the vocation of a librarian, besides the works to which his bibliographical knowledge directed him, numerous were those works, both English and foreign, which, passing through his hands, would not otherwise have been consulted, but which sometimes supplied important materials or suggestions.

But research and observation must have an end. And now arrived at a time of life in which what remains to be done should be done promptly, he commits his studies to the press, entertaining the wish that the reader may derive as much pleasure in a contemplation of the portraiture set before him, as hath been enjoyed gratification by the writer in the process of its development.

London, *April* 30, 1870.

CONTENTS.

CHAPTER VIII.

CHAPTER IX.

CHAPTER X.

CHAPTER XI.

CHAPTER XII.

CHAPTER XIII.

CHAPTER XIV.

CHAPTER XV.

CHAPTER XVI.

CHAPTER XVII.

CHAPTER XVIII.

CHAPTER XIX.

CHAPTER XX.

CHAPTER XXI.

CHAPTER XXII.

CHAPTER XXIII.

CHAPTER XXIV.

CHAPTER XXV.

CHAPTER XXVI.

CHAPTER XXVII.

CHAPTER XXVIII.

CHAPTER XXIX.

CHAPTER XXX.

CHAPTER XXXI.

CHAPTER XXXII.

A BIOGRAPHY OF SAINT LUKE.

CHAPTER I.

THE QUESTION OF IDENTITY.

Λουκᾶς δε και Λούκιος.

THE greatest biographical enigma in the New Testament has been the personality of the writer of the third Gospel. Sharing about an equal part with St Paul in the extent of his contributions to that divine volume, it is wonderful that no adequate attempt has hitherto been made to bring the question of his identity into a course of critical inquisition.

In the authorised version of the New Testament there are the names—*Luke*, Col. iv. 14, and 2 Tim. iv. 11 ; *Lucas*, Philem. 24 ; and *Lucius*, Acts xiii. 1, and Rom. xvi. 21. The object of this argument is to prove that these names, which apparently bespeak three persons, belong to a single individual. The first of these names, *Luke*, is made one with *Lucas*, presently ; for the original word in the first two texts is the same with the third, the three alike being *Loukas*. The variation in the third text may be accounted for by the circumstance that the epistles, from Romans to Jude, were entrusted to seven translators. In two instances the name obtained the English rendering of *Luke* ; but the

A

Epistle to Philemon having perhaps been in the hands of another translator, the name was left *Lucas*, as it stood in the previous versions, which herein followed the Latin Vulgate. There remains, therefore, but two names to be dealt with, *Lucas* and *Lucius*.

Scarcely anything transpires in the early Christian writers concerning Luke besides what is read in, or inferred from, his own writings and those of St Paul; and even some of the notices so derived soon came to be misunderstood. In the second century, Irenæus, attributing the third Gospel (as it is called) to Lucas, wrote, " The Evangelist is indebted for what he relates in his Gospel to those who were witnesses of the life of Christ ;" adding, " he was a companion of Paul." Later in the same century, Tertullian tells the same, with this addition, " The Gospel of Lucas is often attributed to Paul." In the third century, Origen more intelligently said, "Lucas wrote the Gospel commended by Paul in the Second Epistle to the Corinthians, and published it for the use of Gentile converts ;" adding this other important note, " There are persons who regard the name of *Lucas* and *Lucius* as both alike signifying the Evangelist."

In the fourth century, Eusebius wrote, "*Lucas*, by birth an Antiochian, by profession a physician, for the most part accompanied Paul; and being diligently conversant with the rest of the apostles, has left us two books, written by divine inspiration, lessons that are medicinal unto souls which he procured from them. The one is the Gospel, which he professes to have written as they communicated it to him ; the other, the Acts, not of such things as he had received by report, but of what he had seen with his own eyes " (Eccles. Hist., iii. ch. 4).

Fifty years later, in the same century, Gregory Nazianzen says, " Lucas wrote for the Greeks."

What was known concerning Luke in the regions of the

West, was but an echo of the small intelligence of the East; the sum whereof was told by Jerome at the close of the fourth century. Jerome studied for some time in Rome, and afterwards repaired to Palestine, where, in a monastery at Bethlehem, he prepared, by request of Pope Damasus I., a new version of the Bible for the Latin Churches. He also compiled a "Catalogue of Ecclesiastical Writers," which supplies prefaces to several books in some editions of the Latin Bible. His account of Luke relates, "Lucas, a physician of Antioch, as his writings indicate, a follower of the apostle Paul, and his companion in all his travels, wrote a Gospel, of which Paul spake saying, 'We have sent with him the brother whose praise is in all the churches;' and to the Colossians, 'Lucas, the beloved physician, saluteth you;' and to Timothy, 'Only Lucas is with me.' When Paul says my Gospel, he signifies the volume of Lucas. And not only from Paul did he derive his Gospel, who was not with Christ in the flesh, but from the other apostles, as he declares in the beginning of his Gospel; and the Acts of the Apostles he composed as he saw them. He lived eighty-four years. He had no wife. He was buried at Constantinople, to which city his bones, with those of Andrew the apostle, were transferred."

Upon consulting antiquity for evidence, it is discouraging, in all historical researches, to find how fallible and contradictory is human testimony, and how perplexing are the aberrations of tradition. If, as Eusebius and Jerome have said, Luke was a native of Antioch, the present argument fails at the threshold. But is their assertion unimpeachable? Quite otherwise. Dr Lardner, who edited and expounded the largest collection of testimonies for the "Credibility of the Gospel History" ever published, has observed, "The accounts given of Luke by Eusebius, and Jerome after him, that he was a native of Antioch, may justly be suspected. We do not find it in any other writer before Eusebius. Probably it was the invention of some conjectural critic. But all this was taken up without any ground or authority. Jerome only follows Eusebius. He does not seem to have any information about it from others."

It is likewise said by Dr Enfield, in his " History of Philosophy," " Had Eusebius been more free from prejudice, had he taken more care not to be imposed upon by spurious authorities, his works would have been more valuable." And by Leclerc, in his " Life of Eusebius " it is observed, " One may complain of Eusebius because he has inserted several fables in his 'Ecclesiastical History.' " It may be added, Eusebius lived at a period when the allocation of saints' names, and the distribution of their mortal relics, formed a large part of ecclesiastical business, and in which business he himself took no small part.

Antioch was the Metropolitan Church of Syria. Luke had resided there for several years. And if it had been customary to say concerning him, that he was of Antioch, in the same sense that it was said of Jesus that Capernaum was His own city, it required only the stroke of a pen to impart to Antioch the higher credit of having been Luke's birthplace.

And then, with respect to Jerome's testimony, in following Eusebius in one error, he himself stumbles upon another, asserting that Luke in his writings indicates that he was of Antioch ; whereas, in no place in his writings is such an indication to be found. But this is found, that he has written, " Now there was in the Church at Antioch *Lucius of Cyrene* " (Acts xiii. 1).

In these early notices of the Evangelist, the name of *Lucius* has occurred only once. That it is there is an important circumstance for this argument. It transpires about midway between the time of the Evangelist and the commencing ages of ecclesiastical fables. In the passage wherein Origen reports that "Lucas and Lucius were said to signify the same individual," is found just the evidence required: and it is all the more important that it is reported by the father of biblical learning. Of course, as a Greek writer, the Orientals were always accustomed to call the Evangelist *Loukas*, even as an Englishman calls him Luke ; and therefore that those to whom Origen refers were among the more learned of his contemporaries may reasonably be concluded. With others, the identity would soon pass out of recognition. Λούκιος ὁ Κυρηναῖος would soon come to be regarded as another person than Λουκᾶς ὁ ἰατρὸς, Luke the physician.

Moreover, the error being embodied in standard sources of information, the continual assertion by doctors of the Church that Lucas was of Antioch, finally excluded all consideration concerning Lucius the Cyrenian. Hence, finding no account of this Lucius, true to her apocryphal character, the medieval Roman Church invested the name with a fictitious individuality and history, and thereby claimed another saint for its calendar. In that prodigious repertory, the *Acta Sanctorum*, consisting of fifty-six folio volumes, Lucius is conducted from Antioch, and consecrated Bishop of Laodicea ; and his anniversary is fixed for April 22. From that great authority for the legend, of course, no Romanist will ever dissent. By others, misunderstanding the case, no attempt is made to provide Lucius with a distinct biographical status. As specimens of the manner in which this question of the identity of Lucas and Lucius is treated by certain Protestant writers, it is found represented in Dr Smith's large "Dictionary of the Bible," under *Lucius,* "It must be observed that the names are clearly distinct. The missionary companion of St Paul was not Lucius, but Lucas, or Lucanus." And by Dr Alford, under Acts xiii. 1, it is said, "There is no reason to suppose him

(Lucius of Cyrene) the same with Lucas; but on the contrary; for why should Paul in this case use two different names?" By the positiveness of this style, the student is deterred from an inquiry. But, is there, then, no significance in Origen's report? and is an affirmative of the case so utterly beyond the sphere of proof? Perhaps it is not. Peradventure, the case can be so viewed, and such reasons produced as will establish the position that the names Lucas and Lucius mentioned in the New Testament do in fact designate one and the same individual.

The first observation submitted for this argument is, that these names are only different in the respect that one is Greek and the other Latin. During the Roman dominion of Greece, Greek names received a Latin form, and Latin names a Greek form, as circumstances might warrant. Examples of this transformation may be seen by consulting any work on Roman colonial medals and coins. When it is said, with reference to this case, that the Latin form of Loukas (Lucas) was Lucanus, it may be answered, the individual was competent to prefer Lucius. Even at present, Lucas is translated variably in different places in Europe; a person of this name being called in Rome Luca, in Paris, Luc, and in London, Luke. Another observation is, that the occasions upon which the name is found written in its Latin form are both such as warranted its adoption. When it was written by himself, *Lucius the Cyrenian*, Luke was *in the city of Rome*, where he had been accustomed to that name for more than two years. Moreover, as his treatise was addressed to a friend who is supposed to have held a post under the Roman Government, it would seem decorous for Luke, in writing from the capital of the empire, to recognise his own political status as a Roman citizen.

The other occasion upon which the name is written *Lucius* had a similar warrant. Occurring in the epistle addressed by St Paul *to the Romans*, it was so written to suit that circumstance (xvi. 21). At the mention of the name, as it occurs in this place, several critics protest, "This cannot be the Evangelist, because Lucius is here called by St Paul his kinsman." If, by these critics, the Cyrenian Lucius is not admitted to have been his kinsman, here is the case of another supposed person to be examined. Some writers, to escape the dilemma, propose that the verse should be read, "Timotheus, my work-fellow, and Lucius; also, Jason and Sosipater, my kinsmen, salute you." But the case needs no attempt at evasion. It should be observed that the word συγγενής, translated kinsman, is not always confined to the signification of natural affinity; but is also used figuratively. In this same epistle it is used in two senses. It is used in its primary sense, where the apostle writes, "my kinsmen *according to the flesh*, who are Israelites "(ix. 3). Whilst in the present instance it manifestly refers to a kindred *not* " according to the flesh," to a spiritual relationship. The whole epistle is one urging conciliation, grounded on the great argument of the admission of Gentiles equally with Jews to the privileges involved in the covenant of salvation by faith in Jesus Christ. As a Jew, the writer mourns the exclusion of his brethren, the Jews, because of their unbelief; but, as an apostle to the Gentiles, he not only welcomes these, but concludes his argument by affording to both an exemplification of the spirit with which they should "receive each other." This he does by occupying the last chapter of the epistle with a larger list of names of persons, Jews and Gentiles, whom he salutes, than is to be found in all his other epistles combined, and by affixing to each name some expression of commendation and endearment. Thus, of the persons greeted, and of those whose greetings are reported, six are styled "my kinsmen;" the bearer of the epistle is called " our sister;" and the mother of Rufus is saluted as " his mother and mine." So that, according to those protesting critics, here is presented a family-party, and an incongruous one too ; the kinsfolk of the apostle being Jews and Gentiles, Oriental and Western, indiscriminately. But that the expression "kinsmen" is here used with a different signification, and conformably with the lesson of love urged upon the apostle's correspondents in the context, is further manifested by the request with which the salutations are concluded : " Greet one another with a holy kiss ;" that is, the Jew is to kiss the Greek, and the Greek is to kiss the Jew. In short, the word, " *kinsman* " is applied to Lucius in the same spirit that Titus is styled, " my brother " (2 Cor. ii. 13), and that Timothy is called my own son in the faith (Tim. i. 2) ; and also after the example of the Lord when He said, " The same is my brother and sister and mother" (Matt. xii. 50).

If, then, Lucius was not a natural kinsman of St Paul, there remains no obstacle to the identity of the Lucius here in company with the apostle with Lucius the Cyrenian.

And, again, the correlative character of these names appears in the circumstance that, in those instances in which Lucius is mentioned, Lucas is found to have been in the identical situation. Thus, Lucius was a Greek of Cyrene ; but Lucas was a Greek, as by all acknowledged. Lucius was at Antioch (Acts xiii. 1) ; but Lucas is declared by Eusebius, Jerome, and others, to have been of Antioch. Lucius is associated with prophets and teachers ; but Lucas was a prophet and teacher, being an Evangelist. Lucius was at Corinth upon Paul's second visit to that city, and whereby it happened that his name is mentioned in the Epistle to the Romans, written upon that occasion ; but Lucas was a bearer of the letter that preceded and announced the apostle's visit (2 Cor. viii. 18). That among the Christians at Antioch and at Corinth there were two persons, one *Loukas*, and another with that name Latinised, and at the same time, is not likely. Is it probable that

Paul had two companions having a parallel history such as this? Or was the one the shadow of the other?

Finally this argument is not new. There is a reserve of authors, of permanent reputation, by whom it has been perceived and acknowledged that these two names apply to *one* individual only. That profound interpreter of biblical difficulties, Dr John Lightfoot, nearly two hundred years ago, wrote, under Acts xiii. 1, "Why antiquity has so generally held Luke to be an Antiochian is true in regard to his first appearing there under the name of Lucius, though originally a Cyrenian;" and he remarks, in general, "In both Testaments, the Hebrew of the one and the Greek of the other is, upon occasion, flourished with other languages." Hugo Grotius, a prince in literature, in his Commentary, writes, "I think Lucius mentioned Romans xvi. 21, to be no other than Lucius of Cyrene, and I see no reason to suppose that he was another person than Lucas the physician." The very learned Professor Wetstein, who, in his biblical researches, came twice to England respecting collations for his magnificent edition of the Greek Testament, and maintained a correspondence with the great critic Dr Bentley, explains, under Acts xiii. 1, "Lucius, also called Lucas in Col. iv. 14."

Archdeacon Paley, in his "Horæ Paulinæ," says, "A very slight alteration would convert Λούκιος into Λουκᾶς, Lucius into Luke." Bishop Blomfield, a consummate Greek scholar, in his "Lectures on the Acts," unhesitatingly says, "Luke was the same person as Lucius of Cyrene, and of whom St Paul speaks in the 16th chapter of the Romans;" and he explains, that "in addressing these, St Paul would naturally use the Roman form of Lucius in preference to that of Lucas." Granville Penn, in his unbiassed "Annotations," has this emphatic note, "The name was written differently, according to the Greek or Latin inflection; but in the darkening ages which followed, they became distributed to different imaginary persons" (*Supplement*).

And with reference to the practical bearing of the argument, Dr Major, in the Introduction to his " Exposition of Luke's Gospel," alluding to " these testimonies of many learned men," remarks " If these views are admitted, we have some knowledge of Luke's character and history." It may be added, on the other hand, if these views are rejected, there is known only half of Luke's history.

CHAPTER II.

By the evidence that *Lucas* is also *Lucius*, the biography of the Evangelist obtains a beginning. That he was a Cyrenian appears from his own pen. In the books ascribed to him, his name could only be looked for in the Acts of the Apostles; and only there as, in some manner, an agent in spreading the Gospel. And it is just thus that his name is found in Acts xiii. 1. It occurs in a kind of document, the importance of which has never been sufficiently recognised. This is a list of the persons commanded by the Holy Ghost to separate Barnabas and Saul to their apostolate to the Gentiles. If this list was to be given to the Church, there was left for the writer no alternative than to include his own name therein. Accordingly, and with the precision which such a case required, some distinguishing characteristic is added to the name of each of the individuals comprised in the list: his own being set down as Lucius the *Cyrenian* (not *of Cyrene*, as in the common version). In this epithet, the specialty consists in the fact that a person from a country so remote from Syria should be seen to occupy the station in the Church at Antioch that is ascribed to him. By the preservation of this list, a link is afforded to the biography of the Evangelist, without which the clue had otherwise been missed to some of the most interesting points of his history and character.

So inherent in noble minds is the love of country, that, in a narrative describing actions and events, near and remote, and extending over thirty years, and in some of which the writer was himself engaged, it would be expected that some intimations would be found of his fatherland. The manner in which his name is enrolled in the list alluded to is itself one such intimation ; and another intimation is found in his enumeration of the places whence came the multitude of Jews and proselytes that heard, each in their own tongue, the wonderful works of God on the day of Pentecost (Acts ii. 10). In this instance, there is a signification in Cyrenians being mentioned which at first sight does not appear. Cyrene was the most distant place beyond the scenes of Luke's narratives that is mentioned. Nevertheless, the notices given of it discover, above all that is said of the others, the writer's acquaintance with the country. The strangers gathered in Jerusalem are distinguished by the places whence they came, as Parthians, &c., and dwellers in Mesopotamia. But in speaking of those from Africa, it is said, "in the parts of Libya, about Cyrene." Those parts comprised four out of the five cities called the Libyan Pentopolis, namely, Apollonia, Ptolemais, Arsinoe, Teuchira, and Berenice (Hesperis). These cities lay around the coast of the great semicircular promontory of North Africa; whilst Cyrene, the first of the five, stands on a height gradually receding from the shore, surrounded, in a manner, by them all. No stranger to the country, at that period, it may be supposed, would have given a description of it so geographically correct.

Another instance of his allusion to the country is found in the words " Then arose certain of the synagogue of the *Libyans* and Cyrenians," &c. (Acts vi. 9). " The learned Havercamp," says Granville Penn, " was the first who pointed out the error of the present text in its substitution of the word *Libertines.*" And if a criticism is ever to be governed by analogy and correspondence with parallel scripture, this reading of Havercamp must be accepted.

In this place, " Libyans, Cyrenians, and Alexandrians " are grouped geographically on the one side, and "them of Cilicia and Asia" on the other. It is the same in the preceding passage (Acts ii.) There the dwellers in fourteen different countries are specified, including those " in the parts of Libya about Cyrene," not one being denoted otherwise than geographically. Whereas " Libertines " do not denote "dwellers " in any particular country, but a *condition*, being freed-men of any country whatsoever. The ordinary observation made by commentators is, that by Libertines are here signified descendants of Jewish freed-men at Rome, who had been expelled thence by Tiberius. The congregating of Jews and proselytes together in synagogues, according to the several countries whence they came, and the languages they spake, is understood ; but the notion of a separate synagogue for those *Libertines* introduces an unknown item into Jewish archæology. And, besides, why should these, whether Jews or proselytes, that had been captives, have been congregated in a separate synagogue ? They could be under no ban in Palestine. Libistii and Libystani were the names given by the Romans to the people inhabiting the skirts of the colony of Cyrene. Hence, probably, arose the error in transcribing the text. The Jews of North Africa had always enjoyed the protection of the Romans. In Cyrene itself they were numerous. In Berenice, they were almost the sole inhabitants, and possessed a separate Government of their own. And the city of Borium, situate at the extreme east of Cyrenaica, boasted a synagogue which the Jews assigned to the age of Solomon. This synagogue afterwards became a Christian church. It is only reasonable, therefore, to suppose that the Libyan Jews and proselytes should have possessed one, or even more, of the numerous synagogues in Jerusalem.

And another instance of the mention of Cyrene occurs in

the account of the exodus of the disciples from Jerusalem (Acts xi. 20), where it is said, "And some of them were men of Cyprus and Cyrene." Here the former are represented as journeying homewards ; for Antioch lay near the coast which looked upon the island of Cyprus. But it was the reverse with the others, who travelled in quite a contrary direction from Cyrene. There must therefore have been some special reason which determined the mention of these. Is it not explained in the thirteenth chapter, where Lucius the Cyrenian is himself found at Antioch ?

Cyrene is now reduced to a barbarism which renders intercourse with it adventurous. But it wore another aspect in the time of the Evangelist. It then possessed features adapted indelibly to impress the mind of an educated native, and to influence his taste. It adjoined the Latin colony of Carthage, which stood opposite to Italy, as the Greek colony of Cyrene stood opposite to Greece. The latter colony was founded six hundred years before the Christian era, and it retained its language for twelve hundred years, or until, having been first ravaged by the Persians, A.D. 616, its inhabitants were exterminated by the Arabs. It was surrendered by Apion to the Romans, B.C. 97 ; and thereafter was constituted, including the island of Crete, a Roman province, under the name of Cyrenaica. In consideration of the ready submission of the Cyrenians to the commonwealth, they were endowed with the Roman franchise. The prosperity which at that period so abundantly enriched the shores of the Mediterranean was largely shared by Cyrenaica. Geographically, the colony presented a compact appearance, consisting of a promontory stretching into the sea, the land side having been protected from the encroachments of the nomadic hordes of Libya by military stations. The salubrity of this portion of North Africa was proverbial. Its fertility is spoken of with admiration both by the ancients and by recent travellers.

Herodotus relates that the country had three harvests—First, the fruits near the sea became ready for the harvest and vintage; secondly, those of the middle or hilly region, called the uplands; and thirdly, those on the highest lands—so that there were altogether eight months of gathering time. M. Pacho, of Nice, who, in 1826, published, under the auspices of the French Government, the most complete account of the country that has appeared, relates that, when his caravan arrived upon its confines, the hilly character of the country, the forests that adorned the landscape, the height of the trees, the luxuriance of their foliage, and the verdure of the herbage, impressed his Egyptian and Nubian attendants with wonder and delight. And a more recent traveller writes—"The hills abound with beautiful scenes, some of them exceeding in richness of vegetation, whilst they equal in grandeur anything that is to be found in the Apennines. Cyrene was also celebrated for its flowers, and the ground is still enamelled with a rich flora, indicating how fitting it was to be the garden of the Hesperides, or the abode of the lotoseaters " (Hamilton's "Wanderings in North Africa," 1835).

The city of Cyrene stood on the northern or seaward edge of an extensive plateau, whose elevation is about 2000 feet above the level of the sea. From the summit the ground descends abruptly about 1000 feet to a second plateau, which extends nearly to the sea, and terminates in another abrupt descent. The face of the upper slope presents a succession of hills separated by deep ravines (or wadys). The city occupied two of those hills, and is naturally defended on three sides by deep declivities. It is by the ravine divided into nearly two equal parts, most of the buildings being on the western side. The view from the site of the city is magnificent. East and west is an unbroken prospect, as far as the eye can reach, of a plateau beautifully varied with wood, among which are scattered tracts of barley and corn, and meadows nearly always covered with verdure. Ravines, the sides thickly planted with trees, intersect the country in various directions, and afford channels for the mountain streams in their passage to the sea. The Cyrenians took advantage of the descent in terraces to shape the ledges into roads leading along the side of the hill; and the drives are to this day, it is said, distinctly scored with the marks of the chariot wheels indented in the stony surface. Curiously does this coincide with Pindar's description of Cyrene as "a land of goodly coursers, and a city famed for chariots" ("Pythian," Ode IV.) To the north, looking from the summit, the Mediterranean is visible at about a distance of eight miles; whilst the city, beheld from the sea, with its coronal of temples and palaces, presented a distinguished landmark to the mariner. But of that once splendid city, nothing now is visible but scattered morsels of masonry and sculpture. The sacred spring of Cyre, which attracted the first colonists to the choice of the spot for their capital, murmurs a mournful memory. It still flows from its pristine source, but it no longer attracts the pilgrim to its stream, nor inspires the lay of the poet as once he sung—

> "And let me quaff the Cyrenian spring."
>
> —"Propertius," iv. 6.

"The former splendour and importance of this city and the neighbouring country," says Heeren, "are testified by an abundance of noble ruins; a more accurate research into which every friend of antiquity much desires" ("Manual of Ancient History"). Most of its ruins are buried beneath the soil; but sepulchres innumerable appear. The vicinity of Egypt seems to have inspired the Cyrenians with the same reverence for the dead which distinguished that ancient nation. But instead of erecting pyramids, their mausoleums were cut in the everlasting hills. In these, to the extent of two miles around, is beheld a vast necropolis, a true city of the dead. Upon the face of the hills, and following all their sinuosities, terraces were formed, reached by flights of steps. These terraces, according to the height of the several hills, amount sometimes to ten or twelve in number; each presenting a series of façades to sepulchral grottoes, whose elegance, variety of style, and state of preservation, present a striking contrast to the mutilated relics of sculpture that lie scattered about them. Within the sepulchres are still to be found marble sarcophagi, together with many mural inscriptions and paintings.

An exploration of Cyrene was made in the year 1861 by Lieutenant R. M. Smith, R.E.. and Lieutenant Porcher, R.N.; and as the fruit of their labours the British Museum is enriched with nearly two hundred objects, being chiefly marble statues and statuettes, obtained from what is supposed were the sites of temples of Apollo, Bacchus, and Venus. Amongst them is a full-length statue, larger than life, of a queen of one of the Ptolemies. There is a statue of Aristeus, the philosopher. And, more interesting than all, there is a statue of Apollo, to whom the fountain of Cyre was dedicated, and which was discovered in its immediate vicinity. This statue is seven feet seven inches high. It bears the lyre, having a bow and quiver beside it. A serpent is represented twining round the trunk of a tree, which partly supports the statue. In this combination Apollo is symbolised as Ἰατρόμαντις, the oracular physician. This idol often caught the eye of an inhabitant of Cyrene.

The intellectual character of Cyrene was alike attractive. It was fruitful in men distinguished in philosophy and in arts. An academy was founded there by Aristippus, a disciple of Socrates. Aristippus ridiculed the singularities affected by other philosophers, particularly the stately gravity of Plato, and the rigid abstinence of Diogenes.

When asked what he had gained by philosophy, Aristippus replied, " A capacity of conversing without embarrassment with all classes of men."   Eratosthenes, a native of Cyrene, may be called the father of geographical science. Carneades, of Cyrene, was the founder of a new academy at Athens. Whilst the odes of Callimachus take rank among ancient works of genius. Of these odes an edition was edited by the late Bishop Blomfield ; and they have furnished Dr Major with several philological illustrations for his expository notes upon the Gospel of St Luke, particularly in chap. i. 28 ; iii. 4 ; x. 28 ; xviii. 27 ; xxiii. 31.

An allusion to a Cyrenian reputation is found in Athe-neus' *Deipnophistœ*, or Banquet of Philosophers, book xii. 1. A guest says, " You seem to me to be a man of Cyrene " (to quote from the 'Tyndareum' of Alexis), 'and a companion of Timocrates; for in Cyrene, if you invite any one to supper, there presently arrive twelve others, and ten chariots.' Upon this passage Paul Manutius remarks, " This line from the 'Tyndareum' (a play) of Alexis, Atheneus uses proverbially ; he thereby satirises the insatiable avidity of the student Timocrates in inquiring for books for his reading, and for the purpose of editing them. The saying is applicable to a man of an insatiable love of reading, or to one who is never satisfied with other pleasures." *

It is natural that some of those associations by which Luke had been surrounded should abide in the memory of a native, and that some savour of their character should be traceable in his writings, however long he may have been absent from the scenes. Coincidences with his native predilections are plainly found in Luke's record of the circumstances that a Cyrenian bare the cross of Christ to Calvary ; that Cyrenians, being Jews and proselytes,

---

* " Pauli Manutii Adagia," Venetiis, 1591. Small 4to, p. 1896.

formed one of those companies to whom the gospel was first publicly preached by the apostles after the Lord's resurrection ; that Cyrenians were among those who most fiercely opposed Stephen ; and that Cyrenians were in number of those who first announced the gospel to Greeks at Antioch. Nor less obvious are the reasons which would induce the record of these circumstances. They connected Greeks with the earliest annals of Christianity. These notices gratified those for whom the Cyrenian primarily wrote. They commended the gospel in all regions where the Greek language was spoken. And copies of his books being exported from Alexandria, where they were multiplied, those books, as they were the first which conveyed a knowledge of the gospel to the inhabitants of Cyrenaica by writings, so they continued to be the favourite Scriptures in the African churches, as long as those churches flourished.

But besides the internal evidence of the identity of Lucius of Cyrene and the writer of the Acts of the Apostles, there is also external evidence afforded of an important character. In the manuscript copy of the Evangelists and Acts of the Apostles in Greek and Latin, called the ' Codex Beza,' now in the University Library, Cambridge, there is found in Acts xi. 28, instead of, " Then stood up one of them," this remarkable variation, " And when WE gathered about him," that is, about Agabus. The scene here described was at Antioch. But Lucius the Cyrenian was at this moment in Antioch. This appears from the twentieth verse in this chapter, which says, " Some of the men were of Cyprus and of Cyrene," collated with the first verse of the thirteenth chapter, where the name of Lucius is written as one of the prophets and teachers in the Church at Antioch. For the authenticity of that reading, this argument does not plead. It is the unquestionable antiquity of it which gives it importance here. The manuscript was written about the fifth century. And it is not likely that the reading appeared for the first time in this copy, or that it did not appear likewise in some others. But whether or not, its presence furnishes a testimony for the identity of Lucius and the writer of the Acts of the Apostles of an antiquity of at least thirteen hundred years. And further, there exists the same kind of evidence to show that a knowledge that Lucius of Cyrene was the writer of the Acts of the Apostles survived in the East for a thousand years. In both the London and the Paris Polyglott Bibles is printed an Arabic version of the Acts of the Apostles, from an oriental copy, supposed to have been written about the time of the Crusades, wherein the passage Acts ii. 10 is rendered, " The parts of Libya about Cyrene, *which is our country.*" With this supplemental clause critics have been sadly puzzled. Amongst others, Dr S. Davidson, in his " Introduction to the New Testament," following Professor Hugg, represents it as relating to the *translator*, an opinion, however, which is negatived by the accompanying criticism. For after saying, " Internal evidence shows that the books were translated directly from the Greek," Dr Davidson adds, " In the time of the Crusades we could not expect so accurate a knowledge of the Greek in the parts about Cyrene." Now, a reference to history will show that, at the time of the Crusades, the version *could not have been made by a native of Cyrene.* At the date assigned to the manuscript, Cyrene had been in ruins for nearly four hundred years. There could, therefore, have been no student there at the period of the Crusades, nor yet any literature, save what was engraven on the sepulchral remains. Moreover, to suppose that the clause relates to the *translator* himself, is to place him in an unique position ; for whenever was a translator found obtruding an anecdote concerning himself into the text of his author ? A reasonable conclusion is, that the clause is a piece of information relating to the writer of the

Acts of the Apostles, either volunteered as a gloss by the translator, or else already found existing in that copy of the Greek text which was in his hands. And so, in either case, it is an emphatic utterance of antiquity concerning Lucius the Cyrenian.

CHAPTER III.

LUKE A GENTILE.

It does not follow that because Luke was a Cyrenian he was therefore a Gentile. There were then, as now, many Jews in every principal emporium of commerce. But without almost any contradiction he has been adjudged to have been a proselyte ; and if a proselyte, he was of course a Gentile. Evidence that he was a Gentile abounds throughout his writings. Here the deductive process proving this point will be confined chiefly to references to his Gospel.

1. Among the several indications that Luke was a Gentile are the following :—His Gospel has an introductory note. " A reason for this preface," an old commentator says, " is, that Luke had not seen Christ in the flesh, as the other Evangelists had " (Adam Contzen, 1626).

2. The political and chronological notices in his Gospel are those of a Gentile. Matthew, as a native of the country, writes only " Herod the king " (ii. 1). But, as there were other kings throughout the Roman empire, it was natural for a person of another country than Judea to make the specification which is done by Luke in the words, " There was in the days of Herod the king of Judea," &c. (i. 5). Again, in the first verse of the second chapter of his Gospel, Luke writes, " In those days there went out a decree from Cæsar Augustus," &c. No form like this occurs in the other Gospels, this method of computation being inconsistent with the prejudices of Jewish nationality.

Its use therefore indicates that the writer was a foreigner. And a still more significant indication of a foreign hand is found in another chronological form which Luke employs at the beginning of his third chapter. The former data show his relation with Rome : this formula discovers his connexion with Cyrene and Egypt. An elucidation of this peculiarity in his Gospel, like some other antiquarian problems, has been derived from a tomb. Charles Taylor was the first writer who pointed out this remarkable coincidence between the places of Luke's nativity and education and the style here adopted. In his " Fragments " he writes, " On the 24th of January 1821, an Egyptian contract on papyrus, in cursive Greek characters, dated 104 years B.C., from Thebes in Upper Egypt, preserved in the hand of a mummy, was read before the Royal Academy of Berlin by Augustus Boekh. The contract begins thus : ' Under the reign of Cleopatra and Ptolemy, in the twelfth year, which is also the ninth under the Pontiff at Alexandria, under Berenice Philadelphe, under the priests of both sexes who are at Ptolemeus," &c. Here a specimen is afforded of the Egyptian mode of engrossing a date. But mark, he says, the parallel. " The passage in Luke's Gospel reads, ' Now in the fifteenth year of the reign of Tiberius Cæsar, Pontius Pilate being Governor of Judea, and Herod being Tetrarch of Itruria, and Lysinias the Tetrarch of Abilene, Annas and Caiaphas being the high priests ' " (iii. 1). " The association," he continues, " is here apparent. Excepting in the names, Luke's example is a counterpart of the former. But as he is the only Evangelist that affects this precision, it proves that he was of a different country from the others, and accustomed to different forms. After this evidence," adds Mr Taylor, " is it possible to doubt whether Lucius of Cyrene be our St Luke ?"

3. The *geographical explanations* of his Gospel are those of .

a foreigner.   Luke writes, " a city which *is called* Bethlehem ;" " a city *called* Bethesda ;" " Nazareth, *a city of Galilee* ;" " Capernaum, *a city* of Galilee ;" " Arimathea, *a city of the Jews* ;" " the Mount that *is called* the Mount of Olives." Whereas, by Matthew and Mark, being natives of Palestine, the names of these places are given without any expletives. And a passage also occurs in Acts i. 19, which explains concerning the Potter's Field, " that field is called in *their proper tongue*, Aceldama." Certainly a Jew would not have so written.

4. His *genealogy* of Christ is adapted to interest all nations alike. The genealogy drawn by Matthew follows the political and royal ancestry of our Lord, by which He is shown to be the heir to the throne of David, and the Messiah promised to Abraham, the federal head of the Jews, to whom His pedigree is limited. Whereas Luke, regarding Him as the Desire of all nations, continues beyond David to trace His ancestry upwards to Adam, the head and fountain of the universal human family.

5. His *verbal expletives* are such as would be made by a foreigner. For instance, Matthew writes, " Man shall not live by bread alone, but by every word *that proceedeth out of the mouth of God*" (iv. 4). Whereas, instead of the Hebraism of the latter clause, Luke simply says, " but by every word of God " (iv. 4). Again Matthew writes, " Then the devil taketh Him up into *the holy city*." But Luke, neglecting the metonymy used by the Jews, plainly says, " And brought Him to Jerusalem." Again, the other Evangelists, as Jews, in speaking of the temple, of the law, and of the rulers and elders, simply call them such ; whereas Luke, on the first occasion upon which he alludes to them, writes, " The temple *of the Lord*" (i. 9) ; " The law *of the Lord*" (ii. 23) ; " *Their* rulers and elders " (Acts iv. 5). And explanatory of their two principal sects he writes, " For the Sadducees say that there is no resurrection, neither angel nor spirit,

but the Pharisees believe both ;"—a precision in each case which plainly intimates that he wrote as a foreigner, and also in a manner which was proper in a document addressed to a person in a land surrounded by other temples and rites. Concerning this peculiarity, Dr Major observes :— "There occur in Luke's Gospel several instances in which he affords an exposition of things that were new, or would appear doubtful to Gentiles, where he seems only to be carrying on the narrative; his design of relating the same things with the other Evangelists being often accomplished by the difference of only a word. Sometimes he varies from them more designedly. It is observable that in chapter iii. 4–9, Luke quotes no less than *three* verses out of Isaiah xlvi., whereas Matthew and Mark, in their parallel relation, quote only the *first* of them. But it was necessary for St Luke's purpose that he should thus extend the quotation in order to assure the Gentiles, for whom he wrote, that they were destined to be partakers of the gospel, and to see the salvation of God." ("St Luke's Gospel, with English Notes," the introduction.) In his account of the transfiguration of our Lord, Luke avoids the word *metamorphothe* used by Matthew, which would have misled Gentile readers, and expresses the sense by saying "the fashion of his countenance was changed" (*eteron*) (ix. 29). To this note may be added the observation that Luke reports fewer discourses of our Lord in controversy with Jews than does Matthew, his interest in these having been naturally less than that of the Jew.

– 6. His preservation of *prophecies relating to Gentiles*, not recorded by the other Evangelists, seems to evince his own personal interest in them. Two such prophecies are found amid the opening scenes of his Gospel. The first in the declaration of the angel to the shepherds, "Behold, I bring you good tidings of great joy, which shall be to all people." And the second in Simon's ode of welcome, wherein he points to the babe as "a light to lighten the Gentiles."

7. Luke's record of intimations given by Christ of the ultimate *expansion* of His divine kingdom, intimate his foreign sympathies. The appointment of the seventy evangelists (only told by him) as an addition to the staff of Christ's ministers, was such an intimation. This appears in the words, " The harvest truly is great, but the labourers are few; pray ye therefore the Lord of the harvest that He would send forth labourers into His harvest " (x. 2). This intimation afterwards found an illustration in the situation occupied by some of those evangelists, especially by Barnabas, in the Acts of the Apostles. But the plainest intimation of this expansion was that made by our Lord when He charged these same evangelists, along with the apostles, that, as His witnesses, they " should preach repentance and remission of sins in His name *among all nations* " (xxiv. 47).

But besides these particulars, there are other circumstances in the treatment of his subject which tend to illustrate Luke's position as a Gentile: some of which are these :—

1. As a foreigner, he would naturally be inquisitive concerning what were the *personal characteristics of Jesus;* concerning, for instance, His devotional habits. Accordingly, he notices that it was the custom of Jesus to attend the synagogues on the Sabbath-day (iv. 16); that after his public ministry He was wont to retire to desert places (iv. 42; ix. 10). Aptly on this point, Dr Townson has observed, " Luke records instances of our Lord's praying at His baptism (iii. 21); before the choice of His apostles (vi. 12); before He plainly declared to them that He should be put to death, and rise again the third day (ix. 18 and 22); and at His transfiguration, on which occasion Matthew and Mark leave us to conclude the practice of our Lord as a

thing of course ; but Luke is explicit concerning His devotion. And with respect to the inculcation of the duty, the admonition to pray always (xviii. 1), is repeated (xxi. 36). Two parables are given to show the success of frequent and fervent prayer (xi. 5 ; xviii. 1), which occur only in Luke's Gospel. Besides which there are a dozen instances of praising, blessing, and glorifying God mentioned only by him. The adopted Gentile," adds this writer, "wanted to be taught these things more than the Jew trained to the duties " ("Discourses on the Gospels ").

2. As a Gentile, the sympathies of Luke were attracted by what he was informed concerning the *gentleness of Jesus*, and His loving acceptance of sinners, being penitent. Besides what are common with the other Evangelists, he has gathered many charming illustrations hereof into his pages. Indeed, these portions of his Gospel led Renan to observe, "Luke's own tendencies are apparent. He is fond of narratives that bring into prominence the conversion of sinners and the exaltation of the humble." This is said by a sceptic, in a spirit of detraction. Nevertheless, the criticism is accepted as correct. Among Luke's illustrations of this feature of our Lord's disposition are the conversion of Zaccheus and of the thief on the cross ; and the series of parables contained in the fifteenth chapter of his Gospel forms a cluster of such illustrations. With what beautiful simplicity are those parables introduced ! " Then drew near unto Him all the publicans and sinners for to hear Him." Hereupon in the Saviour's teaching follow the parable of the lost sheep (for which every good shepherd is concerned) ; the parable of the lost piece of money (which every person values) ; the parable of the prodigal son (whom every person pities) ; and, the joyful recovery of each being described, the affecting intelligence is added by the Divine Teacher, "Likewise, I say unto you, there is joy in heaven over one sinner that repenteth." Joy in heaven ! What

a sweet preface to the parable that followed! Surely there was given occasion for joy in heaven at that very instant. A reminiscence of the ministry of Jesus like this could not fail to attract the admiration, and doubtless formed the solace, of Luke's own mind, even as his record thereof has been, and will yet be, the solace of millions of his readers.

3. As a Gentile himself, Luke would be careful to inquire concerning Christ's *disposition towards Gentiles*. Accordingly, his Gospel describes several scenes in which this disposition was shown. He relates that, in the first public discourse at Nazareth, Jesus said, "Unto none of the widows in Israel (during a great famine), was Elias sent, save unto a woman of Sarepta of Sidon" (iv. 26). And that although many lepers were in Israel in the time of Eliseus the prophet, none of them were cleansed save Naaman the Syrian (iv. 27). There were two classes of people, not being Jews, who, within the limit of the Lord's journeys, often came under His observation : these were Romans, who held garrison in the several cities of Palestine, and Samaritans. Against both of these classes the Jews entertained a consummate animosity ; against the former, on political, and against the latter, on religious grounds. But Jesus entertained no prejudices. Instances of favours bestowed upon individuals. of both these classes by our Lord are recorded by all the Evangelists. Some of Luke's examples are highly characteristic of the point of view from which he regarded them. A lawyer inquired of our Lord, "Who is my neighbour?" The answer to this question was conveyed by the parable of the Good Samaritan. But Luke alone has preserved this exquisite picture and its moral (x. 29–37). Upon the healing of the ten lepers, nine of them being Jews, and one a Samaritan, Luke relates, Jesus said, "Were there not ten cleansed ? But where are the nine ? There is not found that returned to give glory to God, save this stranger" (xvii. 17–18.) The preservation of such passages as these,

whilst they reveal the benignity with which our Lord regarded Gentiles, argue likewise Luke's own relation to these.

4. An indication of the Gentile consists in *the absence* in Luke's Gospel of the writer's own appearance therein as a teacher. Between his Gospel and Matthew's, there is in this respect a signal difference. In Matthew's Gospel expositions of the relation subsisting between the circumstances of Christ's life and the prophecies which had been made before concerning them are frequent. The publican, it may be supposed, from the promptitude with which he obeyed the Lord's call, had been secretly a devout man, like Nathaniel. He had already searched the Scriptures to see how the character of Jesus, whose conduct he had had opportunities to observe, being a resident in Capernaum, corresponded with those prophecies. And so his sudden call by the Lord did not find him unprepared. Matthew directed the Jews to their own Scriptures. But those for whom Luke wrote did not possess them, nor any divine records to which to appeal.

5. As a foreigner, Luke would be curious to survey *the elements of society by which our Lord had been surrounded.* Besides depicting the great character of Jesus, the Evangelists incidentally, but necessarily and frequently, advert to two classes of the Jews, and to their conduct towards Him. In this, as in every branch of their subject, their accounts substantially agree. It could not be otherwise. For that conduct having been prophetically declared, how many soever might write concerning it, their several accounts must, if true, have a correspondence with one another, and all with the sacred predictions. But in Luke's Gospel this subject is touched much oftener, and is treated more circumstantially, than in the others. And, accordingly, his notices of those classes, namely, the common people and the hierarchy, serve to cast a strong light upon

the progress of Christ in His ministry. Without having
actually witnessed their conduct towards Jesus, Luke had
nevertheless the advantage that he was able to compare the
notices communicated to him concerning them with those
classes themselves. When he visited Jerusalem, the same
high priest and his hierarchy, together with the rulers and
the sects, were still here. Also, the same people among
whom Jesus had walked, and whom He had sought to bless,
were still to be seen on either hand.

6. In his *pictures of the common people*, Luke first records
an announcement made by an angel, that John should
" make ready a people prepared for the Lord" (i. 17). And
truly, it may be said, had there not been such a people, if the
common people had met Christ in the spirit that their
rulers did, there had been no history of His ministry to
record. And that there should be such a people is again
intimated in the prophetic words applied by Christ to Himself, in his inaugural discourse, and which Luke set before
his narrative of Christ's ministry for a text, " He hath
anointed me to preach the gospel to the poor " (iv.) The
fulfilment of this prediction meets the reader in nearly every
page of his Gospel. The class contemplated is found constantly attending the ministry of Jesus, so that He was never
without hearers. It is testified, " They pressed upon Him
to hear the word." Their numbers amounted sometimes to
four and five thousand, besides women and children.

At the beginning of the Lord's ministry—that is, when,
after His baptism and temptation in the wilderness, He
returned into Galilee—Luke writes : " There went out a
fame of Him throughout all the region round about. And
He taught in their synagogues, being glorified of all " (iv.
14, 15). After the raising to life of the widow's son at
Nain, he writes : " There came a fear on all ; and they
glorified God, saying, that a great Prophet is risen up
among us ; and that God has visited His people " (vii. 16).

Nor was this veneration of the people abated by the opposition of the higher classes; for, after an occasion upon which Jesus had justified Himself, in reply to an indignant reproof of a ruler of a synagogue, Luke writes: " And when He had said these things, all His adversaries were ashamed; and all the people rejoiced for all the glorious things that were done by Him " (xiii. 17). And that the people were consistent in their grateful veneration of Christ he shows by representing them as having taken every opportunity to shield Him from the malice of His enemies, observing, " When these sought to destroy Him, they were hindered through fear of the people " (xix. 48, xx. 19). He also shows that it was this apprehension of the indignation of the people that gave importance to the services of the traitor; for what others could not do, Judas promised to effect " in the absence of the multitude " (xxii. 6).

That is a " vulgar error " which says that this same people were those that vociferated against Jesus before the tribunal of Pilate. They did not do so. The prosecution was conducted very early in the morning, *expressly to avoid their knowledge of it.* They who on the day before had welcomed with hosannas the lowly Jesus were not yet in the streets. All was yet silent, except where the prosecution was conducted. At the season of the Paschal Feast, there were many thousands of foreign Jews in the city. These had not seen how Jesus had gone about doing good to people of their own class. They knew not Jesus, except by the misrepresentations of the priests. Jews resident abroad were always zealous to prove their fidelity to the national cause, as represented by the Sanhedrim. Of these, with Judas, the priests, in their conspiracy against Jesus, made their tools. Of these chiefly consisted the multitude who, accompanied by officers of the temple, being Jews, went, guided by Judas, in search of Jesus (xxii. 47); and who, mobbing around the judgment-hall, cried " Crucify

Him." " The criminal usually stood under the *rostra* in a mean garb, where he was exposed to the scoffs and raileries of the people" (Adams's "Roman Antiquities "). This is just what that mob did at this time. Of the same class with that mob were afterwards the murderers of Stephen (Acts vi. 9). Luke had been informed by his witnesses of two companies of the people in relation to the scene of the sufferings of Christ. Accordingly, the time in which they respectively appear in the scene, the place which each occupied, and the difference in their conduct, are accurately marked in his narrative. The multitude just noticed is again brought before the reader, and in exact keeping with its previous position and temper. The people composing this company are associated with the rulers in deriding Christ as He hung upon the cross (xxiii. 35). The company that had heretofore reverently followed Him does not appear on the scene until about nine o'clock, or as the procession passed the street, and thence through the north or Damascus gate to Calvary. And the behaviour of this company is represented as conformable with their previous conduct towards Jesus ; for the people composing it are associated with the women in bewailing and lamenting Him (ver. 27). And in further distinction of these from those that had abetted the enemies of Christ, and now with them derided Him, Luke adds this vivid sketch : " And all the people that came to that sight " (*i.e.*, the casual spectators), " beholding the things which were done, smote their breasts, and returned " (ver. 48). Certainly, this does not describe the mockers. Moreover, in the glimpse that is given of the people that had known Jesus and shared His benevolence, it is seen that after His resurrection, and they had witnessed the signs and the wonders of healing wrought by the apostles, and had partaken the benefits • thereof, when officers apprehended Peter and John in the temple, they took them without violence, for the reason that they feared lest they should have been stoned by the people (Acts v. 26). The rudest populace will neither inflict nor suffer an injury upon their personal benefactors.

7. No less graphic is Luke's picture of *the higher class* of the Jews. The same discrimination of character is discovered in his account of the conduct of the hierarchy, including the sect of Pharisees and the profession of Scribes. He represents that neither John nor Jesus came to preach the gospel to these. And although Pharisees in great numbers attended John's ministry, in the common hope of the advent of the Messiah of their immediate expectation, yet the Baptist hereupon prophetically denounced them as a generation of vipers,—a character which they fully exhibited upon the actual revelation of the Messiah in the humble person of Jesus. In the virtual repudiation of John's teaching, whose prophetic character they did not publicly deny, consisted the hypocrisy with which our Saviour so often charged them. As vipers, they were of their father, the old serpent, the devil. As vipers, they always tracked the path of the Messiah they rejected. The testimony of all the Evangelists shows that they persecuted Christ throughout every step of His ministry ; that no great work was wrought by Jesus, or a discourse delivered by Him to the people, but they were at hand to obtrude their objections, and to raise their cavils against His authority. Jesus had said, " Blessed are they that are not offended in me." But the entire testimony of the Evangelists and of Luke's researches show, that they took offence at His application of the Messianic prophecies. They turned from the passages whereby it was seen that He should touch humanity in its sorrows. They that confessed Him they accounted accursed (John vii. 49), so intensely did they resent a lowly Messiah. As much as they abhorred the Roman yoke, they dreaded a demonstration that threatened a rebellion, which they dared not risk. They, therefore, made a virtue

of necessity, and the motive which they urged upon Pilate was exactly a reflection of their own duplicity: " If you let this man go, you are not Cæsar's friend."

8. As an element of opposition to our Lord, the *malignity of Satan* obtains the notice of Luke in a manner peculiar. With Matthew and Mark, he gives an account of our Lord's temptation in the wilderness. That event would attract his attention as a reverse picture of the fatal temptation in Eden. But beyond those Evangelists, his account has this ominous appendage : " When the devil had ended all the temptation, he departed from Him *for a season* " (iv. 13). Our Lord's ministry was a continuation of the triumph achieved by Him in the wilderness. But when Luke arrives, in his narrative, to the predicted *season*, and writing in common with John, " Then Satan entered into Judas," he adds, beyond this, what Jesus said to the multitude conducted by the devil-possessed one to apprehend Him : " But this is your hour and the power of darkness " (xxii. 53). Hereby the first and the last temptations are connected in Luke's pages. And, as after the first temptation, angels ministered to Jesus, so they did in this. And thereafter they heralded His triumph : " He is not here; He is risen." With the fame of the old serpent, or python, the Gentile was conversant. To him, therefore, the triumph announced in those words was invested with a halo of glory.

CHAPTER IV.

LUKE A PHYSICIAN.

THE knowledge that Luke was a physician is derived alone
from the passage in the Epistle to the Colossians, "Luke,
the beloved physician, saluteth you" (iv. 14). Nevertheless, this simple intelligence being given, the means of its
confirmation are abundant.

Luke's profession, which thus transpires so seemingly
accidentally, is, in fact, not fortuitous. It is only another
example of the plan of much of the New Testament writings, which often furnish, in this manner, a hint which it
is the business of the student to pursue to its conclusions.
Here, for instance, is to be observed the harmony between
the Apostle's mention of this particular concerning Luke,
and the fact of his having been a native of Cyrene. Upon
this coincidence Granville Penn has this intelligent note:
"In truth there appears to be a happy correspondence between the historian's own description of himself as Lucius
the *Cyrenian*, and St Paul's designation of him as Lucas the
physician. As a school of medicine Cyrene was proverbial
(Herodotus, iii. 131). Hence the words ὁ κυρηναιος, 'the
Cyrenian,' and ὁ ιατρος, 'the physician,' may be understood
synonymously."

In contrast with this note, it is represented in a recent
exposition of the New Testament, "There are reasons which
justify the opinion that Luke was a heathen by birth, and
a *slave* in his condition, or at least a freedman. His origin
and *profession* agree with the fact that the Romans were

averse to the practice of medicine, which they left for slaves "
(Webster and Wilkinson).

The opinion that Luke was a slave or freedman, the
whole tenure of his life and literature contradicts ; and the
inference that, because he was a physician, therefore a slave,
is quite unwarrantable. It is true that the profession of a
physician was held in little repute in the early period of the
Roman Republic ; but the disesteem of it had ceased very
long before the time of Luke. It is also true that, even in
his time, families of wealth, maintaining a great establishment, kept slaves skilled in various trades, and among them
was usually one that understood medicine. But the physician must have come to be held in high estimation among
the Romans when Cicero wrote, " The skill of curing and
preserving the body has been thought a divine invention."
Celsus, who wrote his classical " Institution of Medicine "
shortly before the time of Luke, was a Roman, but he was
not a slave.

But Luke was a Greek. And among the Greeks the profession of medicine was held in high estimation. " There
was a law in Athens that no female or slave should practise
it ; and there are extant several medals struck at Smyrna
(*near Antioch*) in honour of different persons belonging to
the medical profession " (" Penny Cyclopædia," vol. xviii.)
Moreover, Luke had studied in those schools of medicine
wherein stood at the head of their profession the memorable
names of Hippocrates and Galen—chieftains—not slaves !

Our blessed Lord himself ennobled and sanctified the profession of a physician. He said, with reference to Himself,
" They that are whole need not a physician, but they that
are sick." And afterwards, describing His ministry, He
said, " Tell John how the blind see, the lame walk, the
lepers are cleansed, the deaf hear, the dead are raised " (Luke
vii. 22). That this summary of our Lord's healing power,
by His own lips, should have been recorded by Luke only,

is consistent with his sympathies as a physician. In studying the life of Christ, he had before him a congenial subject.
The dignity of His power, His mastery over every form
of disease, whether of the body or of the mind, the in-
stantaneousness with which His cures were effected, and
their accomplishment, generally only by a word, must have
raised in Luke, the physician, a singular admiration of Him,
and a curiosity concerning His conduct, which probably con-
duced to his purpose of composing a Gospel.

Dr Nathaniel Robinson, a physician, has observed, " It
is manifest from his Gospel, that Luke was both an acute
observer, and had given even professional attention to all
our Saviour's miracles of healing. Originally, among the
Egyptians, divinity and physic were united in the same
order of men ; so that the priest had the care of souls, and
was also the physician. It was much the same under the
Jewish economy. But after physic came to be studied by
the Greeks, they separated the two professions. That a
physician should write the history of our Saviour's life was
appropriate, as there were divers mysterious things to be
noticed, concerning which his education enabled him to form
a becoming judgment " (" The Christian Philosopher," by
N. Robinson, M.D., 1757).

For specialties denoting Luke's profession, it has been
observed, that where Matthew, in describing the case of
Peter's wife's mother, says she was " sick of a fever " (viii.
14), Luke writes, "taken with *a great* fever " (iv. 38).
And in our Lord's treatment of the case, where Matthew
says, "He touched her hand and the fever left her," Luke
writes, " and He stood over her, and *rebuked* the fever, and
it left her." Again, where Matthew says, "there came a
leper " (viii. 2), Luke writes, " a man *full of leprosy*" (v.
12). Again, where Matthew says, " there was a man which
had his hand withered " (xii. 10), Luke more specifically
writes, "a man whose *right* hand was withered" (vi. 6). And

in the treatment of this case, where Matthew says, " then saith He to the man, Stretch forth thy hand," Luke, as from a note-book, writes, " He said to the man, Rise up, and stand forth in the midst. And he arose, and stood forth. Then said Jesus," &c. " And looking round about upon them all, He said unto the man, Stretch forth thy hand. And he did so ; and his hand was restored whole as the other." Again, where Matthew says, " a woman which was diseased with an issue of blood *twelve years* " (ix. 20), Luke adds this characteristic supplement, " which had spent all her living upon physicians, neither could be healed by any " (viii. 43). And concerning the maid of whom Matthew and Mark say, " Jesus took her by the hand, and she arose," he adds emphatically, " and *her spirit came again* " (viii. 55). In a relation which is given only by himself, he describes, " a woman which had a spirit of infirmity for *eighteen years,* and was bound together, and could in no wise lift up herself" (xiii. 11). And peculiar to his pages are the accounts of the cure of the dropsical man (xiv. 2, 3), the cleansing of the ten lepers (xvii. 12), and the healing of Malchus's ear (xxii. 51). It has also been remarked that, as an important consideration, and in keeping with his professional character, Luke alone of the Evangelists indicates *a medium of cure.* He says, upon one occasion, " the power of the Lord was present to heal " (v. 17). And after an account of our Lord's dispossession of a diabolic spirit, he adds, " and they were all amazed at the *mighty power of God* " (ix. 43). Hereby he puts the cases of our Saviour's healing infinitely above the capacity of all other physicians whomsoever. Further, it is remarked by an American lawyer, " As a physician, Luke would know that deep mental distress frequently induces sleep. But he alone states that the sleep of the disciples in Gethsemane was induced by extreme sorrow (xxii. 45). And he has not failed to mention the bloody sweat of Jesus occasioned by intensity of agony (xxii. 44) " (Greenleaf's " Juridical Examination of the Four Gospels," p. 144).   Besides these examples from his Gospel, it has been added, in testimony of Luke's having been a physician, that in the case of the cure at the " Beautiful Gate " of the man lame from his birth, in specifying that the man's feet and ankle bones recovered strength, he uses the technical term σφυρά, a hammer, which the ankle bone was supposed to resemble (Acts iii. 7).   And it has been likewise observed, that in his account of the disease of which the father of Publius of Malta was afflicted, he employs the term δυσεντερία (Acts xxviii. 8).   It was formerly objected that a dry climate like that at Malta could not produce such a complaint; but the testimony of physicians resident there is afforded to show that dysentery is by no means uncommon in that island in the present day.

As no notice is found concerning Luke between the place of his nativity and his presence in Jerusalem, it will be allowable to enliven the interim by thoughts of what was his probable situation upon quitting Cyrene. Upon "the use of analogy and probable inference as auxiliaries in connecting the materials of biographic representation," it is remarked in an " Essay on the Study and Composition of Biography,"* " Probable inferences often assume the validity of facts where their general tenor and consistency of character seem to warrant the conclusion " (p. 171).

If, as Herodotus reports, " The Libyans were the most

---

* This essay, by James Field Stanfield, is a book of *superlative* value to those about to undertake a biographic composition.   It is the present writer's regret that he so lately became acquainted with its merits. The book consists of 339 pages, in octavo, and was printed in Sunderland in 1813.   The author was a native of Ireland.   In his early days he was a mariner engaged in the African trade. Prefixed to his book is a dedication to the Duke of Gloucester, *President of the African Institution*, and in a list of subscribers is the name of Thomas Clarkson. The author's son, the eminent painter and R.A., born in Sunderland, was named, after that philanthropist, Clarkson Stanfield.

healthy people in the world," there would have been little
inducement for a young physician to remain among them.
It is not, however, to be conceived that Luke passed direct
from Cyrene to Jerusalem.   The important city of Alexandria lay in the way, to whose school of medicine he must
have been attracted.   Theodoret says, " Alexandria was
regarded as the metropolis, not only of Egypt, but also of
Libya."   The city was originally colonised by Greeks and
Jews invited to settle there, under circumstances favourable
to the free action of commercial enterprise and the cultivation
of literary pursuits.   It was divided into three districts :
one for the Jews with their synagogues ; one for the Greeks,
in whose district was situated the palace and museum ; and
the other for Egyptians, where was the Serapion, a temple
containing a figure of that idol.   The population of Alexandria in the time of Luke amounted to 300,000 free citizens, and as many slaves and strangers.   The sovereigns of
Egypt patronised literature with greater ardour than the
rulers of any other country, and by the continued favour
of the Ptolemies, the city became, as a seat of learning, the
most distinguished in the world.   For nearly a thousand
years the cloistered walks, public halls, and ample libraries
of the college were the resort of the most eminent men of
science.   One of the principal founders of this school was
Euclid, B.C. 320.   Students from all countries were attracted by its advantages ; and no disciple of the philosophers was thought to have completed his studies without
partaking its benefits.   The term *museum* is said to have
been first applied to that part of the royal palace of Alexandria appropriated for the reception of the literary works
collected for the use of students.   Seven hundred thousand
manuscript books constituted its glory. Philosophers were its
librarians, among whom had been Callimachus and Eratosthenes, both Cyrenians. "Along with other branches of knowledge, the science of medicine was cultivated in the Alex-

andrian College with peculiar assiduity ; and the faculty is indebted for some very essential improvements to the professors of that school" (Dr Bostock's "History of Medicine").

If, therefore, Luke followed the usual custom of students, he would not fail to repair to Alexandria. And that he did so is intimated by the fact, that his writings partake largely of the Alexandrian dialect. Nor would he confine his studies there to lectures on the medical science, and in consulting the works of Hippocrates and other leading teachers of the healing art ; but he would likewise avail himself of the facilities offered for adding to his store of useful information generally. Here, better than in any other place, he might become acquainted with the various kinds of teaching, physical and metaphysical, which were current ere the doctrines of the gospel had disturbed the schools. He would find in what related to the discoveries and appliances of science much that was interesting and worthy of study. Whilst, nevertheless, he would discover nothing among the wisest of all that were gathered to that emporium of knowledge, but what presented convincing evidence of the failure of the human understanding, unaided from above, to attain a knowledge of the character of the one true God and of man's relation to Him.

At what time Luke first obtained an acquaintance with the Holy Scriptures, which teach that knowledge, cannot be traced. It will be an error to suppose that there were no virtuous heathen. There were always some who groaned under the burden and sin of idolatry ; and who, in the midst of its corruption, were witnesses for virtue. There were those " who, having not the law of God, did by nature the things contained in the law," and whose aspirations were higher and holier than what their idolatrous associations suggested. Such an aspiration, for instance, is that expressed by Cicero in his " Dream of Scipio," " If I were now disengaged from my cumbrous body, and on the way to Elysium, and a divinity should meet me in my flight, and invite me to return, and offer to reanimate my body, I should unhesitatingly refuse his offer, so much rather would I go to Elysium, to reside with Socrates and Plato, and all the ancient worthies, and spend my time in conversing with them." It is hoped that pleasures more blissful than those thus anticipated are reserved for virtuous heathen, through the virtue of the one offering by Jesus Christ for the sins of the world.

Even as the faithful Jew waited for the 'Consolation of Israel,' so the devout Gentile looked for the 'Desire of all nations.' And many more than are usually supposed were those Gentiles who thus hopefully looked for His advent. Of this number was Luke ; and whether he first came to a knowledge of the Holy Scriptures in Cyrene or in Alexandria, a residence in Egypt had its advantages in a religious respect. He had thereby the opportunity to visit the scenes memorable as the theatre of the dreary bondage of Jacob's descendants, and of the signal plagues upon their oppressors which obtained their deliverance. It was here, too, that appeared the first translation from the Scriptures of Moses and the Hebrew prophets. Under the direction of Providence it had been accomplished about a hundred years after the completion of the Old Testament canon, by learned rabbis, employed by a successor to the throne of the Pharaohs, and published in the language which then formed the principal medium of literature throughout all civilised countries. True, the proper benefit of that inestimable boon was long delayed. The mythical books of Egypt were, in the time of Luke, still in the hands of their guardians ; and although a few wise men had gone from the East to Bethlehem to welcome the Messiah, yet there was little perception of that gospel which, fulfilling the Hebrew oracles, should by and by close up the books of the priests for ever.*

* "The Hermetic or Egyptian Scriptures consisted of forty-two books, six of which related to medicine."—*Dr Bostock.*

Nevertheless, there were some devout persons, both Jews and Gentiles, in all countries into which copies of the Greek version of the Old Testament Scriptures had come, who had profited by their publication. Many devout Gentiles became proselytes to Judaism through their means. And although the Jews, who were ordained to be the lights of the world and God's witnesses among the nations, were little disposed to fulfil their vocation, the design was nevertheless accomplished through their captivities and emigrations. In Alexandria the Hebrew Scriptures were read every Sabbath in the several synagogues. And as only a very few individuals, or even families, would be able to possess copies of the Greek version of the Holy Scriptures, it must be supposed that the opportunity of reading them in the synagogues would have been afforded to the devout proselytes unacquainted with the Hebrew language, a provision calculated to be of infinite benefit to all who were led by a gracious Providence to inquire after a knowledge of the God whom those Scriptures reveal. Happily Luke was of this number. And as he loved the truth, and sought to be confirmed in its certainty, and conformed to its purity, he would rejoice to retire to a sanctuary where reading the Scriptures and prayer formed the improving employments. To this privilege he was eligible, as also to all others appertaining to the synagogue, in virtue of his having been accepted as a proselyte.

It would have been during Luke's residence in Alexandria, extending to some years, that he obtained the friendship of Theophilus, to whom he afterwards dedicated his writings. Both being Gentiles, and both proselytes to the synagogue, the intensity of their fellowship was hereby heightened.

That Luke's connexion with Egypt was a tradition in the early period of ecclesiastical symbolising, is shown by his attendant being represented in the apis, or the sacred

bull.   And that the tradition which prompted the symbol
still survives, there is a curious exemplification in a pictorial
edition of " *Les Evangiles*," *par De Sacy*, published in Paris,
1837.   In this edition a portrait is given of the Evangelist,
in which he is represented as an Egyptian, seated holding in
his hands an open scroll of his Gospel.   The portrait is surrounded with emblems characteristic of Egypt and Cyrene ;
and beneath is a figure of the apis clothed with a pall.

CHAPTER V.

How many years Luke spent in Alexandria cannot be known. When he left Egypt he was already in middle life. Charles Taylor has conducted an argument by which he shows, very intelligibly, that Luke was at least fifteen years of age in the first year of the Christian era; and, therefore, about the age of forty-eight when he repaired to Jerusalem. Proselytes, as well as Jews, regarded a visit to the temple at some period of their lives, however distant their residence from Palestine, as a religious obligation. Upon the building of the temple by Solomon, a court was assigned to Gentiles; and upon its consecration, the Divine regards were implored by the king upon those who should ever worship therein. Concerning this class of worshippers, little is noticed until the time of our Lord and his apostles, when it is found that their numerous attendance, from divers countries, at the festivals in Jerusalem, proved to be an important means of publishing to the world a knowledge of the facts of the gospel. But, besides this obligation upon him as a proselyte, the city had peculiar attractions to the devout worshipper. The Divine presence was in a special manner there. The believer had been taught from infant days to regard it with affection and reverence. Its historical associations were of superlative interest; and with the odes concerning it of the Hebrew bards his memory was familiar. The distance from Alexandria to Jerusalem is above 300 miles; and the mode of travelling, in companies, called caravans, is the same now as then. But the most easy, and the most customary, conveyance was by sea to the port of Joppa ; and from thence, a distance of about forty miles, in companies to Jerusalem. All exult at the accomplishment of their pilgrimage. But especially inquisitive of a glance at the diadem-city are those who for the first time approach it, and whose devout affections have already beautified it in their imagination. The different companies—Alexandrians, Cyrenians, Libyans, and Ethiopians—marshal off to their several quarters. Each had their synagogue in Jerusalem, as also had those from other countries, with residences adjoining, in the same manner as at present the Latin, Greek, Armenian, and other Christians have their convents, in which pilgrims are entertained. According to Josephus, there were more than 400 synagogues in Jerusalem. In the case of Luke's visit to Jerusalem was seen an eminent instance of the fulfilment of that word, " Also the sons of the stranger, that join themselves to the Lord, to serve Him, and to love the name of the Lord, to be His servants, even them will I bring to my holy mountain, and make them joyful in my house of prayer " (Isa. lvi. 6, 7). All that met his eye was singular to the visitor. The temple would be the first object of reverent examination. And, although Luke had been accustomed to the sight of priests in Cyrene, and especially in Egypt, where these existed as a hereditary caste, yet the number and decorum of the priests of the Most High God, all in white garments, emblems of their holy functions, would have had an effect on his mind never before felt. The holy spot and its divine service were the attractions of all Jews throughout the world ; never forgotten by those who had ever seen them, and always desired by those who had not. The city, by its side, seemed only to exist for the temple, and by it. Yet here, as almost everywhere else, the visitor found the frailty of human nature discovered

in that bane of many religious communities, *extravagance.*
Although the Jews had been weaned from idolatry by their
captivities, they brought back with them other ways of the
heathen.   Like them, priest and people were found ranged
in sects.   Among the varieties of these, the visitor saw
in the Essenes the type of the ascetic hermits of the desert.
The Essenes of Palestine commonly lived in a state of
celibacy ; they clothed in plainest garments, despised riches,
and formed themselves into monastic fraternities.   And
such sacredness did they covet, that they held the being
touched by any one not belonging to their sect as an impurity which required ablution. He beheld in the Pharisees
a sect equally leavened with paganism, but taking another
development.   In these he saw a sect that courted observation, its members being met in every street and place of
public concourse, and whose numbers, and fantastic cos-
tumes, and paces, imparted quite a scenic effect to the city.
The Talmudists have given some pictures of them beyond
what is seen in the Gospels. They have described, amongst
others, " The *Striking Pharisee,* who, shutting his eyes, as
he walked, to avoid the sight of women, often struck his
head against the wall ; the *Mortar Pharisee,* who, that
his contemplations might not be disturbed, wore a deep cap
in the shape of a mortar, which would only permit him to
look upon the ground at his feet ; and the *Truncated Pharisee,* who, that he might appear to be in profound medita-
tion, as if destitute of feet, scarcely lifted them from the
ground, and so looked like a moving pillar " (Dr Enfield's
" History of Philosophy ").   Perhaps the conduct of these
sectarians suggested that admonition of St Paul, " Be not
righteous overmuch."   It certainly was censured by that
golden maxim and philosophic, " Let your moderation be
known unto all men."

Some persons have thought that Luke was among those
Greeks who expressed a desire to see Jesus. But as that

circumstance is not related by Luke, but by John (xii. 20), it may be dismissed. Dr Edward Burton, in his " Lectures on Ecclesiastical History," says, " There are many reasons which lead me to think that Luke was in Jerusalem at this time" (when Christ was crucified). To this opinion an objection stands in the front of Luke's Gospel. He there relates how he was indebted for his facts to eye-witnesses. That by this statement he virtually excludes himself from their position may justly be inferred. And that he had not seen Christ was the general opinion of the ancients.

Many of the strangers who resorted to Jerusalem would not have directed their attention towards Jesus until the morning of his crucifixion. The circumstance of the execution of a Jew for blasphemy, in the Jew's sense of the case, and for rebellion, in respect of the Roman Government, caused the scene, witnessed beyond the north gate of the city, to attract the presence of many, and to become a topic of conversation by all.*   But when there succeeded the earthquake and the darkness at midday, and the alarm from the temple of the rending of the veil before the holy of holies, and the sight of the exposure of the dead in their sepulchres, by the rolling away of the portals, and the apparition of saints that had been deceased, by these phenomena public attention became intensely aroused. No such a Passover had ever been commemorated since its first institution in Egypt. A feeling of awe would pervade every party, as they assembled around their several festal tables.   The coincidence of those marvels with the sufferings of the crucified, and the three-tongued inscription affixed to the cross, forced the observation of every one, natives and strangers, upon the person of Jesus.   Nevertheless, that

* For an argument for the site of the Crucifixion having been on the *north side* of Jerusalem, and therefore in confutation of the claims of the Church of the *Holy Sepulchre*, the reader is referred to a tract by the present writer, entitled, " The Prophetic Site of Calvary Surveyed."

the impression upon the rulers was far from salutary, is seen in the fact that the disciples sought close retirement through fear of the Jews ; and hence no opportunity was yet afforded to the people of obtaining an elucidation of those mysterious occurrences.

Fifty days intervened between the Passover and the Pentecost. A report of the scene and its accompaniments would have been carried by the Jews returning into the provinces and foreign parts, whereby curiosity was directed towards the next general gathering, which accordingly was attended by a concourse unusually great.

Perhaps Luke arrived in Jerusalem in the interval of these fifty days. His intercourse, at the beginning, would chiefly have been with the Alexandrians and Cyrenians, Jews and proselytes, who seem, from his own narrative, to have been foremost in aiding the priests in their conspiracy against Christ, and in persecuting His followers. The first notices, therefore, which he received concerning Jesus would be perverted. The Pentecost was eminently a thanksgiving festival. Its law of observance is given in Lev. xxiii. 15–17, and Deut. xvi. 9–12. Herein was made a national acknowledgment of the faithfulness of Jehovah to His covenant in respect of the fruitfulness of the goodly land to which the visitor had come prepared to enjoy all its hallowing associations.

On the gladsome morning of the first day (so beautifully significant of the Christian Sabbath, being the first day of the week) the avenues to the temple were thronged at an early hour by Jews bearing their harvest-loaves. And lo ! the foremost had hardly approached the altar, and ere the first offering was presented, there was heard spoken again the ominous name of " JESUS OF NAZARETH ! " An anxious stillness instantly prevailed. All eyes glanced towards the gate through which Emmanuel had been often seen to enter. Anon the mystery was solved. The apostles, having just descended from their retirement in the upper room where the Holy Ghost had baptized them as with fire, had come into the court of the temple. "Endued with power from on high," they instantly comply with their Master's injunction. Beginning at the temple, they do not hesitate to face that great concourse, and stand forth prepared to turn the shame of the recent Paschal into a triumphant Pentecost. With a dozen tongues wanting one, they expound in as many languages the marvels by which the city had been alarmed upon the occasion of the crucifixion of Jesus, and forthwith proclaim the gospel of the resurrection.

A rumour of mysterious occurrences at the temple spread through the city with electric speed. Among the devout men from every country that had come to the festival were some from Cyrene (Acts ii. 10). With these Luke (if, as is supposed, he was at Jerusalem at this time) would hasten towards the temple. His inquiring mind would be intent to ascertain what the rumours truly signified. With the multitudes wending towards the scene, he would be ready to forbode some new marvel. Arriving at the temple, it was there, probably, that he first saw the apostles. Surrounded by crowds of earnest listeners, the humble Galileans, their countenances beaming with supernatural intelligence, and exercising a miraculous gift of speech, must have been objects of wonder unto him : nor less wonderful their revelation of the fact of the resurrection of Jesus from the grave. The answer of Peter to the mockers, his candid explanation of the phenomenon, his adducing the testimony of the prophets to its character, and also to the necessary resurrection of the Holy One, formed a train of exposition which the education and intelligence of Luke could instantly appreciate.

At this period, Luke's narrative of the Acts of the Apostles plainly touches his own history. And although setting himself in the shade, as became his character, yet the feelings with which he regarded the events he records are transparent. Approval of the doctrine and conduct of the apostles, and admiration of their mighty ministry, shine forth in every sentence of his pen. The entire structure of his narrative discovers this sentiment; every fact related being so disposed as to co-operate with their teaching, and to accredit and commend it. Following the apostles step by step, and with undiminished admiration, he reports—1. Peter's discourse in the court of the temple on the morning of Pentecost (ii. 14–40); 2. His exhortation before the Beautiful Gate on a subsequent evening, in company with John (iii. 12–18); 3. His testimony before the Sanhedrim (iv. 8–12); and 4. His second testimony before the same tribunal, the other apostles being present, after his deliverance from prison by an angel. He relates, concerning " the signs and wonders " which accompanied their ministry— 1. The coming of the Holy Ghost upon the disciples, and its effects (ii. 2–4); 2. The healing of the lame man at the gate of the temple (iii. 2–8); 3. The shaking of the place wherein the disciples were assembled for prayer (iv. 31); 4. The sudden death of Ananias and Sapphira (v. 5–10); 5. The healing of a multitude of sick persons by the hands of the apostles (v. 12–16); and 6. Peter and John's release from prison by an angel (v. 19). And how deep was the interest which he took in the success of the apostles' ministry is shown by his notation of its great results.

Nor less manifest is his sympathy with the infant Church by his notices of the opposition that was made to it, and concerning which he relates—1. That the priests, with the captain of the temple and Sadducees, laid hands on Peter and John in the temple (iv. 1–3); 2. That on the morrow the Sanhedrim sat in judgment on them (iv. 5–7); 3. That the same apostles were again apprehended and imprisoned by the Sadducees (v. 17); 4. And that at another time they were beaten (v. 40); 5. He describes minutely the martyrdom of Stephen ; 6. And he tells of the scattering abroad of the disciples from Jerusalem by reason of persecution (xi. 19).

These details strongly illustrate an interest taken in the fortunes of the infant Church inspired by personal observation. The Gentiles of Egypt are often subjects of Scripture prophecy. It was written, " Ethiopia " (by which was meant the entire of North Africa) " shall soon stretch out her hands unto God " (Ps. lxviii. 31). Luke became an earnest of the fulfilment of that prophecy. His profession of faith in the historical facts of redemption is expressed in the note prefixed to his Gospel, as also the profession of his fellowship with the believers in Christ. Hence, in his account of the character and conduct of these is found his own portraiture. Having been baptized in the name of Jesus, according to divine prescription, the promise is fulfilled, " Ye shall receive the Holy Ghost " (Acts. ii. 38). In all these privileges Luke shared, and in their exercises bore his part. Under the heavenly influence experienced, all things became new to him and in him. He was among the first upon whom the new dispensation dawned. By embracing the gospel, his knowledge of the Old Testament Scriptures was not superseded, nor his reverence for them abated; rather their value was enhanced. He now found them illustrated and verified by the advent of the " Desire of all nations," and glorified by the illumination of the Holy Ghost. The facts which he was favoured to witness opened a new medium by which to study the Holy Scriptures, and moved him to higher admiration both of the wisdom and the grace revealed in them.

So likewise now did the temple, to which he had come to worship, appear in a new aspect to him. It was no longer the place for offerings for sin, but wherein daily to present the sacrifice of praise ; especially praise for the abolition of all other kinds of sacrifice, " by the one offering of Christ once for all for the sins of the whole world."

Luke's relation to society became also new. Counting all things loss for Christ, he left the company of those among whom his Lord was denied. He forsook the quarters of the unbelieving Cyrenians and Alexandrians, and casting in his lot with the disciples, he repaired to their upper rooms, and henceforth took his commons with them.

In the absence of the reasons for the belief of Luke's presence in Jerusalem soon after the crucifixion, to which Dr Burton refers, but only one of which he has specified, the following summary is submitted :—

1. Luke does not, as in the case of his Gospel, profess in his account of the Acts of the Apostles to be indebted to others for information.

2. His narrative of the Acts bears the marks of an observer by the minuteness of its details.

3. It discovers an intimacy with the persons whose history it records.

4. The deep interest discovered by the writer in their proceedings, intimates that he was a party in them.

5. The studious notation of circumstances which naturally interested him as a Gentile, shows opportunity for observation.

6. It transpires in Acts xi. 19, 20, collated with xiii. 1. " that Luke was at Jerusalem prior to the martyrdom of Stephen " (Dr Burton).

7. He must have collected the materials for his Gospel at Jerusalem before his retirement to Antioch, because afterwards the eye-witnesses to whom, in the preface thereto, he professes himself indebted, were never again found together.

8. From the period of that retirement his account of transactions in Jerusalem ceases, except so far as they were occasionally connected with the affairs of the Church in other places.

CHAPTER VI.

THE inquiry now arises, How was Luke employed during the years that he resided in Jerusalem? He was forbidden, as a Gentile, to engage as a public teacher in the assemblies of the faithful in Palestine. He would therefore have been known only as a disciple and a physician. But that he was engaged in another pursuit besides the business of his profession, is revealed in the first paragraph that proceeded from his pen. In early editions of his Gospel this paragraph appears distinguished from the text. The writer of this biography possesses two Latin copies of the New Testament, one printed at Antwerp in 1526, and the other at Lyons in 1540, in both of which it is so printed.

In the Antwerp copy, the Gospel of St Luke begins in this form :—

EVANGELIUM SECUN
DUM LUCAM.

PRAEFATIO EJUSDEM.

Quoniam quidem multi conati sunt ordinare narrationem, quæ in nobis completæ sunt rerum, sicut tradiderunt nobis, qui ab initio ipsi viderunt, et ministri fuerunt sermonis, visum est et mihi assecuto omnia a principio diligenter ex ordine tibi scribere, optime Theophile, ut cognoscas, eorum verborum, de quibus eruditus es væritatem.

CAPUT I.

F*uit in diebus Herodis regis Judæa, sacerdos quidam, etc.*

This edition is a duodecimo, printed throughout in neat italic type. The initial letter of every chapter is ornamental; that which begins this chapter is an engraving which represents a fox in a pulpit dressed in a monk's cowl, in the act of addressing a congregation of geese, a cock being perched before him upon the middle stroke of the letter F.

The copy printed at Lyons contains, first, Jerome's notice concerning Luke, after which is—

PRAEFATIO.

Quoniam quidem multi conati sunt, ordinare narrationem, etc.

Beneath this paragraph is a symbolical engraving, being the front view of an ox's head, on its poll a winged cap, from which on either side hangs the sacred pall, folded over the expanded horns, each end terminated with a string of beads. On the next page—

EVANGELIUM.

SECUNDUM LUCAM.

Under this title is a print representing Luke in his study, and an ox recumbent behind him. Then—

CAP. I.

Fuit in diebus Herodis Regis Judææ, sacerdos quidem, etc.

This edition is in 24mo, and is illustrated with several neat woodcuts.

Obscured by becoming conjoined with the text, this paragraph ceased to be regarded in its true character of a *private letter* written to accompany the copy of the Gospel sent to the friend who is named the rein. Dr Adam Clarke

is one of the few commentators who regard it in this light.
Letters often afford important materials in biographical
compositions, especially those letters which lay open the
thoughts and purposes of the writer.   Such a precious
document does the biographer possess in this letter of
Luke.   Herein the Evangelist reveals his mind when contemplating his undertaking; he indicates the means he had
taken to prepare his materials; and he points out as by a
prospectus what was to be expected in the book completed.
Bengel beautifully remarks concerning it, "The preface
savours of recent joy, such as would be felt upon coming to
the knowledge of joyful facts."   But more than this, it
discovers the Cyrenian's diligence in seeking to increase
his knowledge of those facts.   Few are the lines of this
letter, but several are its particulars.

1. The letter *notices preceding writers.*   "Forasmuch as
many have taken in hand to set forth a declaration"
(*anataxasthai diegesin*, to compose a narration).   This reference to preceding writers of accounts concerning Jesus
Christ is a piece of intelligence that transpires in no other
place in the New Testament.   It agrees with what would
have been presumed.   It would have been expected that
some accounts concerning the life and death of Jesus would
have been put into circulation.   Those accounts would
have been of various extent and degrees of merit; but of
their value Luke gives no judgment.   In none of them was
the subject treated in a manner adapted to his conceptions
of it.   The defects of the most of them are to be inferred
from the quality of his own narrative.   All those accounts
soon dropped into oblivion.   "The expression 'have taken in
hand' (observes Dr Oosterzee) is happily chosen to enhance
the importance and difficulty of the work."   Of the Gospels,
only Matthew's was written before Luke's, and that had
been confined to the use of Jews, chiefly in Palestine.

2. The letter intimates *the topics treated in the book—*

"Those things which are most surely believed among us" (*ton peplerophoremenon,* ample evidence). The things believed were those things which had come to pass concerning Jesus of Nazareth; those things which Luke afterwards described when he spoke of his Gospel as "a treatise of all that Jesus began to do and to teach" (Acts i. 1). This *sure belief* of himself and his associates in those things is an important affirmation. Made by one professionally accustomed to inquiry, and also to ponder the evidence of things submitted to his consideration, this affirmation stands for a pledge of the integrity of the accompanying narrative. And this pledge being given to a friend sensible of its value, Theophilus would thereby be prepared to repose the same belief in the facts of the narrative that the writer himself had done, as they had been related to him.

3. The letter mentions *the sources whence Luke derived his facts.* "Even as they were delivered unto us, by those who, from the beginning, were eye-witnesses and ministers of the Word" (*ap arches autoptai,* persons who, having themselves seen, were thereby acquainted with the circumstances; *uperetai genomenoi tou logou,* "ministers of the things they declared"—*Cranmer*). To these the Lord had said, "Ye shall be witnesses unto me." From many of this class Luke would have received intelligence by private discourse, and by listening to what they reported in public assemblies. It is therefore intimated, in this clause, that Luke preserved notes of what he heard from the lips of these several witnesses. Never again could the facilities for gaining the information which he sought be so favourable as now. The first fellowship of believers was in Jerusalem. Here was fulfilled the first series of promises that compacted the holy community. Admitted to their assemblies, Luke had the opportunity to listen to the reminiscences that were frequently reported therein concerning

the Lord. He became acquainted with individuals composing the company, from whom he obtained particulars whilst they were fresh in the memory. From simple questions put to these in behalf of his own personal growth in the knowledge of Christ, his inquiries, being extended, soon took the character of researches. At first, his witnesses were found among the company of the 120 mentioned Acts i. 15. Then they were some of the 3000 mentioned Acts ii. 41. Then they were some of the multitude, both of men and women, mentioned Acts v. 14. And then, perhaps, they were some of "the great number of priests that became obedient to the faith," mentioned Acts vi. 7. In this multiplication of believers, obtained from different classes, and even from that class that had been the most censorious observers of the Lord's conduct, there was found a fulfilment of that word, "One soweth and another reapeth." For it must be supposed that a great many of these converts had been prepared for the prompt reception that they yielded to the arguments of the apostles by having previously listened to the teaching of Jesus, and by having beheld some of His divine actions. And so they were competent witnesses for Luke. Moreover, his witnesses included all persons with whom he became acquainted, who could communicate to him an intelligible account of what they had heard and seen in the ministry of Jesus. Some of those were rulers, some scribes, some were citizens, and some plebeians. Some were persons who, having followed Jesus from place to place, listening with wonder and delight to His gracious words, had now cast in their lot with the saints; persons who had enjoyed His conversation, having welcomed Him to their houses; persons who had received benefits of healing, and the mercy of the forgiveness of sins; persons who had shielded Him from the malice of His enemies (there were several of these); persons who beheld His humiliation unto death ; and persons who were of the companies to whom He had shown Himself after His resurrection. Opportunities for obtaining important information, and of that kind which enabled Luke to say that he had traced the things related by him from the beginning, accrued through the circumstance of his profession. It is well known that a physician is a privileged person in Eastern countries. He alone of men easily obtains access to the female members of a household. So that many anecdotes illustrating the domestic life of Orientals, not elsewhere to be read, are found in the pages of travellers being physicians. Much of the interest of Dr Richardson's admirable volumes of travels in Egypt and Palestine, in company with Lord Belmore, are of this nature. When, however, had ever a traveller such a subject for his researches as had Luke ? The ministry of Jesus, by the testimony of all the evangelical writers, was a gospel of tenderness. The meek and confiding were His peculiar care. Among these, from the character of their sex, were women. The daughters of Abraham found His quickest sympathy. He removed their afflictions ; He blessed their infants ; He restored life to their dead. He otherwise, too, put honour upon women. He was born of a woman. He sanctioned by His presence a bridal-feast. He first revealed Himself as the Messiah to a woman, whereby she became the first that announced His advent to the Samaritans. He appeared first after His resurrection to a woman, whom also He appointed to be the first minister to announce the fact thereof to His disciples. Indeed, it is apparent that for a considerable part of Luke's Gospel the reader is indebted to women. The whole of the first section of his narrative is of this character. From whose lips, for instance, but those of women, could have been obtained the notices of the domestic scenes which relate to the birth, first of John, and then of Jesus ? The private character and the minuteness in detail of these discover plainly their source. Who described to the historian the incidents, together with the scene in the temple, upon presenting the Infant with an offering to the Lord, the blessing there pronounced by Simeon, and the piercing words addressed to herself (ii. 35)? Who spake to the historian of the child's growth in stature, and advancement in wisdom and grace, but the fond mother? And who described to him the visit of the Holy Youth to Jerusalem, along with His missing and His recovery, but she who had sought Him sorrowing? Who reported to him the first words of Jesus which are found recorded? They were spoken to His mother: "Wist ye not that I must be about my Father's business?" And who informed him that Mary kept all these things and pondered them in her heart—an observation twice repeated? But Mary was in Jerusalem when Luke was engaged in prosecuting his researches there.

It is remarked by Charles Taylor, "The genealogy in Luke was a private document; and its insertion adds to the proofs of confidence by Mary in Luke, since from her certainly he received it; while his preservation of it coincides with that accuracy we have attributed to his character" ("Fragments," 321).

And, further, with respect to Luke's indebtedness to female witnesses, the expression, so deeply natural, "Blessed is the womb that bare thee, and the paps which thou hast sucked," only a woman would have repeated to him as a piece of intelligence (xi. 27). It is related by Luke only that, in one of his circuits, there followed our Lord, "Mary Magdalene, Joanna the wife of Chuza, Herod's steward, and many other women, who ministered to him of their substance" (viii. 2, 3). And this grateful devotion of women, conspicuous to the last, must have treasured up incidents which none but themselves would be able to communicate.

4. The letter *commends the writer's position, as an argument for his undertaking.* "It seemed good to me also to

write." This slight allusion to his situation with respect to the subject was sufficient for his friend; and its force as a reason for Luke's undertaking equally appears to the reader of his biography. It is perceived that the clause expanded signifies, "It seemed good to me to write this narrative, who stand in a different relation to the subject of it than do those writers to whom I refer; to me, a Gentile and a foreigner in Palestine; to me, who am, nevertheless, infinitely interested in the history of the life and death of Jesus, and in its fulfilment of the Scriptures of Moses and the prophets, of which Scriptures I have been a devout student; to me who, having resided several years in Jerusalem, have had opportunities which few persons, not being Jews, have possessed for obtaining the necessary information; to me, whose profession enables me to appreciate the healing miracles of the Lord; to me who, on all these accounts, am competent to judge impartially concerning the particulars which I have obtained and now relate."

5. The letter declares the *extent of the writer's researches.* "Having had (obtained) perfect understanding of all things" (*parekolouthekoti*, having investigated step by step the things). The word occurs 2 Tim. iii. 10: "Thou hast fully known my doctrine" from the very first— (*anothen*, from the highest point). Here the Evangelist seems to allude to the matters related in the two first chapters of his Gospel. Moreover, from this representation it is to be inferred that Luke's inquiries, being co-extensive with his subject, they therefore reached beyond Jerusalem. As every intelligent sojourner in that metropolis takes the opportunity to accomplish a tour through the provinces, the Cyrenian would assuredly avail himself of the same benefit. Moreover, as his devotion to the Old Testament Scriptures would have prompted a desire to visit their scenes, the requirements of his design as a historian would have determined him to perform the pilgrimage. The

motives which brought him to Jerusalem would have operated with as much force to induce a resolve to visit the scenes where many of the prophecies relating to the ministry of the Messiah had been fulfilled. Besides, the plan of his book, being founded upon the obtaining the reports of eye-witnesses, it was necessary to embrace a sphere as wide as the matter sought. The greatest part of his Gospel is occupied with the relation of circumstances that occurred away from Jerusalem. And as in the places of their occurrence the chief number of his witnesses would be found, so many passages of his Gospel bear the signature of being so derived. In a tour through the provinces, Luke would have visited Jericho, about twenty miles distant from Jerusalem. There, perhaps, might still have resided Zaccheus ; and there, too, the inquirer might have been informed by witnesses of the scene concerning the blind men who received their sight when the Lord passed though that city. From thence, travelling by the banks of the Jordan, now on the eastern, then on the western, he would have met in divers places persons who had attended the ministry and witnessed the miracles of the Lord in those districts. There are said to have been 400 towns and villages in Lower Galilee, which was more level, fertile, and populous than the Upper Galilee. Arriving in the former district, with what feelings would he have looked upon the lake which had borne its Lord upon its waves ! And with what gratification would he have traversed the shores where had been gathered the great crowds, and the most admiring, that had followed the Lord, listening to His teaching, and receiving benefits from His hands, corresponding with the words of the prophet, applied to Himself by the Lord in his first-reported discourse : " The Spirit of the Lord is upon me, because He hath anointed me to preach the gospel to the poor," &c. (Isa. lxv.) There, in the towns adjacent, in Tiberias, in Bethsaida, in Chorazin,

and in the Lord's own city, Capernaum, where so many of
His mighty acts had been wrought, numerous would have
been the disciples who would have rejoiced to communicate
their experiences of His favour to the pious inquirer ; among
whom might have been some of the five hundred disciples
who at once had seen the Lord, according to His own
appointment made to them in Galilee before His decease.
Fruits of Luke's journey or journeys through the Galilees
distinctly appear. Scenes and events in the Lord's ministry,
consisting of some of the richest of Luke's gatherings, and
only described by his pen, are comprised in the eleventh to
the seventeenth chapters of his Gospel consecutively. They
are continued also in the eighteenth chapter ; but some of
the relations in this chapter are in common with other
Evangelists.

6. The letter refers to *the methodical arrangement of the
materials* of the Gospel. " To write unto thee in order,"
that is, in a series or narration (*katheres*, " in order," being
connected with *diegesis*, " a narration "). By this clause it is
represented that, preparation having been made by research, the design contemplated was accomplished by the
reduction of particulars to a descriptive treatise. And
more than this, it embraced the construction of an important historical argument, the particulars being cast into groups rather than into a strictly chronological arrangement. Luke had been a devout expectant of the fulfilment
of the divine prophecies relating to Messiah. He believed
that many of these had been fulfilled in the person of Jesus ;
and his treatise was directed to present a luminous proof
thereof, by the exhibition of facts which he had gathered,
and with accuracy weighed.

7. The letter mentions the *name of the person to whom it
was addressed,* and intimates his *position in society.* "Most
excellent Theophilus." It is quite inadmissible to attribute
to Luke, as is sometimes done, the having placed a fictitious

name in a note prefixed to a book, asserted to be a relation of carefully-ascertained facts ; and it is also contrary to all propriety to suppose that the word *kratiste*, a title of dignity, was not as distinctively applied to the person addressed, as it was by Claudius Lysias when he addressed Felix (Acts xxiii. 26), and by St Paul when he addressed Festus (xxvi. 25). Hence, Dr Lardner says, Theophilus was a man of senatorian rank, and possibly a governor, forasmuch as Luke calls him "most excellent." And furthermore, Bengel says, "Theophilus belonged to Alexandria, as the ancients testify." And this allocation corresponds with Luke's progress from Cyrene. The friendship between Luke and Theophilus would have begun in the Egyptian metropolis, where they prosecuted their studies together ; and from the fellowship in which they are here found, it may be thought, as it has been already intimated, that they had been at the same time devout students of the Scriptures of the Old Testament, in the Alexandrian version.

8. The letter *states the practical design of the book transmitted to this friend.* "That thou mightest know the certainty of those things wherein thou hast been instructed." Having begun the letter with an expression of his own and of his associates' assured belief of the things of his research and scrutiny, the writer concludes with an expression in behalf of his correspondent, in language which seems to be adopted from that by which Solomon recommended the study of his Proverbs : "That I might make thee know the certainty of the words of truth ; that thou mightest answer the words of truth to them that send unto thee" (Prov. xxii. 2). Theophilus was already a believer. As intimate friends, he and Luke would sometimes have corresponded by letters. In these Luke would have given his friend some notices of his situation since his arrival in Jerusalem, and of his experience of the grace received upon an acceptance of the doctrine of the apostles

concerning the Messiah. And thus, if by no other means, Theophilus would have been partly instructed in those things wherein he is by this treatise more fully informed, the design here being similar to St John's, when he wrote, "What we have heard declare we unto you, that you also may have fellowship with us, whose fellowship is with the Father, and with his Son, Jesus Christ." Here, then, is found an example, at that period, of two earnest students engaged in acquiring the knowledge of the mystery which had been hid for ages—the one being in a situation in which he could only have received a partial degree of information concerning those facts which the other, having had ample opportunities to collect, had both obtained and digested.

This letter is of sovereign use in defence of Luke against the misrepresentations to which his character and writings are subjected by certain critics. Only a few specimens of these will suffice to illustrate this remark.

1. The oldest of these misrepresentations is that which says that Luke's Gospel was composed from Paul's dictation. Often refuted, yet this error is still repeated. It is said, in a recent edition of "The Greek Testament, with Notes," "Luke learned his Gospel from St Paul, which that Apostle could only have received in such accuracy, consisting of numerous minute particulars, from revelation" (Webster and Wilkinson, i. 235).

2. Another misrepresentation is that which asserts that Luke's Gospel was composed from a variety of manuscripts, or, as technically said, of "existing documents." This manner of treating Luke's Gospel was uncustomary in England until, forty-five years ago, a translation of Dr Schleiermacher's "Critical Essay on the Gospel of St Luke" was given by Dr Connop Thirlwall, now Bishop of St David's. In that work, after a dissection of the Gospel, the author concludes by asserting, "From beginning to end,

Luke is no more than a compiler and arranger of *documents* which he found in existence, and which he allows to pass unaltered from his hand. His merit is that of arrangement, and his having admitted scarcely any pieces but what were peculiarly genuine and good, the fruit of a judiciously-conducted investigation and well-weighed choice." This sentiment has since been echoed by many writers, German, French, and English.

3. Renan says, "The historical value of Luke's Gospel is weaker than the others, because it is a *document at second-hand.*" Again, he says, "Luke is less an evangelist than a biographer of Jesus—a harmonist and corrector." And again, "He is, in fact, a compiler, *who had not seen the witnesses*" ("Vie de Jesus").

4. By Mr Froude it is asserted, "Of the Gospels separately, the history is lost in legend." "The apostles and apostolical fathers never mention Luke as having written a history of our Lord at all" ("Short Essays on Great Subjects," vol. i.)

All these opinions are manifestly opposed to the professions of Luke in his letter to Theophilus.

1. The opinion that Luke obtained his Gospels from revelations made to St Paul is quite inconsistent with the tenor of this letter. Moreover, if his facts were so derived, is it conceivable that such a circumstance would not have been mentioned by such an accurate writer as this Evangelist? Certainly, a derivation so remarkable had been worthy the attention of Theophilus, in a letter written expressly to inform him of the motives inducing the composition of the Gospel, and of the sources whence its facts were obtained. Luke obtained his facts from eye-witnesses of them. But Paul was not such a witness. The promise made to the disciples relating to facts, spake of a remembrance of what they had previously known. Whereas Paul first saw the Just One and heard His voice when travelling

from Jerusalem to Damascus. Then commenced his knowledge of Jesus, and then he received the first intimation of
the gospel it should be his province to testify. What that
was which he called " my Gospel " is explained in Romans
xvi. 25, and more fully in the Epistle to the Ephesians, the
third chapter.

2. The criticism that calls the sources from whence
Luke derived his facts *documents*, is opposed to the clause
wherein they are declared to be eye-witnesses. For those
witnesses were obviously *persons*, and not " *documents.*"

3. The assertion that Luke *had not seen his witnesses* is
irreconcilable with a fair interpretation of the words of the
letter. For no mention being made of another mode of
obtaining his facts, the plain signification of the statement
must be taken, namely, that the delivery of the facts to Luke
by eye-witnesses was *personal and oral*. Perspicuity must
have been intended in a letter expressly composed to
explain the principles upon which the Gospel was written.

4. The assertion that " Luke is never mentioned by the
apostles and apostolical fathers " is disingenuous at least.
It is disingenuous, because he is spoken of by St Paul, together with his Gospel, although not by his name, 1 Cor.
viii. 18. And then, the apostolical fathers were not historians : they were not critics. They did not foresee that
some of their writings would survive, and become important sources of appeal. Yet it happens that Ignatius
and Polycarp, although they do not mention the name
of Luke, each distinctly quote passages from his writings.
And close after their age Luke is named, and his Gospel
mentioned, by Irenæus ; and soon after him by Tertullian,
as related in the second page of this biography.

Here a testimony respecting the literary character of
Luke, written long before those criticisms were penned, by
an ingenuous sympathiser with our subject, comes in grace-
fully. Charles Taylor observes : " If a writer, in his general

character, be studious, particular, punctual, we pay a deference to his current discourse ; and if he affirm a thing, we rest satisfied of its truth and reality. But persons of strict accuracy seldom trust to their memory entirely on important affairs ; they make *memoranda,* or keep some kind of journal, in which they minute transactions as they rise, so that at after-periods they can refer to events thus recorded, and refresh their memories by consulting their former observations. I believe, too, that this is customary, chiefly among men of letters, men of liberal and enlarged education, men who are conversant with science, and who know the value of hints made on the spot *pro re nata.* My proposition is, that Luke the Evangelist was a person of learning, of accuracy of character, and that he instanced this by *keeping a journal of events,* of which we have traces in his writings."

But to proceed a step further in this vindication. Upon whatever subject God requires our belief, He sets before us proper evidence. But hypothetic *documents* bear no such character. Luke's own "assured belief" was grounded upon the evidence of eye-witnesses ; and the faith of all that have received his Gospel has been grounded upon the correctness of Luke's report of facts received from them. Three of the Evangelists were personal disciples of Christ. And weight is added to the testimony of these three by the corroboration of a fourth writer, who, from another position, undertook to collect and digest facts derived from the reminiscences of witnesses, of whatever situation, and of either sex. And this he did from the very natural motive, that at present being a foreigner, and prospectively, that other readers of his book, being also foreigners, might know the certainty of those things that are related in his pages concerning the person and ministry of Jesus Christ. The other Evangelists wrote without any foreign inducement for their selection of facts. They were of the same nation as our Lord, the same worship, habits, and customs. Their views were limited by their nationality. And herein is the wisdom of Divine Providence to be admired, that another penman should be admitted into the prophetic circle whose sympathies embraced the larger class to be gathered into the Church under the new dispensation, and who regarded the subject of his researches with a wider observation. And the result corresponds with this difference. The particulars preserved by Luke, which are unreported by the other Evangelists, comprise a full half of his Gospel. Such an inquirer was advantageous for the cause of Christian evidence ; whilst his antecedents as a Gentile and a physician combined to give a distinctive charm to this book of Holy Writ. Providential was the presence of such a convert in Jerusalem at the period of his residence there ; and great the occasion for gratulation found in the preservation of this letter, in which is related the nature and extent of his researches during that period.

Had there existed only one of the Gospels, how great a curiosity would it have been, and how great an exercise of faith to yield credence to its account of the teaching of such an unprecedented character as that of Jesus, and to the marvellous display of His power recorded ! And had that one Gospel been either of the three narratives written by Jews, or the one written by a Gentile, in either case, with what prejudice would it have been regarded, and how mercilessly would it have been treated by critics ! That there are four Gospels, composed by four several writers, at different periods and in different places, and that their narratives harmonise in every material point, is a cause for exultant praise to the Divine Inspirer.

CHAPTER VII.

LUKE'S RELATION WITH THE ACTS OF THE APOSTLES.

The First Period.

NEVER has the Acts of the Apostles been expounded from
the point of view of the writer's own person. Essays entitled Luke and his Gospel there are; but none on Luke
and his Acts of the Apostles. Yet in this department
of sacred history he stands alone. No other writer had
taken in hand to set forth a declaration of the things
recorded in this book.

Luke was detained in Jerusalem by the strong interest
he felt in the circumstances that related to the life of Jesus,
and likewise by the new views he had acquired and the
associations that had engaged his affections. In the exciting scenes by which he was surrounded, he discerned a
signal reformation of the Church of God. He recognised
the connexion of those scenes with the previous history of
Jesus, and he beheld how His ministry was being supple-
mented by that of His apostles. Concerning the ministry
of these it is briefly said by Mark, "And they went forth,
and preached everywhere, the Lord working with them,
and confirming the word with signs following." But Luke
undertook to fill up this outline by a circumstantial development. Favourable opportunities are fleeting: the diligent
secure their advantages. He had now become acquainted
with the principal agents of the work of regeneration proceeding. By the reports of these, added to what he

himself witnessed, he obtained fair and accurate intelligence
of all the most important incidents relating to that work.

The city of Jerusalem became to him an observatory.
Accustomed, as he had been, to the elevation of Cyrene,
it may even be thought that both his convenience and
taste would have led him to prefer a residence on the Hill
of Zion. Looking from thence, all appeared to him like
classic ground. Every prospect furnished some illustration
of the histories, familiar to him, which represented the
ingress and egress of kings and prophets, and of their
proceedings in and around the city. Whilst the entire
scenery was invested with a new halo, upon a thought of
the recent presence of Jesus therein.

In this situation Luke was near to the *uperion*, or upper
chamber, where the apostles assembled with the brethren ;
and also was in the neighbourhood of one or more of
the households of the faithful. To obtain a knowledge
of the facts upon which Christianity is founded, and to
give that knowledge a historical fixture, had become the
leading object of his life. In his study would now be
opened two books : one for a series of notes, being
materials for his Gospel, and another wherein to insert
relations designed for his Acts of the Apostles. Those
collections, it may be supposed, were made simultaneously :
those for the Gospel derived from eye-witnesses, and those
for the Acts, some from eye-witnesses and some from his
own observation. The plan of tracing things from the
beginning, adopted in the Gospel, was likewise followed
here. First there is afforded a relation of events connected
with the pre-Ascension period. Besides those particulars
related at the close of his Gospel, Luke had obtained some
others, also different from those related by other Evangelists.
This new relation extends from the fourth to the twelfth
verse of the first chapter. Herein are rehearsed the last
words addressed by the apostles to Jesus, and the last

words of Jesus to them, both being characteristic to the utmost. Theirs expressed their desire for a national restoration : His directed them to a sublimer hope and enterprise, saying, " *But ye shall receive power, after that the Holy Ghost is come upon you : and ye shall be witnesses unto me both in Jerusalem, and in all Judea, and in Samaria, and unto the uttermost part of the earth* " (i. 8). Simple words, but of profound import. Reported to Luke, they fixed his attention. They were prophetic of a proceeding and of a result which touched his sympathies, and which at once provoked and sustained his curiosity. " Ye shall receive power, . . . ye shall be witnesses . . . unto the uttermost parts of the earth." Upon this assurance and this charge of the Lord to His apostles, the entire series of relations contained in this book has a dependence. In his Gospel is shown by Luke how the prophetic Scriptures were fulfilled by Christ. In the Acts it was proposed to show how Christ's own predictions were fulfilled in His Church. The shame of the cross had been borne : that came from man. The glory of the resurrection had appeared : that came from God. To proclaim the Lord's resurrection by infallible proofs, as witnesses, was henceforth to be the sole employment of the apostles, along with a declaration of His life and exposition of His doctrines. In accomplishing their new mission, a geographical order is directed to be observed ; and in that order flows the current of Luke's present narrative, comprising these sections :—

1. The period wherein a testimony was delivered in Jerusalem only (i. to vii.), terminating about A.D. 36.

2. The period wherein the gospel was published in Samaria and the provinces, and was received by devout Gentiles in Cæsarea (viii. to xi.), terminating A.D. 40.

3. The period wherein the gospel was preached to idolatrous Gentiles, and Churches were raised in Syria and Proconsular Asia (xi. to xvi.), terminating A.D. 41.

4. The period of the planting the gospel, and its successes in Europe (xvi. to xx.), terminating A.D. 58.

5. The period of Paul's last journey to Jerusalem, and his imprisonment at Cæsarea (xx. to xxvi.), terminating A.D. 60.

6. The period commencing with Paul's voyage to Italy, and terminating with his prison-life at Rome (xxvii., xxviii.), terminating A.D. 63.

To the first of these periods consideration is confined in this chapter.

The apostles were to receive divine power before they commenced their commission. And Luke preserves an account of the unexpected and amazing manner in which that power was conferred. He tells how it came by a sound of wind and an appearance of fire—the two most potent elements in nature. He explains,—" And they were all filled with the Holy Ghost ;" and he relates the effect thereof : " and began to speak with other tongues "—a miracle whereby they were fitted to commence their new ministry to the world without any other preparation. In like manner do all the miracles recorded throughout the book have reference to a preparation for, or a confirmation of, the testimonies delivered by the apostles concerning Jesus, and to their fulfilling His charge to witness for Him in Jerusalem, Judea, Samaria, and unto the uttermost parts of the earth.

" Power " was given to the apostles to fulfil their Lord's charge to witness for Him in Jerusalem, when " Peter stood forth with the eleven, and charged the men of Judea, and they that dwelt at Jerusalem, with the crucifixion of Christ; and declared, " This Jesus hath God raised up, whereof we all are witnesses," &c. (ii. 32–36).

That charge was courageously fulfilled when Peter and John, having wrought in the name of Jesus a miraculous cure on a lame man, Peter addressed the wondering spectators, and charged them, saying, " Ye denied the Holy One and the Just, and desired a murderer to be granted unto you ; and killed the Prince of life, whom God hath raised from the dead; whereof we are witnesses "(iii. 14, 15).

It was fulfilled in the same manner when those same apostles, having been brought before the Sanhedrim, addressing the council, said, " Ye rulers of the people and elders of Israel, be it known unto you, and to all the people of Israel, that by the name of Jesus Christ of Nazareth, whom ye crucified, whom God raised from the dead, even by Him doth this man stand before you whole." And remission of sins in His name was preached when they added, " Neither is there salvation in any other " (iv. 8-12).

The Lord's charge was fulfilled in Jerusalem when an angel, having delivered those same apostles from prison, directed them, " Go stand and speak in the temple to the people all the words of this life ;" and having obeyed, they were again taken by officers before the council, and being charged by the high priest to speak no more to the people in the name of Jesus, they replied, " We ought to obey God rather than men. The God of our fathers raised up Jesus, whom ye slew and hanged on a tree : and we are witnesses of these things :" and when they added, " Him hath God exalted with His right hand a Prince and a Saviour, for to give repentance unto Israel, and forgiveness of sins " (v. 29-32). And, in general terms, Luke declares, " With great power the apostles gave witness of the resurrection of the Lord " (iv. 33). " And daily in the temple and in every house they ceased not to teach and preach Jesus " (v. 42.) Here the presence of Luke in Jerusalem, his adopted home, is apparent: gratification glistens on his page. The results of these first essays and successes of the apostles are described with numerical exactness. He notices that to the original number of disciples in Jerusalem there was presently added 3000 converts. Thereafter he sets down an aggregate of 5000 believers; and again, as if the progressive increase baffled a ready reckoning, he writes "multitudes were added to the Church daily."

And equally expressive of actual observation is Luke's account of the character and manners of this new community. He does not give it in the form of a summary of received reports, but in sketches interwoven with his incidents. He represents, concerning those early converts, that—

1. They received the word with gladness (ii. 41).

2. They were stedfast in their profession of the apostles' doctrine (ii. 42).

3. They cherished an intimate fellowship (ii. 44).

4. They exercised a fraternal charity (iv. 32).

5. They were instant in prayer (ii. 42).

6. They were adorned with simplicity, or singleness of heart (ii. 46).

7. Their conduct commended them: "They were in favour with all the people" (ii. 47).

In those sketches, depicted with divine conciseness, the student possesses a cluster of the fruits of the Spirit's grace which adorned the members of the normal Church.

As the narrative proceeds, events are described from the Cyrenian's point of view. The foreigner and the proselyte are reflected throughout the historian's selection of intelligence. Other scenes are depicted, and other ministers besides the apostles appear. Mention is made of a circumstance respecting Greek converts, in the words, "And in those days, when the number of the disciples was multiplied, there arose a murmuring of the Grecians against the Hebrews, because their widows were neglected in the daily ministration" (vi. 1). A notice like this may appear unimportant; but its introduction is explained by the personal interest taken in the class by the writer. It is likewise agreeable to his principle of tracing things from their beginning. His associations had been with the Hellenists, in their synagogues ; and the complainants were converts from those communities. Moreover, the notice stands at the head of a series of particulars all eminently illustrating the main design of the narrative. It was connected with the appointment of deacons (literally *ministers* or *servants*) ; and this appointment was connected with the expansion of the Church beyond the limits of the strictly Hebrew element, to which eldership in the synagogues had hitherto been confined. Stephen, Philip, and Nicolas were Hellenists. A ministration to Greeks required a knowledge of their language. These deacons were students of the Septuagint version of the Bible. Furthermore, the naming of Stephen is the occasion for proceeding with the Greek aspect of events. The attention of Luke was naturally attracted to the Greek party opposed to the disciples. He relates, " Then there arose certain of the synagogue of the Libyans, the Cyrenians, and Alexandrians, and of them of Cilicia, disputing with Stephen " (vi. 9). It appears that the Greeks of the south united with those from the north in the discussion. This discussion would be occasioned by the numerous conversions which had occurred among the Greek communities, and of which conversions Stephen had been largely instrumental. For Luke writes, " And Stephen, full of faith and power, did great wonders and miracles among the people " (vi. 8). Whether he now repaired to the Hellenistic synagogues, or the elders thereof sought him, does not transpire. But as Stephen had been elected a deacon on account of his Greek predilections, it is probable that the discussion took place in the synagogues of the latter. The foreign Jews, especially those of Alexandria and Cyrene, were notorious for their tumultuous habits, as general history tells. This whole relation concerning Stephen discovers Luke's own prepossessions. Stephen is the first minister after the apostles concerning whom he writes. Not less does this relation illustrate the historian's method of connecting incidents apparently remote. For the violent death of Stephen introduces another agent. It brings upon the scene a Jew who had been pursuing his studies in Jerusalem, under a famous doctor of canon law, and who, being a native of Tarsus, attended also the synagogue of the Cilicians, and had there listened with passionate interest to the discussions which had been conducted against the testimony of Stephen. Afterwards, he witnessed the accusation of the deacon before the Sanhedrim. He heard his emphatic testimony, borne there in fulfilment of the Lord's charge. He followed the murderers with their victim without the gate. And here it is that mention is first made of this wonderful character, in these words: "And Saul was consenting unto his death" (viii. 1). The complicity of Saul in that deed was shown by his taking charge of the outer garments thrown at his feet by the witnesses whose evidence had been received against Stephen, and who therefore were bound to cast the first stones (Deut. xvii. 7). Such were the circumstances of Saul's first contact with Christianity. He now stood face to face with its first dying champion ; and he had now the opportunity to mark the correspondence that subsisted between the testimony he had heard from his lips and the behaviour of the saint thereafter.

And finally, attesting the power of the apostles and deacons witnessing for Christ at this period, and the success that attended their ministry, Luke seems, in relating how the number of the disciples multiplied in Jerusalem greatly, and how a great number of the priests were obedient to the faith, to exult as if sharing their triumphs.

CHAPTER VIII.

LUKE'S RELATION WITH THE ACTS OF THE APOSTLES.

The Second Period.

THE second section of Luke's second book may be said to commence at the eighth chapter, and to conclude at the eighteenth verse of the eleventh chapter. A recognition of the writer, amidst the scenes described, as a witness of some of them, and as receiving reports concerning the rest of them from the principal agents in them, imparts an interest to his narrative in the manner, though not the matter, of the Commentaries of classic writers of antiquity. Luke's method of writing being remembered, curiosity is sustained by observing how, as a historian for the Holy Ghost, his eye was directed throughout to the events as to a chain, each link of which is connected with the fulfilment of Christ's final charge. A prime example of this concatenation stands in front of this section. Saul was seen, in the previous chapter, a consenting witness to the murder of a disciple of Jesus: he here appears again, and in the attitude of fierce hostility to Christ's followers. "As for Saul," Luke relates, "he made havoc of the Church." But it is just at this seemingly gloomy and critical moment that a new development arises, and our Lord's charge obtains a fulfilment in its second geographical particular. And here it should be noticed, that Luke only produces samples; accomplishing his purpose, as a historian, by a relation of one, and seldom of more than two, illustrations. As a consequence of the persecution to which Saul had committed himself with his party, Luke continues, " *Therefore* they that were scattered abroad went everywhere preaching the Word. Then Philip went down to Samaria, and preached Christ unto them" (viii. 4, 5). This was the first occasion upon which a testimony for Christ was borne to others than to Jews and proselytes. This mission did not originate by the will of man, but was prompted by divine overruling. The result of this visit of Philip is characteristic. The Samaritans had shown their candour by admitting the Messiahship of Christ upon the occasion of His visit to Shechem. And so now " the people with one accord gave heed unto the things which Philip spake, hearing and seeing the miracles which he did" (viii. 6). "And there was great joy in that city" (ver. 8). Here, then, was accomplished that word spoken by our Lord in this place, " One soweth and another reapeth," having by His own ministry there prepared this harvest. Luke proceeds, " Now when the apostles which were in Jerusalem heard that Samaria had received the Word of God, they sent Peter and John " (ver. 14). And to complete the picture, it is afterwards added, " And they, when they had testified and preached the gospel in many towns of the Samaritans, returned to Jerusalem " (ver. 25). Dr Alford well remarks, " It is very interesting to observe, that this same John, who requested that our Lord might permit fire to come from heaven upon certain Samaritans (Luke ix. 54), came down to Samaria with Peter to confer the gift of the Holy Spirit on the Samaritan believers."

By the same overruling disposal that brought the gospel to Samaria, the testimony concerning Jesus was delivered to an African, journeying homeward from Jerusalem. Like Luke, this man had been a proselyte to the Jewish religion. This is to be inferred from his having been found reading a book of Holy Scripture. As an Ethiopian, he would have read the Alexandrian version.* He had doubtless heard, when in Jerusalem, concerning Christ, either from His enemies or His friends. His mind was occupied with the subject, and he was now reading the portion which especially was known to be prophetic of the Messiah. Philip was sent by divine monition to interpret the passage which he so intently read. The candour of the Ethiopian was equal to that of the Samaritans, as also was his joyful reception of the truth. For having, upon his confession of faith, been baptized, it is added concerning him, " And he went on his way rejoicing " (viii. 39). Luke came from Africa; and the writer's own joy seems to breathe in these words. In another respect this anecdote is remarkable. Some of the bitterest enemies of the disciples and opposers of their mission also came from Africa. But Africa is made the first foreign country to which the gospel is conveyed.

Keeping in mind the principle upon which the narrative is conducted, Philip is seen again as an agent fulfilling Christ's prophetic charge. From Azotus (Ashdod), passing through, he preached in all the towns till he came to Cæsarea, where for the present his tour terminated; for here was his home. As the writer was personally acquainted with Philip (xxi. 8), these particulars would have been received from Philip's own lips, in accordance with Luke's professed method when he was not himself the eye-witness.

And now again appears the name of Saul, which stands at the head of a train of events of singular interest. Saul is now found in pursuit of the fugitives, scattered by the violence of persecution. Breathing out threatenings against them, he bare letters from the high priest, directed to the elders of the synagogues at Damascus, that he might bring any of the disciples, men or women, bound to

---

* The Ethiopic version of the Old Testament was not translated from the Hebrew, but from the Alexandrian Greek.—*Ludolph's Ethiopic Psalter, Pref.*

Jerusalem" (ix. 1, 2). Those disciples were not mere terror-striken fugitives. They went everywhere preaching the Word. They were witnesses fulfilling the charge of Christ. They had His warrant. Their Lord had said concerning Himself to the same high priest, "Hereafter shall the Son of man sit on the right hand of the power of God" (Luke xxii. 69). And now a proof was to be given of the fulfilment of that word. Before Saul had reached the gate of the city, and when he thought the objects of his pursuit were just within his grasp, the persecutor is arrested. He is overcome by a light streaming from the throne of heaven. He hears a voice, "Saul, Saul, why persecutest thou me (in these my members)? I am Jesus of Nazareth, whom thou persecutest." Power was in the words. Saul's heart and his purpose are instantly changed. He yields the promptest homage, saying, "Lord, what wilt thou have me to do?" Saul consenting to the death of Stephen—Saul making havoc of the Church at Jerusalem—Saul breathing out threatenings against the disciples that fled before him —Saul prostrate before Jesus—this is the prophetic connexion.

The triumph of the enthroned Jesus was as complete as it was instantaneous. The apprehensions of the disciples, occasioned by the approach of Saul's embassy, were allayed by a revelation made to Ananias, saying, "Arise and inquire for Saul of Tarsus, for he is a chosen vessel unto me, to bear my name before the Gentiles" (ix. 10-16). With unhesitating faith Ananias went into the house to which he was directed, and addressing him, said, "Brother Saul, the Lord Jesus that appeared to thee in the way, hath sent me that thou mightest receive thy sight, and be filled with the Holy Ghost" (ver. 17). Thereupon Saul was admitted by baptism into the fellowship of the saints, whom before he had sought to imprison. And, conferring not with flesh and blood, he straightway preached Christ in the synagogues ; and increasing more in strength as he proceeded, he confounded the Jews at Damascus, proving that this Jesus is the very Christ (ver. 22). Now the animosity of those to whom he should have delivered the letters from the high priest is turned upon himself. They conspire to kill him ; and, escaping their vengeance by the good offices of the disciples, he returned to Jerusalem. Here, when he essayed to join himself to the disciples, they were all afraid of him. A son of consolation, however, is attracted to him. Barnabas took him and brought him to the apostles, and declared the history of his miraculous conversion. It has been thought that Barnabas had been a fellow-student with Saul at the feet of Gamaliel. But this is quite improbable, Barnabas having been too much Saul's senior for such a coincidence. All that can be said is, that the youthful Saul had obtained some acquaintance with him in the sphere of literature, or through the accident of the contiguity of their respective native homes. That they had been previously acquainted with each other is quite consistent with the confidence which Barnabas reposed in Saul's integrity. Soon did Saul justify this confidence in him by immediately repairing to the communities among whom he had acquired his former hostile feeling against the disciples. Their synagogues resounded with his testimony, as they had once with Stephen's. He spake boldly in the name of the Lord Jesus, and disputed against the Hellenists (ver. 29). But having been divinely directed, while engaged in prayer in the temple, to get quickly out of Jerusalem (xxii. 17, 18), and his life having been again threatened, certain of the brethren brought him down to Cæsarea (ver. 30). In this city the disciples were at present secure, under the influence of the police preserved by a large garrison of Roman soldiers. That Saul should have followed Stephen the deacon in bearing a testimony for Christ in the synagogues of the Grecians at Jerusalem, and then, having made proof of his ministry, that he should have followed Philip the deacon, Stephen's companion, to his residence at Cæsarea, are coincidences worthy of observation. Here, too, the mind reverts to the utterance of the Lord's prophetic charge, and beholds in Saul of Tarsus another link added to the agency whereby the great object proposed in that charge was to be fulfilled. How great was this trophy of Christ's power, selected from among His enemies, is intimated in the hush that succeeded the persecutions in which Saul had taken a conspicuous part, and those which were consequent upon his own conversion. For it is added, " Then had the Churches rest," &c.—that is, after Saul's retirement from the scene.

The narrative is continued by some examples of Peter's ministry. " And it came to pass that as Peter passed through all quarters (of Judea) he came to Lydda." The persecution at Jerusalem had not suspended his labours ; they only changed their scene. As examples of his ministry in the provinces, an occurrence at Lydda is related, and another at Joppa. They were both miraculous, and illustrated at once the powers conferred upon the apostles, and the success that attended their ministry (ix. 35, 42). There is related the conversion of Cornelius with his household, and their admission into the fellowship of the saints. And here, again, Luke's method of connecting his history with the text set at the head of it finds an illustration. Whilst Peter tarried at Joppa, a Roman officer at Cæsarea was warned by a vision to send to invite the apostle of Christ to come and instruct him what he ought to do ; being, although a Gentile, a devout man, fearing God with all his house, and praying alway. The sequel conveys an impression of the difficulty to be overcome, which subsisted in the mind of the apostle, to the free admission of a devout Gentile to fellowship, without the intermediate rite of proselytism to the Jewish economy. Christ came to pull

down the middle wall of partition; and He had often intimated in the course of His ministry, and in words addressed to themselves, that the gospel was designed for
"all the world." Left to man, the divine design would
never have been accomplished.

As the messengers from Cornelius drew near to Joppa,
a divine monition was given also to Peter, whereby he was
apprised of their errand, and instructed in his duty with
reference to it. Having travelled thither, they stayed with
him during the night, and he departed in their company on
the morrow. Their discourse may be imagined : Peter's
concerning Cornelius ; and the messengers', who were Jews,
holding Cornelius in great esteem, concerning the novel
doctrine of the followers of Jesus of Nazareth. Arrived at
the house, the earnest curiosity of Cornelius was shown in
his going to meet Peter at the gate, and his reverence for
him in the manner in which he welcomed him (x. 25, 26).
Explanations followed; Peter rehearsed how his scruples
had been overcome ; and Cornelius, for himself and on behalf of his company, declared, "Now therefore are we all
here present before God, to hear all things that are commanded thee of God" (x. 33). And now the first public
witness for Christ to the Jews becomes likewise the first to
the Gentiles. The testimony is identical, excepting, of
course, in what related to the distinct circumstances of the
two parties. On the memorable occasion of his first wit-
ness-bearing, Peter had said to the Jews, "Jesus of Nazareth, a man approved of God among you" &c. (ii. 22). To
the Gentiles he now explains, "How God anointed Jesus
of Nazareth with the Holy Ghost and with power, who
went about doing good," &c. (x. 38). To the Jews he had
said, "Him ye have taken, and by wicked hands have
crucified Him" (ii. 23). To the Gentiles, "Whom they
slew and hanged on a tree" (x. 39). To the Jews he said,
"This Jesus hath God raised up, whereof we all are wit-

nesses" (ii. 32). To the Gentiles, "Not to all the people, but unto witnesses chosen before of God, even to us, who did eat and drink with Him after He rose from the dead" (x. 41). To the Jews Peter had testified, "Repent, and be baptized every one of you in the name of Jesus Christ for the remission of sins" (ii. 38). And now to the Gentiles he says, in answer to what Cornelius had expressed concerning their anxious attitude, "And He commanded us to preach and to testify that which all the prophets witness, that through His name *whosoever* believeth in Him shall receive remission of sins" (x. 42, 43).

A seal was set to this testimony, for, "while Peter yet spake, the Holy Ghost fell on all them which heard the word. And they of the circumcision who came with Peter were astonished that on the Gentiles also was poured out the gift of the Holy Ghost." Hereupon Peter was compelled to challenge his Jewish companions, saying, " Can any man forbid that these should be baptized?" (x. 44-47).

This instance of Peter's fulfilment of his Master's charge possessed a marvellous interest for the Cyrenian. The baptism of Cornelius and his company is an event which furnishes an opportunity to test the relative position of Luke. He has given the history thereof with vivid exactness, and at a length which bespeaks his sense of its importance. Beginning at the last verse of the ninth chapter, the account of it occupies the whole of the tenth chapter, which consists of forty-eight verses. No writer, being a Jew, it may be supposed, would have devoted such a share of attention to the subject, except with a view to controvert the propriety of Peter's conduct, unless he had been, like Paul, a divinely-appointed apostle to the uncircumcision.

But this is not all. There follows thereafter an account, equally graphic, of a council of the apostles and brethren with reference to this innovation, held upon Peter's return to Jerusalem. "They of the circumcision," proceeds the historian, "contended with him." Exclusiveness is a foible of humanity. Like many in every age, the objectors thought that the benefits of the gospel were to be confined to their own party. Those simple men had no thought of subjugating the heathen to the sceptre of Christ. Such an interpretation of His last charge to them belonged to that class of announcements concerning which it was said, "They understood none of those things." Accordingly, their prejudice embodied itself in the form of an accusation of Peter. Peter's defence consisted in a rehearsal of the matter from the beginning, accompanied by an exposition of all its circumstances. His witnesses were produced, being the brethren who had accompanied him to Cæsarea. Moreover, he appealed to the promise of Christ, and to the fact of its fulfilment by the gift of the Holy Ghost to the Gentile converts, as well as to themselves. And he concluded by the modest appeal, "What was I that I could withstand God?" (xi. 17). The candour of the objectors was worthy of their profession as the disciples of Christ. "When they heard these things, they held their peace, and glorified God, saying, Then hath God also to the Gentiles granted repentance unto life."

As Luke was now in Jerusalem, his information concerning this other step in the direction which the gospel was destined to take had been easily derivable from Peter, or from one of those in company with him. This important circumstance concludes the second section of the Acts of the Apostles.

It already appears that the book is not to be regarded as describing the acts of the apostles in general, but quite in a limited sense. It does not give a full account of the ministry of any of the apostles, but only such facts as suffice to afford evidence of the fulfilment of Christ's final charge to them in its essential particulars. All the apostles, in their several spheres, accomplished their share of the great work assigned to them.   But Luke had no opportunity to follow them all, or to obtain information concerning their progresses from eye-witnesses.   Besides, the twelve apostles were ministers of the circumcision ; whilst his own sympathies were with the dawning expansiveness of the Gospel. The fulfilment of Christ's charge, agreeing with the order in which it was expressed, was gradual.   And most skilfully has the historian chosen his materials for an elucidation of ts progressive fulfilment.

CHAPTER IX.

LUKE ONE OF THE FIRST PREACHERS OF THE GOSPEL TO THE HEATHEN.

PERSECUTION had caused the dispersion of Christ's witnesses throughout Judea and Samaria. A similar cause afterwards led to the departure from Jerusalem of others to places beyond Palestine. And by this last exodus of disciples was occasioned the first step taken towards an accomplishment of Christ's prophetic charge in its last geographical particular. The account of this event forms an introduction to the THIRD SECTION of the Acts of the Apostles, and is related in the eleventh chapter, from the nineteenth verse to the twenty-first. Here Luke says, "Now they which were scattered abroad *upon* the persecution that arose about Stephen, travelled as far as Phenice, and Cyprus, and Antioch." The word translated *upon* rather signifies "after the death of Stephen" (Valpy's Greek Testament); so that some time had elapsed before the persecutors turned upon the foreign proselytes. It is added, "Some of them were men of Cyprus and Cyrene, who, when they were come to Antioch, spake unto the Grecians, preaching the Lord Jesus" (xi. 20). The men of Cyprus journeyed homeward. But for the mention of those of Cyrene, some other reason must be sought than what explains the route of the former. It might have been that, being indisposed to go so far away from Jerusalem as to Africa, they chose Antioch, as being, like Cyrene, a free Roman city. That Luke was one of those men of Cyrene is concluded upon the evidence—(1.) that his name, coupled with his country, appears in the immediate sequel (xiii. 1); and (2.) that from this point to the end of the fifteenth chapter, the current of his narrative has Antioch for its centre. Consistent with this evidence is the opinion of Dr Whitby, who, in a note beneath the verse xi. 20, says, "Luke of Cyrene was one of them that came down to Antioch." The date of that exodus is reckoned by some chronologists to have been A.D. 41. Luke had therefore resided at Jerusalem seven or eight years.

This company of witnesses was dismissed as well by the same overruling hand as from the same secondary cause that sent forth the companies of witness-bearers throughout Palestine. Some of them had relations with one place, and some with another. It is said, "They went preaching the Word"—that is, as directed in Christ's charge. They were all of them preachers. The commission was not to be limited to the apostles, nor yet to them and the seventy evangelists. God usually begins to work at a point unexpected by man. Our Lord had said, "They shall lay their hands on you and persecute you." But he added, "And it shall turn to you for a testimony" (Luke xxi. 12, 13). And history confirms the word. In England, for instance, the Philippo-Marian persecution raised an inextinguishable beacon, deterring the faithful from apostasy; and now the faithful of Britain have the honour to be Christ's chiefest witness-bearers to the world.

Notwithstanding the intense brevity of Luke's narrative at this point, the conduct of his company is distinctly described. Their exodus illustrated that word, "I will lead them in paths they have not known." They preached, it is said, to none but Jews only. They carried with them the prejudices of Judea. As yet, neither Jew nor proselyte, being disciples of Christ, comprehended the freedom with which the Gentiles were to be received into fellowship. To the Jews belonged the oracles of God, having been the recipients and guardians of them ; and to the people thus distinguished it was thought salvation was confined. Hence the devout Gentiles, who read the Holy Scriptures in the Greek version, had always joined themselves as proselytes to the Jewish community. And hence, by both Jew and proselyte, no other idea was entertained but that an acceptance of Jesus, as the Messiah of the Old Testament prophecies, required the same initiation. Under this misconception of the design of Christ, the proclamation of the gospel had hitherto been limited to Jews and proselytes. The three thousand converts on the day of Pentecost included no others ; and perhaps Cornelius and his company had hitherto been the sole examples of an admission otherwise than through the conventional gate. It was by this company, and at Antioch, that this spell was destined to be broken.

And now follows the sentence *upon which turns almost the entire future interest of the book:* "WHO, WHEN THEY CAME TO ANTIOCH, SPAKE UNTO THE GRECIANS CONCERNING THE LORD JESUS." "Here," remarks Valpy, "we seem to have the first account of preaching the gospel to idolatrous Gentiles, for there is nothing in the word Ἑλληνιστὰς (Greeks) to limit it to such as were worshippers of the true God" (Gr. Test.) Luke's design was to describe *progress.* Already the gospel had been preached to Hellenists, both Jews and proselytes, in the synagogues at Jerusalem and elsewhere. Also, in the several towns through which this company had come, the preaching had been confined to the synagogues by those that were Jews, and perhaps to some assemblies of proselytes, by those that were proselytes. But at Antioch the curiosity of others than these was awakened by what had been brought to their ears concerning Jesus Christ by the newly-arrived travellers. And nothing could be more natural than that those disciples who were Greeks should now, among Greeks, freely speak of those things of which their heads and hearts were full. They had left the land of miracles. But adding to their recital a declaration of the risen Saviour's charge, that " repentance and remission of sins should be preached in His name among all nations," their words were persuasive : " The hand of the Lord was with them." A benign influence was shed, disposing the hearers to a grateful acceptance of the message. Misapprehension concerning the design and extent of that message was at once banished by the happy result ; for it is added, " And a great number believed, and turned unto the Lord " (xi. 21). That a result so great was unanticipated, is manifest. It was the first time that the message of Christ had been related, and the mercy of it preached, to idolatrous Gentiles. The case of Cornelius was different from this ; for although a Gentile, he was not an idolator. This result set a divine seal upon the proceeding ; and therein that word of Christ received an illustration, " And other sheep I have, which are not of this fold ; them also I must bring, and they shall hear my voice ; and there shall be one fold and one shepherd " (John x. 16). And now was illustrated the testimony of Peter, being the last words which Luke added to his notes written in Jerusalem, " Then hath God also to the Gentiles granted repentance unto life " (xi. 18). How gratifying must the thought ever have been to Luke, that to him appertained the honour of having been one of the very first witnesses for Christ to the heathen !

Tidings of this display of divine grace beyond Palestine, and towards heathen, were received by the Church at Jerusalem in another temper than upon the occasion of the conversion of Cornelius. A deputy was despatched, and one that betokened the considerate feeling that now prevailed : " They sent forth Barnabas, that he should go as far as Antioch " (xi. 22). Than Barnabas, none could have been more suitable for this delicate mission. He was named " a son of consolation." He had given his property for the solace of brethren impoverished by persecution. And having been a native of Cyprus, his sympathies were not likely to be so contracted as if he had been a Jew of Palestine; but he would be more free to embrace the new class of ingathered disciples. The repetition of the phrase, "*as far as* Antioch," seems not only to indicate distance, but also to express what, in Anglican terms, would be called the extra-parochial character of the movement.

The sight that Barnabas came to witness was one which heaven itself had in suspense awaited. The case of the Gentiles was intimately and necessarily connected with our Lord's ministry. His charge to preach the gospel of the remission of sins in His name to all nations, and to the uttermost parts of the earth, constituted His invitation to every person indiscriminately to partake with all believers the promised grace of the new covenant. Like all prophetic events before their fulfilment, the promise had appeared dim and shadowy to the most discerning student. But now the light had shone, the fact was realised. "A great number had believed, and turned unto the Lord." The link of proselytism was broken. Believers had stepped directly from the ranks of the idolaters into fellowship with the saints. And like as Simeon welcomed the infant Jesus, so, with respect to this infant Church, " Barnabas, when he came and had seen the grace of God, was glad." And—O divine charity !—the simple term of communion proposed to the new converts by this " good man " was, an unswerving fidelity to Him unto whom they had turned: " He exhorted them all, that with purpose of heart they would cleave unto the LORD " (ver. 23).

CHAPTER X.

In travelling as far as Antioch, Luke and his company had consulted their convenience. They repaired to a place remote from the influences that fanned the persecution from which they sought to escape. But the hand of the Lord, which was with them, conducted them hither for a higher purpose than their mere security. They had witnessed many of the interesting scenes connected with the fulfilment of Christ's charge in Judea. And little as they expected it, they had come to a place where they would behold a still wider accomplishment of its great purpose.

Antioch was distant 260 miles from Jerusalem. It was built partly on the lowest slope of a mountain, and partly in the valley through which flows the Orontes, the chief river of Syria, and which runs its course to the sea at a distance of nearly twenty miles. The city was overlooked by mountains; one of which, Mount Casius, is so high that the rising sun may be seen from its summit when the bottom of it is still in darkness. Strabo, who wrote shortly before Luke went thither, describes Antioch as consisting of four distinct quarters, each having a wall of its own, and the whole surrounded with a common wall. The several walls marked the successive additions which had been made to the city.

Antioch was eminently adapted for commencing the design contemplated in the last particular of Christ's charge. Next to Rome and Alexandria, it was the principal Oriental

city of the empire. With Africa on one side of it, and
Europe on the other, it was more central than either of
those cities, whilst its population was of a more cosmo-
politan character. Libanius, the sophist, who was a native
of Antioch, describing the city, says, " Sitting in its market-
place you see before you the inhabitants and manners of all
the cities of the world." And he adds, " Within and without it every art and device are employed to make life desir-
able." The words " without it " include an extensive park,
five miles distant from the city, in which, amidst a grove of
laurels and cypresses, was a temple raised by Antiochus
Epiphanes, wherein was enshrined a splendid idol of
Daphne. The games and pleasures here pursued were of a
character so extravagant that the phrase " Daphnic manners" became a proverb. By the Latins, the city itself was
often called "*Antiochia apud Daphnem.*"

By the events which followed the arrival of Luke and his
company, Antioch came to possess a renown next to
Jerusalem in the early annals of Christianity. In Antioch
was laid the first foundation of the Gentile Church. Here
Chrysostom was born, and here he delivered his " Homilies
on the Acts of the Apostles." Antioch was the theatre of
several ecclesiastical councils. A list of its early bishops is
given by Eusebius. The Crusaders took the city from the
Turks in 1098, by whom it was erected into a Christian
principality. Resumed by the Turks in 1269, it rapidly
decayed. And now, of this once opulent and luxurious
mistress of Syria, it is impossible to form an idea, such as
is attainable of some other obsolete cities by their architec-
tural remains.

At Antioch, Luke was in a new element. The men of
Cyrene were not regarded in this city as strangers and
foreigners, as they had been at Jerusalem. They stood in
the relation of fellow-citizens to the Antiochians, who,
like the Cyrenians, possessed the privilege of the Roman

freedom. The fact that the historian was himself one of those men of Cyrene is verified from his having, fortunately for his biography, inserted his name and country in the narrative just in relation to this time and place. As the future historian of the Church, it was advantageous for his purpose that Luke was set in a position to observe the planting of the gospel at this important station. For, whereas in Jerusalem, not being a Jew, he had no part or lot in the ministry; there having been no such bar here, he is now found classed with prophets and teachers. In that situation no other testimony could have been received with more respect than Luke's by the Antiochians. The fact that he was not a Jew gave weight to his representations. He had no hereditary prepossessions like those prevalent in the minds of Jews. He had made himself acquainted with the whole history to which the faith of inquirers was invited. He had attended for the space of seven years upon the teaching of the apostles. He had received, with them, the gift of the Holy Ghost. He was familiar with their ways in Christ. And ever since his conversion he had been in active sympathy with the divine purpose to bless the world by the gospel of Jesus. In the deliberations, therefore, concerning the exigencies which the rapid gathering of a Church, under circumstances so novel, would occasion, Luke's long experience, and his habits of observation, rendered his counsels invaluable.

Again, Luke's method of a historical combination, as of links in a chain, receives an illustration. Of those that sold their lands to provide for the poor saints at the first ingathering of the Church, Luke specified only the name of Barnabas. Upon Saul's return to Jerusalem, and when the disciples, incredulous concerning his conversion, shunned him, Luke represents Barnabas as having brought him into their company, and, by a narrative of the circumstances of his conversion, inspired them with confidence towards him.

And now Barnabas, with whom by these anecdotes the reader has been made acquainted, visits the Church at Antioch. When God works, all hindrances vanish. Not only can He raise up of stones children unto Abraham, but, having raised them, He can dispose the children of Abraham to regard this new progeny as brethren. Barnabas, the Levite, was so disposed. When he came and had seen the illustration of the grace of God in the converts here, "he was glad; for (or because)," adds Luke, "he was a good man, and full of the Holy Ghost and of faith." When this expression of his friend's admiration is sanctioned by the Inspirer of Holy Scripture, these characteristics must have been bright indeed. Barnabas was a man of great benevolence. He exulted in leaping over the wall of separation, to behold the enriching of the world with an affluence of grace. He was fitted for a ministry, in this new field, by a large endowment of the gifts and graces of the Holy Spirit. Perceiving the design of Christ with respect to these sheep of another fold, he rejoiced to gather them. His character harmonised with the interesting business of the embassy with which he had been entrusted. And how Luke shared the happy feeling of his friend is seen in the words with which he records the result of Barnabas's conciliating ministry. "Much people," he says, "was added to the Lord" (xi. 24). This result of preaching the remission of sins through faith in Christ crucified seems more illustrious here than even in Judea; for there the people had been prepared by a previous revelation through the prophets; but here the result rested simply on a reception of the testimony for Jesus borne by His disciples, the divine influence being present with teacher and convert, compensating the want of any preliminary indoctrination.

By Luke's method of composing his narrative it is shown how God had already prepared another, and a special, agent for this new field of evangelical harvesting. Already the reader is acquainted with him. It has been seen how it was said concerning Saul by Jesus Christ, "He is a chosen vessel unto me, to bear my name before the Gentiles." And it will now be seen how at Antioch these words received their primary verification. An accession of agency had brought new success. The success gave occasion for more labourers. Barnabas had laboured at Antioch about a year. His faith prompted an appliance of redoubled power. He desired help in this new field of enterprise. The relation concerning Saul which he had made to the disciples at Antioch, and the fact of his designation to the ministry of the Gentiles, came to his mind. He resolved to acquaint him with the exigence, and to invite him to share his labours. For this purpose he must travel to Tarsus. Tarsus was the chief city of the adjoining province of Cilicia. It stood near to the Cilician coast, as did Antioch the Syrian, whilst both looked towards the island of Cyprus, which stood in the bay that washed both those shores ; the three places having a triangular relation to each other, and the neighbourhood of the three becoming the theatre of the first dawning of the gospel upon the Gentile world. The situation of Saul during the interval of his retirement from Jerusalem to Tarsus, and his going from thence to Antioch, has always presented a difficulty to his biographers.

But it is submitted whether a key to it is not found in a *word*. In the English version the narrative proceeds, "Then departed Barnabas for to *seek* Saul" (xi. 25). But this version represents only half the truth. The word in the original text, *anazetesai*, does not signify simply *to seek*, but is a compound, having a prefix of intensification, and which, rendered literally, is *to seek back ;* signifying, of course, to seek diligently, or to seek a restoration (of the object in question). The same word had been used by the Evangelist to express the anxious search of Mary for her missing son (Luke ii. 44). And, certainly, did he not intend to convey the same meaning, he had not employed it here. What, then, is this word intended to reveal? It intimates, at least, that Saul was *in obscurity*. But how is this intimation corroborated? The only notice that occurs concerning him during this interim is a notification made by himself in his Epistle to the Galatians of an excursion made into Arabia (Gal. i. 17). Whether that excursion was made in this interim signifies little here. It is sufficient that no fruits of that journey anywhere appear. So this notice only adds mystery to the difficulty sought to be solved. It remains, then, to revert to the account of his coming to Tarsus from Jerusalem, related in the ninth chapter of the Acts. There it appears that his preaching, when he arrived in Jerusalem from Damascus, had had the effect of increasing the persecution that raged against the Church; and as a precautionary means, both for Saul's safety, whose life was sought by the Jews, and also for the sake of the Church, the brethren removed him from the seat of danger. And it is recorded, as an immediate consequence of his absence, "Then had the Churches rest in all Judea and Galilee" (ix. 31).

Passing from the ninth to the twenty-second chapter of the Acts, there is there found an allusion made, several years afterwards, by Saul himself to his situation at this period. It is found in his speech addressed from the steps of the Castle Antonia to a mob of infuriate Jews, that, in a trance in the temple, Jesus had warned him, "Make haste, and get speedily out of Jerusalem, for they will not receive thy testimony concerning me; depart, for I will send thee far hence unto the Gentiles" (xxii. 17–21). Much, therefore, as Saul might have wished to preach Christ where he had formerly blasphemed Him, Jerusalem was not to be the scene of his ministry. His mission was to preach to the far-off Gentiles.

But reverting to the chain of events, the terms in which his dismissal from Jerusalem is expressed should be noticed. First, it is said, " *They brought him down* to Cæsarea," being a safer place for him than Jerusalem. Peter afterwards retired to the same city, to avoid apprehension again, after his deliverance by an angel from prison.

But it is not written concerning Peter that he was " *brought* down," but that " he *departed*, and went to another place " (xii. 17). And, secondly, as though Saul's removal to Cæsarea was not security enough, " they *sent him forth* to Tarsus "—that is, by a ship (ix. 30).

From these premises, the inference derivable is, that Saul's situation at Tarsus was one of almost *constrained retirement.* It was from this condition that Barnabas was divinely directed to release him. And with this inference agrees the language in which the anecdote is related. It says, " And when he had *found him*, he *brought* him to Antioch." But for the clearer perception of the argument, the expressions employed to describe both his *dismissal* and his *restoration* should be read in conjunction.

The first combination—*Saul's dismissal :* " They brought him down to Cæsarea " (ix. 30). *Saul's restoration :* " And when he (Barnabas) had found him, he brought him to Antioch " (xi. 26). .

The second combination—*Saul's dismissal :* " They sent him forth to Tarsus " (ix. 30). *Saul's restoration :* " Then departed Barnabas to Tarsus, to seek back Saul " (xi. 25).

So Saul's appointed place of labour was neither Jerusalem nor Tarsus, but Antioch of the Gentiles, and thereafter the world. And then there is to be noticed the beautiful consistency of this argument with the prophetic chain of Luke's narrative. Here is beheld that " good man, and full of the Holy Ghost," who, in his love and faith, had, as an angel of peace, first introduced Saul to the Church at Jerusalem, becoming now, in like manner, the medium of the introduction of this "chosen vessel" to his proper sphere ; both the one and the other being unconscious with what punctuality they were accomplishing the divine purpose—the one by the invitation to repair to Antioch, and the other by the acceptance of that invitation.

As a witness of the scene, Luke furnishes a glance of the freeness with which Saul followed the example of Barnabas in joining the assemblies of Gentiles, and also of the unanimity of feeling which marked their conduct. "And it came to pass that a whole year they assembled themselves with the Church" (ver. 26). It is worthy of observation, that they are said to have "assembled themselves with the Church"—*not* the Church with them. It is to be observed, too, that this is the first time that the term "Church" is applied to an assembly of Gentiles. In coming, therefore, to Antioch, Saul was introduced to the first divinely-acknowledged Church, composed of persons brought immediately out of the darkness of heathenism, and who, as converts, were exempt from the burdens of the ritual of that economy which was fast waning away. Heretofore his ministry had been confined to synagogues. Here he became conjoined with a new class of persons, with those of a different culture, and of other habits than the class with which he had hitherto associated. It is most probable, also, that it was now that he first became personally acquainted with Luke himself.

Luke takes care to show how the faith of Barnabas was justified by the result. "They taught much people." By the combined ministry of these remarkable men, public attention was sustained. The number of inquirers increase. Salvation from the doubts and dread that hung upon the heathen mind in all things relating to religion was a new theme for thought ; and the tidings preached by these, of the remission of sins and everlasting life through faith in Christ's name, were doctrines welcomed by multitudes of the weary and heavy-laden.

As an evidence of the interest which the fact of the multitude that adopted these new doctrines had excited, Luke relates, " The disciples were called Christians first in Antioch." The mention of this circumstance would be induced by the fact that Luke was himself a member of the community to which the name was thus originally applied. Upon this notice Dr Lightfoot remarks, " As Cæsarea, the seat of the Roman governor of Judea, first saw the door of faith opened to Gentiles, so Antioch, the seat of the Roman governor of Syria, first hears the name of Christian." This name was not given to the disciples of Christ by way of reproach, as some writers have thought. It had been more clearly observed here than in any other place that the disciples were not Jews, nor yet proselytes to Judaism, neither was their place of assembly a synagogue. And their doctrines being, equally with the Jewish religion, opposed to idolatry, and unlike those of any other sect known in Antioch, it was consequently an alternative, both of reason and convenience, that they should obtain the name which definitely indicated their discipleship. But behind the reasons inducing their new denomination, there was an occult cause of this nomenclature. An ancient prophecy had said, " For the Lord God shall call His servants by *another name*. For behold I create a new heaven and a new earth : and the former shall not be remembered, nor come into mind " (Isa. lxv. 15, 17).

By the relation of an anecdote, Luke shows how the first act of the Christians of Antioch, in their collective capacity, illustrated the appropriateness of this denomination of them, and how truly they had partaken of the instinct of the Household of Faith. Informed by a prophetic utterance that there would happen a general dearth, and knowing that the disciples in Judea were already reduced to straits by persecution, and considering how their troubles would be aggravated by famine, these Christians promptly raised a contribution to alleviate the exigence of their Jewish brethren. And, as a further proof of their sympathy, they " sent it to the elders, by the hands of Barnabas and Saul." Happy brotherhood, and happy messengers, bearing such welcome fruits of a ministry to Gentiles !

CHAPTER XI.

A PARENTHESIS.

In passing from the eleventh to the twelfth chapter of the
"Acts," the reader will perceive that he enters upon a
section which, excepting by the conjunction "Now about
that time," has no connexion with the current narrative. As
this is the only instance, since Luke's residence at Antioch,
that he relates anything besides what concerns the Church
there, or the agents proceeding from thence, as from a
centre of Christian enterprise, this apparent deviation from
his plan attracts curiosity. For this deviation, the importance and instructiveness of the particulars may have been
an inducement. But besides this, his plan required that
the intelligence conveyed by his pen should have been
either observed by himself or communicated to him by a
witness. The events related in this the twelfth chapter,
had occurred before Barnabas and Saul went to Jerusalem
with alms from the Church at Antioch, and were uncon-
nected with their mission. And although, upon their
return, they might have delivered the intelligence to him,
as they received it from others when there, they could not
have stood in the place of witnesses.

That Luke nevertheless did write this section from information conveyed by the lips of a witness, or one so closely
allied to the eye-witnesses as to warrant his acceptance of it,
appears in the sequel. In the verse wherein the return of
Barnabas and Saul to Antioch is announced, it says, "And
took with them John, whose surname was Mark." Mark

had hitherto resided in Jerusalem ; and as he was a disciple of Christ, and intimately related to other disciples there, he had been in a favourable situation for observation. Luke would have been acquainted with him during his recent residence in Jerusalem. Obviously the passages of this section were selected from intelligence now brought by Mark. The consideration that the matter of this chapter was contributed by Mark, whilst the composition was Luke's, lends to it a special interest. The particulars thus afforded are these :—

1. *Herod Agrippa's persecution of the Church of Christ in Jerusalem:* " He stretched forth his hand " (exercised his power) " to vex certain of the Church." The notice of this man contained in this chapter is all that occurs concerning him in the New Testament. He was a grandson of Herod the Great, and the son of Aristobalus, who was killed by that tyrant. The history and character of Herod Agrippa are supplied by Josephus in his Antiquities (xix.)

2. *The martyrdom of James.* The conciseness of this notice is characteristic. No books are so full, yet so brief, as the Holy Scriptures. This needful brevity leaves the student the profitable employment of seeking, by combinations of illus-trative passages, to obtain an enlarged view of the subject under notice. With what success this may be done is shown in Dr Paley's " Horæ Paulinæ." This James is called " the elder." He was brother of John, with whom he had witnessed the miraculous draught of fishes in the Lake of Gennesaret, and thereafter was called by Christ to be a fisher of men. He had been distinguished by having had a separate manifestation afforded to him of Jesus Christ after His resurrection (1 Cor. xv. 7). This James, with his brother, aspired to " sit at the right hand of Christ in His kingdom ;" and in response to the Lord's observation thereupon, declared that " he was able to drink of the cup

that Christ should drink." He had since seen how "Christ suffered, leaving an example that he should follow His steps" (1 Peter ii. 21). And now was fulfilled that word spoken to him by our Lord, "Ye shall indeed drink of the cup that I drink of; and with the baptism that I am baptized with shall ye be baptized" (Mark x. 39). James became the second of Christ's disciples that attained a martyr's crown. And whereas Stephen, when suffering, "saw Jesus standing on the right hand of God," James had been beforehand fortified for his conflict by having, along with his brother and Peter, beheld His glory when they were with Him on the holy mount. The notice that James "was killed with the sword," consists with the kingly power under which he suffered. He was not crucified, as was his Master, under the proconsular rule; nor stoned to death, as was Stephen, under the judgment of the Sanhedrim, and by the hands of a lawless multitude.

3. *The disposition of the Jews towards the disciples of Christ.* The murder of James "*pleased the Jews.*" Their malignity towards the disciples of Jesus was unabated; and in Herod Agrippa they found a power to afflict them which they themselves did not possess. James and his brother had been surnamed Boanerges. Like John and Peter, he had with great energy borne witness for his crucified Lord. This is inferred from his having been the foremost arrested. The "certain" upon whom "hands were laid," were, of course, the more intrepid of the disciples. By the death of James, another prophet was added to the number of those that had been slain in Jerusalem. It is hereby seen, that the measure of the iniquity of its inhabitants was being filled up, as the foretold doom of the mystical Sodom approached.

4. *Peter's imprisonment.* The king "proceeded further to take Peter also." The brevity of the notice of James's death is an indication that Mark had not beheld the scene,

but had only, with the mourners, lamented it.   And whereas that event is told in one sentence, the report relating Peter's imprisonment occupies the chief part of the chapter.   And here, by conciseness of style, combined with minuteness of detail, is produced a picture of exquisite interest.   Mark was familiarly acquainted with Peter, by whom he was called his son (1 Peter v. 13).   What, therefore, looking at all the circumstances, can be more reasonable than to conclude that Mark received the particulars from the apostle's own lips, that it was Peter himself who had related in his hearing how he was arrested—how he had been chained to two soldiers—how he had nevertheless slept—and also how many soldiers were apppointed to guard him, together with their several stations in the prison.   Having been twice imprisoned before, and twice delivered, Peter's tranquillity, in this sad situation, arose from an experimental persuasion of his Master's sympathy with His faithful servant.   Upon a former occasion, he had " rejoiced that he was counted worthy to suffer for the name of Christ " (Acts v. 41).   And having shared both the sufferings and the consolations of Christ, he would afterwards say to believers, " If ye be persecuted for the name of Christ, happy are ye ; rejoice, inasmuch as ye are partakers of His sufferings " (1 Peter iv. 14).

5. *The conduct of the Church in the crisis:* " Prayer was made without ceasing " (that is, several days and nights) " unto God for him."   Mark himself was among those earnest supplicants.

6. *A miraculous deliverance.*   Uniformly doth the New Testament, or covenant, follow the Old Testament as a providential history; and equally, under both, had the prophets a miraculous sanction.   The hostile Jews had thought that, by the favour of Herod Agrippa, their victim was at length secure.   In consideration of the sanctity of the
 eason, Peter was kept in prison until the expiration of the

seven days of unleavened bread succeeding the Passover, when the king intended to bring him forth to the people. The evening of the last of those days had arrived; and, according to the expectation of the Jews, Peter was to have been produced as a spectacle on the morrow. Midnight, with its stillness, intervened.

And here, again, by whom was it told that Peter was now sleeping between two soldiers bound by two chains; that an angel stood by him; that a light shined in the prison; that the angel touched him on the side, and raised him up, saying, "Arise up quickly;" that his chains fell over his hands; that the angel said, "Gird thyself, and bind on thy sandals;" and again, "Cast thy garment about thee, and follow me;" that, following the angel, he left the cell; that, having passed the first and second wards, the iron gate that led into the city opened of its own accord; and that, having conducted him through one street, the angel thereupon departed from him? Certainly, these incidents, so minutely related together with the impressions made by them upon his mind as they occurred, no one could have communicated but Peter himself. And that Mark was in a position to have heard Peter's first relation of them will presently appear.

7. *Peter's retirement to the house of Mary.* "And when Peter had considered," or had recovered from sensations like those by which he had been overcome when on the Mount of Transfiguration, "he came to the house of Mary the mother of John, whose surname was Mark." Peter instinctively turned towards the house of his abode when sojourning in Jerusalem. If, in this case, tradition may be trusted, this house was situated in Zion, or upper city of Jerusalem. It was a house of respectable dimensions, having been entered by a gate opening into a vestibule, or atrium. The hostess maintained a corresponding hospitality. "A gracious woman retaineth honour" (Prov. xi.

16). The names of saints are quoted in Holy Scripture for memorials. It is, therefore, proper that we stand before these memorials meditatively. This Mary was one of the mothers in the new Israel. Her brother, Barnabas, was a Levite, and had, therefore, been a minister in the temple, and he had become one of Christ's own converts. Of him, who sold his estate for the solace of disciples injured by persecution, Mary was a true sister. Her house was a resort of the apostles ; and, perhaps, had sometimes been visited by Jesus himself. It has been thought that it was to her house that the apostles repaired when they returned from the farewell scene with their Lord on the mount overlooking Bethany ; for it is written " they went up (*to Zion ?*) into an upper room, where abode Peter and the rest " (i. 13). And, also, it is thought, that it was in the same room, the apostles being assembled, that the Holy Ghost descended, and conferred upon them the gift of tongues.

Here, on the night of Peter's rescue, " many were gathered together in the upper room praying." Here was " a church in the house," and here one of the companies by whom prayer was made for Peter without ceasing. Perhaps, forming part of this company, were apostles lodging in the house (i. 13). " Peter knocked at the door of the gateway ;" " a damsel came to hearken " (indicative of the fear that prevailed within lest a messenger from the king had come for another victim) " named Rhoda "— (Rose)—a precision only to be accounted for by these particulars having been communicated by a person familiar with the household. " And when she knew Peter's voice," having listened to distinguish, " she opened not the door for gladness, but ran in, and told how Peter stood before the gate." How characteristic of the impulsiveness of the maiden was this rushing to the upper room before having admitted him ! " And they said unto her, Thou art mad," so great was her ecstasy. "But she constantly affirmed that it was so." "Then, said they, it is his angel," or an apparition. They had forgotten, in their grief, Peter's former deliverances from prison. "But Peter continued knocking," whilst the company debated. "And when they had opened"—some of the company went with Rhoda to the door, having been still doubtful of the truth of her report,—" and seeing Peter, they were astonished." Because their prayers had not been answered before, they were losing hope. "But he, beckoning with his hand to hold their peace, *declared unto them how the Lord had brought him out of prison.*" Here, then, was made the first relation of these incidents ; and here, in his own mother's house, had been, at the same moment, Mark ; but who, having since travelled to Antioch, was now at Luke's elbow. Thus, obviously, appears the reason why Mary is distinguished " as the mother of John " (Mark), instead of the sister of Barnabas, which would otherwise have been a more appropriate designation. Can there be a doubt that from the lips of Mark were entered into Luke's note-book the particulars related in this chapter ?

8. *The disappointment of the persecutor.* This was expressed by his conduct, for when he had sought for Peter, and found him not, he examined the keepers, and commanded that they should be put to death. "And " (having committed this other act of cruelty) "he went down from Judea to Cæsarea and abode." In Jerusalem, Herod Agrippa was a worshipper in the temple of Jehovah ; in Cæsarea, he was a pagan. How different was his conduct from what was afterwards that of the heathen magistrate, Gallio, at Corinth !

9. *The death of Herod Agrippa.* This was an event of public notoriety. His death at Cæsarea is recorded by Josephus (Wars, ii. 11), whereby a testimony is afforded of the carefulness of Luke to admit only what was authentic.

Luke's account, however, is given more at length than that of Josephus. And, moreover, as a physician, Luke describes the symptoms of the disease which preceded the king's death, and also, as a prophet, proclaims its retributive character : " An angel of the Lord smote him." Herod Agrippa had been three years Tetrarch before he was a king, and had reigned three years in Palestine. He died A.D. 44. Probably " his hand had been stretched forth to vex the Church " much of the latter term.

10. *A cheerful conclusion.* The killing, by the hands of officers of the king, of an apostle of Jesus Christ—the putting, by the same hands, another of his apostles into prison —the loosing of this apostle from the dungeon by an invisible power—the execution of the soldiers appointed for his guards—the arrogant exhibition of himself in the theatre at Cæsarea by Herod Agrippa—the sudden judgment that there befel him, were all circumstances calculated to fill the public mind with awe, and impressively to call attention again to the facts concerning the crucified Jesus, and the doctrines proclaimed by His followers. Jesus had foretold to His disciples, " They shall lay their hands upon you, and put you into prison, and bring you before kings and rulers for my name's sake. *And it shall turn to you for a testimony*" (Luke xxi. 12, 13). This prophecy now received a fulfilment. And, for a conclusion to his account of the persecution of the Church by Herod Agrippa, Luke affirms, " *But the word of the Lord grew and multiplied.*" The design of his whole book of the Acts was to report the progress made by the gospel nathless opposition. And by this conclusion of the Parenthesis is explained the motive which led to its insertion into his book.

CHAPTER XII.

THE last verse of the twelfth chapter makes a proper beginning to the thirteenth chapter of the Acts, the scene again being Antioch. "And Barnabas and Saul returned from Jerusalem, when they had fulfilled their ministry, and took with them John, whose surname was Mark." This is the first appearance of Mark in history. It is thought by some that the young man, who, in his Gospel, is represented as having escaped from the hands of the officers in the garden of Gethsemane, was himself, because that he only mentions that simple incident. He was the youngest of the Evangelists, being at this time not more than thirty years of age. With much gratification, Luke would have welcomed him to this field of service, where, from his acquaintance with evangelical history, he would prove for him a valuable auxiliary.

The return of Barnabas and Saul brought joy to the brethren. The Church is prosperous. It is in the condition of its first love. The freshness of their emancipation gives a glow to the piety of its members. Grateful love is the element of their lives. They are taught that the gospel is to be preached throughout the world, and, as Christians, they are ready to promote their Lord's design. A new development of the divine plan succeeded at this stage; and it is in an enumeration of the chief pioneers in the holy ministry thereof that Luke's name for the first time occurs. This section of his history begins, "Now there were in the Church that was at Antioch certain prophets and teachers." The names of these follow in the order of seniority; and not inaptly may those that are mentioned be regarded in the light of representative persons.

BARNABAS, the *first* named, represents the *Levites.* He was chosen from an honourable condition in society. But his advantages were relinquished for Christ. He is said by Eusebius to have been one of the seventy evangelists, which is probable. If so, he received his commission directly from the hands of Christ. Consequently he was one of Luke's eye-witnesses; and along with other topics, their fellowship would prompt the relation which Luke has preserved of the mission of that class of ministers. The admirable commendation of him by his friend has already been noticed. That Barnabas had the positiveness which belongs to a fitness for great undertakings, the incident of his contention with St Paul illustrates; whilst it likewise shows that he partook of the infirmity often stumbling sanguine minds (xv. 39). But oh! how well does Barnabas deserve the grateful remembrance of every Gentile who has partaken the " consolation " of the gospel !

SIMON NIGER, the *second* named, represents the *Africans.* These played a very different part in the civilised world than they do now. They were found in all the great emporiums of the East, prosecuting, along with people of other complexions, the different branches of industry, and even of philosophy. This Simon was a Cyrenian; and he is here called *Niger,* or black, to distinguish him as an aboriginal. The coincidence of this description, and what is related of him in the Gospels, is remarkable (Matt. xxvii. 32; Mark xv. 21; Luke xxiii. 26). Upon the Passover memorable for the crucifixion of Christ he went to Jerusalem, probably like Queen Candace's chamberlain, as a proselyte to engage in the solemnities of the season. He was coming out of the country just as Jesus had passed the north gate, fainting under the beam of the cross upon which the sufferer was to be suspended, when he was arrested by the Roman guards, and compelled to bear it the rest of the distance to Calvary. It should be noticed that this incident was most opportune for the sufferer. Simon's countenance at once declared that he was not a Jew. And of all the thousands of Jews present at that sight, the guards could not have compelled one of them so much as to touch the beam ; for the reason that the doing so would have rendered the individual unclean, and consequently unfit for the celebration of the approaching festival. Moreover, it would have been offering an insult to the whole nation, which the very giving up of Jesus against his convictions shows Pilate could not afford to do. It is little to believe that this circumstance proved a turning-point in Simon's life, and that his conversion to discipleship to Christ dated from the moment of his receiving that burden. That the evangelists should give such a special description of him intimates their acquaintance with him. If they had known no more concerning him than what was observed in that casualty, their words would have been, in the manner of the time, "a Libyan coming out of the country." His name would no more have transpired than does that of the soldier who pierced Christ's side ; whereas, not one only, but three of the evangelists, mention both his name and also his country. And there was a cause for this explicitness. The reason for it is found in the fact that he was in reality *an important agent* in this wondrous scene. After it was accomplished, and the disciples began to study its details under the light of the prophetic Scriptures, they perceived that, as Jesus fulfilled in His own person the type of the scape-goat, so by Simon was fulfilled that of the *fit man*, literally "the man of opportunity," who accompanied the type into the wilderness" (Lev. xvi. 21). And thus Matthew, who so much more than the other evangelists

H

illustrates his narrative by a reference to its fulfilment of Scripture, says, "And as they came out, *they found* a man of Cyrene ;" in other words, the *fit man* of prophetic appointment.   And then, as to the acquaintance with Simon, which enabled them to furnish his name and country, and which also warranted this preciseness, the explanation is found in the same typical Scripture, " And he that let go the goat for the scape-goat shall wash his clothes and bathe his flesh in water, and afterwards come into the camp " (26).   It surely will not be said that it is an undue spiritualising of this Scripture to say that there is seen in it a picture of the man's saving renewal by the Holy Ghost, his baptism by water, and thereupon his acceptance into the fellowship of Christ's saints.

But this is not the only distinction which Simon gained at this time.   A very early Scripture had said, " Cursed be Canaan ; a servant of servants shall he be.   And blessed be Shem, and Canaan shall be his servant " (Gen. ix. 25, 27).   Christ was the lineal representative of Shem, and Simon was a descendant of Canaan.   When, therefore, Simon bare the cross for Christ, he fulfilled this Scripture.   And when also Christ upon that cross expiated the sins of the world, he thereby removed the curse that had followed the descendants of Canaan.   And now Simon is the first of his race to taste the joy of that fellowship "where there is neither bond nor free, but Christ is all and in all " (Col. iii. 11).   No marvel that Simon should remain in Jerusalem, in the midst of this society.   Nor is it surprising to find him accompanying a party of Cyrenians to Antioch.   And here it should be remarked how aptly the mention of his name by Luke as Simon *Niger*, corresponds with the description of him in the Gospels as the Cyrenian.   And, whatever might have been his secular calling, it is observable that he was favoured by Providence, and honoured by the brethren, for his service to Christ.   His wife was a mother in the new Israel. And from the affectionate terms in which St Paul afterwards speaks of her, in his Epistle to the Romans (xvi. 13), one can hardly help thinking that, like the sister of Barnabas at Jerusalem, she had been a daughter of consolation, having accommodated the apostle in the only way in which it had been possible to attain the character which he there gives her—namely, in the assiduities of the domestic sphere at Antioch. Moreover, these distinguished disciples had two sons, who also were men of note in the Church—Alexander and Rufus. It is Mark who adds this information. His acquaintance with the family in this place would suggest the notice, for his Gospel was written afterwards. She had removed with her son to Rome before the apostle wrote, "Salute Rufus, chosen in the Lord, and his mother and mine." Probably she had become a widow. All these particulars correspond with Simon's place as second in seniority in Luke's list of prophets and teachers.

It ought to have been mentioned that his name is here spelt *Simeon*, but so is Simon Peter's (Acts xv. 14); although, in his Gospel, Luke had written both of them Simon. But however this discrepance arose, of the identity in both cases there is never entertained any doubt.

Lucius, the Cyrenian, the *third* named, represents the *inquisitive Greeks*, who, not inappropriately, is found in the centre of the fraternity, concerning whom his habit of notation has preserved important memorials. He was now about the age of sixty, having Barnabas and Simon for his seniors, which may well be supposed; the one having a nephew capable of being a minister, and the other having two sons afterwards notable in the Church. That Luke's name has not appeared before disappoints curiosity. Dr Olshausen, denying that Lucius was the evangelist, makes this assertion—"It is impossible that Luke should have mentioned himself amongst the more distinguished leaders of the Church." But perhaps this, like some other impossibilities that have been treated, may be dissipated by a little reflection.   When residing in Palestine, Luke had appeared only as a private individual.   Not until he was in another country does his name transpire.   At Antioch, in a church of Gentiles, he was an accredited teacher.   And now the occasion does not admit of the omission of his name.   Serving for an official document, a list of those upon whom it devolved to inaugurate an apostolate to the Gentile world, was to be given.   But the list would have been incomplete if Luke's modesty had induced the omission of his own name.   Moreover, did he not afterwards class himself with Paul, Silas, and Timothy, at Troas and at Philippi; and again with Paul, upon several occasions?

The difficulties which have been raised to the recognition of the Evangelist by the name of Lucius have been already discussed in the chapter concerning " The Identity of Luke, Lucas, and Lucius."   It may, however, be repeated here that he wrote his name in that form by which he was known in Rome, where his book of the Acts was written, and by which he had been accustomed to hear himself addressed during his residence there, and which, as a Roman citizen, he would not repudiate.   Had his situation been different, instead of Lucius he had written Lucas (*Loukas*) in Greek, corresponding with the place of his nativity.   And what adds to the force of this explanation is, that Simon the Cyrenian is treated like Lucius, receiving the Latin epithet of *Niger* instead of the Greek *Melas*, both words signifying dark or black.   Had Luke only repeated concerning Simon what he had said in his Gospel, namely, that he was a Cyrenian, the description would not have conveyed the ethnological difference which subsisted between Simon and himself, the former being an aboriginal African, and it would not have been generally known that the Simon of the Gospels and of the Acts were identical.   It was a case, therefore, that suggested the adoption of the popular mode when speaking of natives of Cyrenaica, which distinguished them as the *black* and the *white* Cyrenians. Luke's own name required no such special epithet, as it conveys the idea of shining or fair. It is known that the Greeks of Cyrene (as the Americans before their late war) were very tenacious to preserve the purity of their European descent.

MANAEN, the *fourth* named in this list, represents the *Herodians.* He is designated Manaen the *suntrophos* of Herod the Tetrarch. *Suntrophos* was a characteristic title sometimes borne by the individual through life, according to the station and merits of the partner. As this Herod's father (Herod the Great) was an Idumean by descent, and his mother was a Samaritan, it is probable that neither was Manaen a pure Hebrew. And this agrees also with his position on this side of Luke. Herod Antipas succeeded to the tetrarchy of Galilee about the third year of Christ, and therefore, reckoning Herod and Manaen to have been nearly of the same age, the latter could have been very little younger than Luke. In Manaen we have an example of divine grace bestowed, and of signal honour put upon one who had been brought up in a court. Whilst Herod, with his men of war, had mocked Jesus, and had been accessory to his death, Manaen was here a confessor for that same Jesus, having left his home to seek an asylum from persecution, and was now identified with the disciples of Jesus, and engaged in promoting their consolation. And who may tell the importance of the services of this confessor in the protection of the Christians at Antioch by means of his influence; or the extent of the benefit he conferred in commending the truth to persons among the upper class of society there? The Gospel calls men to salvation; but it likewise calls the saved to a life of sympathetic exertion. The place that Manaen occupies in this list, in company with " prophets and teachers," is at once an evidence of his devotion to the cause of Christ, and a distinguished memorial of the divine favour shown to a member of aristocracy.

It is pleasing to think that to the intimacy of Manaen with Luke we are probably indebted for the graphic description of the scene upon the sending of Jesus by the governor of Judea to Herod (Luke xxiii. 8–12). None of the other evangelists speak of that circumstance, although they could not have failed to know of its occurrence. The supplementary notice, which observes that Pilate and Herod, who had been at variance, were hereupon reconciled, is a piece of secret history which savours of having been brought directly from the precincts of the court : and when oft in friendly conference, Luke may likewise have derived from Manaen some other incidents in his Gospel, but which are not so easily to be recognised. Nor was Manaen the only trophy gained from the palace of the tetrarch. There had been Joanna, the wife of Chuza, his steward, who had had the blissful honour to minister to Jesus in some of his journeys (Luke viii. 2, 3).

SAUL, the *last* in the list, represents the sect of the *Pharisees.* " After the most strictest sect of our religion I lived a Pharisee," are his own words addressed to Agrippa. He is an example of the grace of Christ towards one of the most zealous partisans of the only class of whom our Lord had ever spoken with severity. Saul's natural temperament was the antipodes of Christ's. But, sanctified and controlled, it was made to subserve heroically the fulfilment of the divine purpose 'of the Gospel. Formerly he had taken a commission from a council of the covenanted enemies of Christ, and had furiously fulfilled it. But now he is in a council engaged in projecting the extension of the cause he had sought to destroy. Only the grace of Christ could achieve a revolution like this. At this time Saul was about the age of thirty-eight, being eighteen or twenty years younger than any of his reverend seniors.

Besides those enumerated, there were other prophets and teachers at Antioch. Mark was here at this moment, and perhaps Titus. There had been a Nicolas of Antioch in the primitive Church at Jerusalem, who might have been here, as others likewise. But the narrative only deals with those named in the list.

The solicitude of this company is expressed by the words, "As they ministered to the Lord and fasted." Their attitude was that of practical self-denial. It was a season of anxious inquiry concerning the work of promoting the divine design in Antioch. They were affected with the magnitude of their responsibility. The city was very great, and so was its moral darkness. Their language would be "As the eyes of servants look unto the hand of their masters, so our eyes wait upon the Lord our God." At length a divine revelation is made to them. "Separate me Barnabas and Saul for the work whereunto I have called them." This monition implies—(1) that the disciples at Antioch had *not* understood the import of Christ's charge to the extent of its universality ; (2) that Barnabas and Saul had only laboured in a manner *preliminary* to the greater undertaking proposed therein ; (3) that the signification of Christ's charge is to receive a *further development.* And here it may be asked, How was this divine communication made? Usually God reveals His will through a chosen agent. In this case Barnabas and Saul are excluded, being themselves the subjects of the communication. And of the other three of the company, to which of them will probability point as having, after receiving it, given vocal utterance to the monition, but to him who is in the centre of the group—namely, to the prophet Luke?

The consecration of Barnabas and Saul, in compliance with the divine monition, is described. "And when they had fasted and prayed, and laid their hands on them, they sent them away." Here it is to be observed—(1) there was an interval between the command and its performance ; (2) the interval was spent in an exercise of devout intercession in behalf of those now constituted apostles to the Gentiles ; (3) the three laid hands upon the two. And here it must be thought that the acts of ordination and dismissal were accompanied by a suitable address. In this address allusions would not fail to be made to the inscrutable way in which these servants of Christ had hitherto been led. The period would be reviewed during which they had laboured together in Antioch under the divine auspices, and in happy fellowship : and as well the prayers which they had offered, as their mutual affection, would prompt an expression of assured sympathy with the apostles during their absence. And, again, who is expected to have been the one who spake these sentiments upon that solemnity ? Surely Luke.

The credentials and departure of the apostles are set down together. The credentials are contained in the words, " *So* they being sent forth by the Holy Ghost." This is a very important notice. It affirms that the ordination which had been accomplished having been by divine command, *so* the mission was God's. Moreover, that it was not man's mission appears from the consideration, that the dismissal of the apostles would be regarded as being contrary to the convenience of the Church at Antioch, where they had laboured with so much acceptance and success ; and also from the consideration, that it must have been equally contrary to the inclination of those by whose hands they had been separated unto their calling.

Here it should be observed,—1. That apostles were an intermediate order, endued with an authority none since them have professed. Where, then, is a succession of apostles ? 2. That the first and the last persons on this list were chosen to be apostles from Antioch ; and that these were the only Jews of the company. But the first apostles to Gentile countries must needs have been Jews; because none but Jews could have fulfilled the injunction, that to the Jews the gospel was first of all to be preached. And this could only have been done in the synagogues, wherein none but Jews were permitted to minister. 3. "And "here," adds Charles Taylor, "we ought not to overlook the wisdom of the appointment made by the Holy Ghost in uniting Barnabas and Saul in the same mission: one was the oldest, the other was the youngest, of the teachers at Antioch: the sedateness of one would temper the fire of the other: the character of Barnabas as a son of consolation, as ' a good man,' mild, courteous, a man of experience, who had long been a companion of the apostles, and was familiar with their views of things, admirably combined with the fervour of his younger friend, whose greater activity and promptitude would induce and enable him to improve every opening, to spend and be spent in all directions, to discern possible advantages, and to act on the contingencies in cases to his less vigorous partner might appear dubious, if not imprudent, or which he might think himself not altogether competent to."

Nor will the student fail to admire the chain connecting the dismissal of Saul from Jerusalem by the brethren there, and his recovery by Barnabas from the retirement to which he had been consigned at Tarsus with his present appointment, along with that same tried friend, to this apostleship of the uncircumcision. Several writers assert that Saul had already been made an apostle by the words addressed to him from heaven in his progress to Damascus. Was he then an apostle before his baptism by Ananias? This is surely a strange position to be taken. But that this ordination at Antioch constituted his appointment to an apostleship, is manifest by the consideration that, had his ordination dated from the miraculous appearing of Jesus to him, his appointment hitherto, although it had satisfied himself, would not have been adequate proof for others; whereas a divine command, executed by those who were delegated to ordain, was within the scope of acceptable evidence. It was Jesus who had called Barnabas to be an evangelist, and Saul to be a chosen vessel to bear His name to the Gentiles. And now it was the Spirit of Jesus that said, "Separate me Barnabas and Saul to the work whereunto I have called them." The call, therefore, was one thing, and the ordination another. Harmonious herewith are Paul's own subsequent representations throughout his history. A reference to this ordination is set in the front of almost all his epistles as his claim for recognition as an apostle. He denominates himself "an apostle of Jesus Christ, by the will of God;" this will having been expressed to Luke and his associates. These inscriptions of his Epistles are worthy of especial notice. Together with the formula of benediction with which every epistle is concluded, they furnish a key-note to the apostle's entire correspondence.

The dismissal of the apostles is related in the words, "They departed unto Seleucia, and from thence they sailed to Cyprus." Seleucia was the nearest port on the Mediterranean. It was consistent that, as the native country of Barnabas, Cyprus should be chosen for the first field of missionary operations. In this mission Luke and his associates beheld the commencement of a new epoch. The divine purpose had been moving on from age to age, shadowed for a season, yet during the season promising the outstretching of the divine arms and the gathering of all people into their embrace. The Holy Ghost had said, by the voice of the prophet, "It is a light thing that thou (Messiah) shouldst be my servant, to raise the tribes of Jacob, and to restore the preserved of Israel: I will also give thee for a light to the Gentiles, that thou mayest be my salvation unto the end of the earth" (Isa. xlix. 6). This

Scripture was now fulfilled; Messiah, in the person of Jesus, had appeared. He had charged His disciples, saying, " Go ye into all the world, and preach the gospel to every creature." A ministry to the Gentiles had been ordained; and now the agents in the ordination of these pioneers stood upon the threshold of that revolution which was destined to bless the world.

In the ordination of apostles to Gentiles is observed another important link in the chain connecting the prophetic charge of Christ with its progressive fulfilment. It is usually reckoned that this ordination was solemnised A.D. 45.

CHAPTER XIII.

A REPORT OF THE FIRST CHRISTIAN MISSION.

THREE of those who had ministered in word and doctrine in the Church at Antioch having departed, there remained as its teachers Luke, Simon, and Manaen, and probably some others. Among these, the Evangelist was the chief; and upon him the care of the Church must now have largely devolved. Those teachers who had fasted and prayed in view of their situation before the appointment of the apostles to their sphere of labour, had a new incentive to do the same under their present burden of responsibility. But, besides the care of the Church, their sympathies would be constantly drawn to the mission. They had engaged, along with the members of the Church, in a measure novel to the world. Never had any sect adopted such a method of propagating its tenets. There may, therefore, have been among them some waverers to discourage the undertaking. Perhaps some, being Jewish converts, had opposed it. For neither had the Jews ever witnessed for God in the world after this manner. Nevertheless, the happy experience of the grace of the gospel upon themselves, as Gentles, influenced the majority of the members of the Church to hopefulness. And, elevated in faith by the teaching of the Word, prayer was made by the Church continually in behalf of the consecrated band and the success of their enterprise. During the absence of the apostles there must have occurred many incidents at Antioch concerning which curiosity craves to be informed.

But however interesting the character of the Church, and important the work in which, with his coadjutors, Luke was engaged, the relation of those incidents being beside his design, he proceeds in his narrative to follow the course of the apostles. This he does in the 13th and 14th chapters of his history. To understand the order of events as they concern Luke himself, reference must be made, first of all, to the passage wherein the announcement is made of their return (xiv. 26, 27). Every word of this passage is important, and is also pregnant with the writer's feeling of gratification. It relates—(1) "From Attalia they sailed to Antioch, from whence they had been recommended to the grace of God for the work which they had fulfilled." (2) "And when they were come, and had gathered the Church together, they rehearsed all that God had done with them; and how he had opened the door of faith to the Gentiles." By the words, "And when they were come," the fact of the continued residence of Luke in Antioch is evident. Here Paul and Barnabas are represented as rehearsing before the congregated Church the incidents of their mission; and Luke appears before the reader as being again seated beside his friends, filled with grateful admiration of the grace bestowed upon them, and with love and reverence for their persons. That was a happy meeting for the Gentile Evangelist; and, charmed with the anecdotes related by the apostles to the assembly, and with their heroism and success, he reduces the substance of their acts and addresses to a narrative adapted to the plan of his history, after the same manner that he had incorporated the communication received from Mark, which occupies the 12th chapter. The REPORT of their proceedings, thus derived, fulfils two essential parts of his plan—namely, that which relates to the fulfilment of the Lord's charge, and that which concerns the admission into his pages only of those things either observed by himself or obtained from the

lips of agents or eye-witnesses.   This Report describes what
is commonly called Paul's first journey.   It is preceded by
an intimation of the discontinuance of the Hebrew name
Saul, and of the future use of the Roman *Paul*, conformable
with the appointed sphere of his labours.   The narrative now
reverses the order followed in the previous naming of the
two apostles, Paul being placed before Barnabas, albeit the
latter was the senior.   The course of their journey seems to
have been influenced by personal predilections ; for Cyprus
was the native country of Barnabas, and the provinces in
Asia Minor were contiguous to Cilicia, the birthplace of Paul.
It is observable, moreover, that the Report contains only a
sample of the proceedings of the apostles.   In Cyprus only
two places are mentioned—one at one end of the island,
and one at the other end of it ; and only two incidents—
one of opposition, and one of success.   Yet there were
several towns in the island, and the time occupied there
must have been considerable ; and that it was a time of adventurous trial appears from the notice that Mark relinquished the mission as soon as the company returned to
the continent.   Of places visited in Asia Minor only six
are mentioned, and of particular incidents only three.   Yet
the apostle spent nearly twelve months in the provinces
specified.

Besides its historical importance, the Report invites attention as a continued illustration of the writer's method.
With Him by whose grace the Evangelist wrote the past
and present are the same.   Hence the undeclared but sensible link which is preserved throughout the holy records,
each portion having a prophetic correspondence with another.   Here the correspondence goes back to our Lord's
manifestation of His person to Saul of Tarsus ; to the exclamation of this chosen vessel, " Lord, what wilt thou
have me to do ? " and to the divine communication made to
the prophet at Damascus, "I will show him how great things

he must *suffer* for my name's sake "—premonitions which all found their fulfilment in Paul's history. The incidents of this journey seem to have been selected by Luke to show how the doctrine preached in Asia Minor, and the results following, corresponded with what had been witnessed of the fulfilment of Christ's charge in Jerusalem. In the discourse delivered by Paul at Antioch in Pisidia is shown the manner in which he preached the doctrine which in Judæa he had formerly sought to destroy. It corresponds largely, and in some parts literally, with the discourse of Peter on the day of Pentecost, and with that of Stephen before the Sanhedrim. In the cure of a cripple at Lystra there is a marked correspondence with the miracle performed upon the cripple by Peter and John before the Beautiful Gate at Jerusalem. Here, he who had witnessed and abetted the martyrdom of Stephen was himself stoned until left for dead. Like Peter and John at Jerusalem, who, undismayed by scourging and imprisonment, upon their deliverance, returned to the temple to proclaim again the gospel ; so here, Paul and Barnabas, retracing their steps, boldly revisited every place from which they had been expelled, confirming the disciples, and declaring to them, by word and example, that " we must through much tribulation enter the kingdom." And equally did the parallel extend to the results of the mission ; for as in Jerusalem there were thousands of whom it was said, " they glady received the word,"—" they were filled with the Holy Ghost "—" the Lord added daily to the Church such as should be saved ;" so, in speaking of " what God had done with them " in Asia Minor, Paul and Barnabas now testified how, when, upon the " contradiction and blaspheming" of the Jews, they turned to the Gentiles, justifying the act by words of prophecy how the Gentiles, when they heard them, " were glad, and glorified the word of the Lord ;" how, " as many as were ordained to eternal life believed ;" how " the disciples were filled with joy and with the Holy Ghost ; and then, finally, in their declaration, that "God had opened a door of faith unto the Gentiles," was found an illustration of the leading argument of Luke's book.   And what gave to the relation made by the apostles its deep interest to the Antiochian Christians was the evidence that the object of their solicitude was gained, whilst the great success of the mission tended to confirm themselves in the faith, and also to establish their claims to be regarded as a church of Christ, Gentiles though they were.

The peculiar phrase, " *the door*," in relation to preaching the gospel, does not occur again in the New Testament, except as written by Paul, by whom it is twice employed, namely, 1 Cor. xvi. 9, and 2 Cor. ii. 12.   Its Pauline character sanctions the view which has been here taken of the derivation of Luke's REPORT.

CHAPTER XIV.

AFTER their return to Antioch, Paul and Barnabas "there abode *not a brief time* with the disciples." And although Luke was in their company, yet, in accordance with the plan of his narrative, he produces only a single occurrence of the period, being one which bore an important relation to the work of fulfilling Christ's charge to spread the gospel. In this work he had taken an active part ever since he left Jerusalem. Having "put his hand to the plough," every impediment to the progress of the work was regarded by him with consistent anxiety. Such an impediment is described, together with the conduct of the Church in relation to it, in the 15th chapter, from the 1st to the 35th verse. This passage forms another of those literary pictures which probably obtained for him the credit of having been a painter. This tablet embraces the several particulars ensuing.

1. *A litigious party.* "Certain men that came from Judea." These are spoken of by Paul in his Epistle to the Galatians as "false brethren unawares introduced, who came privily to spy out our liberty which we have in Christ" (ii. 4).

2. *The dogma of this party.* "They taught the brethren, saying, Except ye be circumcised after the manner of Moses, ye cannot be saved." Circumcision here included all the existing ritualism of the law. These men admit of no compromise, but abruptly pronounce the dismal alternative of their own judgment.

3. *A controversy.* "When, therefore, Paul and Barnabas had no small dissension and disputation with them." The mention only of these does not preclude the probability that Luke and others, deeply interested in the subject, took no part in the debate. But here were fortunately Jews taking part with Gentiles against Jews. By this exclusive mention of his two friends, Luke gave honour to whom it was pre-eminently due. It was now that Paul was led to study the question of the pretended continued obligation of Mosaic ritualism, and that he came to declare his conviction of the efficacy of the grace of Christ above all, and to the exclusion of all other grounds of salvation, as after-wards expounded in his Epistle to the Galatians.

4. *A deputation appointed.* "They (that is, the Church) determined that Paul and Barnabas, and other of them, should go up to Jerusalem unto the apostles and elders about this question." This question had been agitated in Antioch before, Peter himself having urged it (Gal. ii. 11). Therefore, both for their own welfare, and for the interest of Gentile churches in other *places* and in all times, the Antiochians determined to appeal to those who had the mind of Christ, having been His personal ministers. The propriety of the appointment of Barnabas to this mission appears from his having been one of the elders of the Church at Jerusalem, and that he had come to Antioch as their messenger upon the tidings having reached them of the conversion of Gentiles here. Influenced by an enlarged charity, he had *not* enjoined circumcision ; nor had there ever been offered any remonstrance by the apostles at Jerusalem against the omission of it. Peter had before admitted Gentiles to baptism on the same terms ; and the question had, upon that occasion, been debated and settled in favour of the freedom of Gentiles. Consequently, Barnabas repaired to Jerusalem to obtain a formal ratification of a principle which had already been conceded. Paul went as an agent that had received

a special appointment to the great work in progress.   He
says that he went by revelation (Gal. ii. 2).   He went to explain the manner in which he had executed his trust, and
to set forth the results.   The "certain other of them" included Gentle converts, among whom was Titus (Gal. ii. 3).

This is the first appearance of Titus.   Dr George Benson
supposes that he belonged to Antioch ("Planting Christianity," p. 389).   And with this agrees the fact that he was
a convert of Paul's, as the designation of him, "my son in
the faith," implies (Titus i. 4).   It also consists with his
accompanying this mission in the character of a representative of those whose cause was to be argued at Jerusalem.
A visit to the apostles and brethren there would be a good
preparative for his future ministry.

5. *The journey of the deputies to Jerusalem.*   "And being
brought on their way by the Church."   The expense, therefore, of the journey was provided by the Christian community of Antioch.   This godly custom of the Church is
spoken of in the same words in the third Epistle of John,
ver. 6. 7.   Nevertheless, it is amusing to observe, how
some commentators, and of the most recent date, regarding
the Church at Antioch as *already* a great corporate body,
see in this journey a "public embassy" brought on its way
by a suitable "escort!"   (Webster and Wilkinson's note
thereupon).

At this point Luke ceases to be the observer, and writes
from the report made by Paul and Barnabas *after* their return to Antioch.   His picture, however, retains its character, bearing an impress of his deep personal interest in
every part.   Here, then, leaving Luke at Antioch, the
narrative follows the deputation.

6. *A touch of sympathy occurs.*   "They passed through
Phenicia and Samaria, declaring the conversion of the Gen-
tiles; and they caused great joy unto all the brethren."
This intelligence was gratifying to Luke, who had been in

company with the party by whom the gospel was first preached in Phenicia.

7. *The reception of the deputies by the Church at Jerusalem.* " And when they were come, they were received of the Church and of the apostles and elders." This was the second time Paul and Barnabas had come from Antioch deputed by the Church to Jerusalem. Upon the former occasion they had been the bearers of the first-fruits of the conversion of Gentiles in the form of a contribution to the poor brethren of Judea. That loving embassy was not forgotten. And the deputation was welcomed accordingly. But prior to the announcement of the object of their present mission, Paul obtained a private interview " with them of reputation " (Gal. ii. 2). To these, before the subject of the mission was publicly debated, he would adduce the warrant of his apostleship. This preparatory conference was, moreover, prudential, as it regarded his situation with Peter, whom Paul had warmly opposed at Antioch on the very question upon the merits of which this apostle would now be found in the position of an adjudicator.

8. *A public audience.* " And they declared all things that God had done with them." These are the same words employed to introduce the Report made at Antioch of the first missionary journey of these apostles. It is probable, therefore, that the events of that journey formed a chief part of what they here " declared."

9. *An opposition.* " There rose up certain of the sect of the Pharisees which believed, saying, that it was needful to circumcise them, and to command them to keep the law of Moses." The " certain men " who were the occasion of the present debate, belonged to this party. With Jews, and especially those that had been Pharisees, it would have been difficult, perhaps impossible, to cast off the habits of thought and practice nurtured in Judaism. Conformity with its peculiarities had not been formally prohibited.

The belief in Jesus as the Messiah abolished the rites of sacrifice, but the temple and synagogue were visited as before by the devout disciple. There was no sudden departure from the national customs. And none but Jews had been admitted bishops in Judea until after the misfortunes of the Jews in the reign of Hadrian had suggested the choice of a Gentile as a means of marking more fully the difference that existed between Christian Jews and the rebellious.

10. *A second audience.* "And the apostles and elders came together to consider this matter." The debate, therefore, had been adjourned, that the subject might be referred to the especial consideration of these; and this resolution was agreeable, also, with the express intention of the mission. The Pharisees, however, renewed their opposition.

11. *Peter's apology for the Gentiles.* "And after much disputing, Peter rose up." From the glimpse of his speech conveyed in the condensed report of it preserved by Luke, it must have been very impressive. And admitting, as the company did, a divine interposition in the case of the conversion of Cornelius, to which it immediately referred, the argument was conclusive. No word of opposition appears after this. The speech was a triumph for the Gentiles. Here was the apostle of the circumcision admitting the burdensomeness of ceremonial ordinances, and openly pleading that the yoke should not be put upon the neck of the disciples. But even more striking are the words with which, as one of those to whom the appeal was made, he delivered his opinion. Against the objection of the Pharisees, he takes a lower ground for Jews than could ever have been conceived. The extent (geographically) of the work among the heathen compared with what was witnessed among themselves, and the abundance of gifts and holy influence bestowed upon preachers and converts,

led him to invert the natural order of thought when he concluded, " We believe that through the grace of Jesus Christ we shall saved *even as they*,"—or, more literally, "*in the same manner as they.*" In all this the policy of Paul's private interview with Peter appears ; nor less so the candour of Peter. This is Luke's last notice of this distinguished apostle ; and it is inexpressibly gratifying to find it is so admirably characteristic.

12. *The hearing given to the deputies from Antioch.* Peter had argued the case from the point of view which his own experience suggested. He had thereby secured a favourable hearing of what should be advanced from other experiences. "Then all the multitude kept silence, and gave audience to Barnabas and Paul, declaring what miracles and wonders God had wrought among the Gentiles by them." The change in the position of the names of these apostles marks Luke's exactness. Barnabas was heard first, having been an original member of the Church here. As no outline of the address of either of them is given, it is to be concluded that the substance of what they declared was an echo of the Report made at Antioch concerning their recent missionary tour. "The miracles and wonders which God had then done by them" were adduced as the signs and evidences of their apostleship to the Gentiles, and also of the divine acceptance of these through their preaching. And even as Peter produced his witnesses when arraigned in the case of Cornelius, so Barnabas and Paul were provided with theirs in the persons of Titus and others, being examples of the grace bestowed upon the uncircumcised.

13. *An appeal is made by James* to the divine design concerning the Gentiles as revealed in prophecy; and his opinion is expressed in conformity therewith. This was James the son of Alpheus, and a cousin or kinsman of our Lord. The assembly being now in possession of the facts of the case, James stood up as an interpreter of those facts.

He quoted a prophecy; and he showed how those facts fulfilled it. And he inferred that God had foreseen and decreed what they had heard. Both his speech and the whole of the proceedings show how reluctant the Jews had been to admit the Gentiles to communion except through the gate of proselytism. They had acknowledged God's sovereignty in conferring the gifts of His Spirit in the case of Cornelius and his household, seven years before, yet they seem only now to awaken to a due perception of the divine design with respect to Gentiles, notwithstanding that perhaps already the number of members composing the Church at Antioch exceeded those in the Church at Jerusalem, whilst those in fellowship in Phenicia, Syria, and Asia Minor probably exceeded those in Palestine. The intelligence brought by Barnabas and Paul concerning the gifts and grace bestowed upon those converts forced the conviction upon the assembly expressed in James's speech. This speech must have been of considerable length compared with what is quoted. Its conclusion harmonised with the feeling which had been elicited, " *Wherefore I judge*"— not " my sentence is," which is a glossarial turn; but literally, as in the Roman vulgate, *Ego judico*, in the sense of expressing an opinion. The same Greek verb is used, and in the same sense, Acts iv. 19, " Judge ye," and in 2 Cor. v. 14, " We thus judge," or conclude. The judgment proposed by James was, " that we trouble not the brethren which, from among the Gentiles, be turned (are turning) to God." A commentator remarks, " It is well Peter had not said this." But Peter had said the equivalent when, as a defendant in his own case, he concluded, " Forasmuch then as God gave them like gifts as unto us, what was I that I should withstand God " (xi. 17). Peter *then* meant to say, " I simply obeyed God ;" and *now* both he and James mean to say, " Let us obey God's voice as spoken to us in the facts which have been brought under review." Peter says,

" Let us not put a yoke upon them ;" James says, " Let us not trouble the brethren." Where, then, is the priority of these holy men ? It had been forbidden by their Master, and it is not found here.

But James further recommended that a letter should be written, including a *proviso* requiring abstinence from a moral impurity very prevalent among the heathen, and from certain other things regarded as impurities by Jews. This caution was suggested from the fact that there were synagogues in the chief cities of the world, in which Jews and proselytes were wont to meet together to read the Holy Scriptures. The injunction was, therefore, grounded on the principle of avoiding giving any offence. Happy had it been for the Church in subsequent ages if the spirit prompting this caution had been held sacred ! The conduct of James on this occasion harmonised with his own description of the particular grace which it discovered (Epistle of St James iii. 17, 18).

14. *The decision of the assembly.* This seems to have been unanimous, the *proviso* having silenced the Pharisees. And now the apostles and elders and the *whole Church* concurring, action succeeds conference. And emulating the fraternal consideration of the Church at Antioch in both this and their former mission to Jerusalem, they too " chose men out of their own company to send to Antioch with Paul and Barnabas, namely, Judas Barsabas, and Silas, *chief men* among the brethren." A Barsabas had been selected as a candidate for the apostleship along with Matthias (i. 23). Here is another of the name chosen for his qualification to be their representative in an assembly of Gentiles. '

15. *A document furnished to the deputies.* The production of this affords another instance of Luke's exactness. It also shows the important light in which this controversy and its termination was regarded by the Gentile Churches.

The document would henceforth serve as their charter. It bears an impress of the effect produced by the statements of Paul and Barnabas. It is no technical manifesto. Its tenor is entirely conciliatory. It addresses and greets as "*brethren*" the Gentiles of the Church at Antioch and of the churches which had been founded by the two apostles. It repudiates the conduct of those who would "subvert their souls" by the imposition which it had been the object of the present mission to frustrate. It speaks of the delegates as "our *beloved* Barnabas and Paul." And, in allusion to what had been related by them, it recognises them as "men that had *hazarded their lives* for the name of Christ." It intimates the mission of Judas and Silas to ratify by word of mouth the sentiments therein expressed. And in imparting the result of the deliberations concluded, it professes that they had been conducted under a divine influence. "It seemed good to the Holy Ghost and to us," &c.

It is usual to *un*dignify this fraternal assembly at Jerusalem by denominating it the "*First* Council of the Christian Church." Did it, however, belong to the category of councils, commonly so called, it should be accounted the *second* council; the first having been the deliberation concerning Peter's admission of Gentiles to baptism seven years before. Between this assembly and the proper series of ecclesiastical councils, those who have read anything of their history find, among other important discrepancies, that *here* was no exclusion of unofficial brethren; *here* was no golden chair, as at Nicæa, no formulary of belief imposed, no anathema pronounced, and no scenes afterwards of the disputants engaged in mortal strife, as between Arians and Athanasians. A note of a recent expositor under this place is curious. It represents the organisation of the Church for settling controversies to consist of—"1. The bishop (James being *president*); 2. The apostles; 3.

The presbyters, *as deliberators;* 4. The brethren, giving force to the decree *by a reception of it* " (Bishop Wordsworth).

One other observation claims a place. It should be noticed with what skill the account of this embassy is introduced and conducted. It serves a double purpose. It disposes for ever of the Judaising question. And, in accordance with the prime plan of the narrative, it also serves for a link in its prophetic chain. Of the score or more that would speak in such an assembly, besides Barnabas and Paul, only two are named; and of the specches of these only a tithe is produced. But these two were deemed pillars in the Church. And the passages selected from their speeches are such as serve emphatically the design of the report. Peter's speech had an allusion embracing the whole question of the acceptance of Gentiles. But the special step in advance is found in the quotation by James of a prophecy uttered by Amos. " After this I will return, and will build again the tabernacle of David," &c. " That the residue of men might seek after the Lord, and all the Gentiles upon whom my name is called, saith the Lord, who doeth all these things " (ix. 11, 12). By the application of this prophecy to the case before them, the assembly set their seal to the work in which the servants of Christ were engaged in Syria and Asia Minor, in fulfilment of a charge primarily made to the very persons composing this assembly, but whose real meaning and extent they had been backward to understand.

By the action taken upon this occasion, the apostles and brethren at Jerusalem remitted Barnabas and Paul to their work as *apostles of the uncircumcision.* Thus did that prophecy receive a fulfilment, " And He shall speak peace unto the heathen." And here was a beginning of that end, " And His (Messiah's) dominion shall be to the sea, and from the river even to the ends of the earth " (Zech. ix. 10).

CHAPTER XV.

WHEN the deputation returned from Jerusalem, Luke was still at Antioch. This is involved in his words, " So when they were dismissed, they *came* to Antioch " (xv. 30). He witnessed, therefore, what he relates concerning the subsequent proceedings here. A special call of the Church having been made, similar to that upon their return from their first missionary journey, Paul and Barnabas in an assembly of the Church related the circumstances of their embassy, and delivered the epistle of the apostles and elders at Jerusalem : upon the reading of which the Assembly, Luke says, "rejoiced for the consolation " (xv. 31). How obviously is the eye-witness reflected in this note. Exultation is in the words. The writer welcomed the return of his friends. A summary of the report of their successful mission he entered into his note-book, as he had done of their missionary tour. He also rejoiced in the visit to Antioch of the delegates who accompanied them. These he had probably known during his residence in Jerusalem. But to see them again, and upon such an occasion as this, was unspeakably pleasurable. It was also a triumphant moment for the Church at Antioch. The capacity of Christianity for universal diffusion had been upon its trial. The object of the mission had been gained. There was evidence, written and oral, of its success ; and the gratification was commensurate. His notice continues : " And Judas and Silas, being prophets also themselves, exhorted the brethren with many words," and confirmed the terms of the letter, as they had been instructed to do, " by word of mouth." They reviewed its different clauses, each of them at some length, adding their personal testimony to the feelings of fraternal concord which the letter conveyed. The mention that Judas and Silas were prophets is made to impart weight to their testimony; and it also bespeaks the writer's personal sympathy with them; for Luke likewise was a prophet. His notice that " they tarried there a space " seems to divulge the happiness he had derived from their visit; whilst every such opportunity of intercourse with the agents in the great work whose history was confided to his pen by the Holy Ghost, added to the interest of his narrative. Nor less indicative of personal fellowship and sympathy is the notice of the farewell given by the Church to these visitors: " They were let go in peace from the brethren to the apostles." The force of this description is only to be appreciated by those who, like these brethren, have the peace of God shed abroad in their hearts. It was a public and grateful act of courtesy. It embodied an acknowledgment of benefit conferred by the deputies, and of the grace with which they had fulfilled their mission. They were dismissed with benedictions to the revered apostles and elders at Jerusalem. It would appear that Luke had enjoyed the pleasure of the society of these eminent brethren, and the Church their services, for some time. But although having received this formal dismissal, Silas did not return with Barsabas to Jerusalem. The words, " Notwithstanding, it pleased Silas to abide there still," are not found in some manuscripts. But whether they belong to the text or not, the words following imply that he remained in Antioch : " Paul *also* and Barnabas continued in Antioch teaching and preaching the word of the Lord, with many others." Among the others engaged in edifying the Church are to be recognised, besides Silas, Titus and Mark, with Luke himself. The many teachers and preachers found in Antioch was an evidence of the triumphs which the gospel had achieved in that city. Never again was this same company of athletes found together. The period approached in which each of those named should receive, under the divine guidance, new appointments. "And some days after, Paul said unto Barnabas, Let us go again and visit our brethren in every city where we have preached the word of the Lord." But this pious design was to be frustrated by a simple incident. And here again is obtained an illustration of the truthfulness of Luke's narrative. His love to both these men was like that of Jonathan to David, yet the occasion of their separation must be told, and told it is with rigid exactness. The natural affection of Barnabas led him to propose that Mark should again accompany them, as upon the occasion of their first missionary journey. To this arrangement Paul objected, upon the prudential consideration that "Mark had withdrawn from the work at Pamphylia." What a vivid glimpse of diverse character in these apostles does the historian here afford! He had pronounced Barnabas "a good man," expressive of his benevolent disposition. And here it is seen in his relation as an uncle. Paul's temperament admitted no compromise with the decision of his judgment: it was impatient with every obstacle to his sole purpose of fulfilling his Lord's commission. "And the contention was so sharp between them, that they departed asunder, the one from the other; and so Barnabas took Mark, and sailed unto Cyprus" (xv. 39). That Paul's objection to the wish of Barnabas was justifiable is never questioned. But justifiable also, as the sequel proved, was the resolve taken by Barnabas. Barnabas was better acquainted with the hopefulness of Mark's character than was Paul, and he was a less rigid judge. And that Barnabas had formed a correct

estimate of it is evident by Mark's subsequent perseverance
in the labours of the ministry, as witnessed by his having
become the companion of Peter, and likewise, at a future
period, of Paul, who, in a letter to Timothy, bare this testimony of his usefulness : " Take Mark, and bring him with
you, for he is profitable to me for the ministry (2 Tim. iv.
11). So, when the uncle was deceased, those eminent
apostles succeeded in an affectionate appreciation of the
nephew. As both Barnabas and Paul were the servants of
God, who appointed to each his sphere of ministry, so this
dissension was overruled for the advantage of the great
cause to which they were alike devoted. Many have since
been the divisions which, in like manner, have served to
promote the spread of the gospel.

The relation of Barnabas to the Church of Christ possesses a singular interest. In the ecclesiastical record by
Luke, Barnabas has appeared pre-eminent in fulfilling
Christ's charge to preach the gospel in " all the world," as
distinguished from Palestine. He has been seen as introducing to the Church at Jerusalem a convert that became
the most energetic of any preacher of the gospel, and
afterwards as conducting him to a ministry to Gentiles
at Antioch. He has been seen associated with that
preacher, and labouring with abundant fruitfulness in Antioch, in Cyprus, in Pamphylia, in Pisidia, in Iconium, at
Lystra; and also as uniting with him in securing for
Gentile disciples liberty from the yoke of Jewish ritualism.
How those services, along with his own association with
him as a fellow-labourer at Antioch, had endeared Barnabas
to Luke, the narrative of the latter attests ; grateful admiration of him being refulgent throughout the three chapters
wherein the particulars of his ministry are related. By
the absence of any future mention of Barnabas, it is again
seen how strictly Luke adhered to the plan of his narrative. Not even his friendship for that apostle allured him.

By his separation from Paul, Barnabas deviated from the track of the gospel's chiefest course, upon which course Luke kept his eye, and regulated his history; recording only circumstances which were either witnessed by himself or reported to him from the lips of the agents themselves.

The regret felt at the termination of opportunities to proceed with notices of his friend's progress, may, in some measure, be conceived by the reader on reflection. A feeling of sadness is occasioned by the thought that nothing further is reported in the historian's page concerning a character so interesting, and one to whom every converted Gentile is deeply indebted. But, that Barnabas pursued his ministry with unabated devotion and success, there is found an indication in the reference made to him by his former coadjutor in the first Epistle to the Corinthians ix. 6. This mention of him, whilst it shows that Barnabas was known in Greece, affords likewise a testimony of Paul's reverend remembrance of him.

As Barnabas was at least twenty years older than Paul, the period of his future ministry must have been brief. It is related in martyrologies that he suffered death at Cyprus A.D. 54. A legend concerning him adds, that Mark buried him in a cave in that island, and that in the year 485 his bones were discovered therein. Portions of them are pretended to be still held in many ecclesiastical reliquaries. That the estimable character of Barnabas, and his eminent services, had left a very grateful impression upon the Churches indebted to his labours, is manifest from the advantage taken thereof to foist into publication an apocryphal epistle bearing his name. So soon were the Churches infested with forgeries!

Between the departure of Barnabas to Cyprus and that of Paul from Antioch there was a brief interval. And, therefore, the fifteenth chapter might have concluded with the thirty-ninth verse; verses 40 and 41 being made to commence the *sixteenth* chapter.   And from this point the narrative might appropriately receive the title of

"THE ACTS OF THE APOSTLE PAUL."

Henceforward this apostle is the sole commanding figure in Luke's pictures, but around which several interesting characters are occasionally grouped, inviting the attention of the reader.   This portion of Luke's second treatise begins with the sentence, " And Paul chose Silas, and departed, being recommended by the Church to the grace of God" (xv. 40).   From which it appears that the choice of Silas for his companion being intimated by the apostle to the Church, it was sanctioned by a valedictory benediction. Silas was in every way qualified for his new appointment. He was a Jew of the Hellenistic class.   His relations with these parts were, it is probable, similar to those of Barnabas, and had determined the choice of him by the brethren at Jerusalem as one of their delegates.   The same relations would also have their influence in inducing his resolution to abide at Antioch, instead of returning with Judas Barsabas to Jerusalem.   An important qualification for Silas's companionship with Paul consisted in his having been, as a native of a colonial city, like himself a Roman citizen (Acts xvi. 37).   It is highly probable that the liberty of action enjoyed by the teachers at Antioch was mainly attributable to all of them having possessed this privilege. It often served for a panoply in other places.   Moreover, Silas possessed a sterling character.   He came to Antioch recommended as " a chief man among the brethren at Jerusalem."   He was, therefore, no novice.   In years he might be only a little older than Paul.   He was evidently of a courageous constitution.   This is discovered by his promptitude in complying with Paul's election of him. He had in Jerusalem listened with emotion to the relations made to the assembly by Paul and Barnabas.   The account of their journeys, their adventures, and their successes, and the fact of their having " hazarded their lives for the name of Christ," brought him instantly into strongest sympathy with their persons and ministry. And Silas possessed, withal, the amiable qualification of a buoyant and cheerful temper. The prison cells at Philippi afterwards attested this.

How apparent in this appointment is the hand of Providence! Silas is sent on a mission to Antioch. Instead of returning with Judas Barsabas to Jerusalem, he remains. Paul requires a companion. He makes choice of Silas, who accepts the proposed ministry. And when the object and results of his ministry are considered, it will be concluded that every circumstance connected with his appointment to it was directed by the Divine Master. It is descending, but it may be quoted as a foil, that in Silas is presented another example of traditionary muddle. Like several others he bare a Greek name, which, upon occasions, was Latinised. He has consequently been split in two, and consecrated Silas, *Bishop of Corinth*, and also Silvanus, *Bishop of Thessalonica!*

From the persecution that drove Luke and his company to Antioch until this time was about ten years, or from A.D. 41 to 51. Next to the seven years which preceded that persecution, and during which the fulfilling of Christ's charge had been confined to Palestine, these last ten years formed, strictly speaking, the most important of any period in the history of the Christian Church since its first organisation. The progressive power of the gospel had been more largely proved at Antioch than in Jerusalem. To the Jewish mind the notion of a crucified Redeemer was even more abhorrent than to the Gentile. The Jew was familiar with the expectation of a Messiah ; but having looked for Him under a widely different character than that in which He appeared, he stood in the attitude of vexatious dis-

K

appointment. The Gentile also entertained a hope of a Saviour; but having only a dim hope, and the object of it being undefined, his prejudices were sooner overcome, in the feeling of the absolute need in which the universal world stood of a Redeemer.

In reviewing his residence at Antioch, Luke might well have rejoiced. He had here witnessed glorious evidence of that conclusion of the apostles and brethren at Jerusalem, "Then hath God also to the Gentiles granted repentance unto life" (xi. 18). He had been honoured to be an agent in sowing the minute seed; he had been permitted to stay and cherish the tender plant, and to witness the happy fruits of the culture bestowed by the servants of God with whom he had been united in this interesting and beneficent labour. Antioch had responded to the voice from Jerusalem. And now the world was responsive to the voice from Antioch.

Disinclined to interrupt the course of the narrative of events connected with Luke's residence at Antioch, the following specimen of modern criticism has been deferred. Dr Alford, at present an authority, writes in his " Prolegomena to the Acts :"—" Whether Antioch may have been the place of Luke's own conversion, we know not; but *a peculiar interest evidently hangs about this preaching at Antioch in the mind of the narrator, be he who he may!*" In these words, a mystery is confessed. The expositor having approached a gate of the city, seems to discern the person of the writer of the Acts of the Apostles therein. Yet, when he comes to the text wherein *Lucius* is represented as engaged in a ministry in the Church *at Antioch*, he unhesitatingly declares—" *There is no room to suppose him the same with Luke.*" Thus gravely is the gate shut against a solution of the acknowledged mystery.

CHAPTER XVI.

LUKE'S GOSPEL PUBLISHED.

LUKE is still, it is to be supposed, in Antioch. No particular of his biography, it seems, can be touched, except in the form of an argument. The fogs of perverted tradition have hung so thickly upon his memory, that any attempt to set it in the light is regarded with jealousy by those who have committed themselves to the opaque views thence derived. With many the starting-point of an inquiry has been, " What saith tradition?" instead of, " What is to be deduced from Scripture ?" From this cause the particular now to be considered has remained clouded in mystery. No precise intimation of the time and place of the first publication of Luke's Gospel being found, the legends of the Latin Church have been by many writers followed, which assign its publication to the period of his residence in Rome—that is, to about A.D. 63. But here not only is the motive originating this representation to be suspected, persons and events being known often to be misplaced in order to swell the credit of that city in ecclesiastical history, but the representation is opposed by the claims of the East. Those claims rest on no slight foundation. All the early Greek copies of the Gospel were produced in the East. Upon the front or at the end of some of these copies, the scribe has intimated the date when it was judged that the Gospel was originally written. The same is likewise done upon early Syriac and Arabic versions of it. Some say it was published fifteen years, some twenty, and some twenty-

two years after the Ascension. In some of the inscriptions
a place is also assigned of its publication. In some, this is
said to have been Asia Minor, or some province thereof is
named ; in some, Macedonia ; and in some, more specifically, Alexandria. Following these intimations, the question is plainly carried back to the East. But by the want
of harmony in those statements, the student is driven to
an examination of another class of evidence. He is led to
inquire whether a solution of the problem may be obtained
in pursuing the subject by considerations of probability and
the coherence of events. The books of Luke and the
epistles of his friend Paul, the apostle, are before him ;
and the exercise is both pleasing and profitable.

Among the considerations which will aid this course of
inquiry are the following :—

1. It will be observed that Luke spent about ten years
at Antioch. This was the longest residence that he made
at any one place after he left Cyrene.) The eight years he
had spent in Palestine prepared him for the work that
devolved upon him here. He was also prepared thereby
for the task of composing his Gospel. And although at
first his time would be occupied in aiding to found the
Church, and afterwards in endeavours to extend its influence and limits, yet, especially towards the latter years of
his residence at Antioch, he may be supposed to have found
leisure for writing, besides his notes of current events, or
the Acts of the Apostles, his former treatise entitled his
" Gospel."

2. It must be supposed that, when the time arrived in
which the record he had prepared should be required, its
publication would not have been deferred. While the
preaching of the gospel to Gentiles was confined principally
to Antioch, the publication of the written record of the
gospel would not be pressing. There were persons here,
Luke being of the number, who occupied themselves in

making oral relations of the incidents of our Saviour's life, and in furnishing to their audiences reports of his parables and discourses. But that a demand for a written gospel had arisen in other places at least is witnessed by facts. During his residence here, the first regular mission to the Gentiles had been successfully accomplished. A large field had hereby been opened. Many churches of believers had been gathered. Inquirers waited to be informed. It was impossible to supply all these with teachers competent to afford an oral account of the facts of the gospel sufficiently copious and exact. But Luke possessed the means of meeting the exigence ; and the return of the apostles to the scenes of their former labours, together with the requirements of new places to be visited, offered a proper occasion for the issue of the desiderated document. Can it be thought, other considerations concurring, that the boon was withheld ?

3. Antioch offered conveniences for the publication of his Gospel unequalled by those of any place of Luke's subsequent abode. To have published it in Rome—that is, the Greek original—is quite inconsistent with probability. True, Greek books were much prized in Italy by the learned and by collectors of curious books, for these existed then as now. But all those books were imported. Most of the lighter class of Greek literature was obtained from Athens. Neither were Greek scribes to be found in Rome by whom the Gospel could have been multiplied ; nor were the readers there for whom the original was designed and adapted.

4. Some writers prefer to claim Cæsarea for the place where it was written. Drs Conybeare and Howson, in their account of St Paul's imprisonment there, write : " A plausible conjecture fixes this period and place for the writing of Luke's Gospel under the *superintendence* of the apostle of the Gentiles." But invalidating this conjecture

are the considerations that, for the two years which Luke spent in Cæsarea, he had resided ten years in Antioch. Moreover, the identical objection stands here as against Rome with respect to the language of the place. Cæsarea was essentially a Roman colony, having been the residence of the Roman governor and his court, with a large garrison of Italian soldiers, whilst the rest of the inhabitants were chiefly Jews. Whereas, differing from those cities, Antioch possessed a metropolitan character in relation to the eastern provinces of the empire, and especially with respect to the Greek-speaking peoples. And then, concerning the other particular of the conjecture. Was that which it insinuates the true situation of Luke with respect to the composition of his Gospel? Is it to be suspected that an evangelist was not as competent for the work of his own vocation as an apostle was for his? Is it hereby pretended that Luke did not write as directly under the superintendence of the Holy Ghost as did Paul?

As a great seat of industry and commerce, books were included among the productions of Antioch. This city was likewise the chief seat of the Gentile branch of the Christian Church and missions; and as practical copyists were here easily attainable, so the means of distributing the copies were ample. The precious gift had only to pass from the scribes into the hands of the Church, and those Christians who had shown how well they understood the obligation of spreading the gospel by missions would not fail, with similar alacrity, to undertake the dispersion of the written Word, "the sword of the Spirit."

5. It is important to notice the claim which scribes of Alexandrine copies of Luke's Gospel have asserted for its original publication at Alexandria. That this refers to Alexandria in Egypt is frequently denied by critics, who affirm that it signifies Troas. But a demurrer to this criticism is, that although this city was originally named

Alexandria Troas, its former appellation had been dropt by the Romans. In the time of the apostles it was known as *Troas.* Luke's habit of exactness would lead him to be careful to distinguish this city from the Alexandria with which he had formerly been acquainted, and also from all others, for there were no less than a dozen places of that name, according to the gazetteers; and it is quite improbable that the original name should have been adopted by him so long after its disuse, or that the scribe having, in five previous instances, written Troas in the text, should name it Alexandria in the inscription. This remark applies to the Greek copies; and in agreement therewith is the inscription set before the ancient Syriac or Peshito copy, and also the Persian, made from the Syriac, which reads: "The Holy Gospel of Luke the Evangelist, which he uttered and preached at Great Alexandria." With this evidence accord the opinions of those learned critics, Grabe, Mill, and Wetstein, who each say that Luke's Gospel was published at Alexandria in Egypt. But how is this claim of Alexandria in Egypt to be reconciled with the foregoing considerations in behalf of Antioch? The answer is easy. The Gospel may be said to have been published at Antioch and Alexandria *simultaneously.* It has been seen that Theophilus, to whom the Gospel is addressed, abode at Alexandria. A beautiful coincidence is found in this circumstance; for it is to be observed, when the Gospel was published, authors frequently sent their productions to some distinguished man, or prefixed his name to it, in order, by the dedication of a work to him, to testify his esteem, and also to enlist his influence. If he accepted the gift, he was considered bound to introduce it to the world as *patronus libri.* It was hence his part to provide for its publication by means of transcripts and to spread its fame. This usage was followed by Lucius the Cyrenian, in the dedication of his book to Theophilus of Alexandria. By this dedication Luke imposed the same obligation upon his friend, whose duty it became to multiply copies of it, and to distribute them among those for whose use it was particularly composed; his object being the same as that expressed by the poet—

> " My little book
> To one is sent;
> But is for all designed."
> —*Martial*, Sat. vii. 96.

It should be remembered that there is nothing fortuitous in Holy Scripture. No item is found there except for an important reason. That reason may have slipped from recognition, but it is sometimes recovered by study, and sometimes by accident. It was not enough, then, that merely as a personal friend of Luke's the name of Theophilus should have been set in the front of the sacred narrative. Theophilus must have been a person not only in repute in the Gentile Churches, but also known by the leading members of them as a coadjutor in the work of evangelisation. By these deductions it appears that he was so. He is found in the roll of Christ's ministers, fulfilling His command to publish the gospel throughout the world. There is, moreover, a significance in Luke's mention of his name, in the circumstance that it tended to accredit the record to the African Churches, amongst whom Theophilus, as a magistrate, would be extensively known. And there was, likewise, a singular propriety in commending its publication to a resident in a city where the business of literature was patronised and facilitated by its magistrates.

It is impossible to refrain from expressing admiration at the providence which secured the combined action of these two friends in spreading the word of the gospel at points so remote from each other; the churches of Syria, Asia Minor, and Europe on the one side, being supplied by Luke and his allies, and those of North Africa, on the other side, by Theophilus. How, therefore, early copies of the Gospel written here came to bear the signature of Alexandria, finds a solution irrespective of the obsolete Alexandria of the Troad.

6. A confirmation of the truthful current of the foregoing deductions being sought, is at hand. Although, from the neglect of Luke's biography, the inconvenience has arisen of an overlooking, or contradicting, the allusions made to him in St Paul's epistles, yet a few writers have perceived some of them notwithstanding. In the First Epistle to the Thessalonians, it is written, "For yourselves know perfectly"— ye have exact and accurate knowledge thereof—"that the day of the Lord so cometh as a thief" (v. 2) : the allusion being to Luke xii. 39, 40. Bishop Wordsworth, having explained the apostle's words by the paraphrase above given, observes, "This could hardly be unless they had some written evangelical document with which they were familiar, such as a Gospel multiplied by means of copies, and read in religious assemblies."

If this annotation be correct, a recognition of Luke's Gospel is found in the first of the epistles written by St Paul. No other Gospel than his had then reached the Greek Churches ; and so, in the possession of this document by the Thessalonians, there was witnessed a fruit of Luke's mission to Philippi, where he abode when that epistle was written. Again, the Second Epistle to the Corinthians was conveyed from Philippi by Titus and Luke. In this epistle the latter is described as "the brother whose praise is in (or by) the Gospel throughout all the Churches " (viii. 18). This notice of Luke was written about seven years after Luke had quitted Antioch. Had it been written a few years sooner, there had not been sufficient space for his having acquired the wide-spread fame which is here expressed ; or had it been written some years later, it had not so well supported the present argument : for it might have been objected that his Gospel had been published at a later period, and consequently issued from another place than Antioch.

7. With respect to the book itself. The process of writing was so tedious that authors were in the habit of dictating their thoughts to scribes skilled in the art. It cannot be known whether Luke's Gospel was originally written on papyrus or on the inner bark of certain trees, these having been the ordinary materials upon which *books* were written. Writing on separate folios or leaves, and binding them together, had been introduced by Julius Cæsar. And probably Luke's two treatises were issued in this manner. But *epistles* were then always written on parchment, and kept in rolls. St Paul possessed both kinds of writings (2 Tim. iv. 13). Writings being composed of letters which were all capitals, could not be compressed into a portable form, such as modern types enable them to assume, so that books were seldom of a size smaller than what is termed quarto. From the first a large demand must have existed for copies of the Gospel. Obvious, therefore, was the propriety of sending the first transcript of it to Alexandria where the business of copying and supplying books was followed as are now the professions of printing and publishing in London and in Paris.

8. A Christian is sometimes captiously asked to point to the originals or autographs of the writings of the New Testament. Than this demand nothing can well be more unreasonable. Can an objector any better inform us of the existence of autographs of any of the classical or other writers contemporary with the evangelists and apostles? It has been well explained—" Of the fate of the autographs of the apostles, or rather of their amanuenses, nothing certain is known. These original copies would be much perused in the different Christian communities ; and as the ancient papyrus was exceedingly frail, they would speedily

fall into fragments : nor in those days, when materials for writing were scarce and dear, would a transcript be taken which was not absolutely necessary, or while the original could be had or was legible. In those days, also, of persecution, the writings of the Christians were exposed to accidents peculiar to themselves " (" Palæoromaica," by Dr Black, p. 56). It might be imagined that by the invention of printing no difficulty had thereafter been found in the preservation of copies of the early editions of the Holy Scriptures. But what is the fact ? Of the first edition, for instance, of the New Testament in English (Tyndale's, 1525), which was printed fourteen centuries after the original manuscripts were written, not a single copy exists ; only a fragment consisting of thirty-one leaves, which is shown as one of the rarities of the British Museum. And of the second edition of the same book, only two copies are now to be found ; both of them being imperfect. And to speak of another very popular book, published a hundred and fifty years later, namely, the " Pilgrim's Progress," 1668, only a single copy of the first part of it is known to survive. No books, indeed, of which numerous copies were issued are more rare than early editions of the Holy Scriptures, and books which, like them, have been much read and studied : for the simple reason that they were worn out by frequent use.

9. With respect to the methods by which Luke's Gospel was put into circulation ; presuming that it had already been given to the Church at Antioch, a favourable opportunity was afforded for introducing it to other Churches by the missionary labours of Paul and Barnabas, of Silas, Timothy, Titus, and others. The Christian communities which they had already gathered would receive it from their hands with avidity. And its importance, as an auxiliary in spreading a knowlege of the facts upon which the faith of Christians was founded, being felt, copies would be re-

quired wherever Churches were founded. Upon the elders of the several Churches it devolved to provide for the perusal of the precious document. It was necessary that access to it might be obtained by those in whom the preaching of the gospel had excited a desire for its perusal. By the expensiveness of books the custom was induced of affording an easy access to them by their possessors. In the mansions of Roman citizens there was usually a room, called the *tablinum*, furnished with books, the walls being covered with tablets and other writings, and of which the owner was accustomed to afford the use to his friends. Houses in the East were provided with an apartment which answered the same purpose. They were built like castles, being entered by a gate conducting to a square or court, around which stood the building, generally of two stories. In the upper story was a principal room, called in the Gospels the *guest-chamber*, having an entrance from the court by a flight of stairs; and although there might be other chambers upon the same floor, this was distinguished by the name of the *upper-room*, and was at once the domestic sanctuary and the saloon for the entertainment of visitors. The same arrangement still exists. Mr Lane, in describing a house at Cairo, says concerning this apartment: "Sometimes the walls are ornamented with inscriptions from the Koran, &c., in Arabic, which are written in an embellished style, and enclosed in glazed frames" ("Modern Egyptians," vol. i.)

What, therefore, the *tablinum* was to the Romans, and the synagogue to the Jews, the *upper-room* was to the early Christians; and therein not only did they preach, pray, and "break bread," but convenience was afforded in them for the publication of the Christian Scriptures, for the public reading of these, and also individually by those of the congregation who did not possess copies of them; the books, as usual in such apartments, being placed upon shelves, and the parchments (epistles) either in cylindrical boxes, or unrolled and suspended against the walls in the manner that maps and pictures are at present. This, then, was the sanctuary or the Church in the house. Some such a sanctuary had Mary the mother of Mark at Jerusalem; so had Aquila and Priscilla at Ephesus, Philemon at Colosse, Nymphas at Laodicea, Gaius at Corinth; and so had the apostle Paul in his own hired house in Rome.

A glance downwards will show how traces of this method of providing for the reading of the Holy Scriptures are found throughout successive centuries. Tertullian, A.D. 200, speaks of it in his "Apology," where he says that the apostolical epistles were read in the churches; and he particularly refers to their being still found in the Church at Philippi, a Church which at first and for several years had been under Luke's charge. Perhaps no Church before about the beginning of the third century possessed the whole of the books of the New Testament. Some had but one or other of the gospels; some only certain of the epistles, according to vicinage to the places where was the greatest facility for obtaining them. And what with casualties by fire, the oft sacking of towns, and the eagerness with which the Scriptures of the Christians were sought for the purpose of their destruction by Pagans and Jews, it could not be expected that they would be otherwise than scarce. No wonder, therefore, that we read of some confessors having taken pains to commit some or the whole of several books of the New Testament to memory. In the year 325 it transpired at the Council of Nicæa, that a number less than three hundred of the Christian Scriptures were only known of by the members of that Council; several of whom not being able to write their names, were little competent to aid in remedying the deplorable deficiency; nor, indeed, was that scarcity ever obviated so long as books could only be multiplied by manuscript.

After the political establishment of Christianity, the provision for reading the Scriptures was transferred from the upper-room to buildings called *basilikas* and churches. About the year 400 Pantinus had inscribed over an apartment attached to the church at Nola two lines in Latin, having this signification:

> " If any one is piously disposed to meditate
> in God's law, here he may sit and employ
> himself in reading the Holy Books."

The corruptions of what mediævalists call the "*Holy* Catholic Church" rapidly progressed. The writings of the prophets and apostles were superseded. In the place of these, worshippers were invited to admire bones and other relics said to be those of martyrs and saints, and the walls were desecrated with pictures. Before a picture of Jesus the worshipper was instructed to say, "Lord help us;" before a picture of His mother, "Pray to thy Son for us;" before a picture of a martyr, "Pray for us." In these terms did Pope Gregory III. write to the Emperor Leo, A.D. 727. Literature was still in churches, but instead of the narratives of the Evangelists, it consisted of the dreamy legends of hermits and monks.

Shortly before the great Reformation there was scarcely a Latin Testament in any cathedral church in England, though the Latin was the authorised language for the Scriptures and service-books. Instead of the Holy Gospels, the apocryphal legend called the " Gospel of Nicodemus " was affixed to a pillar in the cathedral at Canterbury. And, as an illustration of this kind of perversion within observation, the visitor to Windsor Castle may still read the following inscription in St George's Chapel :—

" WHO LEYDE THYS BOOKE HERE? THE
REUEREND FFADER IN GOD, RICHARD BEAU-
CHAMP, BISSCHOP OF THYS DYOCESSE OF
SARYSBURY. AND WHERFOR? TO THYS EN-
TENT, THAT PREESTIS AND MINISTERS OF
GODDIS CHURCHE MAY HERE HAVE THE
OCCUPACION THEREOF, SEYYING THEREIN
THEYR DIVYNE SERVYSE, AND FOR ALL OTHIR
THAT LYSTYN TO SEY THEREBY THER DEVO-
CYON."

This book was a breviary, which was fastened by a chain
to a ring in the wall, but it has long since been removed,
and replaced by a copy of the Bible in English. By
Edward VI. and Queen Elizabeth Bibles were ordered
to be placed in all churches in like manner. Of the
custom of exhibiting the words of Holy Scripture by the
primitive Christians in their places of worship, the texts
inscribed upon panels in earlier foreign Protestant churches,
and likewise the tablets suspended in our own churches
exhibiting the Ten Commandments, the Lord's Prayer, and
the Apostles' Creed, are obvious relics.

CHAPTER XVII.

LUKE AT TROAS.

ACCORDING to certain modern authorities on biblical subjects, Luke's biography commences here. They affect to
know nothing concerning him until he is found using the
personal pronoun " we " (xvi. 10). One of these authorities
says, " The first ray of historical light falls on the Evangelist when he joins St Paul at Troas " (" Smith's large
Dict. of the Bible "). Consequently, to those who adopt
these guides, all that has been advanced in the preceding
pages of this biography will be regarded as so much romance.
There is surely something mysterious in this repudiating
the history of the Evangelist before this period. Can it be
conceived that to an inquirer no trace of Luke's personal
history should be discernible until he came to Troas, notwithstanding that he had been a disciple nearly twenty
years, that he had published his Gospel four or five years
before, and that more than half the matter of his Acts
of the Apostles had transpired? It could not well be.
And, by a not surprising inconsistency, some of these same
authorities confess to apprehend that Luke may have witnessed some things which he relates in chapters preceding
this period. For instance, Drs Conybeare and Howson,
although strongly declaring against the identity of Lucius
and Luke (vol. i. 129), yet admit, " It is highly probable
that they (Paul and Luke) had already met and laboured
together *at Antioch*" (vol. i. 261). It cannot be pleaded that
there is any difference in the character of Luke's composi-

tion when the article "WE" comes to be used. There is no formal conclusion of what precedes it, and no mark of a section newly commenced. No explanation accompanies the change. But it occurs as familiarly as if this recognition of the writer had been apparent throughout, whilst the biographical harmony of the parts remains unbroken. To the question, then, that arises, " Why does Luke, contrary to his previous custom, now write in the first person ?" it is answered : The information which the use of the word " WE " implies now *became necessary.* The fact of his having notified his presence at Antioch, and the reason thereof, will be remembered. And now, his presence elsewhere is intimated, and in a manner the most simple. As long as he resided in that city, what he wrote as a witness there, and what concerning occurrences in other places from the report of others, is easily distinguishable. But it would be otherwise upon his departure from thence, unless some intimation was afforded of the occasions when he was present in the scenes which he proceeds to describe.

As Luke never returned to Antioch, his departure thence formed a new era in his life ; a fact also indicated by the circumstance which has just been explained. He had bid farewell to his associates there, in contemplation of entering upon some other important sphere of ministry. And it may be thought to be certain that these, together with the whole Church, united in a prayerful commendation of their friend to God, as in other instances of the departure from thence of brethren to scenes of labour. The reason for his visit to Troas must be sought in a consideration of his character and employment as a prophet divinely intrusted with a historical development of the fulfilment of Christ's charge. The Apostle Paul, whose ministry he now chiefly had in view, had compassed a large part of the continent of Syria and Asia, and his absence from Antioch became, therefore, so much extended, that if the narrative was to continue to partake the marks of the writer's being a sharer in and a witness of the enterprises, as well as a reporter from the lips of the Apostle and his companions, it would be necessary for his purpose to follow him. Added to this reason, he doubtless also purposed to extend hereby the circulation of his Gospel, which he had recently published at Antioch. Certainly, a journey or voyage of 600 miles had not been undertaken without strong inducements by one having attained the age of sixty-six. But above all this, as he had been divinely directed to Antioch, so was he now to Troas. He had been favoured to see much of the prophetic charge of Christ fulfilled, first in Palestine, and then in Syria ; and he was destined to witness and to record a still wider fulfilment of it.

By coming to Troas, Luke passed from the greatest city in the east to the greatest city in the west of the continent upon which he stood. He was now on classic ground, a district of fabulous and historical fame. Troas was built by order of Alexander the Great, about B.C. 320; and its rapid decline dated from about A.D. 339, in consequence of the establishment of Constantinople as the metropolis of the eastern dominions of the Roman Emperor. Although it took the name of the district, it was some distance from the site of the ancient city of Troy. Convenient for commerce, it was erected on the coast of the Ægean Sea, and near to the mouth of the Hellespont, having in its front a natural basin for its harbour. In honour of the hero by whose command it was built, it was called *Alexandria Troas*. But having been constituted by the Emperor Augustus a Roman colony, its name was changed to *Augusta Troas*. Afterwards the double designation was dropped, and it bore in the time of Luke simply the name of *Troas*. Coins having each of these inscriptions are to be seen in numismatic cabinets. The name of Troas had not become obsolete in the fourteenth century; but by the unclassic Turk it is now called *Eski Stamboul.*

The city was seated on a hill of several miles in extent, having an aspect sloping from the summit towards the sea. Behind the hill lay a deep valley, from which again arose the chain of hills which constitute Mount Ida. The other sides of the hill terminate in extensive plains. When Luke beheld it, the prospect of the city from the shore presented a noble sight. Behind him was the natural harbour, built around with massive stones, and ornamented with columns of marble; whilst there extended from the shore a pier whose limit and strength are still indicated by the rippling of the waves in passing over it. In the plat forming the foreground of the city was laid out the stadium or race-course, from whence, arising in easy ascent for two miles, appeared the numerous dwellings, interspersed by the public buildings, whose magnificent character is gathered from the ruins of those of them which have retained their individuality. The principal of these consist of a theatre, an odeum or music-hall, two temples; and, crowning all, being distant nearly three miles from the shore, the Palace of Priam (erroneously so called), being, according to the best authorities, a gymnasium, bearing a resemblance to the baths of Diocletian at Rome. Three expansive arches are seen in its front, ornamented with mouldings of white marble, the centre arch being approached by a noble flight of steps.

Several large pedestals, without the statues that had surmounted them, are found in different places. Upon one of these, seen by Chandler, was an inscription to "Caius Rufus, flamen (or high priest), of the divine Julius and of the divine Augustus." Other remains, some of a stupendous size, consist of columns (monoliths) almost equal to that called Cleopatra's Needle in Egypt, marble soroi (sarcophagi), and fragments of architecture, which lay scattered for miles both within and beyond the limits of the city, the port being literally choked with them. Dr E. D. Clarke observes : " Long before the extinction of the Greek empire, the magnificent buildings of this city began to contribute the monuments of its ancient splendour towards the public structures of Constantinople ; and at present there is scarcely a mosque in the country that does not bear testimony of its dilapidation by some costly token of jasper, marble, porphyry, or granite, derived from this wealthy magazine." He adds, " After all that has been removed, it is wonderful so much should remain."

The walls, thick and solid, which encircled the city, are still standing, but are covered with earth up to within a few feet of their height, and present the appearance of a boundary to a forest or to a neglected park ; for such is the character of the whole site upon which the city stood. " Covered," says Sir C. Fellows, " by a forest of oaks, it is impossible to see its ruins collectively."

Works of public utility were on a scale of corresponding magnitude. A valley, comprehended within the walls, and partly artificial, was divided in its whole length by a large common sewer, into which the waters of the city were discharged, and whose outlet, for size and workmanship, was not inferior to the great work of the kind constructed by the Tarquins at Rome. Also, an aqueduct of massive stone structure, which conveyed water to the city, is still seen crossing the country on the side next the Hellespont, extending several miles.

By the prescribed limits of Luke's narrative, curiosity is again disappointed. At what period he arrived in this great city ; and how long he had been here before he was joined by his friends, is not even to be guessed. He was an Evangelist, and therefore, whatever time he had spent here had been employed in endeavours to spread the knowledge of the gospel. As there are no incidents given concerning the introduction of the gospel into Troas, it may be supposed that it had been already brought hither by persons who had come from some of the provinces which had been visited by the apostles. Consequently, Luke had found in this " city set upon a hill " the accommodation of a house, where, in an upper room, two or three or more were accustomed to meet together in the name of Jesus. Only the name of one Christian resident in Troas —that of Carpus—is mentioned in the New Testament (2 Tim. iv. 13). Paul had lodged with him ; but this was several years afterwards, and when Troas had become an important rendezvous for the mission on this side of Asia Minor, as Antioch was on the other side of it.

How refreshing in this distant place must it have been for the Evangelist to welcome the Apostle and Silas. Accompanying them was Timothy, who, during the Apostle's former visit to Lystra had heard the tidings of the gospel ; and had also heard concerning the preacher's having been stoned and cast out of the city for dead ; or, perchance, had witnessed the scene, even as Paul himself had witnessed the stoning of Stephen, but with this difference, that Timothy's heart was affected with sorrow. Upon his present journey, and his revisiting Lystra, the Apostle found this youth " a disciple well reported by the brethren " (Acts xvii.) The same report was also given of him at Iconium ; for he had already become an evangelist by the laying on of the hands of the Presbytery (1 Tim. iv. 14). Being now introduced to Luke, the latter had the pleasure to welcome him as the Apostle's " son in the gospel, and fellow-labourer."

But soon was Luke's gratification subdued. The mysterious relation which he received from the lips of his friends was of a character new and bewildering. The progress of Paul and Silas through the places visited by the former on his first journey had been cheering and prosperous. By their visitation of them "the Churches were established, and increased in numbers daily" (xvi. 5).   From those parts they had proceeded through the midland provinces of Phrygia and Galatia.   But now came an arrest. They were forbidden by the Holy Ghost, by whom they had been sent forth, to preach the Word in Asia, or to go into Bithynia, the place which they next proposed to visit.   The Asia here mentioned was a portion of what is now called Asia Minor, about a fourth of it, which was constituted a distinct province by the Romans as *Asia Propria.* It included Mysia, Lydia, Ionia, and Caria, with a part of Phrygia.   The divine injunction which Paul and his company had received, expressed doubtless in the usual way— that is, by a prophetic utterance of one of the party— brought them prematurely to Troas.   The intimation so received amounted to a prohibition to preach the gospel in the Troad, or in any district on this side of the continent. Hence a dilemma.

CHAPTER XVIII.

LUKE'S VOYAGE TO EUROPE.

In coming to Troas, with the primary intention to maintain his correspondence with Paul and his party, Luke followed the track the gospel was destined to pursue. And as the angels that witnessed the marvel of the first day's creation could not have foreseen what would succeed, no more could those engaged in this mission, having witnessed the first success of their testimony, have conceived the course and extent of its future progress. It is true that prophecies with which, as a student of Holy Scripture, Luke was familiar, spake glowingly of the increase of Messiah's dominion. But prophecies have never been clearly comprehended until illustrated by their fulfilment. Luke might think that what he had witnessed of their illustration was privilege enough for the present generation. And he might have concluded that there was work enough for his companions during their lives, and for more labourers, and for a long time to come, in the vast field of the continent upon which he then stood. In accomplishing their ministry, the Apostle and his coadjutors had reached only a portion of this great field. Many important places of Asia Minor remained to be visited ; and these, after the first announcement of the gospel in them, had to be revisited for the confirmation of the converts, and the consolidation of the Churches raised ; as in the case of some of those places included in this, Paul's second journey. To be arrested, therefore, in their course by the "*Spirit of Jesus*" (for so read some of the most ancient MSS.), whose charge they were in the act of fulfilling, would throw them into the utmost perplexity. The presence of his venerable friend, at this conjuncture, must have proved a source of comfort to the Apostle. His counsel and their mutual prayers would tend to sooth the conflict that arose in the minds of the missionaries. Genius had sealed the district in which this band of Christ's ministers were now delayed with an imperishable fame. No visitor could avoid reflections upon the scenes of the great song of Troy. That song is a tale of wars. From those reflections Luke would turn to the perusal of odes suggesting thoughts more suited to his mood. In these he read, concerning a greater chief than the greatest that imparted interest to those scenes—

> " He shall speak peace unto the heathen,
> And His dominion shall be from sea to sea,
> And from the river
> To the ends of the earth."
> —*Zech.* ix. 10.

By this light a scene lay before him, transcending that enchanted by the magic of Homer. From the face of the hill-built city, musing in an upper room, his eyes fell upon the expansive sea, studded with islands, whilst far on the right flowed the Hellespont, mingling its waters with the Ægean. A spectator of this scene records : " The beauty of the evening in this country surpasses all description. The sky now glowed with rich tints of the setting sun, which, skirting the western horizon, raised, as it were, up to our view the distant summits of the European mountains " (Chandler). The land which Luke saw afar off was destined to become a scene of the triumphs of the Prince of Peace, whose servant he was. But how soon it should become so, he was as yet unconscious.

This crisis in Luke's history was as interesting as it was ambiguous, when lo ! there came a messenger from the very scene upon which his eye gazed and his mind had mused. " A vision appeared to Paul in the night. There stood a man of Macedonia, and prayed him, saying, Come over into Macedonia and help us ! " Soon the clouds vanished. The mystery of the prohibition to proceed in their projected excursions throughout Asia Minor was explained. A new direction was to be taken by the evangelical band. And here it is that, in speaking of the effect of this vision upon the judgment and conduct of the Apostle and his two other companions, Luke expressly includes also its effect upon himself by writing, " And after he had seen the vision, immediately WE endeavoured to go into Macedonia, assuredly gathering that the Lord had called US for to preach the gospel unto them " (xvi. 10). The unusual mode of this intimation shows that an extension of their mission to the European continent had not only not been contemplated, but that a fear of outstepping the limit of what they deemed, for the present at least, the extent of their commission, had to be overcome in the mind, particularly of him to whom the vision appeared. The opening of the door to the Gentiles, of which this is the *third* special instance wherein Jews received a commission to bring Gentiles into the fold, had upon each occasion to be authenticated by a special revelation. Whereas the prompt interpretation given to the vision by the Gentile prophet shows how little such an apprehension had possessed his mind.

If any evidence was wanting that Luke, reticent though he was concerning himself—being only once before mentioned—yet took an active part in the Christian ministry, it is supplied here. Speaking concerning this passage of Luke's history, it is said by Charles Taylor, and with proper emphasis: " I am not pleased with the inferiority ascribed to Luke by writers who make him merely an attendant on St Paul in his travels. His language is not consistent with that opinion. He says : ' A vision appeared to Paul, and immediately WE endeavoured to go into Macedonia ;' and that 'The Lord had called US to preach the gospel in Macedonia.' He does not say, nor does he mean, Paul determined, and we obeyed ; no, he esteems himself equally entitled to give his opinion, and equally called to the expedition." And with this expostulation, it may be added, agrees the entire contexture of Luke's conduct. He had been a believer in Christ before Paul's conversion ;—ere Paul came to Antioch Luke had established, along with his companions, a Church, whose growing interest had occasioned Paul to be invited hither ;—he was one of the three directed to separate Paul for the ministry which he now pursued ;— and he was found at this station before Paul, and *not* accompanying or following him. All this is contradictory to the oft-echoed statements that Luke was Paul's assistant or disciple.

From this moment Troas took an important place in the annals of the apostolical missions. It became another rendezvous, from whence the agents thereof proceeded in the new direction of their labours. Here they might at once obtain and communicate intelligence concerning the work of God on either continent. It is spoken of as such a station, Acts xx. 5, 6. It is twice so referred to in Paul's epistles. And of the Church established here, with its upper room, an anecdote transpires in Acts xx. 7-12.

The associate-authors, in whose Life of St Paul the Apostle's travels are so carefully traced, have given so little attention to the writer of the book from whence all that relates to that Apostle (except the notices contained in his his own correspondence) is derived, that, like some other modern writers, they only begin to recognise him at Troas. Depicting the situation of Paul at this place, they relate : " Among those who were busy about the shipping in the harbour, were the newly-arrived travellers, Paul, Silas,

Timothy, and that *new* companion, Luke, the beloved physician" (Conybeare and Howson, chap. viii.)

By the absence of particulars wished to be known concerning Luke's sojourn at Troas, further than what has been noticed, observation is again directed to the brevity of the notations in parts of his narrative. This brevity often challenges the exercise of the imagination, and it justifies any amplification that may be made by legitimate inference —that is, harmoniously with the time, the place, and the characters of the text, and of its correspondences. The intimate relationship of every Christian heart with the topics of the narrative warrants this indulgence. Here, for instance, the departure of the company is summed up in the words, "Therefore loosing from Troas, we came with a straight course to Samothracia, and the next day to Neapolis" (xvi. 11). No ship is mentioned, and no embarkation. Both are left to be understood. Yet never did ship leave that beautiful harbour bearing such an important freight. Compared with this freight, that of "Cæsar and his fortunes" dwindles into insignificance. In that little company pacing the deck, what an interesting group was seen ! all chosen vessels to carry the blessings of salvation to the quarter of the globe destined most of all eventually to illustrate the divine power that attended the preaching thereof.

There walked Luke, who had been called by divine grace, having, by an acquaintance with the literature of true religion, had his mind prepared for the light and bliss of the gospel. His place in this new expedition is consistent with his having been one of the company by whom the gospel had been first preached to the heathen. Among the first that brought the gospel into Asia, he is now privileged, also, to be among those who first bear its tidings to Europe. Having enriched the Churches of the former by the publication of his narrative of the life of Jesus, he now conveys copies of it to aid in spreading a knowledge of Him in the latter.

In close converse with this venerable man was Paul, who, in the divine foreknowledge, had been separated for this service from his mother's womb, and who had already proved his armour. His own previous rebellion against Christ, and persecution of His saints, ever present in his remembrance, induced an energy in his speech and actions which bespake the intensity of the zeal with which he evermore sought to fulfil the charge of Him whom he now gloried to serve.

Near to these, and joining them in conversation, was cheerful Silas, younger than Luke, but older than Paul, for he had been a prophet and " a chief man among the brethren " in Jerusalem when the latter had accomplished his first missionary tour. Free from the bondage of Jerusalem-Judaism, and possessing the Roman franchise, the sympathies of Silas, sanctified by love divine, were unrestrained to people or place ; whilst of his fitness for partnership in this enterprise, the best evidence is afforded in his presence here by the choice of the Apostle.

There, too, was youthful Timothy, half Gentile, half Jew, and mother-taught, the adopted son of the Apostle, eyeing the three with affectionate interest, and listening, as became his intelligence, to the discourse of his seniors. Having had no past experiences beyond the vicinage of home, his situation, in all its aspects, had for him the interest of novelty.

> " In sight of Troy lies Tenedos,
> An isle renowned." *

Glancing at this object, and steering northward, the island of Lemnos was passed, then the island of Imbros ; then arriving before the lofty Samothracia, the ship was moored until the morning. Sailing thence a distance of sixty miles, they passed the island of Thasos, which lays nearly opposite Neapolis ; for the Ægean is a sea of islands. At

---

* Est in conspectu Tenedos notissimâ famâ insula. — *Virgil* ii. 21, 22.

length they approached their desired haven. The wind having been favourable, they had not been driven out of the direct course. And now, with more than the curiosity of travellers who for the first time look upon foreign scenes, with holy aspirations and subdued wills, these Christian pioneers gazed from the ship's side upon the land to which they had been invited, the voice still lingering in the imagination, " Come over and help us ! "

CHAPTER XIX.

The First Part.

GREECE was divided by the Romans into the two provinces of Macedonia in the north, and Achaia in the south. Neapolis lay between the river Nessus, which divided Thrace and Macedonia, and the river Strymon, both of which flowed into a bay of the Ægean Sea. It was a port of some importance; but the activity imparted by commerce has vanished, and its name has been changed by the Turks into Cavalla. A recent traveller relates : " The aspect of the town is still striking, standing principally on a projecting mass of rock, which rises abruptly from the sea. On the summit stands the fortress, with its round and square towers. A strong wall, apparently of Saracenic construction, surrounds the town. A short distance in the background, a fine aqueduct of Roman work, in good preservation, connects Cavalla with the neighbouring mountains. The appearance of this range of mountains is extremely wild and barren ; masses of granite, partly overgrown with low shrubs, with here and there a stunted tree; the *Via Egnatia* (a Roman road), in tolerable preservation, still used, sweeping round the bay, and disappearing among the rocks and glens, impress the mind with a feeling, that much in that stern landscape is unchanged since the Apostle of the Gentiles commenced his ascent of those bleak mountains on his way to Philippi" (M. A. Walker, " Through Macedonia to the Albanian Lakes," pp. 11, 12).

The distance from the port to Philippi is about ten miles. In travelling that road the missionaries crossed the scene of another great conflict, one within the ken of then recent history. On the plains of Philippi were fought the battles between Roman republicans and imperialists. Brutus, the conspirator against Cæsar, after the assassination of the latter, retired to Athens, where he beguiled himself with literature, whilst also he prepared for an expected assault upon him by Marcus Antonius, who had persuaded the people to avenge the death of Cæsar. Upon the march of this avenger with Octavianus (Augustus), Brutus and Cassius prepared their armies for the encounter in a plain near Philippi. Here, as it is related by Plutarch, one night, when, overcome by watching, Brutus was reading alone in his tent by a dim light at a late hour, his army around him being wrapped in sleep and silence, he thought he perceived something enter his tent, and saw a spectre stand silent by his side. "What art thou?" he inquired. "Art thou a god or a man, and what is thy business with me?" The spectre answered, "I am thy evil genius, Brutus. Thou wilt see me at Philippi." To which Brutus calmly replied, "I will meet thee there." This apparition is represented by Shakspeare as "Cæsar's ghost." The battle ensued. It was fiercely contested, and ended in the defeat of the republicans. Thereupon Cassius fell upon his own sword, receiving for his eulogy by Brutus, upon being informed thereof, "He was the last of the Romans." A second battle near the same spot ensued. In this conflict Brutus had obtained a partial advantage, but perceiving himself surrounded by a detachment of his enemies' soldiers, and preferring death to being made a prisoner, after the example of his friend, he threw himself upon the point of his sword.

Philippi was situated in a plain, having a mount, whereupon was erected its acropolis or fortress. Beside the city flowed the Gangas, or Gangites, a river which, with other streams, fertilise the neighbourhood. By Augustus, and in commemoration of his victory near it, it was constituted a colony of the Roman empire ; and at the period of the visit of this company it was a flourishing and important place. It is no longer a city. Its beauty has long since perished. Only a single ruin of any magnitude is found to memorialise it ; other ruins, scattered in confusion, are covered with the streams, which, uncurbed by industry, overwhelm the plain.

Luke's position in his narrative is now incontestably ascertained, and also the reason for the personal discovery of himself is apparent. In coming to Europe, he followed the progressive advance made in the fulfilment of Christ's charge by the most energetic and interprising of all those who had received it. The plan of his narrative required that he should be within the sphere of Paul's ministry, to whose history it is henceforth confined. It was therefore expedient, upon the Apostle's passage to another continent, to reveal the fact of his own companionship with him, that he might preserve his claim to authenticity as a witness of his progress, or as receiving intelligence from the Apostle himself. And besides this reason, it was proper, as in the case of the ordination of Barnabas and Saul at Antioch, to record who were the persons appointed to this memorable embassy.

Luke was now in another climate, and in the midst of different associations than those at Antioch. Yet the change could not fail to be pleasurable to a colonist who had never before visited the country from which his fathers emigrated. Whilst brevity and brightness characterise his sketches of the incidents of the mission, the interest is heightened by the assured knowledge of Luke's personal share in them. In reviewing these divine sketches, there is observed—

1. *A suspense.* This seems to be indicated by the words,

" And we were in the city abiding certain days " (xvi. 12). Having arrived, probably, early in the week, some days were spent by the missionaries in reconnoitring their new field of labour. In this interim, perhaps, no friendly door was opened to them. Nor did they find any welcome corresponding with the invitation that had directed their steps hither. On their part, they made no announcement of their errand ; but they modestly waited a discovery of the Master's directing hand.

2. *A place of worship visited.* " And on the Sabbath we went out of the city by a river-side, where prayer was wont to be made." The company repaired to the only place in the neighbourhood in which Jehovah was worshipped. More than one stream flowed in the neighbourhood. This was a minor one. It was a retired spot, removed from the heathenish associations of the city. Some writers say it was a grove. But it was not so. Groves were character· istic of idol worship, in continuance of the serpent's place in Eden. The places wherein Jews met for worship were usually tabernacles, or dwellings of some kind, indicating the social character of true worship ; God herein condescending to " dwell with man." It is still a rule in towns wherein are found ten families of Jews, for these to form a synagogue. From the absence of any description of the place " out of the city," it is to be supposed that it was but a simple apartment. Everywhere the synagogue offered a refuge for those that discerned the abomination of idolatry. At Thessalonica there was found a great multitude of Greek proselytes, belonging to the superior class of the community (Acts xvii. 4). Perhaps the prayers of this congregation had often been in harmony with the request of the Macedonian of the vision at Troas.

3. There is described *the first announcement of the gospel in Europe* by the missionaries. " And we sat down and spake unto the women that resorted thither." The appear-

ance of these four strangers could not fail to have excited the notice of the pious worshippers. But curiosity would soon turn to surprise, when these undertook the conduct of the worship. The expression, "WE spake," shows that the writer was a speaker on the occasion. It has been remarked—"It would seem that at that time there were no Jewish men in the city; for Paul and his companions, at that rural place, only spake to women who were assembled there" (Lechler and Gerok).* If men had formed part of the congregation, Luke had not said "WE;" for he, as a Gentile, was precluded from publicly discoursing in a synagogue. Consistently with what had been his special study, and with his acquired character, it cannot be doubted that Luke's address consisted of some particulars of his Gospel. And for those in the congregation who, as God's elect, had often spoken one to another on the subject of the "Desire of all nations," and had "waited for the consolation," how profound would be the attention given to the intelligence that fell from his lips! Was the report brought to their ears by this stranger credible? would be the prompt inquiry. But before this inquiry found expression, Paul, taking up the subject, proceeded to shed upon the narrative which had been given, an exposition such as may be conceived by a reference to his teaching in his epistles. With the friendly and personal character of Paul's epistles the lover of Holy Scripture is familiar. It is easy, therefore, to imagine the manner in which his arguments were conveyed. In confirmation of Luke's statements, he would revert to the explorations made by the Evangelist to obtain these facts from eye-witnesses of Christ's life and ministry. He would glance at the circumstance, that what had been related to them had been gathered by the loving industry of a proselyte, having gone from Africa to Jerusalem, where he had

* Nulli viri sed solæ fœminæ ad orationem convenisse.—*Fromond, Comment.*, 1654.

heard and embraced the glad tidings of the gospel. He would speak of his own conversion, and of the visions he had had of Christ, and how he had been appointed by him to be his apostle to Gentiles. He would tell of the call of himself and companions to Macedonia. And turning to Silas and Timothy, he might invite them to speak concerning their own conversion, and of their toils and consolations in the service of Christ.

4. *The first convert.* "And a certain woman named Lydia, a seller of purple, of the city of Thyatira, who worshipped God, heard; whose heart the Lord opened, that she attended unto the things which were spoken of Paul." No wonder, after the statements made, and the application of them by the Apostle, that such an incident should have followed. Here the accurate pen is observable in the mention of the place from which Lydia came in Asia Minor, and of her occupation here; for Thyatira was famed for the excellence of its purple dye, a colour much esteemed by Orientals. Luke's expression, "Whose heart the Lord opened," corresponds with the words of the Apostle, afterwards addressed to the Philippians, "For unto you it is given to believe in Christ" (i. 29); and again, "For it is God who worketh in you" (ii. 13). So the first convert in Greece was obtained without a miracle. These devout women were conversant with the Old Testament Scriptures. They waited for the promised Messiah. Prepared for the truth, they perceived its beauty and adaptation to their aspirations. From the promptitude of Lydia's conversion, it is not too much to suppose that others of the congregation, upon reflection, and under the effects of subsequent teaching, became believers and disciples likewise.

5. *The first Christian baptism in Europe.* "And when she was baptized and her household." Baptism is a reasonable service. As "a water of separation," baptism was received by proselytes, being Gentiles, upon their admission to

the privilege of Jewish worship. This baptism Lydia had already received. The baptism of John was administered as a pledge to be taken of repentance and the forsaking of sins, and also of a belief and expectance of the Messiah, whose approaching advent that prophet announced. In the teaching of the Apostle Paul, baptism was symbolised as a going down with Christ unto death, leaving therein all the sins of the previous life, and the rising up out of the water as a resurrection with Christ to a new and spiritual life (1 Cor. x. 2 ; Rom. vi. 3, 4). Faith accepts the covenant, and baptism is a seal thereof. Lydia now submitted to this second baptism, probably administered by Silas. With respect to the baptism of her household, it is to be concluded that she had no husband, or he had been a sorry one, to be undistinguished in the group. It is also to be concluded that she was a matron. If she was of the age between forty and fifty, which is probable, her children, if her household comprised any, would be of an age to comprehend and to sympathise with their mother's views. And as she was a "devout woman," there can be as little hesitation in supposing that her household had formed part of the congregation by the river-side ; that they had attentively listened to the facts and arguments by which she had been persuaded to become a Christian ; and that they too had been savingly influenced by them. All this, being consistent with probability, may be reasonably accepted. For again, it must be remembered, that it is Luke's plan to give only the principal features of the case, leaving what is subordinate to be conceived by the reader.

6. *Lydia's hospitality.* "She besought us, saying, If ye have judged me to be faithful to the Lord, come into my house and abide." The terms in which this invitation was given affords a beautiful evidence of the humble and grateful feelings of the "opened heart." "If ye have found me faithful to the Lord." How sweetly do these

words read! how they breathe humility! Here was a disciple, fit companion for the saintly penitent that washed the Saviour's feet with her tears. Could Lydia's appeal, " Come into my house and abide," be rejected?—the matronly character of the hostess being fixed by the note, " And she constrained us." Here, then, was an asylum for the prophets. In this first convert in Europe was found another example added to the number of hospitable matrons whose memorials are conserved in Holy Scripture. Here was another heroic woman, not deterred from entertaining the servants of the Lord by the adverse circumstances by and by appearing. Here was another sister of consolation, like the Mary who had her house on Zion, where abode Peter and other apostles. Here Paul found another mother, like the wife of Simon Niger at Antioch. Under this roof was for the moment gathered the first Christian household, the fruit of the invitation of Lydia's guests to Macedonia. It was the exclamation of Libanius, the pagan teacher of philosophy at Antioch, " Ye gods, what women have the Christians! "

More stirring scenes ensue; and Luke now embodies in his pages sketches of novel interest, all proposed to illustrate the royalty of Christ in the progressive spread of His gospel. What had occurred since the arrival of the evangelistic company in Philippi was marked by the repose of social intercourse, begun in the place of prayer, and continued in the domestic circle of the first convert's house. At appointed times they continued to resort to the former. And all had gone on smoothly there, and with benefit to those who had the happiness to partake the influence that attended inspired instruction. But the tidings brought were not to be confined to that assembly, however much its numbers might increase by the interest which the presence of the missionaries created. Their message was to each pagans likewise. The people of the city must be

awakened. Hitherto no signs of welcome had met them
answerable to the pathetic invitation that brought them
here. But at length, and from an unexpected quarter,
public attention is aroused.

6. There is depicted *an interruption of the missionaries by
a Pythoness.* "And it came to pass that as we went to
prayer, a certain damsel possessed of a python spirit ($\pi\nu\varepsilon\tilde{\nu}\mu\alpha$
$\pi\acute{\nu}\theta\omega\nu\circ\varsigma$), met us, who brought her masters much gain by
uttering oracles." The same followed Paul and us, and
cried, saying, These men are the servants of the most high
God, who announce unto us the way of salvation " (xvi.
16, 17).

By the rendering of the English version, "possessed with
a spirit of divination," the precision of the Greek text being
neglected, a very principal feature of its interest is missed.
The Greek mythology wore two aspects, one suited to the
intelligent and meditative, and another to the vulgar and
licentious. But the devil worked in both. And all their
"gods many," however sublimated some of them were by
art, and set before the eye in fascinating forms of poetry
and sculpture, only veiled an imposture, and enticed to
satanic orgies.

The subject of serpent-worship (*Ophialatria*) is treated
by the learned Jacob Bryant in his "System of Mythology," and since in a volume entitled "The Worship of the
Serpent traced throughout the World," by J. B. Deane.

This worship formed one of the earliest elements of idolatry.
It existed in Chaldea. In Egypt, the serpent was worshipped
under the names *Canoph* and *Ob,* or *Oub,* whence is derived the
name of the tapering column, an obelisk. It was common
to Babylonia and Syria. In the narrative concerning the
woman of Endor (1 Sam. xxviii. 7), she is called *Oub* (a
Pythoness), whereby it appears that this oracle of the
Canaanites had not been suppressed. From the East, the
worship of the serpent spread into Greece, and, by a

favourite legend of that country, Python is represented as an immense serpent produced from the mud left on the earth after the deluge of Deucalion. It is said to have lived in the caves of Parnassus, where it was sought and slain by Apollo, whose victory was celebrated by the Pythian games. Nevertheless, serpent-worship survived, and appeared in nearly every mystery of the Greek and Roman Pantheons. The pictures of Medusa, with a head covered with writhing serpents instead of hair, represent one feature of the fable. In some of the rites by which pythonic mysteries were celebrated, as in those of Bacchus, women appeared in that manner, wearing live snakes in their hair; and holding snakes in their hands, they ran about, and with frantic gesticulations and yells, screamed the name, Eva! Eva! By this poor daughter of hapless Eve, strange as it appears, was uttered the first public announcement of the character and object of the mission to Macedonia, in which Luke bare a part. This she did, when she cried, saying, "These men are the servants of the Most High God, which show unto us the way of salvation." It consists with the power of God to extort a testimony from the enemy. So Balaam, instead of the curses desired from him, and suggested by the demon of his worship, pronounced blessings upon Israel. And so the man possessed by a devil cried, in the presence of Jesus, "I know Thee whom Thou art, the Holy One of God" (Luke iv. 34). But this damsel did more; she cried to be emancipated. The devil within her could not hinder her recognition of the power by which alone her liberation would be effected. She cried, moreover, as a representative person. The spectral suppliant at Troas had said, "Come over to Macedonia and help us!" And in her case was symbolised, in one important form, the condition of need for which help was required—the condition of those who, being without God, are led captive by the devil at his will, which all Python worshippers were. The announcement by the possessed damsel was public, and it was repeated on several successive days. Hereby attention was thoroughly drawn to the missionaries. Her words were regarded by the people as oracular. To these they were couched in mystery; for what knew the idolators concerning the Most High God, or concerning the salvation of which she spake? or what, indeed, did she herself know concerning them?

7. There is described, *The exorcism of the demon by Paul's invocation of the name of* JESUS. Still the principal figure of the narrative stands foremost; so strictly does Luke maintain the integrity of his plan. He had just written, "The same followed Paul and *us;*" now he writes, "PAUL, being grieved"—that is, at the cries and persistency of the possessed one; and being in a situation similar to that in which He whose name he was about to invoke once stood—turned, and said to the spirit, "I command thee, IN THE NAME OF JESUS CHRIST, to come out of her." The faith which prompted this authoritative word was answered. Power accompanied it. "And the spirit came out of her the same hour." Thus at Philippi came off the first conflict with the gods of fable in Greece; and, in the words of Milton, "the fen-born serpent was slain by a pure beam of God's Word." * This is the first time that the missionaries were confronted by the idolatry of Europe; and the promptness, beyond all the fabulous prowess of Apollo, with which the "servant of the Most High God" expelled the "python spirit," whilst it fulfilled the oracular words that had resounded through the streets of Philippi, struck dismay into the supporters of superstition.

8. *The enemy's retaliation.* "When they saw that the hope of their gains was gone, they caught Paul and Silas,

* In a tract printed in 1641, or twenty-six years before the publication of "Paradise Lost."

and drew them into the market-place to the rulers, and brought them before the magistrates." By "her masters" is suggested that the damsel had belonged to an idolatrous establishment of some sort. The loss of "their gains" is all their grief. Idolatry is becoming bankrupt, whilst the damsel, by her emancipation, gains all; for it must be hoped that it was perfected by her divine adoption. Lydia was competent to become her instructor concerning the further import of the word "salvation."

Paul and Silas were brought, evidently with violence, to the market-place, where a mob followed, to abet, by their clamour, the applicants for reprisals. In the market-place was the forum, where sat the magistrates, or *prætors*, as Philippi was a Roman colony. The charge was preferred in the words, "These men, being Jews, do exceedingly trouble our city." These two, out of the company of four, were known to be Jews by their physiognomy and appearance. They both wore flowing beards, after the manner of Jews in all countries. Whereas Luke, being a Greco-Roman, wore his beard trimmed short, as is seen in the busts and medals of Romans of the period; whilst Timothy's youth and costume left him undistinguished.

The charge was manifestly false in respect of disturbing the city. The accused had conducted themselves with exemplary modesty. They had gone out of the city to exercise their worship, and the word spoken to the demon had been unaccompanied by any mark of ostentation. Moreover, an obvious benefit had been conferred by the cure of the patient, and the injury sustained by her masters was an accident of the case which had no remedy by law. Nor does this, their real grievance, seem to have been urged at all; but the course taken was to excite popular feeling against them, "*being Jews*," which, notwithstanding the smallness of the number of those in Philippi, and their unobtrusiveness, it was not difficult to do. Jews were everywhere in disfavour, partly because their religion was testimony against idolatry—thus Pliny the Elder charges them with a " contempt of the gods"—and partly because of their impatience of the Roman government, manifested on frequent occasions by their resistance to civil authority. Thus Cicero, in his oration for Flaccus, calls them " our enemies," and further says concerning them, " That nation has shown by arms its feeling towards our supremacy." And so here advantage is taken of the prejudice in a second clause, which sets forth, " And they teach customs which are not lawful for us to observe, *being Romans.*"   Perhaps this clause was suggested and added to the charge, from a knowledge that the reigning Emperor, Claudius, had banished all Jews from Rome, a circumstance which happened about this time.   And as a colony of the empire was apt to regard proceedings at the capital as proper precedents, the magistrates at Philippi would be disposed to decide the case according to the wishes of the accusers and their friends the mob.

9. *The treatment of Paul and Silas by the magistrates.*— " And the multitude rose up together against them ; and the magistrates rent off the clothes of Paul and Silas, and commanded them to be beat ;" that is, by officers called *lictors ;* and having been " beaten with many stripes, they were committed to prison, with a charge to the jailor to *keep them safely.*"   A suspicion seems to lurk under the command given to the jailor that the magistrates were not quite at ease concerning the possibility of an exercise, by the prisoners, of a power that might set the judgment of the court at defiance, but to which contingency they were unwilling to make an allusion.   The real occasion of the prisoners having been dragged to the forum was known to every one concerned in the case ; and, therefore, it is impossible to say how much the mysteriousness thereof prompted this excess of caution.

CHAPTER XX

LUKE IN PHILIPPI.

The Second Part.

WHERE, at this crisis of the mission to Macedonia, was Luke, who has described the scenes and incidents just reviewed with such divine vividness? He had probably witnessed the proceedings against his companions until they were conducted away to prison. Afterwards, accompanied by Timothy, he returned to the house of their hospitable hostess. The company gathered there consisted now of the Evangelist and his young companion, with Lydia and members of her household, being also disciples, and probably a few sympathising friends, who had obtained a knowledge of what had happened to the missionaries. Luke sets down no note of his reflections upon the sad occasion, nor yet concerning what were the feelings and discourse hereupon of the company. The object that occupied his pen was absent. No doubt the inexperienced converts would be ready to utter expressions of dismay, both with respect to the condition of Paul and Silas, and also for the course of the gospel at Philippi, which they would regard as hereby checked. But their sobbings would have become hushed when Luke, with dignified composure, informed them concerning the case of the imprisonment of Peter at Jerusalem, and what had been the conduct thereupon of his friends in the house of Mary. And thereafter, having advised the adoption of the course pursued upon that occasion, the night would be spent in prayer. To describe the manner in which the exercise was conducted on such an occasion and by such suppliants, may not be attempted.   It is left to be imagined.

That true watch-night was succeeded by a morning of painful suspense.   Now was first known by the converts at Philippi, in its deep meaning, that "fellowship in the gospel" of which the Apostle afterwards spake so gratefully in the front of his epistle to them.   But soon these clouds should disperse: "Weeping may endure for a night, but joy cometh in the morning."   Answer to importunate prayer was not to be confined to the disciples in Jerusalem. For anon another coincidence with Peter's case followed. Before the hour of noon the beloved friends, whom the company thought to be immured in prison, stepped across the threshold.   In an instant all was changed.   The interview was reviving.   Pleasurable greetings ensued.   By Luke and Timothy, their companions would be welcomed as given back to them by their Divine Master.   By Lydia their reappearance was hailed like a deliverance from a wreck, whilst the presence in her family of more than one joyous Rhoda would impart heightened animation to the scene.

After a short interval for repose, "Paul and Silas related to the company what the Lord had done with them and for them, as Peter had done after his release from prison."[*] Brief as had been the period of their separation from the company, it was thronged with incidents the relation of which fell upon the ears of the new disciples as beyond measure marvellous.   Agreeably with his plan, it was from the REPORT now made that Luke framed his narrative of the prison experience of Paul and Silas at Philippi, and of their deliverance.   In this narrative, therefore, the reader has the gratification to be informed of those incidents as from their own lips.

* Lorini, Comment. in Acta Apost., fol. 1605.

1. *There was reported the prison experience of Paul and Silas.* The night had been spent in a very different manner than their friends had imagined. The jailor fulfilled the command of the magistrates to the utmost of his means. They were in a deplorable situation. But they did not lose their self-possession. There was no whispering with bated breath concerning their discomfort. They were again arrested in their progress ; but not by a divine monition, as in Mysia. At midnight they prayed and sung praises. Their Master had forewarned them what they should endure in fulfilling His charge, and had promised His presence should be with them to the end of the world. Hence their strong confidence. Such confidence Peter possessed when in prison, and he slept. Such confidence Paul and Silas possessed, and they *prayed in hymns*, that is, their prayers were sung aloud in the words of psalms suitable to their condition. Herein the cheerful temper of Silas was illusrated, and its advantage felt. The notice that the singing was heard by the other prisoners is not set down without some signification. The prisoners heard notes, not of songs of hardened bravado, but strains of devout import, which, accompanied by the immediately succeeding solemnity, might have left upon them a salutary impression. Perhaps some of them afterwards became inquirers concerning the " way of salvation."

2. *Their deliverance by an earthquake.* " Suddenly there was a great earthquake, so that the foundations of the prison were shaken, and immediately all the doors were opened." In this phenomenon Paul and Silas simply discerned a summons for their deliverance. And besides the usual effects of an earthquake, the Report sets forth the miracle of the loosing of every one's bands.

3. *The jailor's conduct.* He is startled out of a sleep which had probably been disturbed by dreams of the mysterious exclamations of the damsel whose dispossession of the

demon had brought Paul and Silas under his charge, and having still ringing in his ears the peremptory order which he had received concerning them. There was the man's dread of consequences to himself had the prisoners escaped. There is his conduct upon being assured from the lips of Paul that they were all safe. There is seen how the thoughts of his heart are now revealed, and how instinctively he regards Paul and Silas as "servants of the Most High God;" how he inquires, as for life, concerning his own salvation; how the heart of this man, of roughest occupation, was opened; how he makes all the reparation in his power for the wounds which had been inflicted upon them; how, forgetting his fears, he himself brings them out of prison; how he conducts them to his own residence; how he sets meat before them; how he listens with wonder and gratitude to the brief teaching of Paul answering his inquiry of "What must I do to be saved?" And here it may be observed, that by the question itself, and also by the answer to it, "Believe on the Lord Jesus Christ, and thou shalt be saved, and thy house," it is evident that he had been informed of the language of the damsel when following the Apostle and his companions, and that he was aware of the terms of the invocation by which the dispossession had been effected.

4. *The jailor's household.* The reader may fancy how the members of the jailor's family hastened their attentions; how they hearkened, with sympathising interest, to the doctrine brought to their ears by their remarkable guests; how all was new to them, and how all that was said was felt to be suitable to their moral wants. A happy event for the jailor had been the custody of these servants of Christ. Accepting their message, it is related, "he rejoiced, believing in God with all his house" (ver. 18); and thereupon "was baptized, he and all his straightway" (ver. 17). So that here, in one of the last places in the

city where such a result would be expected, was added another household to the fellowship of the saints.

5. *The effect of the earthquake beyond the prison.* The earthquake had shaken the whole city, and the magistrates were the first to connect it with the men whom the day before they had committed to prison. The apprehensions were realised which led them to give stringency to their charge to the jailor concerning Paul and Silas. Such was their conviction of the relation between these and the phenomenon, and so great was their alarm lest another shock, still more portentous, should follow, that they send their officers to deliver a message, commanding the jailor to " let those men go." And there is thereupon the counter-message of Paul and Silas, wherein they declare their Roman citizenship. They had not pleaded the possession of this privilege to avoid suffering; but now they desire the magistrates, as a testimony of the injustice of their conduct towards them, to come themselves and escort them into the city. "And they came, and besought them, and brought them out." Here, therefore, officers of the " strong man armed " were reduced to a parley with the ministers of the stronger. Moreover, this public act, subsequent upon the earthquake, amounted to a new and grave advertisement of the mission of the latter to Macedonia.

To his account of the incident which had been related to the company by Paul and Silas, Luke adds, " And when they had seen the brethren, they comforted them." Besides what was otherwise proposed for this purpose, great would be the comfort which the brethren derived from the assurance which the Report gave them of their Master's presence with His servants. Moreover, "having seen before their own eyes the examples of the Apostle's boldness in the faith, of his devotion to the Lord, of his triumph and enthusiasm for His cause, of his rejoicing amid all his trials, of the wonderful dispensation by which he had

been delivered, the faith of the Christians had been peculiarly confirmed and strengthened" (Neander on Philippians, p. 3).

So the object of the mission suffered no hindrance by
the casualty; but, in language like that afterwards addressed
to the Philippians by the Apostle from Rome, they could
say concerning it, "The things which happened unto us have
fallen out rather for the furtherance of the gospel" (i. 12).

6. *The departure of Paul and Silas from Philippi.* The
happiness of this reunion was of short duration. For,
upon descending from the Acropolis, where it is to be supposed both the forum and the prison were situated, the
magistrates, haunted with dread of the presence of Paul
and Silas, "requested them to depart out of the city."
With considerate generosity, they yielded to the solicita-
tion; and after the visit to the house of Lydia which has
been described, they departed, and travelled to Thessalonica. But their departure was not premature. There
was a great work before the Apostle. It was not fit that
he should abide at Philippi, as he did at Antioch after his
first visit to that city. The request of the magistrates,
and his own generous compliance therewith, may be regarded, therefore, as having been directed by the Divine
Master to speed His servants' progress. Not until six
years afterwards did Paul visit this city again. By the
departure of his two friends, Luke was left for the present
with young Timothy for a colleague. It is often represented that Luke accompanied Paul on his missionary
journeys. But Luke did not itinerate. He had resided
more than nine years at Antioch, and in Philippi he remained other six years. And his continuance here is,
equally with the departure of his friends, to be regarded
as of divine overruling. At this point his biography
again loses the advantage of his pen. No more anecdotes
relating to his residence here are found, whereby to en-

liven the page. Yet something may be deduced concerning this period of his history from sundry considerations. His position at Philippi, although he was a Roman citizen, was somewhat perilous. At Antioch he had been shielded by the multitude of sects existing and permitted there, and of which Christianity was taken to be one. At Philippi all was intolerance; and it had been seen by the inhabitants, at the very outset of their acquaintance with the Christians, that their doctrines were subversive of their idols. That opposition to the Christians was continued, and that, with his flock, Luke endured persecution from the idolators, is attested by those words in Paul's epistle to them : " And in nothing terrified by your adversaries; for unto you it is given in the behalf of Christ, not only to believe on Him, but also to suffer for His sake " (i. 28, 29). The persecution, which is thus dignified as a benefit to themselves, turned likewise to be a benefit to their cause, by keeping public attention upon them, and so bringing the more thoughtful to repair to the assemblies of the Christians to learn what was there taught concerning the Most High God and concerning the Lord Jesus Christ, the invocation of whose name before them had been attended with a power above that of their demons.

Upon the departure of his two friends to Thessalonica, Luke had been left with Timothy for his companion for a brief season. This was a happy providence for this young minister. As a student of divine knowledge, an opportunity was hereby afforded to him to become fully instructed from the lips of this learned Evangelist in those facts which constituted the basis of the doctrines taught and preached by the Apostle who had recently chosen him to be his assistant. Timothy joined Paul at Berea (xvii. 14).

That Luke had a *divinely-appointed ministry in Philippi*, appears from his own observation : " Assuredly gathering that the Lord had called us to preach the gospel to them "

(Acts xvi. 10).   That his ministerial character is recognised by Paul is seen in his Epistle to Philemon, where he is called " my fellow-labourer " (ver. 24). And that he had been claimed by the Holy Ghost for His minister, the evidence appears in his having been commanded, with other prophets, to separate Paul and Barnabas to the apostleship to Gentiles.   And how he delighted to recognise the presence of the Lord the Spirit is witnessed in every page of his apostolical history.   So Luke in Philippi was the first *Episcopus*, or Christian bishop, in Europe.   The particulars of his labours during his residence here are not revealed. But the character of them may be inferred.   A person of Luke's intelligence, and with a mind fraught with the information obtained in the schools of Cyrene and Alexandria, and afterwards by his experiences in Palestine and Syria, would soon attract the esteem of persons loving knowledge, and especially of those who sought the highest kind of knowledge, that which maketh wise unto salvation.

Agreeing with what had been his studies, Luke's method of public preaching would have been historical.   This method (the preaching from a historical platform) is now the rarest of any, although the best calculated to promote faith ; and as it is, also, the most interesting method of teaching, if more followed, it might tend to check the brain-softening evil of religious novel-reading.   In the historical department, he stood on solid ground.   A copy of his Gospel laying before him, he would expound its facts by reference to the Old Testament prophets, confirming the several particulars of the narrative by an account of the witnesses from whom he had received them.   It cannot be doubted that the religious services conducted by Luke were of the most simple character, corresponding with his writings.   He did not invite the curiosity of the mere seeker after novelties.   "His style," remarks

Bishop Horne, " is singularly animated, affectionate, and pleasing."

Luke's *social relations in Philippi* are also easily inferred. Here, at the very beginning of the divine cause in the city, were Christian *households*, to which rapidly must have been added others. In these, the reign of love was fostered, whereby there would have been repeated scenes such as Luke had beheld in Palestine, and he had himself promoted in Antioch. Soon would the benefactor of those households be established in their grateful veneration, and his visits be hailed in their domestic circles. Ah ! how would he whose feelings were so deeply in sympathy with the innocence and simplicity of children, as his pictures thereof testify, have loved to visit " the happy home," to converse in holy fellowship with the host and hostess, and to catch an inspiration from the cheerfulness of the striplings— the hope of the world—himself blessing all, and blessed by all !

And then, beside his pastoral ministry in Philippi, Luke would have engaged *in his special occupations in the province of sacred literature.* His situation in this city was convenient for his purpose. It was favourable for obtaining information concerning the progresses of St Paul, necessary for the continuance of his notes for his book of the Acts. In this frontier city he stood as upon a watch-tower, being not far distant from Asia Minor on one hand, and having the cities of Greece before him on the other, both having become the extensive scenes of that Apostle's labours.

Alike favourable was his present situation for his object of supplying copies of his Gospel to the several Churches gathered in Macedonia. Dr Macknight has remarked, " Here we may suppose Luke employed these six years in composing and making copies of his Gospel, that he may have sent to the Churches in these parts." But that his Gospel had already been composed at Antioch has been argued in a previous chapter of this biography. And indeed, the Word of truth must have been largely distributed along with the oral teaching, which he probably likewise delivered during circuits taken in Macedonia, where such a flourishing condition of the Churches came to exist as that which was happily witnessed. Luke had come hither at the first that he might follow the progress of the gospel, and, either as a witness thereof, or as being in close correspondence with the chief agent herein, he might continue his record.

His notes of events, although excessively brief in some places, yet, like so many lights set at chosen stations, direct and guarantee the sure path of the traveller; whilst the epistles of St Paul, confirming their integrity, serve to interest and to cheer by their correlative notices.

CHAPTER XXI.

NOT until an interval of six years after the events just narrated does any notice of Luke again · occur. Those years, it has been seen, were spent in a ministry at Philippi, and in visitations of the infant Churches in Macedonia. During those years Paul accomplished a great work in planting Churches in Greece, and thereafter in extending the triumphs of the gospel in Proconsular Asia ; particulars of which were obtained from time to time from eye-witnesses by Luke, and incorporated in his narrative testimony, having this appropriate conclusion : " So mightily grew the Word of the Lord, and prevailed " (Acts xix. 20).

At length, after two years' residence at Ephesus, Paul's ministry there drew towards a close ; the first intimation thereof having been given in a letter (the first) to the Corinthians. In that letter he requested that they would make a weekly collection in behalf of the poor saints in Judea, and added a notice of his intention to pass the ensuing winter at Corinth (1 Cor. xvi. 1–6). With this intention Luke had been aware, for he writes : " After those things were ended, Paul purposed in the Spirit, when he had passed through Macedonia and Achaia, to go to Jerusalem " (Acts xix. 21).

And now the current of the narrative approaches towards Luke's own sphere. Messengers arrive at Philippi from the Apostle, who are thus announced : " So he sent into Macedonia two of them that ministered unto him, Timothy

and Erastus ; but he himself stayed in Asia for a season "
(ver. 21, 22). These having been engaged in collecting
funds in Asia, for the purpose mentioned in the letter to
the Corinthians, are now sent to complete the collections
made for the same purpose in Macedonia.

Paul's ministry at Ephesus having concluded in a blaze
which would tend to excite attention to his doctrines, and
to the Church he had founded there, he left that city,
and, in fulfilment of his plan, he turned his steps towards
Greece. At Troas, according to a previous arrangement,
he ought to have found Titus returned from Corinth. His
absence caused the Apostle a double disappointment, for he
looked anxiously for tidings of the manner in which his
expostulatory letter to the Corinthians had been received,
and to be informed what fruit it had borne. Titus had
gone to Corinth expressly to observe all this, as also, by his
ministry there, to advance the objects proposed by that
letter. And the non-arrival of Titus occasioned him, besides, this inconvenience—having parted with Timothy, he
had no help to support him in a promising opportunity of
usefulness at Troas. For once he was under the pressure
of discouragement. He wrote : " When I came to Troas,
and a door was opened to me of the Lord, I had no rest
in my spirit, because I found not Titus, my brother; but
taking my leave of them, I went from thence into Macedonia " (2 Cor. ii. 12, 13).

In this mood Paul came to Philippi, where, upon his
arrival, he found no abatement of his trouble ; his language
being, " For when we were come into Macedonia our flesh
had no rest, but we were troubled on every side ; without
were fighting, within were fears " (vii. 5).

Happily the suspense was of short duration. And as
he had before emerged from under a cloud, so now, by the
arrival of Titus, who joined him at Philippi, his anxieties
were dispelled ; and, inspired by happier feelings, he

wrote, " Nevertheless, God that comforteth those that are cast down, comforted us by the coming of Titus. And not by his coming only, but by the consolation wherewith he was comforted in you, when he told us your earnest desire, your mourning, your fervent mind towards me, so that I rejoiced the more " (vii. 6, 7).

This visit of the Apostle to Philippi formed another leading event in the life of Luke. With what feelings two such friends, and upon such an occasion, greeted each other, can only be faintly conceived ;—one being the chief agent in the great work of evangelisation, and the other the historian of that work ; and the hearts of both of them alike burning with devotion to the Master, by whom the sphere of each was appointed. The communications of the Apostle to his friend concerning his labours and troubles in Greece and Proconsular Asia, are reported in the seventeenth to the nineteenth chapters of the Acts. In their conversations, Luke, in his turn, would have related how the Church over which he had presided had flourished under the sensible influence of Christ's fulfilled promise ; how the minds of the converts were illumined, like those of the first, to an immediate perception of the truths announced ; and how their growth in the knowledge of the gospel had been quickened by an experience of its power. After so long an absence, Paul would have been introduced to a multitude of new friends. And it was by the opportunities afforded by this visit that he became acquainted with the prosperity and character of the Church at Philippi. Reminiscences of this occasion of his fellowship with its members pervade the epistle afterwards addressed to them.

The collections throughout the Churches in Macedonia having been completed either before Paul's arrival or soon afterwards, it was proposed that, whilst he remained a while at Philippi, a deputation should be sent to Corinth, to further the object of the fund, concerning which the Corinthians had before been advised. It was upon the occasion of the departure of this mission that this, the *Second* Epistle to the Corinthians, was written. The chief topics of this epistle are three : the first concerns the report brought by Titus of the temper in which the former epistle had been received by the Corinthian Church. *This topic* occupies the first two chapters. The *second* topic consists chiefly of a vindication of the writer's character as an apostle of Christ, and of the consequent divine authority of his teaching. In the degree that heathenism or Judaism prevails in a Church, the spiritual element of Christianity is opposed, and those with whom " Christ is all " are contemned. This was witnessed at Corinth. Less than two years had sufficed to change the feelings of some of the fickle Corinthians towards the Apostle and his doctrines. " False apostles " having been admitted, the writer expresses the " fear lest, as the serpent beguiled Eve, so the minds of his correspondents should be corrupted from the simplicity that is in Christ." The vindication of himself and his teaching is treated at large from the third to the seventh chapters, and is again resumed at the tenth chapter. Throughout this vindication there are not wanting those occasional gushes of holy thought and discourse which form such a quickening property in all the Apostle's writings ; a sublime example of which is contained in the fifth chapter. The *third* topic of the epistle relates to the business of the collection. This topic is treated in a long parenthesis, occupying the eighth and ninth chapters. In these chapters, which almost seem like a distinct document, the Apostle reminds the Corinthians of the request which he had made to them twelve months before, to gather contributions in behalf of the poor brethren in Judea : he informs them of the alacrity with which the churches of Macedonia had engaged in the business ; he incites his correspondents to liberality by setting the poverty of these against the wealth of the Corinthians.

He says, " We desired Titus, as he had begun, so he would also finish in them the same grace also " (viii. 6). Further, he expresses gratification that God had put into the heart of Titus to be forward of his own accord to accept this service (ver. 16, 17). And thereafter follow two clauses which, next to the subject of Luke's identity, involve the most debated points that occur in his biography. The first clause is : *" And we have sent the brother, whose praise is in the gospel, throughout all the churches "* (ver. 18). The second is this : *" And we have sent with them our brother, whom we have found diligent in many things, but now much more diligent upon the great confidence which he has in you "* (ver. 22).

The question here arising is, Who were these two persons that, *not* being named, are thus described ? Every companion of the Apostle, whether having been with him when the letter was written or not, has been claimed for one or the other of them. Concerning the first of them, some say he was *Barnabas.* But Barnabas is excluded, forasmuch as that he was not in Macedonia when the epistle was written, nor had he been in Paul's company since he parted from him at Antioch, at which time he was succeeded by Silas (Acts xv. 39, 40). *Silas* has been proposed. But Silas had not come from Ephesus with Paul on this occasion, and therefore he could not have been the brother. Nor could *Timothy* have been the brother, for he was joined with Paul in writing the epistle. Neither could *Mark* have been the brother, for he had gone with Barnabas. After these, resort is had to the list of six of Paul's companions, who went before him from Macedonia, and tarried for his arrival at Troas (Acts xx. 4). Of those, *Aristarchus* is generally preferred. But he likewise is excluded, there being no other previous notice of him than that, along with Gaius, he was caught by the incensed Ephesians (Acts xix. 29), a notoriety quite unequal to that of this brother. In behalf of another of the six, Dr Stanley, in his exposition of the verses, says, " *If it were worth while* to hazard a conjecture, it would be that one of the two may have been *Trophimus.* He, like Titus, was one of the few Gentiles who accompanied the Apostle.   An Ephesian, and likely to have accompanied him from Ephesus now, he was, as is implied of " this brother," whose praise, &c., is well known, *so well known* that the Jews of Asia at Palestine immediately recognised him ; he was also especially connected with the Apostle in this very mission of the collection " (Acts xxi. 29).   " It also appears that he was with St Paul on his return from this very visit " (xx. 4).

But neither will this plea save Trophimus from exclusion ; for the fact of his having been *so well* known as to have been afterwards recognised by Jews from Asia at Jerusalem is very far from answering the fame of the brother, whose praise or fame in or by the gospel had extended to the Churches in Greece as well as Asia.   Again, in behalf of Trophimus and Tychichus, it is said, " We are informed that Trophimus and Tychichus (both Ephesians), *were with St Paul at Corinth* (Acts **xx.** 4) " (Conybeare and Howson).   But was it so ?   Where is this related concerning these persons ?   Certainly not in this verse, nor yet in any preceding verse.   Had they been in Corinth with Paul, their names, it must be supposed, would be found mentioned along with those in Romans xvi., written in Corinth.   The verse (xxi. 4) simply records the names of persons at Philippi who were prepared to accompany Paul to Asia—Trophimus and Tychicus standing last in the list, probably for the reason that they were the juniors.   Eventually, however, according to the next verse, instead of sailing in company with Paul, they went before and tarried at Troas.   Neither of them was in Paul's company when he wrote this epistle. And what is more, this is *the first appearance of their names in history.*   So, there is no evidence whatever to show that they had acquired the character of these deputies.

But besides those associates mentioned (Acts xx. 4), there was another person in Paul's company when now in Philippi. This person is not named; but his presence is revealed by the little word US. No difficulty is felt in interpreting this pronoun as signifying St Paul and the narrator of these incidents himself. Nevertheless, concerning this other companion of the Apostle, Dr Alford, upon reviewing a regiment of candidates, plainly avers the claims for Luke to be "*altogether without proof;*" and he further declares, "*the identity of this brother must remain in uncertainty.*"

These seem great discouragements, but they do not create despondency. The arguments of this chapter were framed long before either of these expositors was consulted; and their objections have only instigated to a closer examination of the writer's positions, and a more studious essay to confirm them.

And, first, for the *direct evidence*, or that which regards the concurrence of Luke's history with the terms of this commendation of the brother. By the prefix of the definite article *the* is denoted a pre-eminence of fame, whereby all competitors are excluded. And, secondly, by the terms "whose praise is in (or by) the gospel throughout all the Churches," is described an agent in publishing the gospel, whether by preaching or writing, or by both, whose labours herein had been co-extensive with the sphere of the Apostle's own successes. But than the concurrence of Luke's history herewith, nothing can be more exact. Luke was known personally or by reputation to all the Churches which had been raised by St Paul. He had been among the first who preached the gospel to the heathen. He had spent several years at Antioch as a chief in council, occupied in establishing a Church there. He had been honoured to be one of those who were commanded by the Holy Ghost to separate two apostles to the ministry by which those

Churches had been raised that are here represented as acknowledging their obligations to the brother. He was a partner with Paul, Silas, and Timothy in the enterprise of the first mission to Europe. He had fulfilled an extended ministry at Philippi, where his habit of inquiring of every messenger concerning the progress of the gospel gave him a celebrity throughout all the Churches. He had published a written Gospel, copies of which had been carried by Paul and his fellow-labourers to all places visited by them, whereby each new community had become possessed of the narrative which formed an authentic text of the Apostle's preaching. If the Apostle Peter mentions the writings of St Paul as those of " our beloved brother Paul " (Ep. iii. 15), does it not appear to be an agreeable coincidence that the Apostle Paul should be found treating *his* writings and speaking of *his* person in a similar manner, who has composed notices of the ministry of both of them ? Indeed, that some allusion to his great services in the gospel should find a place in St Paul's correspondence is just what would be hoped for. And if, by the circulation of his Gospel, Luke's fame had reached places where he was hitherto personally unknown, as at Corinth, where could a mention of him more appropriately occur than upon the occasion of his first introduction to the chief Church that had hitherto been raised in Europe ? Surely nothing is more natural than such a circumstance.

But this is not all. Grateful confidence in this " brother " is expressed in the clause, " And not only that, but who was chosen of the Churches to travel with us (ver. 19),— rendered by Wiclyf, " the felowe of our pilgrimage unto this grace." Having in the former clause expressed his own sentiments concerning the brother, St Paul appends this note declarative of the estimation in which he was held by the Churches whose contributions had been gathered also with the design further to accredit his mission. Upon this clause Dr Macknight has this remark: "This is the second declaration concerning the person sent. It agrees very well with Luke; for, having lived so long in Macedonia, he was well known to the Macedonian Churches, who, by making him their messenger to Judea, showed their great respect for him." Harmonising herewith, do not the emphatic words, "*And not only that*," seem to breathe forth gratification felt by the writer at the prospect of having such an admirable companion in his journey to Jerusalem?

Proceeding to the *circumstantial evidence* of the case, the identity of "the brother" and Luke is confirmed by the following particulars :—

1. After Luke's arrival at Philippi, as related Acts xvi. 12, there is no notice of his having left that city until the occasion of this mission to Corinth.

2. Luke's name appears at the end of the epistle as having, along with Titus, conveyed that document to Corinth; and although the subscription was probably added by a scribe who had inferred the notice from 2 Cor. viii. 18, yet there it is, an echo of antiquity at least.

3. Luke is found to have been at Corinth at the time that Paul was there on the business treated of in the epistle. This is seen in the occurrence of the name Lucius among the salutations delivered under Paul's hand in the Epistle to the Romans, written during the Apostle's visit (Rom. xvi. 21).

4. Luke was in Paul's company when he had returned from Corinth to Macedonia, on the eve of commencing his journey to Jerusalem (Acts xx. 6).

5. When the rest of Paul's company had preceded him from the shores of Europe, having deferred his own departure, doubtless, for an important reason, *only Luke is with him*—a distinction both harmonising with the terms in which *the brother* had been commended by the Apostle, and

in keeping with the honour of having been appointed to be his companion in the mission.

6. Luke's identity with the brother in question is recognised by some of the Fathers, and has been so by the Latin Church from time immemorial; a lesson appointed for Luke's anniversary being 2 Cor. viii. 16–24. Origen writes: "The third Gospel is that according to Luke, commended by Paul in the second Epistle to the Corinthians." Grotius observes: "Neither am I dissatisfied with the opinion of many ancients, but I accept the application of 2 Cor. viii. 18 to Luke." This identity is recognised by Wetstein in his large edition of the Greek Testament, and by Dr Whitby in his Commentary. And long after the preceding argument was composed, the writer was gratified to find that Bishop Wordsworth, in his edition of the Greek Testament, affirms the application of this passage to Luke by a series of observations, of which some are these—

1. "We need not disparage the application made of these words to St Luke by ancient writers, Origen, Primasius, and St Jerome." 2. "The words seem plainly to point to some *written document*, circulated, like St Paul's own epistles at this time, *by copies through the Churches*, and probably *read* publicly in them, as those epistles were." 3. "There is a peculiar propriety in the fact that St Paul, the inspired Apostle of the Gentile Churches, here sets his apostolic seal on that Gospel which was specially designed for Gentile use." 4. "Observe, also, the person here mentioned was chosen and appointed by the suffrages of the Churches to be St Paul's coadjutor, to convey the alms of the Gentile Churches to Jerusalem. This incident confirms the supposition that the person in question was St Luke, as St Paul's intimate friend and companion, who was more likely to be associated with him." 5. "The person in question was *also* well known and highly esteemed by all the Churches for his labours in the *gospel*, and he was chosen

for that reason."   6. "If St Luke's Gospel had been written and circulated, it would have recommended him for such a mission."   7. "To praise such a person was inexpedient.   He whose praise is in the gospel needs no other praise."

And withal the Bishop adds this challenge : "*Has it ever been proved that St Paul does not refer to a written gospel, and consequently to the Gospel of St Luke ?   Certainly not.*"

Upon a survey of these several considerations, it follows, that as they meet in the history of no individual besides Luke's, those persons who have been proposed for *the brother* in question are rather to be regarded as having been among those who, in their several Churches, had published the brother's praise.

Equally disputed is the question concerning the identity of the individual referred to in the words, " And we have sent with them another brother."   " Still less," writes Dr Alford, " can we determine who this second brother is." Here, then, is another historical dilemma.   This doubtful question likewise is here sought to be pursued to an issue. Sometimes a clue to the solution of a problem is found by the student unexpectedly.   In this case the person to whom evidence points is one whose name, it is believed, has not hitherto been mentioned by any writer in relation to the inquiry.   The particulars here to be examined are two— 1. " *Whom we have oftentimes proved diligent in many things.*" 2. " *But now much more diligent upon the great confidence which he (this brother)* had in you ;" not, as in the English version, " *I* have in you," which is contrary to the sense of the clause (2 Cor. viii. 22).

Here, again, it must be premised that the inquiry is limited to those only who were in Paul's company when these words were written.   His companions here, as far as known, were few.   They were—1. Timothy, who, as he was joined with the Apostle in addressing the letter, and

remained with him at Philippi, could not have been the
person described; 2. Titus, whose name is mentioned in
the letter; 3. Luke, whose claim has just been argued; 4.
Erastus, whose arrival at Philippi, along with Timothy,
was noticed at the commencement of this chapter. In
respect, therefore, of the necessary condition of being one
of the company present at the writing of the letter, Erastus
is the only other possible candidate known. And his claim
is further confirmed by a reference to the notices fortu
nately elsewhere found concerning him. It is here said,
" Whom we have often proved *diligent in many things.*" The
being " diligent in many things " signifies something else
than preaching. It refers to the conduct of affairs, *pollakis,*
in various ways. Now in the Epistle to the Romans,
written when Paul had followed the deputation to Corinth,
not the name only of Erastus occurs, but also his secular
position is added; the words are, " Erastus, the *Chamberlain of the city, saluteth you* " (xvi. 23). The original word
oikonomos is employed by Luke in his Gospel (xii. 42),
where it is translated *steward.* By the Romans this officer
was called a *Quæstor.* It is probable that Erastus was one of
Paul's converts during his first sojourn at Corinth : but it
does not appear that, upon his embracing Christianity, he
relinquished his office in the city.

In Acts xix. 22, as it has already been seen, Erastus is
represented as having been at Ephesus, and is described as one
of those who ministered to Paul. By this notice is discovered
the lively interest with which Erastus regarded the Apostle's
person and work. Dr Paley remarks : " It appears, from
various instances in the Acts, to have been the practice of
many converts to attend St Paul from place to place "
(" Horæ Paulinæ "). So Erastus had followed his father in
the gospel to Ephesus, where his zeal had been quickened
at witnessing how mightily the Word of God grew and prevailed through the Apostle's ministry. What the nature of

the assistance was that Erastus rendered to Paul is suggested by his previous occupation. He brought to his friend's assistance, "in many things," those abilities for business which his office at Corinth required, and which were habitual to him. The business of the collection for the poor brethren in Judea, which had been commenced a year before, much occupied the Apostle. Upon repairing to Ephesus, therefore, Erastus zealously engaged in promoting that object. And, in its management, who could have been more competent than the Quæstor? God provides all kinds of agents for His service.

In coupling Erastus with Timothy in the errand from Ephesus to Macedonia, is seen a proof of the appreciation of the previous services of the Chamberlain; the more so, as, according to the narrative of the context, the parting with Timothy, at the time, must have been attended with much inconvenience to the Apostle. They brought no letter addressed to the Churches in Macedonia. The recommendation of the object for which they sought alms was left to their own exposition of its claims. Their mission was successful. And the response made by the Churches to their application is gratefully told by Paul in his address to the Corinthians in behalf of the same object (2 Cor. viii. 1-6). When, therefore, "after a season," Paul having come from Ephesus to Philippi, had received their report, it was natural that he should now wish to unite with Titus and Luke in the same undertaking at Corinth Erastus, whose diligence in the business had already been so amply proved elsewhere.

The second particular specified concerning this other brother is this: "But now much more diligent upon the *great confidence which he has in you.*" A single sentence will suffice upon this. Who better than the Quæstor of the city could have possessed the knowledge of the Corinthians that would have inspired this confidence?

And, to complete this view of the case, it should be added, that in coming from Ephesus to Macedonia, and in going from Philippi to Corinth, Erastus was in the proper course of his way home. Also harmonising with this chain of coincidences is the information contained in a subsequent notice of him, made when Paul was in prison at Rome (2 Tim. iv. 20), where the Apostle imparts the intelligence to Timothy, " Erastus still abode at Corinth ;" a very naturally-made memorandum, signifying that Erastus was not absent from home on any errand like that in which he had once gone in company with Timothy to Asia and Macedonia. If there be any solidity in this exposition, how valuable appear the sacred scintillations which furnish the ground of this argument ! Within a circle of four passages, including the primary one under consideration, there is traced a portrait worthy to be viewed in the scriptural gallery. Yet so little has this " worthy " been recognised, that *not* even the name of *Erastus* has a place in that biblical treasury, Dr W. Smith's *large* " Dictionary of the Bible." No wonder, therefore, that Tychichus and Trophimus are proposed therein for these anonymous brothers.*

The importance with which this mission was regarded is manifest from the ninth chapter of the epistle, wherein its object is forcibly urged throughout. And than the three persons composing the embassy, no more important agents

* Since the above observation was made, an *Appendix* has been published to Dr Smith's Dictionary, wherein the name " Erastus " appears as representing *two* persons—1. *Erastus* " with Paul at Ephesus, and sent thence with Timothy to Macedonia (Acts xix. 22)." 2. *Erastus* " the Chamberlain of Corinth, Rom. xvi. 23, and mentioned 2 Tim iv. 20." This curt method of dealing with such a question ought not to satisfy a student. How much of the interest of Scripture characters is lost when they are duplicated in this manner ! In the very valuable " Lexion Universale " of Hofman, 4 vols. folio, 1698, is a notice of *Erastus*, in which the several instances wherein the name occurs in the New Testament are applied to *one* individual.

were at hand. Nor yet, had more suitable persons been sought from afar, could there have been found any that were better adapted than these to accredit its object in the eyes of the Corinthian Church. These were—1. Titus, who, in the absence of Paul, acted as an *Episcopus* at Corinth ; 2. Luke, a venerable servant of Christ, and benefactor to *all the Churches* that had been raised by apostolic teaching ; 3. Erastus, "the Chamberlain of the city," and withal a zealous disciple of the Lord Jesus. Hence appears *a reason why*, instead of the names of the last two of these being given, their characters are portrayed. It was to do them the more honour. This metonymical method of speaking of them was alike complimentary to themselves and also to the Corinthians. By the report of Titus, as well by that of others visiting Corinth, and also by their use of his Gospel, the Church there could not fail to have become familiar with the reputation of him who, in supereminence, was the *Evangelist of the Gentiles.* Of course, they both knew and honoured the Chamberlain of the city. Paul preferred character to name. When mentioning the names of beloved friends, he not unusually couples therewith a descriptive epithet. And sometimes omitting the name, he denotes them only by their character and services, as in the instance of the women at Philippi (Phil. iv. 3).

But more than this. Besides this expression of the mind of the Churches of Macedonia, by whom the deputation was appointed, there follows another clause in the epistle, which especially manifests Paul's own personal sentiments towards the deputies. He had written in another place concerning himself : "Need we, as some, epistles of commendation to you, or from you ?" (iii. 1). Yet, for the reason that false apostles had challenged his commission, he had entered into a large vindication of his authority. So, for the reason that the authority of the brethren forming this deputation might likewise be questioned by the querulous, and thereby their errand hindered, it became as expedient as it was agreeable with his own generous nature, that he should put under the same seal his own personal estimate of them, which he does by adding this impressive certificate : " Whether any do inquire concerning Titus, he is my partner and fellow-helper ; or *our (two) brethren*, they are the messengers of the Churches, and the GLORY OF CHRIST" (viii. 23).　No encomium can surpass this, and no comment can heighten its lustre.

CHAPTER XXII.

LUKE IN CORINTH.

IN going direct from Philippi to Corinth, the customary course was by sea; and as it was likewise the least fatiguing, it is presumed that this was the course taken by the delegates, Luke, Titus, and Erastus. The Ægean is a true Polynesia: it is starred with islands, and the navigation is for this reason troublesome. As the ship was brought every night to a mooring, the time occupied in the voyage would not have been less than four days, the distance being about two hundred miles. The traffic on this sea was a hundredfold above what it is now. Ports which were thronged with shipping are no longer ports at all. Luke's mind would be differently exercised upon this voyage than when, six years before, he traversed this sea from Troas. During that period, the Word of the Lord had sounded forth into all the principal towns of Greece, and from them had been wafted to the coasts and to some of the isles upon which his eyes now glanced. Grateful sentiments would possess the mind of the Evangelist, prompting conversations by the way, encouraging his companions to perseverance in the work to which they had put their hands.

Having at length turned into the gulf that stretched towards the Corinthian isthmus, the city of Athens was discerned on the right, four miles distant from the shore. The harbour of Cenchrea was entered, between a temple on either hand, and the mole was ornamented with a brazen statue of Neptune. From the ship, the travellers stepped into a scene which at once bespake the importance of the city of their destination. The harbour of Cenchrea was commodious, and the town of considerable extent. The distance from hence to Corinth was eight miles. Conducted by his companions, who were familiar with the neighbourhood, Luke was instructed in the various features of the intervening scenes. All corresponded with what had first met the eye. A temple of Diana was passed, and on both sides of the road were found, at intervals, tombs which, by their affecting inscriptions, wailed a voice to the travellers. At the terminus was a grove of cypresses dedicated to mourners; and near the gate of the city was pointed out the sepulchre of Diogenes, the great exemplar of austerity, both subjective and objective, as the learned would say. That philosopher, having been captured, during a voyage, by pirates, was sold to a Corinthian, who appointed him tutor to his sons. By Plato he was called the "mad Socrates." The instance of his uncouthness exhibited upon the interview with him of Alexander the Great, is too well known to need to be repeated. He died at the age of ninety, B.C. 324.

Corinth, with its surrounding scenery, presented a spectacle animated and picturesque. The city was five miles in circumference, and, including its Acrocorinthus, ten miles— embracing together a very large population. "The Acropolis of Corinth," Mr Dodwell says, "is one of the finest objects in Greece. It stands majestically 1800 feet in height, and forms a conspicuous object at a great distance— being seen from Athens, which is forty-four miles distant" ("Tour in Greece," vol. ii., p. 187). The isthmus, upon which athletic games were celebrated every three years, is a natural curiosity. At its narrowest part it is four miles, and at the widest eight miles broad, and it is about eight miles in length. It was contiguous to this narrow junction that the metropolis of Achaia was situated. In

the centre of civilisation, and with the unique advantage of
having ports on either side of the isthmus, it grasped, as
with two hands, the traffic of the countries east and west.
By the poets it was called "the city with two seas" (Bi-
maris). Despoiled by a general of the Roman Republic, and
thereafter forlorn for a hundred years, it was re-established
by Julius Cæsar, when it again repaired its fortunes. The
opulence of its inhabitants was relieved by a profuse expenditure. By their patronage, the arts flourished among
them beyond all other places, except Athens. Architecture,
statuary, and casting in brass, were here carried to their
highest perfection. With specimens of these the city was
magnificently adorned. And, along with its sister city of
Athens, it was visited by students in art from every land,
as Italy is visited now.

Eighty years after the period of Luke's visit, Pausanias,
a man of learning and taste, having made a tour in Greece,
composed what served the *dilettanti* of those days for a
Handbook descriptive of the principal objects of art existing
throughout the country. Fortunately this book has survived.
Without the information contained therein, the knowledge
concerning those objects would have been very fragmentary ;
for, excepting those which have been gathered into the
museums of Europe, scarcely a relic of them is to be seen
on the spot. Even to Luke, who had been familiar from
his youth with the displays of important cities, the number and character of the objects that everywhere met his
eye must have been exciting. Exceeding in artistic display all other localities was the Forum. This spacious
place was entirely surrounded by public buildings, and
otherwise adorned with columns and statues the pride of
the Corinthians, and the admiration of visitors. Among
the more characteristic of those objects, as told by Pausanias, there was a temple of Mercury, the divinity of commerce ; there was a temple of Fortuna, the daughter of

Oceanus, within which was a statue of the goddess in Parian marble; there was a temple dedicated to "All the gods," which of course included the "Unknown God" whom the Athenians ignorantly worshipped. Around the Forum were numerous statues, mocking, as it seemed, the throng at their feet. Among these were three of Jupiter, who was held in great reverence by the Corinthians, being, as was said, the father of Corinthus. One of these statues was nameless; the second was called Jupiter the *Terrestrial;* and the third Jupiter the *Highest* ($\Upsilon\psi\iota\sigma\tau o\varsigma$). There was a much-admired wooden image of Bacchus, "gilt," says Pausanias, "in every part but the face, which is *adorned with vermillion,*"—a becoming visage at least! And, conspicuous above all, being in the centre of the Forum, there was a statue, in brass, of Minerva, a daughter of Jupiter, patroness of the arts, having for its base a bas-relief of the Muses. Surmounting the propylæ at the north side of the Forum were two gilt cars, one bearing Phæton, and the other the Sun. Having passed through the porch, there was seen, just beyond, the fountain of Pirene, so named from a nymph, who, in the language of fable, dissolved into tears at the death of her daughter, who had been accidentally killed by Diana the huntress. Thence the road, lined on either side with sacred objects, ascended circuitously to the Acrocorinthus. The summit of this hill being of wide extent, upon it was built a town, with its several temples and statues. Here was a temple of Tranquillity, into which no person was permitted to enter; and, high above all, a temple of Venus, to whom the hill was dedicated. It is said that to this shrine, in the more luxurious days of the Corinthians, were attached a thousand female slaves dedicated to the service of this vile myth; and that these priestesses, as they were called, contributed greatly both to the gaiety and to the wealth of Corinth. After descending the hill, the isthmus was next visited. Here also numerous objects attracted notice. Besides a theatre and a stadium, there were a temple of Jupiter Capitolinus ; a temple of Neptune, whose property the isthmus was said to be ; and a temple of Palæmon, in the precincts of which was a subterranean adytum, wherein, it was rumoured, Palæmon was still concealed. Near this temple was a statue of Ino, the mother of the said Palæmon, who threw herself, with her son, from a cliff near this place into the sea. Here, likewise, were statues of Bellerophon, son of the Corinthian king, Glaucus; also of Pegasus, the winged horse, upon which Bellerophon mounted into the air, and fought a chimera. Among the tombs on this side of the city was a sepulchre of the two children murdered by their mother, Medea, over which was raised an image of Fear, represented as a woman of a dreadful aspect. The harbours on each side of the isthmus were regarded as especially under the guardianship of Neptune—Leche and Cenchrea having been, it was said, his offspring. Besides these, many more objects and fables are described in the *Corinthiacs* of Pausanias, every interesting locality having had its patron god.

Drawn by a witness, and he a heathen, the foregoing picture commands attention. It affords authentic illustration of the monster evils with which the servants of Christ had to deal in fulfilling His charge among the Gentiles. By the scene before him, Luke could apprehend what were the emotions of Paul upon his first arrival in this city. He could feel how, without a divine admonition, his departure from hence might have been as speedy as had been his departure from Philippi. He could understand how, in view of the mad idolatry of this place, and of the fanatic persecution of him by the Jews, the mighty encouragement was needed, which in a vision was afforded to him, saying, "Be not afraid, but speak, and hold not thy peace : for I am with thee, and no man shall set on thee to hurt thee ; for I have much people in this city" (Acts xviii. 9, 10).

How the Apostle complied with this admonition was afterwards told by Luke (Acts xviii. 11). Of the consequences of his obedience to the heavenly vision, a memorial survives in his twin epistles to the Church gathered in that city. The occasion for writing the first of these was intimately connected with the idolatrous element of the place. A residence of eighteen months amidst its scenes had imparted images to the writer's mind which the opportunity naturally reproduced ; and the correspondence of those images with the description of the realities by Pausanias, whilst it stamps authenticity upon the correspondence, imparts to it, likewise, an obvious speciality.*

The epistle begins with three peculiarities. The *first* of these is, that, besides to the Church at Corinth, the letter is addressed " to *all that in every place* call upon the name of Jesus Christ ;" the *second* peculiarity is, the addition of the clause, "both their Lord and ours,"—that is, the Lord of believers in every place ; and the *third* is, that He upon whom they call (whom they worship) is denominated LORD six times within a few lines, or from the second to the tenth verse. A reason for this reiteration is found in the writer's jealousy, the grounds for which immediately appear. Idols and idolators are mentioned in the epistle twelve times, being eight times oftener than they occur in all the other of Paul's epistles together. Christ came to abolish idols (Isa. xlii. 5–8). He commands His servants to plant His gospel beside them. Paul had planted it amidst a forest of idols at Corinth. And here is witnessed his anxiety to promote its fruitfulness. Moved by a remembrance of those scenes and objects, he speaks of " things offered in sacrifice to idols," and of " the idol's temple " (viii.) And teaching by the figure, so familiar to his corre-

* " Corinth, a sight oppressing the spirits " (" Sights and Thoughts in Foreign Churches," by F. W. Faber, 1842, p. 500). How great the change since the visit of Luke !

spondents, he transfers the term "temple" to the persons of believers, saying, "Know ye not that ye are the temples of God?" (iii. 16) ; and again, "Your body is the temple of the Holy Ghost " (vi. 19).

Also strongly reflecting the associations of the writer's visit to Corinth are the rebukes occasioned by the clinging to heathenism of the converts, who, as they had been accustomed to say, "I am a disciple of Socrates," "I am of Epicurus," "I am of Zeno," now said, "I am of Paul," "I am of Peter," "I am of Apollos." Nor less so is the frequent occurrence in the epistle of the word *wisdom*, and of those passages in which the wisdom of God, as discovered in the gospel of the cross of Christ, is set forth against the wisdom of their philosophers. Eminent among those passages are three : The first is that which expounds the nature and privilege of the believer's fellowship with God, a theme which is called "the wisdom of God, in a mystery," and which, although argued in terms as philosophical as divine, will be for ever a mystery to all except the *spiritual man*, for whom its exposition stands for a charter against all claims made to enfetter him. This remarkable passage is comprised in the second chapter.

Another of those passages in which the excellence of the gospel beyond the philosophy taught by the heathen is set forth, is the eulogium of *Charity* contained in the thirteenth chapter. The divisions of the wise among the heathen were accompanied by the *odium philosophorum*, or hatred of one sect towards another. Whereas the Churches of Christ should be like the tribes of Israel, as seen arranged in their several encampments, their tents in goodly order, east and west, north and south, the Divine Presence from the centre shining equally upon them all, and where none was before or after another : the golden chain that should preserve this goodly order, and hold together the numerous peoples of diversified complexions, both physical and intellectual, gathered into the divine fellowship, being just this simple, lovely grace of CHARITY.

And the other remarkable passage suggested by a comparison between heathen and Christian wisdom or teaching is that on the *Resurrection,* contained in the fifteenth chapter—a passage which, like a light shining upon the tombs that enclosed their dead, instructed the living by an argument never before conceived by them, in the evidences of a blessed immortality, as well for the body as the soul of the righteous. And whereas the epistle is addressed " to all that in every place call on the name of Jesus Christ our Lord," like the discourses of Jesus Christ in controversy with the Scribes and Pharisees, its teaching, grounded on the defects of a Church, is intended for a solemn lesson to every Christian, and throughout all ages.

Luke was acquainted with that epistle. And now, with a vividness which only the sight could impart, he recognised the impress upon it of all by which he was surrounded. And when ever had the scene been looked upon by a more intelligent observer? In one sense it had no novelty for him. He had been surrounded from his early days by objects of art peculiar to a high degree of civilisation, and, therefore, the sight would occasion to his mind no sudden emotion. Nevertheless, there was much in it that stirred his sympathies. In coming hither, he had passed on to another step in his sphere of observation. He had often heard spoken those proverbial sayings : " The brass of Corinth," " the pleasures of Corinth," "the pride of Corinth," and that other popular expression, " the Jove of Corinth." And, as the painter looks upon a new and striking scene influenced by devotion to his art, so Luke's reflections all rushed to one point. A new illustration was obtained for his page. A conquest for Christ had been achieved in Corinth.

That word, " I have much people in this city," had been

realised (Acts xviii. 10).   Here, as elsewhere, Paul had turned away many people by his preaching, "They be no gods which are made with hands" (Acts xix. 26).   By the epistle (the second to the Corinthians) brought from Philippi, Luke was introduced to this new community of believers. Himself the only stranger of the three messengers, the warm heart of hospitality kindled towards him.   Oh, how sweet was Christian fellowship then!   How rapturous to embrace an inspired servant of Christ, and he on an errand to their own doors!   Of all the candidates for his company as a guest, it is probable that he who had been his fellow-traveller, the city chamberlain, had already secured that gratification.   Luke's fame had preceded him.   As their benefactor in the gift of the gospel of facts, upon which the preaching of the doctrines they had received was founded, he was welcomed by the disciples in the spirit in which he was commended to them by their teacher.   Curiosity would have been their first feeling towards him, love and gratitude thereafter abiding.

Every illustration of the power of the gospel was precious to Luke.   This visit afforded him many such illustrations.   Besides those whose irregularities are censured in the former epistle, there were those in Corinth who had kept themselves unspotted, and were living in the freshness of first love, and with the activities that characterise it (1 Cor i. 2; vi. 11).   In Corinth commercial associations were the chief; and as Jews were found in all such places, they abounded here.   Among the trophies of Paul's labours and perils in this city were two rulers of synagogues.   Five of his converts from Corinth visited the Apostle at Ephesus, either drawn thither by business, or attracted by the doctrine and example of their teacher.   Sosthenes, once a Jewish ruler, and, like Paul, at first a persecutor, being associated in the inscription of the epistle addressed from thence to the Corinthians, thereby endorsed all its expostulations and counsels. Admirable are such examples of fidelity. Auxiliaries in the great evangelical enterprise, the gratitude of posterity is ever due to those zealous merchants of Corinth.

If it had been Luke's business to record his own progress, it is probable that his narrative would have shown how he took the opportunity from Corinth to visit the sister city of Athens. To indulge the supposition, it may be thought that he might have gone thither in behalf of the same cause for which he came to Corinth—to obtain contributions from the Church there for the fund intended to be conveyed to Jerusalem ; or, he might have been prompted hereto by other inducements. Having come to the wealthiest city of Greece, he would desire to visit also the most learned, and, according to popular opinion, the most religious, of its cities, being said to present but one great altar to the gods, by reason of its numerous statues and temples. Luke would naturally wish to walk through a city of so much renown, and to compare its features with those of other great cities known to him. He would wish to follow the footsteps of his friend, especially when the trip could be so easily accomplished. A few hours' sail, on some fine morning, would bring him to one of the three ports of Athens. He had received an account of Paul's triumph there from the Apostle's own lips. But the relation as given (Acts xvii. 16–34), contains features which seem to indicate more than a verbal report. Besides a description of the manner and terms of the Apostle's proclamation of the sublime truths of his mission, a regard is had to the scenic circumstances thereof. The picture is completed by the accessories of the spot. And these are wrought in with a truthfulness to nature that has often attracted the admiration of travellers.

Here is a picture by the Earl of Carlisle : " What is admirable and wonderful is the harmonious blending of every detached feature with each other—with the solemn mountains, the lucid atmosphere, the eternal sea, all wearing the same unchanged aspect as when the ships of Xerxes were shivered on that Colian cape beneath ; as when the slope of the Acropolis was covered with the Athenian audience, to listen under this open sky to Æschylus and Sophocles ; as when St Paul stood on Mars Hill, and while summit above and plain below bristled with idols, proclaimed with the words of a power, to which not even Pericles could ever have attained, the counsel of the true God." Very emphatic is what follows :—" Let me just remark, that even the impressive declaration of the Apostle, that God dwelleth not in temples made with hands, may be seen in effect when we remember that the buildings to which he must have almost inevitably pointed at the very moment were the most perfect that the hands of man have ever reared, and must have comprised the Theseum below, and the Parthenon above him. It seems to have been well that ' art and man's device' should be reduced to their proper level, on the very spot of their highest development " (" Diary in Turkish and Greek Waters," pp. 180, 189).

It is related in the Acts (xvii. 34), a woman named Damaris believed. Perhaps Luke was entertained at her house, and had the opportunity to appreciate her character, or wherefore is she added to the list of women he delighted to honour ? for there were also other women at Athens who believed.

At Philippi a jailor had been one of Paul's converts : here the only individual named of the " men that clave unto him was one of the magistrates in the supreme court of judicature, Dionysius the Areopagite. Of course this worthy has a legendary history. A quantity of literature has been attributed to him, having for titles, " The Heavenly Hierarchy," " The Ecclesiastical Hierarchy," " Mystical Theology," together with epistles to Titus, to

John the Evangelist, to Polycarp, and to others. But fortunately for his credit, the existence of these books is not to be traced further back than the fifth century; of which period these titles have a strong odour, and the contents a stronger relish. Yet of these *Opera* published under the name of Dionysius the Areopagite, four editions in folio have been issued, three of them with large annotations. With the literature attributed to him, the legends concerning his life correspond. According to these, he was consecrated a bishop by the hands of Paul; he travelled to Jerusalem to meet the apostles who repaired thither from all parts of the world to be present at the last hours of the Blessed Virgin; he visited Rome, where he was entertained by Pope Clement; in his nineteenth year he repaired to Ephesus, to enjoy an interview with John the Evangelist. And to this day at Luxemburg, in a church dedicated to him under the name of St Denys, is pretended to be shown his skull, on the crown of which is the mark of a white cross ! His portrait was painted on a wall of Justinian's re-erection of the Basilica of Saint Sophia (Holy Wisdom) at Constantinople. His anniversary is marked in the callendar for the 9th of October.

But to return with Luke to Corinth. The arrival of Paul, being the last visit to that city, formed another interesting event for Luke. His words concerning it are, " And when he (Paul) had gone over those parts (Macedonia), and had given them much exhortation, he came into Greece " (xx. 2). Paul had much wished this visit. When at Ephesus he had written to the Corinthians, " Now I will come unto you when I shall pass through Macedonia, and it may be will abide, and winter with you " (1 Cor. xvi. 4, 5); and when he had reached Philippi, he wrote the epistle of which Luke and his companions were bearers, wherein he expressed his intention to follow the messengers shortly. As he visited other places in Macedonia besides Philippi, it may have been above a month after they left him that he came to Corinth. Upon the Apostle's former visit to that capital, in obedience to the Lord's assurance, " I have much people in this city," he had remained there eighteen months, " preaching Christ crucified, in demonstration of the Spirit and of power " (Acts xviii. 11 ; 1 Cor. ii. 2-4). During that period he had enriched the Church by his two Epistles to the Thessalonians; and now, during his present visit, was written his Epistle to the Romans. Besides the weighty argument discussed therein, an interest belongs to this document in respect of its having been the last epistle written by the Apostle during the period in which he exercised his ministry at liberty. In the Apostle's recent letter to the Corinthians, Luke was spoken of otherwise than by his name. But in the epistle now written to the Romans, he is mentioned by his Roman name, *Lucius.* Here, then, occurs another landmark in Luke's biography, proof being hereby afforded that he was now in Corinth, having here remained until the Apostle's arrival. It stands in a group of names of persons whose salutations Paul conveys to the Church at Rome. The names are these—1. Timotheus, my work-fellow ; 2. Lucius (Luke), *equally so ;* * 3. Jason, a Gentile of Thessalonica (Acts xvii. 5, 6) ; 4. Sosipater or Sopater, a Gentile of Berea (Acts xx. 4, 5) ; 5. Gaius, a Gentile, who is described by the Apostle as " mine host, and of the whole Church," signifying that he entertained the Apostle, and perhaps Timothy, and also that he afforded accommodation for the assemblies of the Church, so he was a man of position and substance : he was one of Paul's early converts in Corinth, and one of the few whom Paul baptized with his own hands (1 Cor. i. 14) ; 6. Erastus, a Gentile, the chamberlain of the city, or quæstor, an officer to whom belonged the receipt and expenditure of the public

* *Lucius pariter.* So paraphrased by Dr Gagnæus in his Paraphrasis in Epist. ad Rom. Paris, 1533, 8vo.

P

money ; 7. Tertius, a Gentile, the Apostle's scribe at the moment ; 8. Quartus, a Gentile (Rom. xvi. 21-23). By these notices the reader is introduced to some of the saints with whom Luke was associated in Corinth. But besides these, there belonged to this city other brethren of note who may be supposed to have been absent at this moment. 1. Sosthenes, the Jewish ruler (Acts xviii. 17), and associated with Paul at Ephesus (1 Cor. i. 1) ; 2. Stephanas, baptized by Paul (1 Cor. i. 16, and xvi. 15, 17) ; 3. Fortunatus, a Gentile ; 4. Achaicus, a Gentile (1 Cor. xvi. 17) ; 5. Crispus, who had been a Jewish ruler, and baptized by Paul (Acts xviii. 8) ; 6. Justus, a Gentile (Acts xviii. 7) ; 7. Chloe's family, Gentiles (1 Cor. i. 11).

The Epistle to the Romans was composed in the house of Gaius. And to this hospitable place Luke would often resort, and, with the company by whom the writer was surrounded, enjoy the communion of saints. Here was the Apostle of the Gentiles, himself a Jew. Here was the Evangelist to record the fulfilment of their Master's promised grace. Here were Jews and Gentiles ; both those who had before been proselytes to Judaism, and those who had stepped at once from paganism, all one in Christ. Here were converts of Corinth, entertaining with loving hospitality the true athletes, inspiring them by their grateful benignancy in the great work which takes them from place to place, and which had brought them here—teachers and converts, all disciples of the Christ of love. Happy reunions were those in the house of " mine host " at Corinth !

The epistle now addressed to the Romans was itself an expression of love, not only from the writer, but also from the friends by whom he was surrounded. It was a memento to persons who had stood in an interesting and personal relation both to Paul and to these. Curiosity is excited upon observing that, of persons named at the close of the epistle, and saluted as being in Rome, there are a score more than those who are named as saluting them. And an observation, likewise, of the notices appended to some of the names and the epithets bestowed upon others, adds to the student's inquisitiveness concerning them. It has been remarked, " It appears probable that the persons here named had formerly been residents in Asia or Greece, where the Apostle was acquainted with them." (Moses Stuart, 'Commentary on the Romans'). Another step may show how they came to have been residents there. Upon turning to Luke's account of the arrival of Paul on the occasion of his first visit to Corinth, it is told, that "Paul there found Aquilla a Jew, and Priscilla his wife ; because that Claudius had commanded all Jews to depart from Rome " (xviii. 2). This expulsion of the Jews from Rome is also mentioned by Suetonius. And that many of them were led to repair to Corinth in particular, is suggested by a note in the Corinthiacs of Pausanius, where he says, " At present none of the ancient Corinthians inhabit Corinth. But the inhabitants consist of such persons as were sent into it by the Romans." The new city having been colonised from Italy by Julius Cæsar, consequently intimate relations must have subsisted between the Corinthians and Rome, and from which not even Jews, being natives of Corinth, would have been exempt. Hence, upon their expulsion from Rome, a multitude of Jews, who had formerly belonged to Corinth, would return hither with their families, whilst others would find their way to various places in Greece and Asia, where Paul and his coadjutors were labouring. The inference is, that the aforesaid salutations were from Romans to Romans—Paul and Luke, as citizens by privilege, others as descendants of Roman colonists, including Jews and Gentiles, men, women, and households.

It is probable that the Church at Rome was originally composed of some of those Jews and proselytes who had been in Jerusalem upon the occasion of the passover succeeding the crucifixion and resurrection of Christ, when they heard those events expounded to them in the Latin language from the lips of an apostle with a miraculous demonstration. The expulsion of the Jews from Rome might seem detrimental to the infant Church there, but in one view it was rather advantageous to it. Hitherto unvisited by apostles or evangelists, the disciples in Rome were only imperfectly instructed in the economy of the gospel. They were now driven forth to the scenes of its chiefest triumphs, and for the space of four or five years they were mingled with the favoured communions raised and fostered by apostolical ministration.

The salutations with which the epistle closes are useful here. Circumstances are mentioned in connexion with some of the names which tell of an acquaintance and a former companionship with the Apostle and with those who from Corinth salute them. It is hereby seen that some of those named were disciples before their dispersion. Some had been in Christ before Paul himself. Some had been his fellow-labourers ; and some had found, in their exile, a new and divine citizenship under his ministry. The Emperor Claudius died A.D. 54, and thereafter many returned to their Latin homes. From that time Paul counted in Rome many interesting friendships ; and friends like those named must be kept at any price. Such would have been the judgment on both sides. The case of the couple that stand at the head of the list of salutations may be cited for a sample of all. When Paul first went to Corinth he found those energetic Christians there, and he joined them as a fellow-workman at their occupation in trade. Two years afterwards, they were at Ephesus, being the only persons named in the First Epistle to the Corinthians as saluting them ; and in a little more than a year from that time, or at the date of this Epistle to the Romans, they were again in Rome.

Little can it be doubted, therefore, that the friendships thus formed occasioned Paul's present correspondence. Before the departure of his friends, it would seem, he had agreed to visit them at a convenient season. That he had so appointed, seems to have been known to Luke, who probably, in order to follow the progress of the gospel, already contemplated to bear him company. Paul being still at Ephesus, and Luke at Philippi, the latter quotes, saying, "After I have been there" (Macedonia, Achaia, Jerusalem), "I must also see Rome" (Acts xix. 21). And now having come into Achaia, and before taking the next step of going to Jerusalem, the letter is written apprising his friends in Rome of his intention to fulfil his engagement. The Apostle begins his epistle by expressing that he committed himself to the enterprise by prayer; "making request," he says, "if by any means *now at length* I might have a prosperous journey by the will of God to come unto you" (i. 10), "for I long to see you;" adding, "Now I would not have you ignorant, brethren, that oftentimes I purposed to come unto you, but was let hitherto" (13). All this obviously intimates pre-arrangement. And upon resuming the personal part of the epistle, towards its close, the subject again stands foremost. Paul was a man of order as well as of earnestness. He must conclude one department of his work before he enters upon another. He furnishes the reason for his previous delays, by noticing the character and extent of the work in which he had been engaged. He tells his correspondents that, as " the minister of Jesus Christ to the Gentiles, through mighty signs and wonders by the power of the Spirit, I have fully preached the gospel from Jerusalem (in the south) to Illyricum (in the north), for which cause I have been much hindered from coming to you" (xv. 19-22). And observing, "Now having no more place in these parts," he proceeds to inform them of his plan, namely, of taking Rome in his way to Spain, after that he had gone to Jerusalem. And he beseeches them to unite their prayers with his own, that having accomplished his errand to the saints there, he may thence come to them with joy by the will of God (xv. 23–33).

The whole epistle bears a strong impress of the circumstances under which it was written. The lurid picture of idolatrous pagans contained in the first chapter, is immediately connected with the preceding intimation of visiting Rome. Paul had preached at Athens and at Corinth, the chief seats of idolatry, as also learning and the arts, among the Greeks. And now he writes, " I am ready to preach the gospel to you that are at Rome also. For I am not ashamed of the gospel of Christ : for it is the power of God unto salvation to every one that believeth, to the Jew first, and also to the Gentile." The picture is produced to show that neither was he ignorant of the colossal evil against which he was about to oppose there, as elsewhere, the preaching of Christ crucified.

So likewise the divine argument that follows, comprised in chapters ii. to xi. inclusive, whilst the subject of it might have been suggested by information given to Paul by his friends in Rome, is yet strongly linked with the epistles to the Corinthians and Galatians. Not having, as in their case, any remonstrances to make with the Romans on the ground of inconsistency with teaching previously received from him, it is resolved into a treatise, supplementing, as it were, those epistles, as they concerned the position of Jew and Gentile in the economy of the gospel, and setting a seal for ever upon the doctrine so acceptable to all who know they have no other plea for salvation than free and unmerited grace through faith alone in Christ Jesus. About this *encyclical* there must appear to many persons something very unsatisfactory for the dignity of the Romish Church that now is. No bishop is named, no priest, nor yet is there any official minister addressed, or so much as alluded to. But instead thereof, the Christians then in Rome are presumed to have been "able to instruct one another" (xv. 14). Moreover, the letter, instead of being sent by the hands of a legate, was despatched by a humble *deaconness*, proceeding from Cenchrea to Rome on her own secular affairs.

There now only remained for Paul and his companions to conduct the business with the Church at Corinth which had chiefly brought him here. The Corinthians had been exhorted a year before to contribute, along with other Churches, towards a fund to be conveyed to the poor brethren in Jerusalem (1 Cor. xvi.) And having complied with the exhortation, and also with the request contained in the letter recently brought to them, the collections would have been completed. In this letter Paul had said, " And when I come, whomsoever ye shall approve by letters, will I send to bring your liberality to Jerusalem. And if it be meet that I go, they shall go with me " (1 Cor. xvi. 2–4). Accordingly, an appointment was now made of the persons who should be the almoners. Already Paul had designed to visit Jerusalem soon after this season, and therefore he was chosen for a deputy of the subscribers to the fund. Luke, who had wished to accompany his friend, was chosen by the Churches to travel with Paul, and so might be regarded as a deputy of the Philippians, Aristarchus being the deputy of the Thessalonians, and Trophimus of the Ephesians.

The appointment of such a company attests the importance with which their mission was regarded; and from the length of time during which the collections were gathered every Sabbath-day, and the situation of the contributors, as those rejoicing in their recovery from the darkness and slavery of degrading superstitions, it may be thought certain that a munificent offering had been prepared. The Apostle and Evangelist, in love, and in obedience to a divine monition, had brought the gospel into Macedonia and Achaia; and now they take back with them, as a fruit of their labours, an expression of grateful sympathy for the poor brethren of Judea—the acceptance of this trust being the last and crowning act of their ministry in Greece.

CHAPTER XXIII.

AT this point begins the fifth section of the Acts of the Apostles, the date being about A.D. 58. Here another important stage in Luke's life is reached. It had been the intention of Paul to sail direct from Achaia to Syria, having his eye and affections fixed upon Antioch, as a stage to be visited on the way to Jerusalem. But this design was frustrated through his enemies, the unbelieving Jews. He was informed that a party of these had conspired to way-lay him when he should proceed to the ship, and of course for the purpose of killing him, as on other occasions attempted. But the Lord had more work for His servant to do. Instead, therefore, of going down to the port of Cenchrea, he turned towards the opposite direction, and took the road to Philippi. Whether, with his companion, they went thither by land, or in part by sea, is not known. At Philippi they found several brethren who had been engaged in a ministry in Macedonia (Acts xx. 4). These, upon Paul and his companion's arrival, preceded them to Asia, whilst the former remained to indulge for a brief space in a farewell fellowship with their beloved Philippians. Besides, it may be supposed that there would be several things to set in order before their departure from Europe. After farewell addresses, doubtless embracing a review of what God had wrought by their ministry and that of their brethren, they at length bade the last adieu. They had come to Greece at the first in company, and they leave that continent together. The combination in the narrative of Paul and Luke by the pronouns *us* and *we*, intimates the closeness of their fellowship, and also the special position of Luke in the embassy. Those that went away before, Luke says, "tarried for us at Troas; and we sailed from Philippi after the days of unleavened bread;" that is, a week after the passover, or about the end of March. The voyage to Troas was more tedious than when they came from thence to Neapolis upon their first coming to Europe. The passage then had been performed in two days, whereas now, to return, the voyage extended to five days.

The brethren who went before and awaited them at Troas were—

1. *Sopater* (one of the Bible-searching nobles) of Berea. The three most ancient manuscript copies say, "*the son* of Pyrrhus." Sopater, or Sosipater, had been at Corinth when Paul and Luke were recently there (Rom. xvi. 21). With the wonderful tendency existing with some editors for multiplying the persons mentioned in the sacred books, Sopater and Sosipater are not allowed to be the names of one individual.

2. *Aristarchus of Macedonia.* He had laboured with Paul at Ephesus, and had been used with violence in an uproar raised by the craftsmen (Acts xix. 29). Somewhat more than two years after this notice of him, along with Luke, he accompanied Paul to Italy.

3. *Gaius of Derbe.* He had laboured with the Apostle, and had suffered along with Aristarchus at Ephesus. It may be supposed that this Gaius was another person than "mine host" of Corinth. The name Gaius occurs five times in the New Testament, yet the only notice taken of it in Dr W. Smith's *large* "Dictionary of the Bible" is this: "*Gaius,* SEE *John, the second and third epistles of.*" But even in this curtness there is an error, for the name does not occur in John's *second* epistle.

4. *Timothy of Lystra.* He is properly paired with Gaius by reason of the contiguity of their residence. Timothy seems to have remained in Macedonia during Paul and Luke's visit to Corinth, and he was still at Philippi upon their return thither.

5. *Tychicus,* and *Trophimus of Asia.* This is the first notice given of these two. Of the company congregated to meet Paul, only Trophimus is mentioned in connexion with the visit to Jerusalem (xxi. 29).

Upon Paul's former passage through Troas, he had found there an effectual door opened for his ministry. The door being still open, his abrupt departure, on that occasion, is now compensated. Seven days were devoted to this service, and aided by the goodly company that attended him, those would prove days of refreshing to the Church at Troas. By the three copies S., V., and A., Luke appears in the reading, "Upon the first day of the week, when WE came together," &c. (xx. 7). From the picture given of this farewell-service the day before the departure of the company, it is seen that the interest of the Church in the exercises of the week was maintained to the last. The meeting was held in a guest-chamber upon a third floor, and the discourse of Paul was extended until midnight; so, although the Apostle prescribed, "Let all things be done decently, and in order," he seems to have known nothing of *uncanonical hours.*

A young man sought relief from the pressure and heat of the place by sitting in one of the windows—not a window having a frame with glass, but movable lattices. Overpowered by sleep, induced by long attendance and the ascending stream of heat, he lost his balance, and fell to the ground—probably not into the street, but into the court common to large houses. Here, apparently, was a calamitous termination of the week's devotions. How painful would it have been to the travellers to have gone away with the sad impression received by the death of the youth under those circumstances ! But Jesus was with the spirit of His servant, prompting the faith which, exercised for the recovery of the deceased, was answered. The hand of Faith touched the hand of Omnipotence. To the joy of all, Eutychus was restored to his friends ; and so an impressive seal was set to the ministry that had been conducted during that memorable week. Although the dawn approached, the congregation did not disperse. Paul again ascended to the apartment. He brake bread with the assembly in a true love-feast, and resumed his discourse with a new emphasis, as it would appear, to a people whose hearts were attuned to faith and joy by the miracle just witnessed.

A few hours having been taken for repose, the time arrived when the company must commence their journey. From hence the Evangelist's narrative partakes the character of a panorama. Sketches of the successive scenes are given with a simplicity and power which only the hand inspired by the eye that witnessed them could have delineated. In the first scene, the Evangelist himself is revealed, and in a manner calculated to excite the reader's sympathy. He writes, " And WE went before to ship, and sailed unto Assos, there intending to take in Paul, for so he had appointed, minding himself to go afoot " (xx. 13). Upon this personal notice of the Evangelist, Charles Taylor pertinently remarks, " If I am not mistaken, we discover tokens of elderly weakness in this circumstance. Luke preferred proceeding by ship as less fatiguing. He might now " (adds Mr Taylor) " be about seventy-four or seventy-five years of age." The notice equally shows that, at this period, Paul possessed a vigour not often enjoyed by men of his age. The distance he walked was nearly twenty miles, over a Roman road, but a mountainous district. Assos was a seaport of Mysia. " The view of this city, at that time, from the sea was striking: in the foreground was an extensive cemetery, covered with huge sarcophagi of granite; thence a flight of steps led to a terrace and porticoes, and the principal gates of the city; the baths and edifices of the lower town filled up the scene, with the theatre, acropolis, and its temples rising majestically behind. The walls of the city were five miles in circuit. The acropolis is a rock of granite of very steep sides" (Dr Hunt in "Walpole's Turkey," vol. i., pp. 129, 130). A traveller wrote in 1838, "I found the whole front of the hill a wilderness of ruined temples and theatres. All the buildings were of the solid Greek style, and the friezes much ornamented" (Fellow's "Travels in Asia Minor").

In few ancient writers is the manner of sailing, previous to the discovery of the magnetic needle, more fully illustrated than by Luke. From the succession of places which he mentions, it is seen how carefully the ship "hugged the land," as sailors say. After the embarkation of Paul at Assos, several places are named at which the ship touched. On the fourth day of the voyage Miletus was reached, a seaport of Caria, distant beyond Ephesus thirty miles. Here the company landed. The ship had passed over the Bay of Ephesus, but Paul would not put into a port there, lest, by going up to the city, he should get into any entanglement which might detain him. He had bidden farewell to the disciples there some months ago; but his expectations of a return to the scenes of his triumph in Asia had suddenly vanished. Since his embarkation he had received intimations which led him to conclude that his adieus to his friends in those parts were final. Apprehending that he would have no opportunity, besides the present, of a personal interview with those at Ephesus, he sent a message to request the ministers of the Church there to meet him at Miletus. These were those called in the Epistle to the Ephesians "the faithful brethren," and here, by the historian, *presbuteroi*, elders, and by the Apostle himself, *episcopoi*, which the English version in other places translates *bishops*, but here *overseers*. The number of those ministers that came from Ephesus is not known. It is probable that they met Paul and his company at the house of a disciple at Miletus.

All these incidents are eminently illustrative of the general plan of Luke's history. Nothing is related as being of fortuitous occurrence. Everything is connected either with the past or the future. Paul spake as a prophet in his address to the elders. That address touched a new chord. No revelation was made to him now, as formerly, promising protection and assuring success. On the contrary, his language is, " And now, behold, I go bound in spirit unto Jerusalem, not knowing the things that shall befall me there, save that the Holy Ghost witnesseth in every city, saying, that bonds and afflictions abide me " (xx. 22, 23). " And now, behold, I know that ye all, among whom I have gone preaching the gospel, shall see my face no more " (25). Again Paul spake as a prophet when, with respect to themselves, he warned them, saying, " Take heed, therefore, . . . for I know this, that after my departure shall grievous wolves enter in among you, not sparing the flock. Also of your own selves shall men arise, speaking perverse things, to draw away disciples after them " (28–30). How the scene that ensued touched Luke's sympathies is witnessed in the notes which, having jotted on his tablet, he afterwards transferred to the historic page. They are, " And when *Paul* had thus spoken, he kneeled down and prayed with them all " (observe their position in prayer), "and they wept sore, and fell on Paul's neck, and kissed him " (an example of the kiss of charity); " sorrowing most of all for the words which he spake, that they should see his face no more. And they accompanied him to the ship." So concluded Paul's ministry in Asia. The tender heart realises the solemnity of that procession.

Having, with his company, gone on board the ship, Luke's feelings are again denoted. He describes the separation from the Ephesian brethren by words which signify "*tearing ourselves* from them," but which are coldly translated in the English version, "after we had gotten from them" (xxi. 1). Patara, to which place the ship was bound, was reached on the third day. This city was situated beside the river Xanthus, in Lycia. A fine collection of Xanthian marbles, selected from the ruins in the neighbourhood by Sir Charles Fellows, and deposited in the British Museum, is described in his "Travels in Asia Minor," p. 421 to 456. At Patara a ship was found about to proceed to Phenicia. This was the longest reach they had made, and the most distant from the land ; for, by sailing on the west side of Cyprus, the circuit of the great bay in which that island lay was avoided, and a direct course taken to Tyre. At this port the company landed, "for there the ship was to unlade her burden."

This was an interesting stage of the journey for Luke. The city of Tyre and its fortunes and misfortunes were familiar to him as a student of the Bible. Some of its inhabitants had gone forth "to hear Jesus, and to be healed of their diseases" (Luke vi. 17). And, along with the men of Cyprus and Cyrene, who, journeying from Jerusalem to Antioch, preached the gospel in Phenicia, Luke himself had been associated. That had been about eighteen years before the time of this visit. Christianity had not, it would seem, greatly flourished here, yet there were some disciples found, upon being sought after. With these, seven days were spent upon this occasion by the evangelical company. Here it was repeated to Paul, by disciples speaking by the Spirit, that "he should not go up to Jerusalem." No other particular of what transpired at Tyre is recorded. But again Luke depicts a farewell scene, and, like the last witnessed, the picture is accomplished by a few strokes: "And they all brought us on our way, with wives and children, till we were out of the city; and we kneeled down on the shore, and prayed. And when we had taken our leave one of another, we took ship, and they returned home" (xxi. 5, 6). The representation of the movement of this procession is in keeping with what was the geography of the place; the city having stood at some distance from the shore—some part of it on the high mainland, and some on an island, but connected by a mole. In the interest taken in the departure of the company by the "women and children," is not the ministry of the benevolent physician, during those seven days' sojourn, to be traced? And does not the specifying these notify his gratification in receiving from those "daughters of Tyre" this mark of their grateful affection? And then, how refreshing seems the kneeling for prayer in the cool of the sea-breeze, and within hearing of the ripple of the waves!—how lifelike the leave-taking!—and how naturally do the words, "And they returned home," intimate that from the ship's deck the writer's eyes followed the retiring group until lost from view!

The last port to which the company sailed was Ptolemais, now called Acre, renowned in modern history by its heroic defence, sustained successfully, under the generalship of Sir Sidney Smith, for two months against the assaults of Bonaparte's army. This place being distant twenty-five miles from Tyre, the voyage would have been made during the same day. The next day was spent with the disciples found there. And upon the day following, the company travelled by land to Cæsarea, the distance being about twenty miles. The first circumstance mentioned by Luke, upon the arrival of the company in Cæsarea, was one of special interest to himself: "They entered the house of Philip, one of the seven deacons." He had known Philip when, heretofore, he abode in Jerusalem. His sympathies had, at an early period, been drawn to him as one whose ministry had been directed to Gentiles. The meeting of such friends would have been refreshing ; and many were the passages of each other's subsequent experience in the ministry of their divine Master which they would mutually recount. In Philip's house the company of delegates abode during their stay in the city, which extended to " many days ; " not more than ten or twelve, as the season of the Passover approached, which Paul wished to spend in Jerusalem. With characteristic respect for the female branches of the house, Luke mentions the "four daughters " of his friend ; and he sets it down as noteworthy, that "they prophesied." What this term signified, as applied to them, must have been fully understood in the days wherein the prediction of Joel, quoted by Peter (Acts ii. 17), was manifestly fulfilled : this, at least, it signified, that they were devoted deaconesses or servants of the Church, and, in Paul's language, " fellow-labourers " with the " faithful brethren."

The only other incident having occurred during their sojourn here which is related, is an intensified remonstrance that was urged against the Apostle's proceeding to Jerusalem. By the arrival of Agabus from that city, they were put in possession of what was there known to be the evil intentions of the Jews against the Apostle of the Gentiles ; and in an enunciation accompanied by a symbolical action, Agabus emphatically declared what awaited Paul in Jerusalem. Like the brethren in other places, those of Cæsarea renewed their entreaties that he would proceed no further ; and in which entreaties they were joined by those of Paul's company, who seem hitherto to have refrained from any interference with his design. Luke himself, having heard the testimony of one whom he knew to be eminently endowed with the prophetic spirit, spake apprehensively ; for he writes, " And when we heard these things, both WE and

they of that place besought him not to go up to Jerusalem."
Moved by their fears, thus impressively confirmed, they
were able, besides repeating the cautions he had received,
to urge that the object of their deputation to that city could
be fulfilled without his presence there ; and that here, just
on the border of the land, he would be in a place of safety,
as he had before found, when he had been suddenly brought
hither from Jerusalem by disciples (Acts ix. 30). Cæsarea
having been the great citadel and chief residence of the
Roman Governor of Palestine, no Jew dared to move
riotously there. By the added solicitations of his own
company, Paul's feelings were overcome. He had already
perceived the danger which he approached, and had expressed his conviction thereof to the elders of Ephesus.
But he acted under an impulse stronger than all by which
he was opposed. "He went bound in spirit." The conflict was great. Magnanimously declaring his readiness to
die in Jerusalem for the name of the Lord Jesus, he
triumphed, albeit in agony. " What ! mean ye to weep and
to break my heart ? " was the language of a counter-re-
monstrance. And it prevailed. " And when he would not
be persuaded," Luke meekly says, " we ceased, saying, The
will of the Lord be done ; " concluding that his friend's resolution was divinely prompted.

CHAPTER XXIV.

JERUSALEM REVISITED.

A LIVELY picture of the departure of Luke and his company is sketched by his pen. His words, "We took up our luggage," imply the act of packing it upon the backs of beasts of burden; whilst the clause, "and went up to Jerusalem," presents to the imagination a cavalcade of grotesque appearance to an European, but made familiar to the reader by the prints which often accompany books of travels in the East. The distance to Jerusalem being above fifty miles, not sooner than the next day towards even could they have finished the journey. Arrived before the Bethlehem gate, the luggage was unloosed, and the travellers conducted to their quarters. Luke was once more in Jerusalem. Externally all appeared unchanged. There was the Temple; there the palaces of Zion; here the streets with which he was familiar; surrounding all were the everlasting hills. But he felt otherwise than he had been wont among these scenes. The anticipated pleasure of the visit was clouded by the remembrance of the forebodings that he had heard expressed by the way. Some of the disciples of Cæsarea had accompanied the party on the journey. By these they were conducted to the house of "Mnason of Cyprus, an old disciple," with whom it had been appointed that they should lodge. The unusual speciality with which their host is described is suggestive. The mention that he was of "Cyprus," seems to connect him with the memories of Barnabas, and Mary his sister, who, by this time, were most likely deceased. By the term "an old disciple," is probably signified an *originul* disciple,—one of the converts in the great pentecostal season ; and, therefore, one with whom Luke had been acquainted when he had formerly resided in Jerusalem. It bespake no small degree of courage, knowing the temper of the Jewish people towards them, to have entertained these servants of Christ. And here, on an imperishable page, the name and hospitality of this ancient Israelite have a memento.

Under the two opposite aspects of society found here, it is pleasant to glance upon the first. Besides the welcome received from their venerable host, several of the brethren having obtained intelligence of their arrival, hastened to embrace them. To the feelings hereby inspired expression is given by Luke in the words, " And when we were come to Jerusalem, the brethren received us gladly." Eighteen years had well-nigh removed from the city all with whom he had been then acquainted. Seated in the host's guest-chamber, he would learn that none of the apostles were in the city except James ; and to many of his inquiries concerning individuals he had here known and loved, he would receive replies that would send his thoughts, in following them, either to heaven, or to far distant lands. He had departed from this city before any thoughts had been entertained of the conversion of Gentiles, irrespective of Jewish proselytism. He had been one of those who first held the office—never before heard of—that of a Gentile prophet. He had welcomed the co-operation in a new field of Christian teaching of Barnabas and Paul, and had seen how their labours therein had been sanctioned, by himself having received, along with fellow-elders at Antioch, a divine command to ordain them to an apostleship to the Gentile world. With Paul he had been in correspondence throughout all his missionary journies ; and he was now by his side, a joint-deputy with him from Gentile Churches to the saints in Jerusalem, and bearing fruits of the reality of their mutual brotherhood. After the repose of the night, the business of the mission was begun. Luke's notes proceed : " The day following, Paul went in with us unto James, and all the elders were present." This was a private meeting at the house of James ; its privacy arising from danger to be apprehended by a more public advertisement of the presence of Paul in the city. " And when he had saluted them,"—that is, first personally, and then officially, producing at the same time the letters from the Churches represented by the deputation,—" he declared particularly what things God had wrought among the Gentiles by his ministry." This was the third report of the kind that Paul had made to the elders in Jerusalem. The first had been when, in company with Barnabas, he brought alms from Antioch ; and the second, when he came with the embassy from the same place, upon the circumcision controversy. Since the last of these occasions, the progress made in the conversion of Gentiles had been a hundred-fold. He had travelled far and wide ; scarcely a place of note between Palestine in the south, to Illyricum in the north, having been unvisited ; and when he was about to quit his ministry in Europe, he could exult, saying, " Now thanks be unto God, who always causeth us to triumph in Christ" (2 Cor. ii. 14). A practical illustration of the character of the Gentile converts was now placed before James and the elders, being the offerings which it was the business of the deputation to convey. "And when they had heard Paul's rehearsal," and had received from his hands this token of sympathy, " they glorified the Lord" (xxi. 20).

But this bright sunshine was of short duration. Almost without a moment's suspension of breath, James intimated how well grounded were the fears which had repeatedly been expressed concerning the dangers to be apprehended for the personal safety of Paul in Jerusalem (xxi. 20–24).

It is true, that he spake only with reference to the prejudices of the Jewish Christians ; but this only makes more obvious the hostility against Paul of the Jewish mind in general. "Many thousands of Jews that believed were so zealous for the law," that they suspected him of being an apostate, and regarded the freedom from its ceremonials which he permitted among his Gentile converts as impious. The advice given to Paul by James concerning the Nazarite vow could have found no echo in Luke's mind. And it seems only to have been set down by him because it was the first link in the chain of succeeding incidents.

Luke had not spent a week in the pleasures derived from a renewed intercourse with old friends, and from the acquirement of new ones, before the forebodings that had been uttered throughout the journey to Jerusalem were verified.

Paul was engaged in the temple fulfilling the vow recommended to his observance by James, where he was found by some of his old enemies, Jews from Ephesus. They knew Trophimus of the same place, and having just before seen him in company with Paul in the city, they concluded that he had gone with him into the temple, having passed into a court forbidden to Gentiles. The cry of sacrilege ran like that of fire; and, at the time of a festival, a very few minutes sufficed to bring together a mob heartily disposed to join in wreaking vengeance. They now do, as they would have done fourteen years ago, had Paul not departed suddenly by divine command. Luke writes, "They drew him out of the temple." This would have been on the north side of it. And by the expression, "they went about to kill him," it is signified, that they were in the act of drawing him towards the adjoining gate in the east wall of the city, to the spot that had witnessed the martyrdom of Stephen. But they were arrested ere the gate was reached. Tidings of the riot were carried to the Captain of the garrison in Fort Antonia, (from which a flight of steps conducted to the street), who, attended by soldiers and centurions, " ran down unto them." Whereupon the mob suspended their blows, " and the captain took him, and commanded him to be bound with two chains ; " that is, in token that he intended to act lawfully towards him, having rescued him from an illegal execution. And so was fulfilled the prediction of Agabus that he should be bound, being delivered into the hands of the Gentiles (xxi. 11).

The account of his capture, together with the report of Paul's noble defence of himself and testimony given for Christ, which it had been permitted him to make to the " men, brethren, and fathers," that thronged the streets and the stairs, as also of his subsequent treatment in the castle, would afterwards be obtained by Luke from his own lips (xxi. 30–40, xxii. 1–29). But Luke might have had the opportunity to witness the next public scene into which his friend was brought. To this scene Paul was introduced by the captain, who was as discreet in judgment as prompt in action. The castle or tower had been erected to restrain the Jews from revolutionary movements in the temple ; and to their riotous conduct upon occasions the captain would have been accustomed. In the course he now adopted, he acted justly towards all the parties concerned, and, in the end, he thereby furnished himself with another proof of the intemperate conduct of Paul's accusers.

The action of the captain, and his motive for it, are thus described by Luke : " On the morrow, *because* he would have known the certainty wherefore he was accused of the Jews, he loosed him from his bands, and commanded the chief priests and all their council to appear, and brought Paul down and set him before them " (xxii. 30).

As the hall of the high priest, in which the council was held was on Mount Sion, the course taken by the military escort, to avoid attracting a crowd, would have been through the gate towards which Paul was yesterday being hurried. And passing beside the wall flanking the east and the south sides of the temple, a gate would be entered which led to the Hill of Sion. It was through that gate that Jesus had been conducted by officers of the temple from Gethsemane, by the bands of the high priest.

Paul having been set before the council by the captain and his officers, with what a gaze would its members regard him! The character of that gaze may be surmised by the gaze that was once set upon Jesus in that same hall, and also by the gaze that was afterwards set by the council upon Stephen. That gaze, however, did not disconcert the captain's prisoner; for Luke's description of the scene begins with the words, " And Paul earnestly beholding the council" (xxiii. 1). Dr Alford says, " 'Earnestly beholding' seems to describe that peculiar look connected probably with *infirmity of sight.*" But this guess is quite inconsistent with Luke's method of composing his narrative. A particular such as this he would only note for the reason that it illustrated the incident in hand. Several years ago Paul had been acquainted with members of this council, and his scrutinous eye would be directed to discover whether now any of those might be recognised. Moreover, being probably, like many highly intellectually-gifted persons, a physiognomist, he would wish to scan the temper through the face, and to obtain thereby a perception of the attitude of the assembly towards himself. This intense glance at his judges is as natural as it was politic. The practice of taking such a glance is observed by orators upon every important occasion, as this was. And, besides all this, that "earnestly beholding" his judges by Paul, testified the intrepidity of his own temper, and also his confidence in the faithfulness of the Master, for whose cause he stood there.

It was soon perceived that no more moderation was to be expected from the Sanhedrim than from the mob. Paul had uttered only one sentence, when the high priest commanded them that stood by him to smite him on the mouth. Whereupon Paul said unto him, " God shall smite thee, thou whited sepulchre ; for sittest thou to judge me after the law, and commandest me to be smitten contrary to the law." Paul stood there as a prisoner, but he was also a prophet. And not from any feeling of personal indignation, but as delivering a solemn sentence, divinely prompted —a sentence whose fulfilment should by and by be witnessed by some that heard it pronounced—did he utter those words. " And those that stood by said, Revilest thou God's high priest so? And Paul said, I wist not that he was the high priest." Paul might well have supposed that an order like that which had been given had not proceeded from the proper president of that august assembly. And both Paul's supposition, thus expressed, and also the prophetic character of his sentence upon the man, are justified by subsequent history. It need hardly be said that this was another Ananias than he before whom Jesus had been brought. Concerning this Ananias, Josephus says, that " he had been high priest when Quadratus was president of Syria, by whom he was deposed." And it does not appear that he was ever restored, but that the office was vacant at this time, so that he was only high priest nominally, and president of the Sanhedrim accidentally. Concerning the death of this man, Josephus relates, that " he was slain (*smitten*) during an invasion of the city by a band of robbers" (Antiq. xx.) This happened about six years afterwards. The proceedings of the council, as they concerned Paul, were abruptly terminated. This exordium, suggested by the survey of its members that he had taken, was all the defence which he had the opportunity to deliver. " Men and brethren," were his words,

" I am a Pharisee, the son of a Pharisee : of the hope and resurrection of the dead I am called in question this day. And when he had so said, there arose a dissension between the Pharisees and the Sadducees ; and the multitude was divided" (xxiii. 6, 7).   That was a remarkable session, wherein the accused was thus able, from a knowledge of its composition, to set the venerable council into a blaze of controversy among themselves.   Nevertheless, although, by the terms of that exordium, the anger of one party was seemingly abated towards him, the rage of the other was redoubled ; so that " the captain, fearing lest Paul should have been pulled in pieces of them, commanded the soldiers to go down and to take him by force from among them" (ver. 10).

And now Luke's admirable picture conducts his friend to another scene.   " And he" (*the captain*) " brought him to the castle."   Here Paul was in durance, but he was beyond the reach of his foes.   He was in the custody of the only person in Jerusalem who had power to protect him.   That he was not consigned to a dungeon, but to an ordinary apartment, may be inferred from what has been seen of the considerate conduct of the captain towards him.   Never did the castle enclose such a captive.   During the quiet here obtained, Paul pondered his situation.   He could not fail to have reflected upon those words he had quoted to his audience from the stairs of the castle, " Get thee quickly out of Jerusalem, for they will not receive thy testimony concerning me."   He would, perhaps, have called to mind the correspondence that preceded his coming hither—his letter to the Romans, wherein he apprised them of his intention to visit Italy, after having gone to Jerusalem, and wherein he requested them to join him in prayers, " that he might be delivered from them that do not believe in Judea" (xv. 24–31).   He would remember that, upon starting on the mission from Corinth, his life had been threatened by the laying in wait of Jews. And he would reflect upon the several instances in which he had been besought not to proceed further upon the journey. And perhaps these and similar considerations caused him to question the propriety of the course he had pursued, seeing it had terminated so inauspiciously, as it appeared. He had received no divine direction to undertake the journey hither, like that which sent him, with his colleagues, into Greece, although, having taken the step, and when on the journey, he professed himself to be "bound in spirit" to execute his purpose. And then, with respect to Paul's feelings. What these were may be imagined by a reference to what had been his conduct in the dark dungeon at Philippi, and also by passages contained in the two epistles already referred to, and which, as they were the last he had written, expressed his most recent experiences. In both of those epistles love pants for language by which to express devotion to its object. "Who," he writes, "shall separate us from the love of Christ? Shall tribulations, or persecutions, or peril, or sword?" (ix. 35). And to the Corinthians, "Therefore I take pleasure in infirmities, in reproaches, in persecutions, in distresses, for Christ's sake" (xii. 10). And here he had just illustrated his love for Christ by fulfilling a ministry for Him in the face of His enemies, earnestly and faithfully, after the examples of the apostles Peter and John, and the deacon Stephen. Yet how little soever he was daunted by the sufferings now endured, his mind must have been shaded by a feeling of disappointment, in that his arrest seemed to render doubtful his hope of reaching Rome.

Presently all Paul's anxieties were hushed. It was now night, the season when, at a short distance from this castle, Jesus having been in an agony, angels had ministered unto Him. And now, in Paul's extremity, *"the Lord stood by him"*—that is, by a personal interview, as He was seen several times before His ascension by the disciples, and had already been seen by Paul himself. " *And he said, Be of good cheer, Paul.*" The Master's voice, and His familiar, gentle words, fell upon his ear as the soft zephyrs, soothing all to peace, peace. " *For us thou hast testified of me in Jeru-salem* "—an expression of approval, and a recognition of His servant's zeal, sweetly rekindling the confessor's confidence —" *so must thou bear witness also at Rome* "—an answer to the special difficulty of the case.

Oh ! what wonder, witnessing this intimacy of Christ with His servant, at those frequent and impassioned expressions of admiration of Him that pervade his writings !

And then, in these words of the Master was included a message to Paul's companion. How Luke himself interpreted that message will be seen presently.

CHAPTER XXV.

WHERE was Luke on the morrow after his companion's imprisonment? He would certainly have visited him early. His business in Jerusalem was now centred in the object of his chiefest reverence among men. Having followed that object with his sympathies whilst pursuing his ministry, how anxiously would he hasten to repair to him now ! Knowing the peril to which he was exposed yesterday, he would be impatient to afford the solace which the presence and converse of a friend can communicate. Access to him was easy, by the good-will of the chief captain. But Luke had been anticipated. Ah, loving friend ! the object of thy quick sympathy had, in the interim, been visited by a faster Friend than even, thee ! The Lord had stood by him, and said, "Be of good cheer, Paul ; for as thou hast testified for me in Jerusalem, so thou must bear witness also at Rome." And the day did not close before another link was added to the chain of contingencies that should lead to the fulfilment of His word. Another visitor arrived. The Apostle had a nephew in Jerusalem ; perhaps pursuing his studies here, as his relative had done before. With eager interest he had followed the case of his uncle ; and having discovered what was the next intended step of his enemies, he hastened to apprise him of the intelligence he had obtained. In the youth's report Paul instantly recognised a message from his divine Master. And he at once requested an

officer to introduce his young visitor to the captain. The
notes of Luke relating the conversations that followed
hereupon, and the action taken, bespeak his near intercourse with the parties. There is the action of the officer,
and the words with which he introduced the youth to the
chief captain : " So he took. him, and brought him to the
chief captain, and said, Paul the prisoner called me unto
him, and prayed me bring this young man unto thee, who
hath something to say unto thee." There is the courteous
reception given to the youth : " And the chief captain took
him by the hand, and went aside privately, and asked him,
What is that thou hast to tell me ? " There is the statement made by the informant, and the sensible request by
which it was accompanied : " And he said, The Jews have
agreed to desire thee, that thou wouldest bring Paul to-
morrow unto the council, as if they would inquire somewhat of him more perfectly. But do not thou yield unto
them ; for there lie in wait for him more than forty men,
which have bound themselves with an oath, that they will
neither eat nor drink till they have killed him : and now
are they ready, looking for a promise from thee." There
is the chief captain's caution to the informant upon dis-
missing him : " So the chief captain bid the young man
depart, and charged him, See thou tell no man that thou
hast showed these things unto me " (xxiii. 18–22). The
plea of the conspirators requesting Paul to be set before
the council again was plausible, as yesterday he had been
hindered from proceeding beyond the commencement of his
speech. Upon succeeding in this plea, the plot contemplated
an attempt upon his life, somewhere between the steps of
the castle and the entrance to the high priest's palace,—a
bold adventure, knowing that the same precaution would
be taken in conducting him as was taken before. In the
rapid business that ensued, Luke witnessed the last scene
which he ever had occasion to describe in Jerusalem. The

moment was critical, but the captain's tactics were equal to the emergency. He cut off all attempts at a negotiation on the subject by an instant removal of his prisoner from the city. "He called unto him two centurions, saying, Make ready two hundred soldiers to go to Cæsarea, and horsemen threescore and ten, and spearmen two hundred, at the third hour of the night" (nine o'clock). "And provide beasts that they may set Paul on, and bring him safe unto Felix the governor" (ver. 23, 24).

Of the beasts ordered to be provided for Paul, surely one was intended for his companion. A hasty salutation given by the considerate captain, the stairs descended, the horses mounted, an exit would be made through the adjoining gate. Few persons being outside the walls at that hour, the nearest course was taken to reach the road to be pursued. Thus, in less than a week after his arrival, was Paul hurried from Jerusalem. Perhaps he had been no longer time here when he was hurried from it fourteen years ago. But now he goes away never to return. It could have been no common danger that Paul had escaped, to have required nearly five hundred soldiers to conduct him forth. The conspirators were countenanced by most of the priests and elders, and had they the opportunity to act, they would have been supported in their enterprise by the people generally. And the frequency and frenzy with which the Jews were accustomed to revolt against the government of the Romans explains the captain's precautions. Surrounded by the armed host, Paul and his companion rode together during that night, musing on their strange situation ; reflecting how it differed from expeditions which they had formerly made in company ; and comforting themselves in the confidence that no less now than then they were moving under the guidance of their divine Master. When they reached Antipatris, a garrison-town thirty miles distant from Cæsarea, the infantry were left to return to Jerusalem, the horsemen alone forming the guard to the end of the journey.

Arrived at Cæsarea, the cavalcade rode straightway to the residence of the governor, to whom the officer entrusted with the errand delivered the chief captain's letter, and also presented Paul before him. The letter related how he had rescued Paul from the hands of the Jews, who would have killed him—how he had brought him before their council, but that nothing had been laid to his charge worthy of death or of bonds—how, having been told that the Jews laid wait for him, he had promptly sent him to Felix, and had ordered the accusers to prefer their charges before him. The letter having been read, and a question put to the prisoner and answered, the governor decided, "I will hear thee when thine accusers are also come." In that letter the name of the chief captain for the first time transpires; and it is a relief, in the midst of scenes so sad, to observe the moderation and justice discovered in the conduct of this agent in the incidents under review. It would appear that Claudius Lysias's regret for the wrong he had ordered to be inflicted upon Paul, being a Roman citizen, had wrought in his mind a patriotic interest for him; and his sympathy would be augmented by the manliness (worthy, as he would think, of a Roman) exhibited before a factious tribunal by one whose ordinary behaviour he had found to be singularly gentle and conciliatory. This letter is one of several curious documents transmitted in the historian's page. It was evidently written with an intention to convey a favourable impression of Paul's case; and it as evidently had an important influence upon the treatment he received here. It is withal composed with skill. It hides, for the writer's own benefit, the particulars originating his discovery that Paul was a Roman; but it sets forth the fact of his being a Roman, as a reason for the caution he had exercised in his treatment of him, and also for the transfer of him to the governor himself. The whole of Luke's account of this person's conduct reflects his esteem for him. But that which would give additional emphasis to it was a recognition in him of an instrument executing the design of the divine Master in the preservation of His servant's life, and sending him forth in the direction by Him intended.

And here succeeds another series of scenes carrying on the prophetic chain of Luke's record. A courier was dispatched to Jerusalem citing Paul's principal accusers to repair before the governor; and the promptitude with which the summons was obeyed manifests how unrelenting was their animosity against him. " After five days, Ananias, the high priest, descended with the elders, and with a certain orator, Tertullus." And here again the *quasi* high priest and his satellites appear in their instinctive character. They both detested the Roman government and despised its rulers; yet, by the mouth of their Roman orator, they seek to win the favourable judgment of Felix by flattery. Paul being called forth, and Luke standing by him in the character of his *patronus*, Tertullus addressed the governor this exordium : " Seeing that by thee we enjoy great quietness, and that very worthy deeds are done unto this nation by thy providence, we accept it always, and in all places, most noble Felix, with all thankfulness." Whereupon he urged his charges against Paul, declaring that he was a mover of sedition among the Jews throughout the world, being a ringleader of the sect of the Nazarenes—that he had gone about to profane the temple ; and thereafter concluded with a reflection upon the conduct of the governor's deputy at Jerusalem (xxiv. 1–8). This done, the prosecutors from Jerusalem arose and testified that " those things were so."

Paul's defence was unimpassioned. It simply reviewed the clauses of his impeachment, refuting them *seriatim*—1.

By a statement of what his religion really was; 2. What had taken him to Jerusalem; 3. What his conduct had been in the temple; 4. He reminded his accusers that they had neglected to bring proper witnesses; and 5. He declared that themselves had failed to prove what they affirmed. The witnesses that should have been produced were manifestly the persons who had arrested him in the temple, inasmuch as that his alleged conduct therein was the chief point for the consideration of the governor. But besides this defect in the prosecution, the governor regarded the absence of his deputy, whom they had likewise blamed, with still greater jealousy. He therefore deferred his judgment, saying, " When Lysias, the chief captain, shall come down, I will (*shall then*) know the uttermost of your matter." But as it does not appear that this witness ever came, it is probable that Felix was glad to fix the ground of his deferring judgment upon that plea. Moreover, to add to the grief of the venerable plaintiffs, he commanded *the* (not *a*) centurion to keep Paul, and to let him have liberty, and that he should forbid none of his acquaintance to minister or come unto him. Felix was partly prompted, perhaps, to give this direction concerning Paul's acquaintance by seeing Luke and other of his friends by his side. " The centurion was the commander of the horse who had the charge of Paul from Jerusalem " (Valpy). So Paul was remitted, with these favourable instructions, to the care of an officer who had already received a kindly report of his charge from the lips of the governor's deputy at Jerusalem. It was only as a prisoner of state that Paul could have been secure from the hands of his unscrupulous enemies.

Such is the first scene in Luke's description of the Lord's providence for Paul's protection at Cæsarea. His situation as a prisoner was here improved. He was now lodged in a palace. Having his books, of which he was still a student— as every man of intellectual power must be who possesses opportunities—and with a servant to open his door to every visitant, his lot must have been regarded by other prisoners as enviable. Almost as well by silence on every topic, except the one immediately before him, does the specialty of Luke's plan appear. How interesting to the reader would be a glimpse of the Apostle's prison-life at Cæsarea! How much is it desired to know what were the principal exercises of his mind there;—what had been within the compass of his ability to accomplish for the benefit of others;—what messages he sent to the Churches which his indefatigable labours had raised! But, concerning everything of the kind, the historian's pen is silent; and nothing is told until the next incident arises illustrating the fulfilment of the Lord's declaration, "Thou must bear witness also at Rome."

Now, then, Luke perceived what message was conveyed to himself in the words addressed by their Master to Paul in Jerusalem. In the declaration, that Paul must "witness at Rome," he recognised a direction for the conduct of his own steps. "I accepted the engagement," he would say, "to accompany my friend thither. And although checked in our course, I am assured that, whatever betides, we shall go to Rome. I must, therefore, patiently abide the will and the time of Him who gave His servant that assurance." The business of Luke's companionship with Paul, the Lord's prisoner, therefore, may be reckoned from the moment of the Apostle's committal to custody here. There was something solemn in this suspense. To wait the course of events which involved Luke's own position, required much of patient faith, especially when to the bodily eye all seemed to conflict against the thing hoped for. This suspense, likewise, required a firm friendship in the companions on either side. But such a friendship was that which subsisted between these companions. It was a bright exemplification of the new brotherhood established by the gospel. The difference of their nationalities, instead of repelling sympathy, enhanced it. The Jew, appointed an apostle to Gentiles, and burning with zeal to fulfil his mission, clung to the Gentile, whose whole intelligence and abilities had been so steadily devoted to the service of his Lord. Nor could the Gentile allow a limit to his gratitude to the Jew who had sacrificed everything that is reckoned precious that he might accomplish that ministry. To a man of Paul's temperament, the monotony of a prison-life must have been excessively irksome. Benign, therefore, was the Providence that supplied him at that season with the services of a companion who was so entirely adapted to be his comforter. Then were illustrated those words, " I was in prison and ye visited me." And who may tell the solace afforded by the attendance of such a visitor upon such a prisoner ! With what reverence would the object of sympathy be approached! And by the prisoner, how wistfully would the known footsteps be expected! What music was in the familiar voice of the visitor! What comfort in his varied communications! Who has not been favoured to behold the eye sparkle upon the approach of a friend, and the face thereupon lighted up with an indescribable vivacity? The proverb says, ' As iron sharpeneth iron, so a man sharpeneth the countenance of his friend :"—his presence sometimes beatifies it.

Not Silas, not Timothy, would have been so well adapted for the Apostle's companion now. These were more consistently employed in their usual work of evangelisation. But Luke had not been an itinerant; and both his habits and his advanced age rendered an accommodation to the providential requirements more easy to him than to them. Henceforward, the constant companion of Paul, excepting in sharing his bonds, Luke would be the principal medium of the Apostle's communication with the outer world. Now is more fully seen the terms upon which these eminent servants of Christ had mutually stood throughout their acquaintance and correspondence. In the instance of the Apostle's friendship with our Evangelist is a grandeur that sets it above the most eminent examples thereof in history. Before his conversion, it had been impossible that Paul should have formed such a friendship: his nationality would not have permitted it. As a Jew, he partook of the pride and bigotry that induced a scorn of the Gentile, any contact with whom would have been regarded as a defilement. And although Luke was a proselyte to the Jewish worship, he would have been met by a Hebrew of Hebrews *only at the gate.* Equally adverse to such a friendship was Paul's natural temperament. Paul possessed a mighty will. Courageous and firm of purpose, he courted enterprise. He felt himself capable of whatever he proposed, surmounting everything, as a swimmer the waves before him. In contending for the faith, he gloried in the strife, as an athlete rejoiced in the games. With such a temper it might be thought that he had never been capable of a strong affinity with a person of Luke's disposition. Luke was calm and unimpassioned. Thoughtful and studious, convictions were received by his mind calmly, and their dictates were followed with steady step. Avoiding itinerancy, he preferred a limited sphere wherein to exercise his quiet ministry. Passages are found which illustrate the difference of their dispositions before the period of their friendship. When, by the persecution by Paul and his party, the disciples were scattered abroad, Luke, following the prudential advice of our Lord, retired from Jerusalem, and travelled as far as Antioch. But when Paul, some years after his conversion, revisited Jerusalem, although his life was threatened by his old associates of the Sandhedrim, he boldly preached in the name of the Lord Jesus, until the disciples snatched him away to Cæsarea, and from thence sent him back to Tarsus. How does this conduct of the Apostle recall the case of the boldness where-with Luther, in the fifteenth century, faced the Diet of Worms, and also his rescue from the designs of that council by his disciple the Duke of Saxony. A similar correspond-ence is found in the celebrated friendship of Luther and Melancthon with this between Paul and Luke. In each of these examples of friendship, the sanguine and the phlegmatic coalesced by the force of an admiration for quali-ties which, not being possessed by the individual himself, he nevertheless admired. And in both of these examples there existed, besides, the influential motive of a mutual pursuit. The object of the Apostle commissioned to gather Gentiles, and that of the Gentile Evangelist, was one. To promote a revival of spiritual religion was alike the object of the vehement Luther and the gentle Melanc-thon. And the inspiration impelling the conduct of all these friends was the same. The love of Christ constrained them. Paul's appreciation of Luke's character is ex-pressed in an encomium stronger than has ever been uttered (2 Cor. viii. 23). Luther's emphatic language concerning his friend, addressed to Reuchlin, was : "Our friend Philip Melancthon, the extraordinary man who excels other men in almost every quality, and who I so much love and ad-mire." On the other side, Luke's admiration of Paul's character is shown in an appropriation of half his second book to an account of the ministry of his friend, and also in a companionship with him in his protracted imprison-ments ; whilst Melancthon's admiration of Luther was illustrated by numerous publications in justification and in aid of his labours, and also shone forth in the fine oration which he delivered upon the event of the Reformer's death. Surely, the alliances of those valiant men with friends so admirably qualified to hold up their hands, to counsel them in their enterprises, and to solace them in their dangers and discouragements, were links in the providential chain by which, in their respective ministries, they were conducted. The duration of those remarkable friendships was in each case nearly the same, namely, about a quarter of a century. Friendship is always charming; but Christian friendship is a rivulet flowing from high heaven, beautifying and refreshing the earth.

In walking about Cæsarea, Luke beheld a city different from all others in which he had heretofore resided. The buildings were comparatively new, the city having chiefly been built by Herod the Great, and all in a substantial style. Here were a theatre, and temples, and statues, with all the gear of idolatry, as in cities distant from Palestine. Here the Roman governors lived in their own element. A great military garrison, consisting of Italian soldiers, reserved for exigencies often occurring, gave a martial aspect to the place. Commerce also flourished by the attraction of a commodious harbour, obtained by the construction of a mighty breakwater. Here, therefore, as in all such places, the money-seeking Jews were found in numbers; but the heathen population exceeded them.

During his detention here, Luke became accustomed to the associations peculiar to a maritime port. Often would his anxious eye glance across the expanse towards the land he sought to visit, and then would arise the wish that soon the summons he awaited might be given which should enable him to embark. In the meantime, besides his almost daily fellowship with his friend in bonds, there were fellowships to be cherished and enjoyed in the city. Philip and his daughters would introduce him to several estimable friendships. If he had not already obtained them, he might now have secured those exact particulars concerning Cornelius, a centurion belonging to the garrison here, which form such an interesting picture in an earlier chapter of his narrative. Among the Christian community here, his own person and ministry would excite a peculiar interest. His origin as a Cyrenian, his profession as a physician, his experience as an evangelist, his position as a historian of the Lord's life, and his presence now in Cæsarea as a comforter of the imprisoned Apostle, would all concur to cause him to be regarded as no ordinary visitor among them. Perhaps, as in other places where he had resided, he might sometimes have exercised his ministry by relating facts, both those obtained several years ago in Jerusalem and those which concerned the progress of the gospel in Asia and in Greece. Some writers have supposed that he occupied himself here in composing his Gospel. But that this was not the case has been shown in a previous chapter, devoted to the consideration of the time and place of its publication.

Not to write his Gospel, which had been issued eight or nine years before this period, but to witness another step in the history of Paul's ministry, was Luke conducted hither ; and also thereafter to write a section of his second treatise, whereby the Church of Christ is enriched with a series of sketches of surpassing interest and incalculable value (chaps. xxiv., xxv., xxvi.) It had been revealed concerning Paul to the prophet Ananias at Damascus, " He is a chosen vessel unto me, to bear my name before the Gentiles, and kings, and the children of Israel." How he had fulfilled this prophetic word among Gentiles appears in many chapters of Luke's narrative. How he fulfilled it before the children of Israel was seen in his carefulness to begin his ministry in every place at the synagogue. How he fulfilled it in Jerusalem has just been noticed ; and now it obtains a fulfilment in the third particular at Cæsarea.

In the class of incidents which Luke should here describe, he possessed a great theme, and worthily did he execute it. On the one hand, here were rulers and princes seated on thrones of judgment, surrounded by their retinues of courtiers ; and on the other, the Lord's Apostle, a prisoner before them. Never before did those rulers look upon such a prisoner. He discovered no fear. There was no hesitation in his speech. Candour and truthfulness hallowed every word he uttered. He felt that he was there for another purpose besides the parrying the attacks of his enemies; that he had a lesson to read to his judges, a message to witness for Him for whose cause he testified there as everywhere. And admirably is all this represented in Luke's page. The prisoner appears with the dignity of a prophet. Courts are gathered to listen to his testimony. The decision of the judge is deferred to give an opportunity for a succession of auditors. And the scene moves on, only to consummate a divine purpose.

Of the four appearances of Paul before the tribunal of the governor at Cæsarea, the first has been noticed. His second public appearance was before the same magistrate. The former appearance had been judicial, but this one seems to have been commanded for the gratification of the governor's wife. Antonius Felix had been Procurator of Judea five or six years, and being married to a Jewess, he had become familiar with the peculiarities of those he governed. By the frequent riotings which he was called to suppress, he acquired a character for severity ; and by the testimony of Tacitus, he was, besides, mean and profligate. Drusilla, whom he had taken for his wife, was a princess, the daughter of King Herod Agrippa I., and so sister of Herod Agrippa II. She had been married to Azizus, king of Emesa, from whom Felix seduced her. That characters such as these should have desired to inquire concerning " the faith of Christ," shows how much public attention had been moved towards the subject, and also with what curiosity the person of Paul was regarded. They had now the opportunity to hear the gospel expounded by the lips of its most notable preacher, and they embrace it. The courtiers and officers standing around, Paul was conducted to his station. The object of the summons was courteously explained to him by Felix. And, anon, the preacher composed himself into his usual attitude for public speaking. He was acquainted with the character of the individuals that occupied the thrones. The terms of his oration are not reported at length. But it is told that he did not conclude it until, like the Baptist before a grandsire of the princess here seated, he had addressed them on the special evils of their lives: " He reasoned of righteousness, temperance, and judgment to come." And it is likewise told what were the effects of this unexpected application of truth to their consciences: " Felix trembled." What solemnity must have reigned, at that moment, throughout the hall of judgment. And when Felix said, " Go thy way for this time ; when I have a more convenient season I will call for thee," with what reverence must the company have looked upon the heroic preacher, as he was thereupon conducted from their presence. Perhaps some of the auditors were permanently affected by what they had seen and heard, and led to make inquiries after the new life of the gospel.

The third appearance of Paul in the hall of judgment occurred about eighteen months afterwards, and was occasioned by the accession of a new governor. This was Porcius Festus, who is represented by Josephus as a just as well as an active magistrate. Three days after his arrival, he repaired to Jerusalem. Paul was not forgotten there. A new high priest, Ishmael, had been recently appointed. His enemies " instantly informed against him, and besought the governor, and desired favour against him that he would send for him to Jerusalem." Festus had of course, upon entering his office, received a report concerning him, and also a representation of the earnestness with which he was pursued by the applicants. And his reply was based upon his knowledge thereof. Instead of sending for him to come to Jerusalem, his accusers were directed to accompany himself to Cæsarea, and prosecute their cause before him there. They did so. And the day after their arrival, the governor having commanded Paul to be brought before his judgment-seat, " they laid many and grievous complaints against him." As upon the former hearing of his case, so now Paul simply repelled their charges, declaring, " Neither against the law of the Jews, neither against the temple, nor yet against Cæsar, have I offended anything at all." Again they had come unfurnished with proof. And again, therefore, judgment was deferred. Failing in their suit, they make another attempt to get him lured into the road to Jerusalem, " intending," it is said, " to lay wait for him in the way, to kill him." So, they were provided with assassins, though not with witnesses. Festus, unaware of their treacherous intent, and willing to do the Jews a pleasure, put the question to Paul, " Wilt thou go to Jerusalem to be judged of them there before me ?"—that is, it was proposed that his accusers should judge him, and that Festus should witness their proceedings. But Paul, knowing their duplicity, and having an eye to his Master's declaration, did not hesitate to reply, " I stand at Cæsar's judgment-seat, where I ought to be judged ; to the Jews have I done no wrong, as thou very well knowest. For if I be an offender, or have committed anything worthy of death, I refuse not to die ; but if there be none of these things whereof thou accuse me, no man may deliver me unto them." " I stand at Cæsar's judgment-seat,"—that is, " I object to the transference of my case to another court than this : and as you decline to decide it, *I appeal unto Cæsar.*" " Then Festus, when he had conferred with the council, answered, Hast thou appealed unto Cæsar ? unto Cæsar shalt thou go " (xxv. 1–12). By this decision his enemies were effectually foiled, and a step was gained towards Paul's transit to Rome—the Lord overruling.

The fourth and last appearance of Paul before the rulers

at Cæsarea was the most remarkable of all. Ere steps had been taken for his transit to Rome, another incident arose to complete the gradation of his auditors. Luke's estimate of this incident is manifest in the extent of his description of it. His account of the preceding appearances occupied each only a few verses, but this extends over the chief part of the twenty-fifth chapter and the whole of the twenty-sixth. The occasion of this arose from the arrival of King Herod Agrippa II. on a visit to welcome Festus to his government. This Herod Agrippa was seventeen years old when his father died, A.D. 44, so, reckoning this visit to Festus to have taken place A.D. 60, he was now thirty-three years of age. Among other matters concerning which Festus conferred with his royal visitor was his custody of Paul. Agrippa having the charge of the temple committed to him by the Emperor, was conversant with the religious aspect of the case against Paul. It was, therefore, natural that Festus should have embraced the opportunity to submit the case to the judgment of the king. Agrippa having been likewise well aware of the existence of Christians, as followers of Jesus the Crucified, curiosity prompting him to see and to hear a statement from the lips of one of the most noted of them, he said to his guest, " I would also wish to hear the man myself." On the morrow, therefore, the king, accompanied by the Princess Bernice, repaired " with great pomp " to the hall of judgment. Magnificence was a characteristic of the Herods. The pride of his father, when, arrayed in royal apparel, he made an oration in the theatre, and thereupon received the homage of a god, and the judgment which then befell him, are recorded in a former chapter. Bernice was the daughter of that same Herod Agrippa, and the sister of Drusilla. She had been married to her uncle, Herod, king of Chalcis, after whose death she lived, on scandalous terms, with her brother, this second Herod Agrippa.

The company having arrived, consisting, besides these persons, of the chief captains of the garrison, and the principal men of the city, " Paul was brought forth." According to Roman custom, he would have been attended, during the audience, by "friends, who, as advocates, assisted the accused by their presence and counsel" (Adam's " Roman Antiquities"). Who these friends were it is easy to conclude. One of them would have been Aristarchus, sent to be his companion by the Macedonian Churches, and the other would have been Luke. Here, therefore, were two witnesses of that interesting scene, having an intimate relation with the prisoner, and with the cause on whose account he was " brought forth." The court having been opened by a brief address, made by Festus, explaining the object of the present audience, Agrippa invited Paul, saying, " Thou art permitted to speak for thyself." How gratefully is felt to be the advantage of Luke's presence now. Following his eye, his pen describes the action of the Apostle : " Then Paul stretched forth his hand." There is given the conciliating exordium, beseeching to be heard " patiently." Then proceeds the oration, in the delivery of which the speaker, sensible of an overruling Hand, rises up to the greatness of the occasion. The oration, which was spoken perhaps in Greek, was framed to fulfil the design of a testimony delivered before a king, and also to meet the king's desire for information. It consisted of an argument wherein the speaker explained that his education, his prejudices, and his zeal, shown as an agent of the Sanhedrim, to prosecute the disciples, had all been opposed to the probability of his ever accepting the claims of Jesus ; that he had come to a knowledge that Jesus was the Christ of the prophets, having received an indubitable proof of His resurrection by having seen the same Jesus, who had also spoken to Him, and who had appointed him to the ministry which he had henceforth pursued, " witnessing both to small and great, saying none other things than those which the prophets and Moses did say should come; that Christ should suffer, that He should be the first that should rise from the dead, and should show light unto the people, and to the Gentiles."

Here the presence of the watchful companion is perceived. He relates that at the word " *Gentiles*," Festus hastily interrupted the speaker. Festus had thought, and had spoken, of Paul's case as if it had related to the Jewish religion alone. He had conceived that he was an enthusiast persecuted on account of some point of controversy. He knew what was meant when he spoke of Moses and the prophets. He was also aware that Paul occupied himself much in reading. But he had not thought that Gentiles were concerned in the subject. Very natural, therefore, was his exclamation, "Paul! thou art beside thyself; much learning hath made thee mad!" And well is Luke's surprise and indignation at this turn in the speech denoted by his observation, that Festus said this with *a loud voice.* Striking also is Luke's report of the masterly adroitness with which the interruption was turned to the advantage of the argument with Agrippa. Now the discourse became personal. Paul rejoined, " I am not mad, most noble Festus; but speak forth the words of truth and soberness." And turning from the Gentile, he appealed to the observer of the law, "For the king knoweth these things, before whom I speak freely; for I am persuaded that none of these things are hid from him." And again, and still more pointedly, "King Agrippa, believest thou the prophets? I know that thou believest." This was the climax; the argument reached the royal conscience, and produced the sentiment that compelled the admission, "Paul, almost thou persuadest me to be a Christian." In a certain style of criticism, this remarkable admission made by the king is represented as only signifying, "Lightly (with small trouble) art thou persuading thyself that thou canst make

me a Christian ; or *I am not so easily to be made a Christian*"
(Dr Alford). Paul's noble answer to the king, contained
in the next verse, furnishes an ample refutation of this
insipid gloss.

That was a triumphant moment for this servant of
Christ. Here was illustrated that sentence of Menander,
" It is the character of the speaker, and not his words only,
that persuades to a confidence in what he says." In Paul's
were combined, and upon this occasion illustriously exhibited, zeal and moderation, candour and courteousness,
dignity and benevolence. His character and discourse were
in beauteous harmony. And the effect upon his audience
was corresponding. It was the voice of all that had sat
with the governor and the king, after they had risen up
and were gone out, " This man doeth nothing worthy of
death or of bonds,"—a declaration similar to that of Pilate
in the case of Jesus, " Behold I have examined him before
you ; I have found no fault in this man touching those
things whereof ye accuse him" (Luke xxiii. 14). But in this
case no other judgment is pronounced than that expressed
by Agrippa to Festus, " This man might have been set at
liberty if he had not appealed unto Cæsar." The true import of this reserve in the king's judgment was known to
Paul and his companions. The Apostle had now finished
his ministry in Cæsarea. Rulers and princes had listened
to his testimony. The divine design for which he had
been brought here was fulfilled. It now remained that
that word spoken to him at Jerusalem should likewise
receive an accomplishment, " So must thou bear witness
also at Rome."

CHAPTER XXVI.

AFTER two years' detention in Cæsarea, the information that at length orders had been given by Festus for the transfer of Paul to Rome, would have been received by Luke with much gratification. Hasty adieus would be made to the brethren in the city, and gladly would he join his friend at the time and place appointed for their meeting. His account of the embarkation and the adventures that succeeded, forms a new and stirring picture, occupying the twenty-seventh and a part of the twenty-eighth chapter of his narrative. In no part of his writings does Luke's own personality so continuously appear as here. He is combined with the circumstances related in those chapters twenty-seven times, by the pronoun *us* or *we*.

Paul was now transferred to the custody of Julius, a centurion of the Augustan band, or the " Emperor's own." The conduct of this gentleman, which was uniformly respectful and considerate towards Paul, it may be presumed was, at the outset, influenced by the report he had received concerning his prisoner from the centurion at the palace, who, besides his own favourable impressions concerning him, would be likely to relate to him the circumstances under which Paul became a prisoner, and his exculpation from fault by the governors and the king. A passage was engaged for the centurion's party—which included other prisoners, with soldiers for guards—in a ship whose destination was Adramyttium, a city of Mysia. This was about the end of August or beginning of September A.D. 61. It was late in the season, but not too late to hope to reach Italy before the coming of the equinoctial winds. Entering into the ship, Luke writes, " we launched,"—that is, from the harbour into the sea,—" meaning to sail by the coasts of Asia." The weather, therefore, was [such as to require cautious sailing. Now again Luke is embarked on the sea, and sailing in the direction from whence, in company with the Apostle, he had formerly come. By the notice, " Aristarchus of Thessalonica being with us," is signified that, along with Luke, he was conveyed to Rome as Paul's advocate and his witness for him in an appearance before the court there, according to the privilege permitted by Roman law in every suit. Aristarchus is first noticed in history as Paul's companion in travel, when, along with Gaius, he was apprehended in the disturbance made by the craftsmen at Ephesus (Acts xix. 29). Afterwards, along with Gaius, he was at Philippi with the company that went before Paul and Luke to Troas (xx. 4). He was sent by the Thessalonians to Cæsarea, to sustain the Apostle in his present affliction. Luke does not intimate that he was a state prisoner ; neither as a Macedonian, would he have been remitted to Rome by the judicature of Palestine. That Paul's denomination of him, " my fellow-prisoner," is figurative (Col. iv. 10), is seen by that other designation of him, " my fellow-labourer " (Philem. 24).

Sidon having been reached on the morrow, Luke says, " Julius, kindly behaving towards Paul, gave him liberty to go unto his friends to refresh himself." So Paul had friends at Sidon. Upon the former voyage he had been " refreshed " by his friends in the sister city of Tyre. He was then at liberty ; and had been warned by them not to proceed to Jerusalem. How significant is the expression " refresh himself" of the pleasure derived by the confessor from " this brief interview with hospitable friends." He had requested the prayers of the Romans, "that he might come to them, and *with them be refreshed,*" —that is, with the comfort of Christian fellowship (Rom. xv. 32). But lower objects for Paul's going ashore here have been proposed. One's eyes seem at fault upon reading, in a modern commentary, "'*To refresh himself with his friends,' was perhaps to obtain that outfit for the voyage which, on account of the official precision of his custody at Cæsarea, he would not there be provided with*" (Dr Alford). Not at all likely is it that, having been treated with courtesy by his keepers, and declared guiltless by his judges, Paul would have been made to wear a criminal's costume. Jesus wore his own garment when He was led to Calvary ; and it was a decent one, or the soldiers had not coveted it. And another commentary proffers this dilution, "*Paul stayed a night on shore, probably having experienced sea-sickness*" (Webster and Wilkinson). Could it have been likely that the commander would have brought his ship into port to accommodate a prisoner, and especially for either of these reasons ? That Paul went on shore at Sidon, that he might be refreshed by a gift of apparel from his friends there, or that he might have an opportunity to repair to a bazaar to purchase a *new outfit ;* or else, according to the other guess, that he required and obtained a respite on land on account of *sea-sickness,* are alike situations so unspiritual as to be altogether inconsistent with the character of Luke's writings.

The narrative continues, "We sailed under Cyprus, because the winds were contrary." Upon the occasion of coming from Asia, favoured by the winds, the ship took the outer side of that island ; now the inner passage was taken. The coasts of Cilicia and Pamphylia being passed, "We came to Myra in Lycia." On the former voyage they changed ships at Patara, a few miles distant on the same coast. Myra was the metropolis of the province. It stood on a high hill, a considerable distance from the shore. As the ship in which they had come hither was bound only to Adramyttium, a city of Mysia, quite out of their route, and another ship being found in the port whose destination was Italy, the centurion transferred his charge to the latter. This seems to have been a larger ship than the former one, having a heavy freight, and many more passengers on board. If the sailing had been slow before, it became much more tedious now ; whilst the winds, which had been contrary, became besides of baffling strength. The distance made from Myra to the extreme length of the coast of Asia, to be followed, was a hundred and fifty miles, which, with a fair wind, might have been accomplished iu a day and a night. Whereas, Luke says, "And when we had sailed slowly many days, and hardly were come opposite Cnidus, the wind not suffering us to reach the harbour, we sailed under Crete." Cnidus, now, Crio, is a peninsula with a harbour on each side as at Corinth ; that on the east being very commodious, and offering a fine station for ships in which to lay up for the winter. From here, therefore, taking the proper course towards Italy, they crossed over to Crete (now Candia), a narrow island forming a sort of natural break-water along the front of the Ægean sea, being a hundred and sixty miles in length, and varying from seven to fifty miles in breadth. Still the weather increased in tempestuousness. And with difficulty clearing Salmone, on the eastern cape of the island, they came to a harbour called the Fair Havens. Here the ship was brought to an anchor, and a brief respite was obtained from the contest with the elements.

Luke had another object in accompanying Paul than what obviously appeared. He came for materials whereby to continue his narrative. And, as a poet catches suggestions for his verse, and a painter pencils objects and scenes for studies in his sketch-book, so Luke took the opportunity to commit to his tablet the particulars of the voyage. His treatment of this part of his narrative is equally exact with the rest of it. It would be difficult to find, in all antiquity, an account of a voyage wherein is given a more careful register of the points from whence the wind blew, and the corresponding results and manœuvres in navigating the ship, than in Luke's page. A writer who has made this account the subject of a distinct and elaborate investigation, aided by personal researches in the Mediterranean, has said : "St Luke exhibits here the most perfect command of nautical terms, and gives the utmost precision to his language by selecting the most appropriate." But, seeming to have slight acquaintance with Luke except on shipboard, the writer herefrom concludes that Luke was a Roman *naval officer.** This is a curious opinion; but it has its match in the case of the exhaustless Shakespeare, whose technical exactness, on certain subjects, has led to the arguing of conclusions by writers concerning his having had other pursuits besides that of a dramatist. One writer has set forth "Shakespeare's knowledge of medicine;"[†] another, "Shakespeare a lawyer;"[‡] another, "Shakespeare's legal acquirements considered;" [§] another, "Shakespeare's knowledge and use of the Bible;"[‖] another, "Shakespeare a Roman Catholic."[¶] And so, arguing from the play of "The Tempest," some writer may by and by publish a treatise entitled, "Shakespeare a *Naval Officer.*"

Soon Luke was committed to another series of observations. Although the centurion and the officers of the ship were warned by Paul of the danger to be apprehended by quitting this harbour, yet, abetted by the most part of the

---

* James Smith of Jordan Hill.   † J. C. Bucknell.
‡ W. L. Rush.   § John Lord Campbell.   ‖ Dr Wordsworth.
¶ Charles Butler, in his "Memoirs of English Catholics;" also in the *Rambler*, No. 7, published in Dublin, 1854; and in the *Edinburgh Review*, Jan. 1866.

passengers, they resolved to attempt to gain the more commodious port of Phenice, situated about fifty miles farther on the same side of the island. Tempted by a softly-blowing wind, the venture was made. But the prospect of entering that port, or any other, was presently lost.

Suddenly the wind veered from south to north, bringing in an instant a hurricane, called by Luke *Euroclydon*, better known by the name of a typhoon. From this moment succeeded a storm furious and protracted. Immediately the ship discovered signs of weakness. All the tactics usual to such a condition were resorted to; and very skilful was the management of the vessel, so far as it was possible to exercise any control over its security and its course. All hands, including Luke himself, were put into requisition,—now in easing the ship, by casting heavy objects overboard; and anon, in relays, for working at the pumps. Eleven days had passed since quitting the haven; and for many of those days neither sun nor stars having appeared, whereby to make the needful observations, despondency prevailed. "All hope," wrote Luke, "that we should be saved was taken away." His language expressed the fear of himself and of his companions that they were threatened with a final arrest. All Paul's anxieties concerned his reaching Rome. On no occasion, perhaps, had Luke observed upon the countenance of his friend more evident marks of perplexity. The fury of the elements was more dreaded than had been the opposition of men. The prospect had become dark indeed; the peril was imminent. The wind moaned around; the restless waves were crested with foam; the ship laboured over the billows, its timbers creaking at every heave. Wearied with anxiety and fatigue, but having no dread of death, Paul retired to his berth, and sunk in slumber. Sleep, sweet and peaceful, succeeded. He arose refreshed; he glanced with composure upon the big waves; his countenance was placid—his appearance dignified. And presently the cause of his confident bearing was revealed. Inviting the attention of officers and others, Paul stood forth in their midst, and, with the majesty of a prophet, said, "Sirs, ye should have hearkened unto me, and not have sailed from Crete, and to have gained this harm and loss. And now I exhort you to be of good cheer ; for there shall be no loss of any man's life among you, but of the ship. For there stood by me this night the angel of God, whose I am, and whom I serve, saying, 'Fear not, Paul, thou must be brought before Cæsar ; and lo ! God hath given thee all them that sail with thee.' Wherefore, sirs, be of good cheer ; for I believe God, that it shall be even as it was told me. Howbeit, we must be cast upon a certain island." His Master's watchful eye was following him, and again, in his extremity, had appeared for his solace. The words, "I believe God, even as it was told me," expressed the principle inspiring his confidence. To none could the intelligence conveyed in this address have come with such welcome as to Luke and Aristarchus. The assurance that they should go to Rome, despite all obstacles, shipwreck included, as it inspired the speaker, imparted also new life to these. For Luke the announcement had an interest herein peculiar to himself, inasmuch as that it furnished another prophetic link for his page.

For a fortnight had the ship been driven about the widest part of the Mediterranean ; sometimes approaching Cyrenaica, near whose coasts lay the dreaded *Syrtes*, or quicksands ; when at length, after the fourteenth day, at midnight, the seamen keeping watch conceived, either by the fragrant smell wafted from the land, or by the sound of breakers, or by both, "that they drew near to some country." At the cry of "Land ! land !" all were instantly alert, ready for every effort to secure their lives. Anchors were cast out to save the ship from a sudden shock. Amidst the confusion of the impending wreck, with an intrepidity inspired by faith, Paul again stood forth, and gave directions that none should be allowed prematurely to leave the ship. And, in prospect of their struggles, he besought them to take food, declaring, " For there shall not fall a hair from the head of any of you ; " and himself taking food in his hands, gave thanks to God, in the presence of them all, and thereafter began to eat. His example was followed ; and all having likewise taken food, they became, like himself, " of good cheer." And now all hands were directed to cast the remaining freight overboard, in order still further to lighten the ship, and so to mitigate the concussion.

Throughout those scenes how unlike was Paul to a prisoner ! Perhaps he was the only Jew in the ship. And his conduct and speech might have been regarded by the Gentile voyagers as some mystic phases of the Jewish religion, had he not for partners in faith his companions, Luke and Aristarchus, who were Gentiles. In any case, God gave him their confidence ; and now, according to the prophetic word, " He gave him their lives." Preparations were made for gaining the shore. The anchors were taken up, the rudder-bands were loosed, the mainsail was hoisted to the wind, and the ship was made to run aground. At once it became a wreck ; and of the two hundred and seventy-six souls composing its living freight, some of them swimming, and some clinging to boards and broken pieces of the ship, " *they escaped all safe to land !* " In the joy common to the voyagers upon their deliverance from threatened destruction, Paul and his company fully shared. But these had, besides, other motives for gratification. Paul's confession, made before many witnesses, of belief in the word of God which had been communicated to him, was now justified ; and their deliverance, taken as a proof of the Divine faithfulness, was a source of delight beyond that of the preservation of their lives. They rejoiced in the deliverance as affording a pledge that, although delayed in their progress thither, they were still on their way towards Rome.   With respect to Luke himself, his pleasure at this moment, and the ground of it, are revealed by his narrative of the perils through which they had passed. The length of this episode, compared with some others of his narrative, whilst it attests his own feelings upon the deliverance, discovers likewise a special reason for his gratification.   The whole texture of it, so impressively illustrative of the plan of his book, reflects his exultation in riveting another link to his prophetic record.   And the story, moreover, reflects an additional illustration of his character.   It shows his *collectedness.*   Found in a novel situation, amidst scenes of confusion, and almost of distraction, by reason of the great number of persons that thronged the ship, yet how conspicuously does it manifest his equanimity.   And it shows his *perseverance.*   He did not neglect his vocation; but, notwithstanding the many inconveniences, and their being so long protracted, he continued to secure notes of the voyage, composed as carefully as any other parts of his history.

That the island upon which they were cast, called by Luke *Melita,* was Malta, the proofs which sundry writers have adduced render certain.   It is the only place now or ever under the British crown which either Luke or Paul ever visited.   The island is about sixty miles in circumference.   St Paul's Bay, as the place is now called, into which the ship was driven, is in the north-east end of the island. Of the several grottoes in the rocky coast, after some centuries, one of them, of course, was selected, by *very* religious people, for the cave into which Paul resorted, and therein has been erected a chapel dedicated to the Apostle's name.

Luke's notes relate the hospitality with which they were received by the natives; * and that their first act was to

* Called *barbarians,* because they were not Greeks or Romans.

kindle a fire, because of the rain and cold. They relate how Paul himself gathered some sticks whereby to add to the benefit; that in the bundle he had unconsciously conveyed a viper, which, upon the application of the flame, started from its quiescence, and fixed its fangs upon his arm; and how he flung it off into the fire, without having experienced the usual consequences of such a misadventure. Whereupon, the spectators concluded, observing that he was a prisoner, that his particular crime had been murder, and that retributive vengeance had overtaken him. But anon, observing that Paul proceeded with his business, indifferent to the casualty, and that none of the symptoms which commonly follow the bite of such an animal ensued, they changed their opinion, and pronounced him a god. This occurrence served to call attention to his person; and would naturally act favourably in respect of his obtaining from the natives their assistance to meet the subsequent necessities of himself and his company. And thereafter a door was opened to the sympathies of the upper class of the people by the miracle performed upon the father of Publius, the chief man of the island, perhaps the Roman prefect. And, also, the interest of the natives in general was won, both towards the person of Paul and towards his ministry as an apostle of Christ, by the assuaging of the afflictions of the many who, having diseases, came and were healed at his hands. What the ministry of these servants of Christ had been besides, is not told: but that they preached the gospel to the people of the island as well, is certain. In return, Luke says, "They honoured us" (Paul, Luke, and Aristarchus) "with many honours." This had not been mentioned unless those honours had been accompanied with the substantial benefits which they needed during the period of their detention; and, that these had not been withheld, is to be inferred from what is added: "And when we departed, they laded us with such things as were necessary." And it may likewise be thought, that, as the presence of the Lord's servant in the ship had been a source of safety to the lives of his fellow-voyagers, so here it was found that the influence Paul acquired among the natives had proved a means promotive of their sustentation ashore.

After having spent the winter season at Malta, instead of at Crete, the voyage was resumed in the beginning of the next year, in a ship from Alexandria bound for Italy with a freight of wheat, and which had wintered in the island. There was nothing fortuitous in the visit of this ship, for Malta lay in its proper course when the voyage by the wide sea was ventured upon. "The Alexandrian ships were sometimes of large dimensions. One is noticed by Hales (*in his "Chronology"*), whose tonnage was 1938, being 180 feet long, 45 wide, and 43½ deep; and that in which Josephus was wrecked, a year after, in making the same voyage, carried six hundred souls." It reflects much credit upon the navigators of the ship which had been wrecked conveying our company, that notwithstanding the many days they had been knocking about, they had succeeded in keeping it under such control as to be found at last hardly out of the true course.

The distance from Malta to the island of Sicily is a hundred miles. There three days were spent at the renowned city of Syracuse. Seventy-five years before the Christian era, Sicily had been the residence of Cicero in quality of Quæstor. Before he left the island he made a tour of inquiry and observation relative to whatever it contained that was remarkable. Upon being shown the curiosities of Syracuse by the magistrates, he inquired for the tomb of Archimedes, who was killed when the city was taken by the Romans, B.C. 212; but, to his surprise, he perceived that they knew nothing concerning it, and even denied that there was any such tomb remaining. Animated, however, by the concurrent testimony of writers, and remembering the verses said to be inscribed upon it, and that a sphere and cylinder was engraved on some part of it, he would not be dissuaded from persevering in the search. Conducted without the gate, where the greatest number of the old sepulchres existed, he presently observed, in a spot overgrown with shrubs and briers, a small column whose head just appeared above the bushes, having upon it a sphere and cylinder. "This," said he, addressing the company, " is the object which I sought." And having commanded the ground to be cleared of the brambles and rubbish, he found also the inscription, although the latter part of the verse was effaced. "Thus," he says, " one of the noblest cities of Greece, and once, likewise, the most learned, had known nothing of the monument of its most deserving and ingenious citizen, if it had not been discovered to them by a native of Arpinum." Archimedes is said to have threatened, if furnished with a fulcrum upon which to rest his lever, that he would move the world. For a moral movement thereof, the Apostles and Evangelists obtained the fulcrum ; and thereby the world is moved.

From Syracuse to the port of their destination was about two hundred and fifty miles. Before the ancient city of Rhegium (Reggio in Calabria) the ship lingered, awaiting a favourable wind to bear it through the Strait of Messina. A south wind arising, the voyage was terminated on the following day, by the arrival of the ship at Puteoli.

This city, now called Pozzuolo, is situated just within a small bay at the northern extremity of the Bay of Naples. It was a place of great commerce, and an emporium for grain imported from Egypt and the coasts of North Africa ; and being, as a principal port, the nearest to Rome, it was here that ambassadors and functionaries of the government were accustomed to disembark from the eastern provinces of the empire. The harbour was spacious, and protected from the turbulence of the sea by a mole of great extent and strength. In crossing the Bay of Naples to arrive hither, a scene lay before the eye which it is impossible for any word-picture to describe. Ancient writers spake of it in terms of rapture; and a modern, speaking of the first glance obtained of it, says, " It was like a scene created by the hand of enchantment." Viewed from the deck of the " Castor and Pollux," the shore, thirty miles in circumference, was seen planted with populous cities, all with public buildings of proportions that at once filled the eye and gratified the taste. There were the cities of Naples, Herculaneum and Pompeii; and behind them, rising in solemn grandeur was the mountain Vesuvius, which, in less than twenty years afterwards, by a discharge of its boiling lava, and the scattering forth of its fiery ashes, entombed the two latter cities.

But to the spectator intelligent and learned, the scene possessed other attractions. After observations in the East, Luke now saw before him what was eminently classic ground in the West. Those enchanting shores had been chosen for the favourite retreats of philosophers, poets, and statesmen. Looking across the small bay in which Puteoli stands, at the distance of three miles, appeared the city of Baiæ, whose luxuriousness was a frequent theme for satirists. The shore from Baiæ, at the one extremity of the bay, to Puteoli on the other, was studded with villas of the aristocracy of Rome. Baiæ has disappeared, its site being, in a great part, covered by the sea; and Puteoli maintains only a shadowy existence, having, instead of above a hundred thousand, not more than ten thousand inhabitants. Relics of some of the objects on which Luke cast his eyes upon landing here are grimly visible. Of the mole, beside which his ship was moored, several arches remain, attesting its wonderful masonry. The amphitheatre, being a vast oval, a few gigantic columns of a temple of Serapis, and some other objects, memorialise periods of a very different character from the present.

But Luke was in no mood to linger over those scenes, nor was he able to appreciate them now. His friend, whom he attended as a companion, had come hither a prisoner: that circumstance spoiled all. But another source of interest, and one more congenial with his feelings, was at hand. "Here," he writes, "we found brethren, and were desired to tarry with them seven days." Here, then, again Paul was kindly treated by the centurion, in being permitted to comply with the invitation. With this pious community Luke and his companions "refreshed" themselves.

Having been gratified with a week's sojourn at Puteoli, Luke adds, "And so we went towards Rome." The knowledge that this was the last journey taken by him in company with Paul, will invest it with a melancholy interest in the mind of the reader. As the distance to Rome was about one hundred and forty miles, it is to be supposed that the journey was performed in an ordinary vehicle of the form of an open waggon, drawn by mules or horses, two or three abreast. The direct road to Rome ran beside the coast to Sinessa, where it came upon the Via Appia, which likewise from this town skirted the coast as far as to Terracina. At this place the highway diverged from the sea-side, and took a straight course to Rome, a distance from hence of about sixty miles.

The Romans, early sensible of the advantages arising from an easy and speedy communication with the different parts of their dominions, bestowed much attention to their highways, commonly called their consular or military roads. These roads, like the railroads of the present day, were carried on, as nearly as possible, in straight lines. Hills were sometimes levelled, valleys filled up, swamps drained, banks raised, ditches dug where inundations were apprehended, and bridges built over rivers and hollows. Thus the great south road derived its name from its founder, Appius Claudius Cæcus, who was consul of Rome in the year A.D. 296, and again in 307. Between each mile a pillar was raised to mark the distance from Rome; and at the end of about every twenty miles stations were established for the convenience of government couriers, and where relays of horses and mules were obtainable, and refreshment might be taken by travellers in general.

The first station reached on this part of the road was Appii Forum, a place, as its name indicates; in which a market was held and justice administered: its distance from Rome was forty-three miles. Horace has described, in humorous terms, a journey which he made with Mecænas along its whole extent from Rome to Brundusium. He says, "This part of our route, which to more active travellers than ourselves was a day's journey, we lazily took two to accomplish." And he represents the place as being "full of boatmen and vulgar innkeepers." Its adjacence to a canal, and the number of inns with which a market-place is usually surrounded, accounts for this description. Upon arriving at Sinessa, Horace and his companion were joined by Virgil, Plotius, and Varius, from their respective residences in the neighbourhood of Puteoli and Baiæ. That was a memorable meeting and fellowship of genius. And the picture of it is not too highly toned, where the poet, describing his companions and his feelings upon the occasion, writes—

> " Souls more candid ne'er trod the earth
> To none am I more strongly bound :
> Oh, what embraces, what joys were there !"
>
> —*Sat.* i. 5.

Now a band of another fellowship than that of mere genius—one of a holier element—travels that road, who also are met by friends that accompany them throughout the rest of the journey. "When," writes Luke, "the brethren heard of us, they came to meet us as far as Appii Forum." Who would have been the friends that manifested such devotion to the Apostle and his companions as to travel so far to meet them, but those who had invited him to visit them, and to whom he had written the letter in which he informed them of his intention to comply with their request? Their haste to welcome him was befitting their having made that invitation. It proved their sympathy with him, and their sorrow that he should be coming to Rome a prisoner; and it justifies the epithets with which several of their names are coupled in the salutations of that epistle. Surely at the meeting of such friends as these, and under such circumstances, it might have been again said—

"Oh, what embraces were there!"

As they were within a day's journey from Rome, the combined parties may have rested that night at Appii Forum, and have resumed the journey betimes on the morrow. *Tres Tiburnæ*, which was the next and intermediate station towards Rome, was of small extent, having three inns, which gave the name to the place. It was probably resorted to by the inhabitants of Rome for recreation, as Cicero speaks of having come hither to celebrate the festival of Ceres. At this station another party of brethren from Rome was found, waiting to welcome the Apostle. These may be supposed to have been some who were less robust than the former, and with the party were probably some of those women who are named with commendation in the Epistle to the Romans. This second manifestation of sympathy for him had an impressive and salutary effect upon Paul's mind. He had been unable to repress melancholy musings on the difference of his situation, upon entering the capital, to what he had expected it

to be when he addressed his epistle to the friends composing those saintly bands. But by this interview his
feelings became elevated. And Luke's pleasure in witnessing the change appears in the observation added to his
notice of the meeting, " Then Paul took courage." They
had proved to him messengers of peace.

From hence, the combined parties moving forward,
they rapidly passed Aricia, a town of infamous repute,
where Diana was worshipped with inhuman rites, whereof
enough appears in the fact, that her priest was always a
runaway slave, who succeeded to the office by killing his predecessor in a match at single combat. Luke had seen the
memorials of the dead beside cities in Africa and Greece.
He came now upon a scene significant both of vanity and
of woe transcending any that he had before beheld. From
Aricia, which was twelve miles from the capital, every
other object—-the celebrated spots on either hand, the fine
eminences, the several temples, the elegant villas, the long
lines of arched aqueducts, all lost their interest with the
traveller by reason of the stronger appeal made to the
imagination by the great number and ever-varying character
of the sepulchres and monuments that thronged the road.
This vast necropolis extended a quarter or half a mile deep
on either side, up to the walls of the city. Monuments of
Romans of renown or wealth, dating a long antiquity, and
stately tombs of recent periods, presented an impressive
illustration of almost every stage in the Roman history.
And even now, after the devastations of all kinds, proceeding
through nearly eighteen centuries, travellers observe that
there is nothing so sublimely melancholy as a journey along
this road in view of the mute memorials, still subsisting, of
those once mighty rulers. It is said by a learned traveller:
" The entrance to Rome from the side of Naples exceeds
anything that Italy can produce, and of which no description can be exaggerated. This is the only road from which

the whole city is actually surveyed" (Burton's " Antiquities of Rome "). But it may be thought that Luke was too much occupied in conversation with some of the brethren who had just joined his company, or engaged in observing the happy effect of their presence upon Paul, to receive the full impression of those scenes. And presently the journey ended; they entered Rome, company after company, through the Porta Capena.

CHAPTER XXVII.

The First Part.

ROME was now entered by the travellers, the period being, as is supposed, early in the year A.D. 62. Luke's long wished-for visit to the metropolis of the world was at length accomplished. The prayer that had been offered by Paul and by his friends here, at his request, " that he might come to them by the will of God," was now answered. This event is the culminating point of Luke's journal. They had started together propitiously from Macedonia, but soon intimations were given of the hindrances that succeeded. Paul's imprisonment seemed an insuperable obstacle ; yet a bow appeared in the clouds. Assurance was given and repeated by their Lord that Paul should testify for Him in Rome ; and the structure of Luke's narrative was set to magnify that word. His account of the several proceedings against Paul in Palestine—his details of the voyage and the shipwreck, all serve to give effect to the issue, and to stamp it as a remarkable record of the divine faithfulness. Although his friend had come as a prisoner from a distant province, yet, by the divine favour, his situation had been attended throughout by several mitigations. After the example of Joseph, the patriarch, when in prison in Egypt, Paul had acquired the esteem, and obtained the obliging conduct towards him, of

the successive officers to whose charge he had been committed. During the voyage, Julius, the Roman officer, had
treated him more like a companion than as a prisoner. He
had consulted his convenience on every occasion. Of course
Paul's respectful acknowledgments had followed ; and hence
mutual esteem naturally arose by the courtesy of the one,
and the pious and befitting behaviour of the other. And
as they had been fellow-sufferers during the tempest and in
the shipwreck, and as Paul's presence had been the means
of saving his life and the lives of all on board, the Roman
soldier and the Christian prophet would naturally come to
entertain for each other mutual sentiments of gratitude and
respect.

Luke now writes, " And when we came to Rome, the
centurion delivered the prisoners to the military commander," called in Latin *Præfectus Prætorio.* The quarters
of the Prætorian or imperial guards was called *Castrum
Prætorium.* It was situated on the north-east, without the
walls of the city, but since enclosed by them. Much of the
said building remains, some parts having been repaired with
the old materials. Thither, therefore, the centurion's
prisoners were conducted. And, as this is the only place
in Rome to which the presence of Paul can actually be
traced, that edifice will be an object of interest to the
Christian traveller.

By the care of Julius, the attention of the prefect was
especially directed to the case of Paul. Having handed to
the magistrate the report of Festus concerning him, wherein
it would have been stated that no criminal act had been
proved against him, the centurion would certainly thereupon offer a representation suitable to his own feelings,
and relate some of the features of Paul's admirable conduct
as observed by him during the time he had been in his
custody. The prefect's attention was hereby engaged towards Paul's case, and the happy effect thereof was

immediate. Instead of sending him to associate with other prisoners, he ordered that he should enjoy the utmost privilege consistent with his position as a state-prisoner. And the gratification with which Luke listened to this adjudication is discerned in his words, " But suffered Paul to dwell by *himself*, with a soldier that kept him." No need is there to question with what class Paul found the accommodation of a lodging. It does not appear that Aquila and Priscilla were in Rome at this time, or he had certainly been seized on by that exemplary couple for their guest. But, in the absence of these, there would have been many who, " given to hospitality," would hail as a privilege an opportunity to afford the Apostle that accommodation. Some of those Christians were now by his side who, having gone forth to meet him, had not retired until they had seen in what manner he was disposed of. By one of those friends he would surely have been received to his home, albeit burdened with the presence of the soldier that kept him.

Thus, then, by the favour of his divine Master's providence, was Paul permitted to " refresh himself with his friends in Rome " (Rom. xv. 32). Nor can it be supposed that his two comforters were separated from him, but that Luke and Aristarchus were likewise invited to the same dwelling. Having come to their lodging, and ere they retired to rest, what communings would arise between these three confessors! How would the sad situation of the Apostle, and yet its alleviations, the mishaps of their journey and its mercies, the novelty of their present situation, the fears and hopes commingling respecting their future ministry, and how far and in what manner it might be prosecuted in their peculiar case, occupy their minds and compel consideration!

Here, again, on the morrow, would their friends gather around them. Here, too, those saints who had not a previous acquaintance with him would come to look upon the face of the writer of the letter he had addressed to them from Corinth, so sublime in doctrine, and so loving in its personal allusions.

Speedily was Paul's ministry in Rome commenced. Following his Master's order, he had always borne his testimony first to Jews. But now he had an additional reason for wishing to address them at the earliest opportunity—the reason being that he might explain the circumstances that caused his coming hither a prisoner. He could not attend their synagogue, so he obtained notice to be given to the principal Jews in the city—which was easy to do, as they resided in a particular locality—of his wish for an interview with them at his lodging. Accordingly, on the third day after his arrival, several attended, to whom he explained his case, as the Jews in Jerusalem were concerned in it, protesting, in conclusion, "Therefore have I called for you, to see you, and to speak with you ; because for the 'Hope of Israel' I am bound with this chain." At this interview his hearers responded with candour, and expressed a desire that he would let them hear him again concerning his doctrine, which they regarded as being one held by a sect that had recently arisen among the Jews.

By a meeting, therefore, of their own appointment, an opportunity was given to Paul to deliver his first testimony for Christ in Rome. That was an eventful meeting, inasmuch as it was also the last occasion recorded of a formal conference held by Paul with a company of Jews. Nevertheless, dispensing with a recital of the arguments of Paul's discourse, Luke only says, in a summary way, " There came many to him into his lodging, to whom he expounded the kingdom of God, persuading them concerning Jesus out of the law of Moses, and out of the prophets." The reason for the historian's brevity, it may be thought, was the similarity of the discourse with those which Paul had formerly addressed to Jews, two of which are given at adequate length, one in a synagogue in Antioch in Pisidia, and the other in Jerusalem, from the stairs of the castle. Luke intimates the earnestness with which Paul spake, and the close attention given to his discourse by the audience, by the note, that they were engaged herein "from morning until evening." He depicts the temper of the Jews by noticing the yielding belief to Paul's doctrine by some, and the persistence in unbelief by others. And he exhibits the effect of the rejection of the gospel by the latter upon Paul's mind by producing the terms by which he concluded his testimony, his application of a prophetic rebuke to them, and the emphatic utterance of his resolve to turn to the Gentiles, who would hear it. This is the last of those historical sketches which have formed the life-spring of these biographical exercises. In observing this, a feeling of sadness is experienced, akin to that of casting a last and farewell glance upon scenes which have been frequented, full of beauty, and fragrant with all that could commend them to the senses, and which, besides, were tinged with that ethereal loveliness which was imparted to them by the companionship of a friend whose intelligence and piety commanded sympathy and veneration.

Here, then, was Luke in that great city, the *Imperium Terris*, as it is named by Virgil. From whatever point regarded, Rome had a remarkable appearance. It occupied seven hills, with their valleys. And although some of those hills are not very distinguishable now, they were all prominent then. Luke had not desired to come hither to gratify curiosity or taste in respect of objects mundane; yet, as in the several cities he had visited before, so here the prominent features of the place would not escape his observation. At every step some object of interest met the eye : palaces and temples adorning the hills, and theatres and other edifices of vast proportions occupying sites in the plains. Indeed, vastness was the chief feature of Rome. Never before had he seen such an assemblage of great buildings. In eastern countries public buildings were chiefly made of marble or stone, and, except in Egypt, were of moderate dimensions. But in Rome, the larger were constructed of bricks, the walls being of great breadth, and their height in proportion. Among the useful as well as ornamental erections were the porticos. These in his walks Luke would have had occasion sometimes to traverse. The Romans were fond of columns. And the shelter from sunshine or showers which colonnades afforded rendered them very convenient, whilst the number and loftiness of the columns fitted them to adorn the great buildings around or beside which they were erected. Paved with Mosaic tiles, they formed pleasant promenades. But besides this, the porticos were used for various purposes, according to locality. Under the shade of some of them magistrates held their courts; in others, articles were exposed for sale; in others, rhetoricians exemplified their rules; in others, lectures were delivered by moralists and sophists to congregated pupils. Babels of philosophy were the porticos where those lecturers were found. There almost every sect, African, Greek, and Roman, were represented; and there harangues might be daily heard from the cynic, who declared the excellence of poverty and filthiness; the epicurean, who, on the ground of the doctrine of life's finality, recommended an indulgence of the appetites, and who commended himself to the tables of the rich at once by the suavity of his manners and the neatness of his attire.

Here Luke might have seen Demetrius, the stoic of Corinth, who was in Rome at this time; and concerning whom Seneca said, "Leaving the nobles clad in purple, I converse with and admire the half-naked Demetrius. And why do I admire him? but because I perceive that in the midst of poverty, he wants nothing. When I hear this excellent man discoursing from his couch of straw, I perceive in him not a preceptor only, but a witness of the truth ; and I cannot doubt that Providence has endowed him with such virtues and talents that he might be an example and a monitor to the present age." One of this philosopher's maxims was : " It is better to have a few principles of wisdom always at hand to use, than to learn many things which cannot be applied to practice." Demetrius was afterwards expelled from Rome for having reflected upon the vices of the Emperor. When he returned to Corinth, he visited Musonius, who had been banished to the Isthmus of Corinth for the same cause. He found Musonius labouring as a slave with a spade ; and expressing grief for the misfortune of his friend, Musonius, striking his spade into the ground, replied, " Why, Demetrius, do you lament to see me digging in the isthmus ? You might lament if you saw me, like Nero, playing upon the harp " (" Enfield's History of Philosophy," vol. ii.)

The number of inhabitants in Rome at this period has been differently computed from two to four millions. But as the suburbs of the city, like those of London, extended several miles around, and were likewise very populous, the lower figures might have related only to the city, and the others to both the city and the suburbs, although, even then, they are generally thought to exceed the reality. Athenæus writes : " Rome presents a people collected from all parts of the globe. The city may be called an epitome of the universe. Here are seen the rich Alexandrian, the beauty of Antioch, the brilliant Nicomedian " (Book i.)

Upon the arrival of our company in Rome, the Emperor Nero was in the eighth year of his reign, having succeeded Claudius in October A.D. 54. His education had been conducted by eminent teachers, the principal of whom were Burrus for athletic training, and Seneca for mental. Both of these had been afterwards honoured and enriched by the favour of the Emperor; and both of them were at that moment the prefects or chief magistrates of the city,—Burrus being the military commander, and Seneca chief of the civil departments. It was to the custody of Burrus that Paul had been committed. Nero had commenced his reign in a manner consistent with what had been the character of their teaching. But soon, like too many young persons, he chose evil counsellors, who prejudiced him against his former ones, suggesting to him that he had been long enough under tutors ; and more than this, who influenced the malignity latent in his nature. Thereafter, upon different pretexts, Burrus and Seneca were deposed. Burrus was poisoned in the next year after the arrival of Luke in Rome ; and two years later, Seneca was made to commit self-destruction. It does not appear, however, that Seneca died a martyr for his "morals," but that he was sentenced to death in consequence of meddling with the broils of the imperial family. Luke may, in the course of his movements about Rome, have seen Seneca. But certainly Paul's situation did not admit the probability of such a circumstance. Paul had formerly seen Seneca's eldest brother, Marcus Annæus Novatus, who changed his name to Junius Gallio, by whom he had been adopted. To Gallio, Seneca dedicated his " Discourse on a Happy Life." As the proconsul of Achaia, Paul had been brought before Gallio by the Jews at Corinth ; but being a Stoic, and following the then Roman rule of toleration in worship, he abruptly refused to enter into the charge (Acts xviii. 12–17).

Absurd as curious is a fictitious correspondence between Seneca and Paul. The letters composing it are fourteen in number, varying in length from five to twenty-five lines each. The correspondence opens with a letter addressed by the philosopher to the Apostle, in which it is represented that the writing of it was suggested by a conversation held with Lucilius in the garden of Sallust, some of Paul's disciples being in their company. It speaks of the writer's having read some of Paul's epistles. All the letters, including the pretended replies to them of Paul, are little more than complimentary. The name of Christ is not mentioned throughout, and they have other discrepancies besides. So that it would be no inappropriate guess to suppose that they were composed, as a frolicsome exercise, by one of Constantine's too quickly-made Christians. Nevertheless, Jerome, in his "List of Ecclesiastical Writers," professes that, on account of those letters, he was induced to number Seneca with the saints : a profound mistake; for, independently of the character of the letters, saints do not engage in plots; neither will they, with intellect intact, die by their own hands.

Important to Luke was his opportunity for an observation of the world of mind by which he was surrounded, in respect to its moral and religious character. That character was conspicuously symbolised by the public buildings. The number and size of the theatres gave evidence of the devotion of the Romans to their amusements; whilst a sight of the chief of them, the amphitheatre, of colossal proportions, would have raised a feeling of awe in the mind of the Christian beholder, knowing that, at seasons, spectators pressed into it by scores of thousands to gratify their taste for the scenes of fatal heroism and sanguinary cruelties therein exhibited. And still does the amphitheatre retain a mournful memory. For therein, not long afterwards, Christians were cast to wild beasts, that wilder men might gloat over the agonies of their martyrdom.

And as the theatres illustrated the sensual tendencies of the population, no less did the temples, which everywhere met the eye, betoken the prevalence of superstition. The number of these in Rome at that period was at least three hundred. Some years later they were said to amount to four hundred. Among the gods to whom those temples were dedicated there existed classes aristocratic and plebeian,—distinctions which, like Swedenborg's doctrine of correspondencies, were adapted to the ranks of Roman society. And as there was no special order of priesthood established among the Romans, the ceremonies appertaining to the superior gods were performed by distinguished patricians, the Emperor himself being the *Pontifex Maximus*, to whom also belonged the magistracy of the temples in general. But there was a further peculiarity about the religious element of Rome. Whatever country had been subdued, the people thereof were allowed to retain their own gods and ceremonies. So that Gibbon says, " Rome being filled with subjects and strangers from every part of the world, who were all permitted to enjoy therein the particular superstitions of their country, it became, hereby the common temple of her subjects ; and," he adds, " the freedom of the city was bestowed upon all the gods of mankind." It was on this account that Rome obtained the name of *Urbs Deorum*. And to suit this catholicity was the object of the Pantheon, a temple dedicated to Jupiter and all gods, an innumerable company ! The varieties of Jupiter alone, white and black, benign and terrible, and of different denominations, were reckoned to be above three hundred by Varro, called " the most learned of Romans," and who had been appointed by Julius Cæsar to be his librarian.

Often must the Pantheon, cased with marble, with its noble portico and circular dome, have been within the vision of Luke in his walks through the city. Standing in the Campus Martius, a large plain beside the Tiber, the Pantheon still remains the most perfect of all the temples of Ancient Rome. The visitor now, however, will see it shorn of its marble casing. Early in the seventh century this building was given by the Emperor Phocas to Pope Boniface IV., who, quite characteristically, after an exor-

cism and a plenteous lustration, deposited therein thirty-
six waggon-loads of *bones* fetched from neighbouring
cemeteries, and placed both the temple and them under
another protectorate, renaming the building, " St *Mary ad
Martyres.*" It is a curious observation that, twelve hundred
years after that consecration, out of the hundred churches
existing in Rome, twenty-six are dedicated to Mary, *one* to
Jesus and Mary, and *one* to JESUS alone! An observation
of the morals of the vast population of Rome was a subject
constantly forced upon the reflecting visitor. Luke saw
their melancholy variance with the purity of the divine
law. Persons living in great cities, where the gospel has
been established for centuries, are nevertheless sensible to
what a mass of corruption they are neighbours. But how
immeasurably greater than this was the corruption of manners witnessed in the Roman metropolis, whose whole community, excepting the few Jews and Christians therein,
was in ignorance of God's holy law! The wisdom of the
Romans in the science of legislation is acknowledged, and
also the excellence of some of the maxims of their moralists.
But this wisdom and excellence only rendered the evil of
their manners the more conspicuous. Their legislature lacked
the breadth that touched licentiousness, and their philosophy was exclusive, neither reaching, nor being intended
to reach, the people in general. The corruption of these, un-
checked by virtuous teaching, was nourished by their public amusements and superstitions ; the former being often
brutal, and the latter libidinous ; whilst the Cæsar now occupying the throne, being a profligate, his example, together
with that of his courtiers, gave a full licence to vice. Luke
had been familiar with various aspects of heathenism, but
never before had he witnessed it under a development so
vile and so vast. By contemporary satirists, the vicious-
ness of the lives of the Romans of all classes was sometimes exposed. But however dexterous at pointing the

barbed arrow were these, they were but lame moralists, as the student of the classics too well knows. Ample is the corroboration found in their pages of the impressive description of heathenism set in the front of the Epistle to the Romans, wherein the vices enumerated are twenty-two in number ;—a catalogue which intimated to his correspondents the writer's knowledge of the monster with which he would have to combat in the chief seat of its empire,—a description which forms a fitting supplement to pictures of idolators occurring throughout the Books of the Prophets.

At this point Luke's narrative, hitherto the delighful fount of his biography, is suspended. That it was not carried forward so as to include Paul's appearances before Nero, and to have completed the argument of the fulfilling of Christ's declaration concerning His servant, has been the regret of many readers, and has raised the cavil of some. The surmises to account for its discontinuance have been various. A reasonable supposition is, that it was regarded by the writer, and by his friends, to have been inexpedient to publish particulars of Paul's proceedings, pending the decision of his cause by the Emperor. Perhaps after that Luke was unable, from some cause now unknown, to put his hand again to the subject. Happily, however, after a long interval, he subjoined to his narrative a POSTCRIPT, wherein an outline is given of Paul's situation when he had been two years in Rome. As Luke's own situation is only to be gathered from that of Paul, this short addendum possesses a double value. Like some of Luke's former summaries, this postscript is largely suggestive. Its intelligence is comprised in five items.

The *first* of these items relates, that "*Paul dwelt two whole years in his own hired house.*" This note is as interesting as it is significant. It shows that Paul used his privilege of a choice of residence to the utmost. His great soul contemplated a great work, although he was in bonds. Here was Rome, and there was the world beyond, and he would reach them both as far as he might. Lodgings were too strait for his temperament and purpose, whether supplied by friends or hired. He required the convenience of an entire house. An idea may be obtained of his situation upon this change of residence by a glance at a house of that place and period. A house occupied by one family was called *domus,* as in Scotland such a residence is called a *self-contained house.* The houses in Rome wore a dull appearance, having no windows like modern ones, but only narrow openings, with wooden folds or slides. The principal entrance was approached by two or more steps. The apartment into which the gate opened was the *atrium,* or hall. This, being a larger apartment than any other, was the audience-chamber, around which ornamental furniture was arranged. It was also used as the *supper-room.* Resembling this apartment were the ancient .baronial halls of England. Beyond this apartment, and opposite the gate, was the *tablinum,* or library ; and on either hand of the hall were other apartments. Generally, there was only one other suite of rooms above. By this change in Paul's residence was added another Christian household to those that existed in Rome. To the reader loving a domestic life, the notice of this feature of the Apostle's life will be regarded with pleasure. Besides other assistants, the household would have required the services of a female manager, who, in this case, would have been a saintly matron, perchance one of the widows for whom the Churches were taught especially to care. Paul's companions, Luke and Aristarchus, would probably have formed part of the family, as would Timothy, upon the occasions of his visiting his father in the gospel. Also, in succession, other fellow-labourers, arriving from their several spheres, would partake the hospitality of the large-hearted host. Here, then, in Paul's own hired house was founded the first college *de Propaganda Fide,* or mission-house, a focus of communication with branches of the great work of evangelisation in the city and throughout the Roman world. Such was the situation of this "ambassador in bonds" in Rome.

The *second item* of the postscript relates, " *He received all that came in unto him.*" Hereby is testified the liberty Paul enjoyed of free intercourse with society, and also his own catholic behaviour. As he could no longer go about doing good, he dispensed his beneficent ministry in a house open to all comers. He had said in his epistle written from Corinth to the Romans, "I long to see you, that I may impart unto you some spiritual gift, to the end that ye may be established; that is, that I may be comforted, together with you, by the mutual faith both of you and me" (i. 11, 12). And now the opportunity to gratify that desire was afforded in his own house.

The *third item* relates, " *Preaching the kingdom of God, and teaching those things which concern the Lord Jesus.*" It was important that this particular should be mentioned; for what is here announced had been the chief object contemplated by Paul in his desire to come to Rome. It had been the thrice-promised word of his divine Master, after his arrest, that he should go to Rome, and there testify for Him. And now the fact of the fulfilment of that word forms the final link in Luke's historic chain. But under other circumstances than those which he had hoped for, did Paul devote himself to his favourite work. He who had gone forth, and for years had fully preached the gospel from Judea to Illyricum, was compelled to confine his preaching to the compass of the *atrium* of his own house.

The *fourth item* relates that Paul's ministry was prosecuted " *with all confidence.*" Paul had declared, when contemplating a visit to Rome, "I am not ashamed of the gospel of Christ; I am ready to preach it to you that are at Rome also." By this item is told the freedom of spirit with which he fulfilled his ministry.   How, in the proudest city in the world, would a Jew be accepted as a teacher, and he a prisoner remitted from Palestine?   Or how would his doctrine be received concerning the claims of a Jew, that had been crucified at Jerusalem, to be a divine Redeemer?   Yet so stood Paul before his audiences at Rome, and such was the doctrine he preached.   With all confidence he preached faith in Christ crucified, and afterwards glorified, as the only way of salvation,—a way so simple that it will never be taken by the proud and self-reliant, but only by the humble and meek ; a way so straight that only the unembarrassed by the vanities of human sapience or the love of the world, can ever enter it.   Besides this way, there are a hundred of other ways by which the world is confounded and souls are lost.   And that Paul felt the gravity of his actual situation, and how much to preach the gospel with all confidence, required a courage inspired by divine grace, is seen in a request which he made to the Ephesians in the letter written at this time, wherein, advising to prayerfulness, he adds, " And for me that utterance may be given unto me, that I may open my mouth boldly, to make known the mystery of God, for which I am an ambassador in bonds, that therein I may speak boldly as I ought to speak" (Eph. vi. 19, 20).

And the *fifth item* confirms the previous particulars, " *no man forbidding him.*"   In this last note the divine Master's overruling hand is recognised.   Paul had been brought by His providence to Rome.   Here he was to bear a testimony for Him.   All hearts are in Christ's hands.   Throughout the various steps of His servant hither, He had caused him to be regarded with favour by his keepers ; so here likewise. And in this postscript, Luke resumes his pen to inform Theophilus and the reader in general, that Paul had been able to prosecute the ministry for which he came to Rome, albeit in bonds, yet without hindrance by the civil authorities, or the opposition of others.

What an example of simplicity of purpose do the lines of this postcript reveal ! And how much Luke was in sympathy with that divine purpose, appears from his having denoted Paul's actual situation in Rome ere he dropped his pen finally.

It has been appropriately said by an expositor under this postscript, " Instead of pouring forth the sigh of unavailing regret that the sacred historian has carried us no farther onward, we should rather speak the language of praise that he has given, by the inspiration of the Holy Ghost, a history of the Church for thirty years after the ascension of the Saviour; that he has recorded the accounts of the first great revivals of religion; that he has presented to us the examples of the early missionary zeal ; that he has informed us how the early Christians endured persecution and toil ; that he has conducted us from land to land, and from city to city, showing us everywhere how the gospel was propagated, until we are led to the seat of the Roman power, and see the great Apostle of Christianity there proclaiming in that mighty capital of the world the name of Jesus as the Saviour of men" (Albert Barnes).

A digression may be permitted here. Besides his other occupations in Rome, Luke is represented by ecclesiastical fabulists to have exercised the art of painting. And, although no original copy of his writings exists, several of his paintings are professed to be preserved in Rome, and in other places in Italy. It is related by the Rev. William Arthur, in his " Italy in Transition,"—" At the Lateran (at the top of the Holy Stair) is a little dark chapel ; you can see through the grating, and read a Latin inscription to the effect that there is not upon earth a spot more holy. No woman may enter. It contains a picture by St Luke, said to be an exact likeness of the Saviour when twelve years of age" (p. 317). Another, being the most famous of those pictures, is the one placed over the altar in the chapel *della Madonna*, attached to the Basilica of the Church of *Santa Maria Maggiore.* By the side of this picture is suspended a Bull by Pope Pius the Sixth, attesting its authenticity. A history and description of this picture has lately been published by the Abbé Milochan, canon of Rennes. In that publication it is said, " To the left (under the cupola), the visitor perceives no other object of his worship than a simple picture, the work of a mediocre painter, blackened by age, for which the sovereign pontiffs have not thought it too much to erect this chapel, than which no chapel in Rome is more splendid ; for the reason that this picture is the first which received the homage of the faithful, the true portrait of the Holy Virgin, painted by the same hand that in the Gospel traced the history of the infancy of Jesus, and his relations with His mother." * According to the representations of this writer, the Romans would seem to have been more indebted to this picture than to Luke's writings. Among other of its miracles, it is said that, upon the occasion of the raging of a plague in Rome, the picture having been carried in a procession, attended by the Pope and priests chanting litanies to the Virgin, the plague was thereupon stayed. Corresponding with the virtue attributed to it, is the marvel concerning it reported to Max Misson, when, in company with the Earl of Arran, he visited the chapel in 1688, namely, that sometimes the singing of anthems by angels was heard from above the picture.† And speaking of another of these paintings, it is said by Mrs Jameson, in her "Legends of the Madonna,"—"Of the many miracle-working Madonnas in Italy popularly attributed to St Luke, the Virgin of the Ara-Celi is undoubtedly Greek, and old and black and ugly as sanctity could desire" (p. 116). If any refutation be needed of the pretensions made con-

* " La Vièrge de Saint Luc, à Sainte Marie Majeure."   Paris, 1862.
† " Voyage d'Italie," vol. ii., p. 215.

cerning those pictures, the following considerations may suffice :—

1. "The profession of a painter was profane and odious in the eyes of the primitive Christians" (Gibbon).

2. There is found no notice concerning any painting attributed to Luke until the sixth century, when Theodore Lector relates that "Eudocia, the wife of the Emperor Theodosius, junior, sent from Jerusalem, about the year 448, the image or picture of the Virgin to Pulcheria, the Emperor's sister, which was painted by Luke the Apostle."

3. Upon the head of the sketch of the portrait which is prefixed to the Abbé Milochan's book, is drawn a small ✠; the presence of which emphatically contradicts all vouchers for the authenticity of the theory as a work of Luke's, that symbol being the "mark" of the prophecy Revelations xiii. 16, 17.

4. The authenticity of those pictures is repudiated by intelligent Italians. In 1766 was published an essay, read to the Academy at Volterra, by Domenico Manni, "Concerning the Error which attributes the Paintings to the Evangelist."*

5. And—alas! for the credit of the Pope's bull of authentication—it appears from Lanzi's "History of Painting in Italy," that the legend affirming that Luke had been a painter arose from confounding him with a Greek hermit of the name of Lucas, who, with other artists, drew those dingy pictures to supply the demand that arose for them among the churches.

An institute of painters was founded at Rome in 1595, called "The Academy of Saint Luke." This dedication had been consistent if it was given in consideration of the obligation of the early painters to his writings. For to these more than to any other parts of Holy Scripture, were they,

---

* "Dell Errore che persiste di attribuirsi le Pitture al S. Evangelista." Firenze, 1766. 4to, 24 pages.

indebted for their subjects. In the academy is preserved a picture of St Luke by Raphael, in which the Evangelist is represented in the act of executing a portrait of the Virgin and Child. There are likewise possessed by the Academy Raphael's own portrait, painted by himself, and his veritable skull in a casket.

There is a portrait of St Luke by Van Sichem, a Flemish artist, painted about the year 1600, an engraved copy of which is now in the hand of the writer of this biography. In this engraving the Evangelist is represented as a Dutch professor, with the bonnet or cap usually worn at that period. Embracing the ideas of a threefold profession, he is depicted seated at a table in his study, with a pen in his hand, and his two books before him : facing him is an easel, whereupon is a picture of the Virgin and Child, and behind him, on a shelf, is a row of bottles and jars.

CHAPTER XXVIII.

The Second Part.

HENCEFORTH the sole source of information concerning Luke's history is to be found in St Paul's epistles written at Rome. In these many are the glimpses afforded of the persons composing the Apostle's band of comforters and fellow-helpers. From Luke's relations with the writer, he was acquainted with his being engaged in composing those letters ; and from the interest he took in the history of the Churches, and welfare of the persons addressed, Paul would have freely communicated to him the topics of his correspondence. Upon the circumstance that in Paul's epistles written in Rome Luke is mentioned only three times, Bishop Wordsworth has these interesting remarks : " Certainly there was something more than accidental in the fact that a person who was so constant an attendant on St Paul as St Luke was in his voyages and imprisonments, and who was chosen by the Holy Ghost to write the history—the only history—of his acts, as well as one of the Gospels, has received so little notice by name from St Paul in his epistles." And after the query, "What can be the reason of this silence ?" the Bishop answers by beautifully saying, "None more probable it seems can be assigned, than that the Apostle would thus show that the blessed Evangelist St Luke acted, wrote, and suffered with a higher aim than for praise, even from the lips of an apostle, and that he whose *praise* is the *Gospel* needed no other praise ; and that the Apostle would not expose himself to the imputation of having purchased the honourable record from the apostolic historian by panegyrising the historian himself."

It is, however, gratifying to notice, that in all the epistles wherein salutations are delivered from the writer's associates, Luke being present, as in that written at Corinth, and in the three written at Rome, his name is found. Admirable are the illustrations of his situation, and highly illustrative of his character are the notices of him, which those instances afford.

The first of this series of letters is the *Epistle to the* EPHESIANS, set, however, by some critics, after the epistles to the Colossians and Philemon. Ephesus had been Paul's chief station in Asia Minor, and from thence had sounded forth the Word of Life throughout the provinces. He had resided at Ephesus at first for a short period, and afterwards during two years. In his address to the Church of Ephesus, therefore, the Churches throughout Asia were likewise included. In this epistle no other name is mentioned than that of Tychichus, the bearer of the letter to Ephesus (vi. 21). Tychichus was a minister of the Church at Ephesus, and had come to Rome to assist the Apostle in his evangelical labours. His arrival was cheering to Paul and agreeable to his companions. His character and services in the gospel would have strongly commended him to Luke, and this opportunity of fellowship with him he would have much prized. To Luke he was not a stranger. He had been of the party that preceded Paul and Luke in going from Macedonia to Troas (Acts xx. 4). That one other name, that of Timothy—consecrated by tradition the first Bishop of Ephesus—is not found in the epistle addressed to the Church of his own diocese, is somewhat perplexing, seeing he was in Rome when the letter was written. The interest taken by Luke in this communication may be estimated by the historical notices of the Church at Ephesus contained in his Acts of the Apostles, furnished to him by Paul himself. To the reader this epistle may serve for a specimen of the Apostle's teaching in Rome. The affluence of thought herein, and the unction crowning every sentence of it, testify his enjoyment of the promised presence of the Master.

In the Epistle to the Romans, composed when Paul was at freedom, and in the full tide of his successes, two classes of persons were addressed—Jews and Gentiles. He therein argued the comprehensiveness of the New Covenant, the admission into it of all believers in Jesus Christ, irrespective of nationalities. Upon his arrival in Rome, having expounded the gospel to an assembly of Jews, who, with the exception of a remnant, rejected his counsel, he declared to them his purpose to turn to the Gentiles. When composing this epistle, surrounded chiefly by Gentile companions, he is seen a believing Jew exulting in the new position of Gentiles before God. After expounding, in his Epistle to the Romans, this mystery, Paul broke forth with the exclamation, "O the depth of the riches both of the wisdom and knowledge of God! how unsearchable are His judgments, and His ways past finding out!" But here having spoken of the grace given to him that he should preach among the Gentiles the unsearchable riches of Christ, in harmony with his situation as the prisoner of the Lord, his feelings flow in the calmer utterance of prayer, and he meekly says, "I bow my knees unto the Father of our Lord Jesus Christ, of whom the whole family in heaven and earth is named, that He would grant you, according to the riches of His glory," &c. (iii. 14–21). The Jews prized the prophetic blessing of their patriarchs; and in this prayer was expressed an apostle's blessing upon the Church of Christ, of every place and of every generation. A Jew pleading this prayer for Gentiles, and he a prisoner for their cause !   What a sight was that for Luke and Aristarchus !

The epistle opens with a note of congratulation to the Ephesian Church upon their accession to a new relationship with God through Jesus Christ.   It is observable that their election and position are illustrated by characteristics peculiar to the Mosaic economy.   Thus the tribes of Jacob were chosen to be a peculiar people unto God : and Paul writes, " According as He hath *chosen* us in Him before the foundation of the world."   They were chosen on the ground of the sovereignty of the divine love (Deut. vii. 7, 8) : and Paul writes, " For by grace are ye saved, through faith, and that not of yourselves ; *it is the gift of God.*"   The Jews received a seal of their personal adoption, as it is explained, " And he received the sign of circumcision, a seal," &c. (Rom. iv. 11) : and Paul writes to the Gentiles. "In whom also, after that ye believed, ye were *sealed* with that Holy Spirit of promise."   The Jews were redeemed from a bondage : and he writes, " In whom we have *redemption* through His blood, the forgiveness of sins, according to the riches of His grace."   The Jews obtained an inheritance in Canaan by divine appointment : and Paul says of the Gentiles, " In whom also we have obtained *an inheritance* according to the purpose of Him who worketh all things after the counsel of His own will."   The Jews had a temple : and he writes, " And are built upon the foundation of prophets and apostles, Jesus Christ himself being the chief, in whom all the building fitly framed together groweth unto a *holy temple* in the Lord."   The Jews had Moses for their chief : and Paul writes, concerning Jesus Christ, " And gave Him to be the *Head* of all things to His Church." The Jews were assigned to be God's witnesses to the world : whereupon Paul writes, "And came and *preached peace* to you which were afar off, and to them that were nigh.   Finally, in the temple was a wall, separating the Gentiles from the holy congregation : and Paul writes, "Who hath broken down *the wall of partition;* now therefore ye are no more strangers and foreigners, but fellow citizens with the saints, and of the household of God."

The Epistle to the COLOSSIANS is the second of this series. It is inscribed, "To the saints and faithful brethren." Here the members of the Church in general precede the ministers, being bishops and deacons, designated by their character only. In this epistle is obtained the first glance of the principal of those who were associated in Paul's " own hired house." In noticing these the grateful hand has set a characteristic signature of appreciation after each name, one excepted. The names, with the notifications affixed to them, are these—

1. " *Timothy, our brother.*" His name is joined with the writer's in the inscription of the epistle.

2. " *Epaphras, our dear fellow-servant, who is for you a faithful minister of Jesus Christ ; who also declared unto us your love in the Spirit*" (i. 7). And again, " *Epaphras saluteth you, always labouring for you in prayers that ye may stand perfect and complete in all the will of God. For I bear him record that he hath a great zeal for you and them in Laodicea and them in Hieropolis*" (iv. 12, 13). Epaphras had come to Rome to take the place of the next-mentioned as a missionary assistant in Rome.

3. " *Tychichus, a beloved brother, and a faithful minister and fellow-servant of the Lord. All my state shall he declare unto you. Whom I have sent for this purpose, and that he may know your state, and comfort your hearts*" (iv. 7, 8). Tychichus had been directed to make a similar oral relation to the Ephesians (vi. 21).

4. " *Onesimus, a faithful and beloved brother, who is one of you. They* (he and Tychichus) *shall make known unto you all things which are done here*" (iv. 9).

5. "*Aristarchus, my fellow-prisoner, saluteth you.*" So denominated, significant of his self-denying service (iv. 10).

6. "*Marcus, sister's son to Barnabas, touching whom ye received commandments; if he come unto you, receive him*" (iv. 10). By this note it would seem that it was known to the Colossians how Mark had formerly been separated from the Apostle. Perhaps his restoration to his companionship had been explained when those "commandments" were given. It is said by Romish writers that Mark published his Gospel in Rome. But (as it has been said before concerning Luke's Gospel) that city was an inappropriate place in which to issue a Greek composition. It is more reasonable to suppose that he wrote his Gospel in the East, and published it when travelling with Peter, who calls him "my son," for the use of strangers (*Hellenists*) scattered throughout the places visited by that venerable Apostle.

7. "*Justus, who* (and Mark) *of the circumcision only are my fellow-workers unto the kingdom of God, which have been a comfort to me*"—that is, being Jews (iv. 11).

8. "*Luke, the beloved physician.*" Luke was personally unknown to the Colossians. But that he was known to them by reputation is to be inferred from the definite article being used, "*the* beloved physician." Here Paul's feelings towards his companion found expression in a manner whereby his correspondents were informed that his medical adviser was by his side ; and so this notice may be accounted as one of those things which, as it concerned the writer's state, might "comfort their hearts" (iv. 14).

In this epistle there seems to be an allusion to Luke's gospel in the words, " whereof ye heard before" (*i.e.*, of the hope laid up in heaven) "in the word of the truth of the gospel" (i. 5). This intelligence may very well be thought to be other than that by *viva voce.* Among the inconveniences occasioned by the neglect of Luke's biography has been the overlooking the allusions to his writings in St Paul's epistles, or the controverting them.

9. "*And Demas greet you*" (iv. 14). This reads sadly, being the only name not followed by some significant particular. Here, then, is a list of nine of the principal of the Apostle's companions at this time, including Luke.

It is usual to find it represented that, because Paul writes, " As many as have not seen my face in the flesh " (ii. 1), he had therefore been personally unknown to his correspondents of Colosse ; but this conclusion ill accords with the structure of the epistle, and especially with the familiar particulars just noticed. May it not rather be thought that those words refer to the considerable number of converts that had been added to the Church there during the five years since Paul was in Asia Minor ?

Tychichus was the bearer of both the Epistle to the Ephesians and this to the Colossians. Ephesus was reached first ; and the Epistle to the Colossians being still in his possession, it may be supposed that, when the former letter had been publicly read, it would have been followed by the reading of the other. The intended mutual use of the epistles in the two Churches is inferred from the note to the Colossians respecting a similar case : " And when this epistle is read among you, cause that it be read also in the Church of the Laodiceans, and that ye likewise read the epistle from Laodicea " (Col. iv. 16). The subjects treated in these epistles were alike applicable to both Churches; and the information concerning the brethren contained in the one epistle would serve to supply its absence in the other.

Dr Paley has occupied twenty-four pages of his " Horæ Paulinæ " in noticing correspondences between the epistles to the Ephesians and Colossians ; and he remarks, " Both epistles represent the writer as under imprisonment for the gospel, and both treat of the same subject. The Epistle, therefore, to the Ephesians, and the Epistle to the Colossians, import to be two letters written by the same person, at, or nearly at, the same time, and upon the same subject, and to have been sent by the same messenger." There are, however, important differences in these epistles. They differ in extent, the Epistle to the Ephesians being the longest of the two. In the Epistle to the Ephesians three chapters are occupied with the doctrinal part, which, in the epistle to the Colossians, is confined to the first chapter. And whereas in the Epistle to the Ephesians, believers are re-presented as "called," as "quickened from death," and as "exalted to sit with Christ;" in this epistle other figures are employed, and they are said to be "translated into the kingdom of God's dear Son." Herein the glory of Christ enthroned is set forth, and His prerogatives, as the Creator of all things, and as the Head of the Church, redeemed by His blood, are described. Adapted to this representation are the practical parts of the epistle ; and, suitable to the figure of a kingdom, there are warnings given against dis-loyalty by idolatrous predilections, forming a prophetic series a fit companion to the tablets confronting Church congregations :—1. "This I say, lest any man beguile you with enticing words." 2. "Beware lest any man spoil you through philosophy and vain deceit, after the traditions of men, after the rudiments of the world" (*doctrines and legends which aim to dethrone Christ*). 3. "Let no man judge you in meats or in drinks" (*a superstitious choice of them, or abstinence from them*) ; "or in respect of a holiday, or of the new moon, or of the Sabbath" (*of ceremonies, and days of heathen or of Jewish observance*). 4. "Let no man beguile you into the worshipping of angels" (*and of course of inferior beings likewise, under a pretence of humility, and contrary to the prerogative of the "One only Mediator"*). 5. "Touch not, taste not, handle not" (chap. ii.)

The Epistle to PHILEMON is the third of the epistles written by Paul at Rome. Extremely brief, yet consisting entirely of personalities, it is of singular interest in the series of letters written under Luke's observation. Paul does not here, as in his epistles addressed to Churches, begin with a note of his apostleship, not now writing as a teacher; but he designates himself, " Paul, a prisoner of Jesus Christ." The Lord having conducted him to Rome, he accepts his situation there as a divine ordination. He likewise describes himself, " Paul the aged." He was at this time about sixty years of age, a period of life at which persons ordinarily do not call themselves " aged." Descriptive of his own sensations, the expression reveals the fact that, physically, he was prematurely old. It intimates how his constitution had been affected by his labours, more abundant than others, by his having been in prisons frequent, in journeyings often, in perils, having suffered shipwreck, in weariness, in hunger, with the care devolving upon him of all the Churches he had raised, and withal oppressed by a distressing bodily infirmity (2 Cor. xi. 23–28 ; 2 Cor. xii. 7).

1. In this epistle are to be noticed *the correspondent addressed*, Paul's estimation of whom appears in the inscription, " Unto Philemon, our dearly beloved ;" a ground of his regard for him being expressed in the description, " and our fellow-labourer." Nor is this all ; but his character is illustrated by the grateful terms in which his services are mentioned, in the verses four to seven. And then, greatly is our interest in Philemon increased when it further appears that he was one of Paul's own converts (ver. 10). They who ignore conversion enjoy not the honour, nor know the happiness, of this relationship.

2. *The subject of the letter.* " I beseech thee for my son Onesimus." And this is said of Philemon's slave. In Europe, slaves were generally white. They came into bondage by having been taken in war, by purchase, by a penal sentence, or by having been born of parents in slavery.

So numerous were slaves, and sometimes so refractory, as to cause trouble to the state. Persons of education and superior abilities were sometimes reduced to this condition. Onesimus seems to have been of this class. It appears from the letter, that having absconded, he had sought to conceal himself in the great population of Rome. He had very likely formerly seen Paul or some of his company at his master's house at Colosse. And now, by some means, he had been led to visit the Church in the house of Paul, and here he had been arrested by Paul's ministry. So, before the master, and now his slave, had been converted from the death of heathenism to the life that is in Christ by the same Apostle. Being acquainted with his master, Paul took Onesimus by the hand, and kept him for a while in his own service. And, as he wished to introduce him to his master, and also to the Christians at Colosse, in his new character, the letter is addressed "unto Philemon, and unto the Church assembling in his house."

3. *Philemon's associates.* These are addressed conjointly with him :—1. The beloved Apphia, (not *our* beloved). Grotius says this name is altered by the Hebrew letters *ph*, from the Greek *Appia;* and he remarks that she was a deaconess, with duties spiritual and temporal, like those mentioned Romans xvi., and Philippians iv. 11. 2. "Archippus, our fellow-soldier,"—that is, as preaching the gospel to the heathen, a perilous enterprise. The message had been sent to him in the Epistle to the Colossians, "And say to Archippus, Take heed to the ministry which thou has received in the Lord, that thou fulfil it " (iv. 17).

4. " *The Church in Philemon's house.*" Here is another particular illustrative of Philemon's position and character, and another reason for Paul's regard for him,—a particular in which he followed Paul's own example in his house at Rome. And, now, to this Church at Colosse and its

ministers, a letter is brought by the converted fugitive, in which, by the Apostle, he is commended to their regards. By favour of tradition, Onesimus is advanced to be the first Bishop of Colosse. But it is plain that Archippus had prior claim to that honour.

5. *The writer's own associates*, who were—1. *Timothy*, who is united with the writer in the inscription of the letter as " Brother Timothy "—not *our* brother, for not the pronoun, but article *the*, is the prefix : this combination intimates that both Paul and Timothy were familiarly known to their correspondents ; 2. *Epaphras*, described as " My fellow-prisoner in Jesus Christ"—not a prisoner of the state, as Paul himself was, which would be inconsistent with his having come to Rome a messenger from the Church at Colosse (Col. iv. 12, 13), but it is said in acknowledgment of his self-denying devotion to the person of the Apostle. The same compliment is paid to him which was bestowed upon Aristarchus in the Epistle to the Colossians (iv. 10) ; who in this epistle is classed as a fellow-labourer; 3. *Marcus;* 4. *Aristarchus ;* 5. *Demas ;* 6. *Lucas*—the four last mentioned being called "my fellow-labourers."

Here, then, Luke's name again appears, and having another designation accompanying it. By this passage is obtained a testimony that Luke was engaged in another ministry than is by some writers allowed to him.

In this place Luke is mentioned with Mark as a " fellow-labourer." That Mark was a preacher as well as a historian is never disputed. And that Luke was the same is witnessed from the time that he was found with the disciples who, quitting Jerusalem, " went everywhere preaching the Word." To regard Luke as a historian is the principal thing with posterity; but here is a testimony showing that he took a general share in the ministry of the gospel. There is nowhere any intimation that Luke had visited Colosse ; but the gracefulness of mentioning his name in this place is apparent, as also in the preceding epistle, and in each under a different aspect; for besides his fame having long been spread throughout all the Churches by his Gospel, he was reverenced by them for his magnanimity in abiding with Paul as his comforter at Rome.

Objections were made to the admission of this epistle into the volume of Sacred Scripture, because it contains no doctrinal or direct religious teaching. But it is to be observed that that teaching had already been given in the epistle to the Church at Colosse, of which Philemon was a member. Its value as a historical document renders it worthy of this distinction. Than this, no letter more characteristic of a benevolent and magnanimous heart was ever penned in Rome. Moreover, what a lustrous example does it afford of the condescending and consoling character of the gospel of which the writer was a minister, and who estimated the soul of a slave as being of equal value with that of a prince!

The Epistle to the PHILIPPIANS is the fourth written by Paul in Rome. Notwithstanding that Luke is not mentioned therein, this epistle possesses a singular value in his biography. It forms a supplement to his own narrative of events at Philippi (Acts xvi.), and it discovers what had been the influence of his teaching there. That this is not a second epistle to the Philippians, instead of the only one, may be attributed to the circumstance that the pastoral care of Luke had rendered a former one unnecessary; otherwise it would have been as likely that a previous letter should have been written to the first Church founded in Europe, as that two epistles should have been addressed to the second Church that was raised here.

In an observation of the historical particulars of this epistle, there are to be noticed—

1. *The Inscription.* Paul and Timothy, the servants of

Jesus Christ. By this inscription Timothy's share in bringing the gospel to Philippi is recognised. "To all the saints which are at Philippi, with the bishops and deacons." Here, as in the inscription to some of the other Epistles, the members in general are put foremost.

2. *A retrospect.* "I thank my God upon every remembrance of you, in every prayer for you making request with joy, for your fellowship in the gospel from the first day until now" (i. 3–5),—that is, from the time that, with his company, he entered into the house of Lydia; and that his personal knowledge of them had been renewed, when he visited them again, six years afterwards, upon the occasion of his going to and returning from Corinth on the business of the collection of alms for the poor saints in Jerusalem. This epistle differs from all the others addressed by Paul to Churches. It is more congratulatory than any of them. Herein no precise theme of discourse or argument is pursued. The subjects touched arise out of the instant occasion of its·composition, and also from remembrances of the history and character of his correspondents, the whole being toned with the sentiments which that occasion and those memories inspired.

3. *A favourable representation of Paul's case.* "But I would that ye should understand that the things which happened unto me have fallen out rather unto the furtherance of the gospel; so that my bonds in Christ are manifest in all the prætorium, and in all other places" (ver. 12, 13). It would have been thought by persons distant from the scene that Paul's work was suspended. With a seeming allusion to his imprisonment at Philippi and its fruits, he speaks of his ministry in bonds and its fruits in Rome. They were manifest in all the "prætorium"—that is, the quarter of the prætorium guards (not the Emperor's palace). Paul's hired house was probably near to the place to which he had been taken upon his arrival. The soldiers

to whom he was successively chained, affected by his conduct and discourse before all comers, would convey the report thereof to their comrades, and, by the Holy Spirit's grace, the impressions made among them were manifest by the conversion of some of them.

4. *An intention expressed to send Timothy to Philippi.* "But I trust in the Lord Jesus to send Timothy shortly unto you, that I also may be of good comfort when I know your state. For I have no man like-minded who will [so] naturally care for your state" (ii. 19, 20). To conclude herefrom, as some do, that Luke was not in Rome when this letter was written, is unnecessary; for Luke did not receive his appointment as an evangelist from Paul. If it had been proper for him to make the visit, Luke would have performed the journey on his own account. Moreover, his advanced age renders unreasonable the thought that he should have gone instead of Timothy.

5. *An expectation of release.* "But I trust in the Lord that I also myself shall come shortly" (ii. 24). This expectation was grounded upon the circumstance that his accusers, having so long delayed to make their appearance to prosecute their charges against him before Cæsar's tribunal, he might hope, by petition or otherwise, to obtain his liberation.

6. *A Philippian messenger.* "Epaphroditus, your messenger" (ii. 25). This person is said by some to have been the same as Epaphras. But an objection to this opinion is found in the definite manner in which each is represented by Paul as having belonged to different communities, upon different continents. Epaphras was a minister of the Church at Colosse, in Proconsular Asia, and Epaphroditus was a presbyter of the Church at Philippi, in Macedonia. The estimation in which Paul held this visitor appears in his designation of him as "my brother, and companion in labour, and fellow-soldier." This last term seems to have

been used in allusion to the soldier to whom Paul was constantly chained wrist to wrist. And so it is equivalent to what had been said concerning two other of his companions, that they were his " fellow-prisoners."

7. *An errand accomplished.* " Now, ye Philippians, know also that in the beginning of the gospel [in Europe] no Church communicated with me concerning giving and receiving, but ye only. For even [when having gone] to Thessalonica ye sent once and again to my necessity. Not because I desire a gift ; but I desire fruit that may abound to your account. I have all and abundance, having received of Epaphroditus the things sent from you, a sacrifice acceptable [to me] well pleasing to God. But my God shall supply all your need, according to His riches in glory by Christ Jesus "—a recompense measured by immeasurable resources." By the designation of Epaphroditus as " my companion in labour," it appears that he was a considerable time in Rome. And by that other, " and he that ministered to my wants," it appears that he came provided with ample means to support the Apostle. Paul had been an almoner of the Church at Antioch, to convey their offerings to the poor saints in Judea. He had afterwards pursued the object of a collection for the. same persons from other Churches. He had likewise gone with this last offering to Jerusalem. And now, he who had pleaded so persistently for the cause of Christ's poor saints, is himself in the condition of a recipient. But as the relief comes from a source which he felt to have been so warmly fraternal, or rather so much in the form of a discharge of a debt—for truly he was a prisoner on account of the Gentiles—his great soul felt no abasement thereby, but exulted at the grace bestowed alike upon both the givers and the receiver.

8. *The messenger's departure.* " Yet I thought it necessary to send to you Epaphroditus" (ii. 25). The reason

for his dismissal arose from a severe illness which he had suffered, and which having been reported to the Philippians, Epaphroditus was anxious to allay their anxiety concerning his health by his immediate return. Moreover, the writer declares that the joy which his return would occasion to his correspondents would alleviate his own sorrow at parting with him. So the friend is restored with this dimissory, " Receive him therefore in the Lord with all gladness, and hold him in reputation ; because for the work of Christ he was nigh unto death, not regarding his life to supply your lack of service toward me" (ii. 29, 30).

9. *Instructions given to Epaphroditus.* " I entreat thee also, true yoke-fellow "—1. " Help those women which laboured with me in the gospel." This describes deaconesses. These were so well known to the messenger and to the Church, and their zealous co-operation with Paul when at Philippi, that this description is given instead of their names. Perhaps one object of their labour had been the aid rendered in the collection made for the poor saints in Palestine. 2. " With Clement also." This person is claimed for *Clemens Romanus;* but that he was a Greek is as likely as that the other persons here mentioned were Greeks. 3. "·And other my fellow-labourers whose names [not registered here] are in the book of life " (iv. 3). 4. " Salute every saint in Christ Jesus." The benevolent heart cannot overlook one of Christ's members, however obscure (iv. 21).

10. *Salutations sent to the Philippians.* 1. " The brethren who are with me greet you." Although not mentioned by name, these were Aristarchus, Demas, Luke, and perhaps Mark. Timothy united in addressing the letter. Disappointment is felt that at least the name does not transpire of him who, with Paul, Silas, and Timothy, had taken the gospel to Philippi, and had afterwards remained the *episcopus* of the Church there. The arrival of a minister must have

been a happy event for Luke, and his protracted stay in Rome a source of much gratification to him. Their conversations together would often relate to the affairs of their Macedonian friends; and by the opportunity of his return, Luke would surely have committed to him various messages to friends, and also would have made written communications to some of them. In like manner, some others of the "brethren" who were acquainted with Philippians would have prepared communications to be conveyed by the same hand. In this view of the case is perhaps found the reason why the names of the "brethren" came to be omitted. 2. "All the saints salute you, chiefly they that are of Cæsar's household." So an advantage of his "bonds in Christ" had been the conversion of some of these.

11. *Characteristic counsels.* As in the epistles to the Ephesians and the Colossians, so in this precepts and cautions have a place. But that these in no manner presume any defect in the conduct of his correspondents is manifest from the words, "Wherefore, my beloved, as ye have *always obeyed*, not only as in my presence, but much more in my absence," &c. (ii. 12); "Let us therefore, as many as be *perfect*, be thus minded" (iii. 15); "Therefore, dearly beloved, *my joy and crown*, so stand fast in the Lord" (iv. 1). Inviting them, saying, "Brethren, be followers together of me," the Apostle cheerfully declares that, whether by his life or by his death, his Master will be glorified, averring, "For me to live is Christ, and to die is gain." He urges his correspondents to "stand fast, nothing terrified by their adversaries; for it was given unto them both to believe in Christ, and to suffer for His sake." From the privilege of suffering for Christ, he urges conformity with Him: "If, therefore, there be any consolation in Christ," &c., "fulfil ye my joy, that ye be like-minded" (ii. 1). [An instance of this fellowship was exhibited when this passage was quoted as a farewell message to the saints

of Bohemia by the martyr Huss, concerning whom Luther said "he deserved to be canonised."] Further, the Philippians are exhorted to exercise "humbleness of mind," upon the ground of the wondrous example of the condescension of Christ (ii. 5–11). They are exhorted, "Do all things without murmurings and disputings." Two persons at variance are addressed : "I beseech Euodias and Syntyche that they be of one mind in the Lord" (iv. 2). The golden maxim is proposed, adapted alike to religious and secular life, "Let your moderation be known unto all men." They are counselled, "Be careful for nothing ; but by prayer and supplication, with thanksgiving, let your requests be made known unto God." As the first fruits of the Apostle's mission in Europe, exultation at the bright example of piety presented by the Church at Philippi begins and is continued throughout the epistle ; and that they might be cheered under their sufferings in behalf of Christ, and share his own happy experience, he urges, "Rejoice in the Lord" (iii. 1) ; "Rejoice in the Lord alway ; again I say, Rejoice" (iv. 4). Notes these are unlike those of a prisoner ; they recall the scene when, with Silas, the writer sang in the jail at Philippi. If it did not transpire that the writer was now in bonds, it might have been thought that this epistle had been written in some favourable situation, as when in the house of "mine host at Corinth," surrounded by the company of friends, whose names appear in the Epistle to the Romans. What an attestation is afforded by this document of the Master's presence with His servant !

The Epistle to the HEBREWS is the *fifth* of those epistles which were written by Paul at Rome. Its authorship has been a subject of much debate. The question itself, and the controversies respecting it, are reviewed, historically and critically, by Professor Moses Stuart, in an Introduction, consisting of *two hundred and forty-eight pages*, prefixed to his Commentary on this Epistle. It is a case, however, in which the evidence so greatly preponderates on the one side, that there is occasion for little suspense in coming to a judgment concerning it. By the absence of an inscription of Paul's name upon the epistle, it became a question in some quarters who was the writer of it ; but it is declared by Jerome, that "the knowledge that it was Paul's production was always preserved by the Oriental Churches." At Alexandria there had been established classes, called catechetical, for the instruction of heathen inquirers in the history and doctrines of the Christian religion. Towards the close of the second century, Clement of Alexandria was the chief leader of this school. He affirmed, in a work edited by Eusebius, " Paul was the author of the Epistle to the Hebrews ; and as it was addressed to the Hebrews, it was originally written in their language, *and afterwards translated by Luke for the use of the Greeks"* (lib. vi., c. 14). Pantænus, his predecessor in the tutorship of the same school, is reported by Clement to have given the same testimony. Might not this knowledge concerning the subject have been obtained by the transmission of a copy of the Greek version of the Epistle by Luke to his friend Theophilus ? In the next century, Origen said the ancients did not rashly hand it down to us as the production of Paul. And as a critic, confirming the account of Luke's Greek version, Origen remarks, " The character of the style of the Epistle to the Hebrews has not the unpolished cast of the Apostle's language, who professes himself to be a man unlearned in speech—that is, in phraseology. Besides, this epistle, in the texture of its style, is more conformed to the Greek idiom, as every one must confess who is able to distinguish differences of style. I should say that the phraseology and the texture belong to some one relating the Apostle's sentiments." That Paul was the writer of the epistle was primarily doubted in the Western Churches ; and to doubts naturally succeeded errors. Some, dissenting from the belief that the epistle was Paul's, attributed it to Clement of Rome, and some to Luke ; but these two having been Gentiles, their claim is properly regarded as incapable of being entertained. By others, Barnabas is said to have been the writer of it ; but if the epistle which is already attributed to him be taken for a specimen of his matter and manner, it was manifest that he was not the writer of the Epistle to the Hebrews. By others, Apollos has been named as the writer of it ; and some German critics, as Bleek, De Wette, and Tholuck, have advocated this hypothesis, and of course with characteristic reconditeness. But besides Luke's notice that Apollos was an eloquent man, and mighty in the Scriptures, there is no pretence for the opinion. No documentary criterion exists whereby to make a comparison, and thereby to judge of the ability of Apollos as a writer. His case, therefore, as a candidate is plainly defective, for want of a prime item of evidence.* For the other side, the propriety of the original report that Paul wrote the epistle appears upon a very slight consideration of the evidence that supports it. An example of obvious resemblance, both to the scope and style of the Epistle to the Hebrews, is seen in the passage 2 Cor. iii. 7-18, wherein a comparison is made between the ministry of the law and of the gospel, and their respective glory ; and then, possessing such examples of argument and graphic power as the Epistles to the Romans, Galatians, and Ephesians, together with the Apostle's orations on special occasions, reported in the Acts, there are afforded grounds whereby

---

* We have just discovered that, arguing this question in favour of Apollos, in above twenty pages of "How to Study the New Testament," Dr Alford asserts, "Nothing will induce *me* to acknowledge Paul for its author."—Again he says, " It has become the *fashion* among English upholders of its Pauline authorship to *laugh to scorn* this and every other attempt to decide the question on its own merits" (pages 90 and 103). Of the existence of this bad FASHION we were not before aware.

to form a judgment on the case by comparison. Those examples afford coincidences of thought and treatment with the composition of the Epistle to the Hebrews which no other existing writings present; and, then, for coincidences as they relate to the situation of Paul, and to the personal notices in the epistle. Since he was sent away from Jerusalem (Acts ix. 30), he had always sought to bring the gospel before the Jews in their synagogues throughout Asia and Greece. From some of these he gathered disciples, but by the majorities his testimony had been rejected; and now, his course being nearly run, it was natural that he who, in his love and grief, had protested that he "wished himself accursed for the sake of his brethren according to the flesh," should be inspired to compose an argument especially adapted to awaken, to instruct, and to exhort them concerning Christ and the doctrines of His gospel. The Epistle to the Hebrews is such a delivery. It possesses the dignity and solemnity of a prophet's address. It is a communication becoming the chosen vessel of Christ. As a composition, it combines the character of a treatise and a hortatory epistle. That it was primarily sent to "the mother of all Churches," the Christian community in Jerusalem, as it is the common conjecture, so it is the most probable one. How deeply interested Paul was in the members of that Church is seen in the solicitude with which he prosecuted the object of collecting for its poor, and the zeal which led him twice to convey the offerings to Jerusalem, persisting in taking the last journey thither, although warned that its completion would cost him his liberty. With the Church at Jerusalem he had long ago debated the subject of the freedom of believers from the ceremonial law, upon the accession of Christ to a *sole* holy priesthood. He had received an intimation, from the lips of James, of the prejudices of the Jerusalem Jews against him as a preacher to the Gentiles

(Acts xxi. 21) ; and as the head of the Churches of the circumcision, to no Church would such an epistle have been so appropriately directed as to the Church at Jerusalem. Other circumstances, which apply to no person but to Paul, and which therefore confirm his composition of the epistle, under the inspiration of the Holy Spirit, are, that he speaks of his correspondents as having " had compassion on him in his bonds," probably when at Cæsarea—an interesting particular, and one hitherto unnoticed (x. 34) ; that he writes, "The saints of Italy salute you," Paul being at Rome when the epistle was written (xiii. 24) ; and that he mentions Timothy, who was peculiarly *his own* minister. Some other coincidences might be traced, but surely these suffice for the argument.

There remains no space here to observe upon the arguments of the epistle, and their accompanying illustrations, and pleadings, and warnings. The great design of this wonderful composition has only been very partially accomplished. It possesses still *its prophetic character.* When the set time of a general awakening of the " dispersed Hebrews " shall come, then will its great value be discerned. In the meantime, to the Jew, touched by compunction for his disbelief, and for the rejection of Christ by his fathers, this epistle serves as a light, like that which shone upon its writer at his own conversion, whilst to the Christ-minded Gentile it furnishes a sublime argument against any acceptance of, and any trust in, an abolished ritualism. That the epistle was written before Paul's liberation appears from the request "Pray for us;" "I beseech you the rather to do this, that I may be restored to you the sooner" (xiii. 19). And that it was written after the epistles which have already been reviewed appears by the observation, " Know ye that brother Timothy is set at liberty, with whom, if I come shortly, I will see you ; " for there is no previous notice of Timothy having been in prison.

Some writers, pledged to an entire original Greek text of the New Testament Scriptures, persist that Paul wrote this epistle in Greek ; but did he address the Jewish multitude as he stood on the stairs leading to the Castle Antonia in Greek? (Acts xxii.) ; and if in Hebrew, who translated his speech as it appears in the Acts but Luke? Or, did Paul speak before the Jewish Council in Greek? (Acts xxiii.) And if upon those occasions he spake in the dialect of the Hebrews, is it reasonable to suppose that he *wrote* to them in another language than their own?

In attributing the translation of this epistle to Luke, it is a beautiful consideration that, besides having furnished his own quota to the code of the New Testament, he was led, by his companionship with Paul at Rome, to add this other service to the cause of Christianity. What a memorable fraternity was that wherein the Jew Apostle and the Gentile Evangelist were united in an appeal, to be protracted throughout all ages, inviting to the

" LOOKING UNTO JESUS ! "—(xii. 2).

CHAPTER XXIX.

THE PUBLICATION OF THE ACTS OF THE APOSTLES.

By universal consent the volume of the Acts of the Apostles is said to have been published in Rome, soon after it was completed, which was perhaps twelve years after the former treatise. It may, therefore, be supposed that from notes which had been made during the entire period of the history, it was composed at the interval of two years between the occurrence of the scene last reported therein and when the postscript was added. Speculations have been raised to account for the blank intervening in the narrative. Already it has been remarked (p. 301), that it would have been prejudicial to Paul's impending case, and also perilous to the Christians in Rome, to have divulged the particulars of his successful ministry there, reaching, as it did, to inmates of the imperial household. And then that Luke closed his history here, shows how strictly he kept within the limits of his plan. He had described the introduction of the gospel into place after place until he had arrived at what he regarded the geographical limit of Paul's ministry. His plan was accomplished; and even Rome, the mistress of the world, allures his pen no further.

Whether the title by which this book is called was given to it by Luke himself, is not known. It would appear from his own words, that he had named it his "Second Treatise" (*logos*), a title which is entirely adapted to its consecutiveness to his Gospel. The title which the book afterwards obtained was evidently derived from the Latin :

acta having been the name usually given to annals, or journals, by the Romans. It is, therefore, to be inferred, that the present title of the book first appeared in the Latin copies, and was thereafter adopted in the Oriental ones by the Greek rendering of *praxeis*, a word which conveys no allusion to the class of literature to which the book belongs, but only to the subject itself, while the Latin title does both. In the edition of the Latin vulgate, printed at Antwerp by J. Tibald in 1526, a copy of which is in the hand of the writer of these pages, this suitable title is prefixed, " *The Acts of the Apostles, or Second Book of the Gospel according to St Luke, addressed to Theophilus.*"

A translation of the book into Latin for the benefit of the Western Churches would soon have been made, and not improbably by Luke himself. And so, in this sense, the Roman Church may boast of its having been published here by its writer.

The book completed, the first copy thereof, as in the case of the Gospel, and for the same intent, would have been despatched, according to the inscription which it bears, to Theophilus at Alexandria. A copy would have been sent to Timothy, that he might introduce it to the notice of the Churches in Proconsular Asia. Copies would also have been sent to the Churches to which the writer had been peculiarly allied; to Philippi, to Corinth, to Antioch. But mark the incoherency of tradition. When Chrysostom, exercising his ministry at the latter city, delivered a course of lectures on this book, he declared, in commencing it, that a reason for the undertaking had been, that the knowledge as to who was the writer of it had failed from the memory of the Church at Antioch.

And then as to the character of the book, regarded as a specimen of ancient literature, this book possesses a remarkable character. The only books that preceded it, to which it can be compared, are the writings of Xenophon, concerning

Cyrus the younger, in Greek, and Cæsar's Commentaries in Latin. But it only resembles these in the respect of its being a narrative. Those writings relate the adventures of warriors. This book describes the progress of a reign of peace, announced by humble heralds, first in Palestine, and thereafter from province to province of the Roman empire, by ministers, of whom Paul was the chief. Xenophon, as a general, followed his hero to Persia. Luke, as a fellow-labourer, accompanied Paul to Italy. The *style* of this book is nicely adapted to its object. It is brief, often to severity, yet it is always perspicuous. It is full in all essential things; often presenting pictures of great completeness, yet is in no place diffuse; and if the volume had been smaller, it would not have admitted those pictures; if larger, it would not have corresponded with the writer's former treatise, or with the proportions of the other narratives in the New Testament. The *design* of this book is similar to that of the writer's Gospel. The Gospel relates to one person, the Lord Jesus. It describes the life and ministry of a spotless character. This book relates the ministry of several persons, being the disciples of Jesus, who had received a commission from Him to preach His gospel to the world, and also obtained strength and ability for their ministry from the Holy Ghost; but who, holy and zealous as they were, nevertheless came short of the perfection of their Master. Like the report which Paul and Barnabas made to the Church at Antioch of their first missionary journey, this book proposes to afford a report of the acts of the Apostles, so far as the writer witnessed them, or obtained intelligence from those engaged in them, or was himself so engaged as a fellow-labourer. Its purpose was one that had relation both to the present and to the future, as much as did any of the other books of the Bible. The *central* position of the book in the series of New Testament Records is appropriate. It concludes the historical portion thereof; and preceding the epistolary part of it, it sheds a light upon both the sections.

The *acceptance* of this book could not fail to have been welcome to the Churches that had received the writer's volume of the Gospel. Several of those Churches were immediately interested in it by reason of narratives contained therein which concerned themselves. And, to put the Churches in general in possession of a history of the introduction of the gospel into several places, and its *progress* thereafter during thirty years, must have been to all as interesting as it was important. And so likewise to successive generations, to possess the notes of one of the witnesses of, and agents in, that wonderful work of regeneration, is a rare advantage indeed.

Of the *benefits* derived from the publication of this book, two of them especially are incalculable. *In it the Churches of Christ possess a treasure of ecclesiastical history.* This book is the only such history. Four are the Gospels; but there is only one account of the Acts of the Apostles and disciples succeeding those narratives. Herein, as in the Gospels, truth shines without alloy. The benefit of this record, in this respect, may be imagined, in some measure, by a thought of the consequence that would have ensued from its absence. Not that there would have remained altogether a blank in history concerning the period it embraces. Oh, no! Ingenuity is prolific; and the fabric of what is called tradition is often ingeniously woven like the lives and adventures of the oriental hermits. What thanksgivings, therefore, ought to pour from the truth-loving heart at the thought of having hereby been saved from an alternative of fables! That this is no exaggerated expression is proved at once by a reference to the histories that pretend to supplement this book. Secular history has not so many examples of writers of uncritical discernment and of credulous capacities as are found in history that is ecclesiastical.   Credulity was that by which the latter class of writers in the early ages regarded the circumstances reported to them, and was also the poise of their judgment concerning them.   In consulting the works of the fathers of Christian history, the first task of modern writers is to seek to separate the chaff from the wheat, the fable from the fact, as they lay commingled in their pages.

The other important benefit of this book to be named here, is *its practical significance.*   It is a history of the renewal of man by divine truth ; and, by a relation of how the truth was delivered, and how received, at the beginning, it serves to inform and instruct in points of paramount interest.   It describes how *the truth was delivered* by ministers who had been instructed by Jesus Christ in person, and who had witnessed the facts concerning Him which formed the basis of their arguments,—how it was delivered with an accompaniment of power which Jesus had declared they should receive by the presence of the Holy Ghost with them and in them.   The book shows how, in this power, the apostles and primitive disciples went forth and pulled down the strongholds of Satan, as at Philippi, Ephesus, and elsewhere.   And a *lesson* conveyed by the record of their proceedings and successes is, that what was the power for this achievement then, must be the power for the same always.   So that no agent can be a successful co-worker with God unless he has an endowment of " power from on high."

And so likewise the relation made in this book of *how the truth was received* upon its first announcement, conveys a lesson of correlative importance.   Great is the benefit of possessing, in the succession of pictures which this book affords, a palpable view of Christianity in its freshest aspect.   Hereby Christians perceive what Christianity is in an embodied form.   They behold in it the manner in which it was first taught and received.

And another lesson conveyed by its details is, that, whether for the revival of communities, or the growth of piety in individuals, the same divine influence that accomplished those results then, is requisite now and attainable now. Subsequent history has illustrated this. Revivals are seasons in which many are quickened. And the history of every revival since the Pentecostal one serves for a testimony of the Holy Spirit's presence and grace with the community in which a revival has occurred.

And then, for the individual instances of conversion, and the subsequent piety of the converts herein recorded, these are produced for examples and incentives to subsequent ages. The conferment of large measures of grace should not be supposed to be confined to the period embraced in the pages of this book. Its pages are prophetic. There is no reason why the grace which then constituted the privilege and formed the believer's character, should not be bestowed as largely on believers now as then. The promised grace extends to the believer's seed of all times. The divine gospel, in all its holy and elevating and saving character, still remains, like its Author, unchanged and unchangeable. The sacred books which reveal its doctrines have been transmitted, in their integrity, from age to age. And the effects upon the believing mind of their truths concerning the atoning death of Christ, and the justifying fruit of His resurrection, and their promises to the faithful, still continue, in all their primeval power, to cheer and to sanctify. Evidence of this has been under every eye. How many bright examples of piety are still witnessed! How true it is that the holy character and tendency of the gospel is now as ever capable of being traced in the conduct of some of its professors; in the sustaining power which it affords in seasons of tribulation, and in the triumphant testimony it enables the believer to bear in death!

But the benefit of the examples in this book are not

limited to those only that are bright.   Examples are given
of defective Christians.   These blot some of its earliest
pages.   Without a notice of these, the lessons to be conveyed would have been incomplete.   These are produced for
warnings. The first two of these examples were of those who
sinned through covetousness.   Then there were Jews who,
convinced that Jesus was the Messiah, nevertheless refused
to relinquish ceremonials which were done away by Him.
These troubled the Churches with their controversial
speech and evil counsels.   And there were converts from
heathenism, who clave to indulgences forbidden to those
called to walk in the purity of the gospel, and who rejected
its restraining grace.   Successors in the spirit of all these,
with varying circumstances, have ever since afflicted the
Church, fulfilling the word of Jesus concerning the growth
of the tares beside the wheat, and also concerning the
offences which must needs come.

This book, then, is a book of historical precedents for the
benefit of the Church in all times.   Addressed to the same
friend to whom the writer's Gospel had been dedicated, it was
written with the same design, viz., that he might know the
certainty of those things that had transpired in the Church
since the conclusion of that record,—a design that was also
prospective, having relation to every convert, at every
future period of the Church's history.   "It is," observes a
judicious expositor, "an invincible demonstration of the
truth of Christian faith; for it confirms the truth concerning
Christ's declaration, 'He that believeth on me, the works
that I do shall he do also' (John xiv. 12); concerning His
power, 'I will give you a mouth and wisdom, which all
your adversaries shall not be able to gainsay, nor resist'
(Luke xxi. 15); and concerning the truth of His promise,
'Lo, I am with you alway, even unto the end of the
world' (Matt. xxviii. 20)" (Dr Whitby).

CHAPTER XXX.

THE last authentic notice that exists concerning Luke finds
him still in company with Paul. This notice occurs in the
Second Epistle to Timothy, being the sixth of Paul's epistles
written at Rome, and the last of all his epistles. In a
biographical respect, this epistle is of transcendent importance. Without it the history of the last stage of the
Apostle's life would have been left a blank, and no further
intelligence would have been found relating to Luke, except what is told by tradition. As the Epistle to the Hebrews may be regarded as Paul's legacy to his " brethren
according to the flesh," so this was a legacy to his " dearly
beloved son " (i. 1). The last letter of a beloved friend is
always regarded with reverent interest ; and this letter,
since it became the property of the Church of Christ, has
been esteemed by its devout members as a precious memorial. It is not, however, to its aspect as containing the last
testimony and advices of Paul to his beloved disciple, that
attention is here directed, but only to the historical intelligence which it incidentally conveys.

Foremost in the intelligence hereby obtained, is the fact
(or strong supposition) that Paul was liberated after an
imprisonment of two years, or somewhat longer. As his
case had hitherto stood, it was reasonable to expect that
when an imperial mandate should have been given for its
adjudication, he would have been acquitted. Of any charge
upon political grounds, Paul had been cleared by the judg-

ment of two successive governors of Palestine. His accusers of the Sanhedrim seem not to have followed their case against him to Rome; and if they had, perhaps the magistrates here would have cared little more concerning it than did Gallio for the charges that were made against him at Corinth. That Paul had anticipated his release, is discerned in passages of previous epistles. To the Philippians he had written, " Him " (Timothy) " I hope to send presently, so soon as I shall know how it will go with me. But I trust in the Lord that *I also myself shall come shortly* " (ii. 23, 24). And to Philemon of Colosse he had written, " But withal, prepare me also a lodging, for I trust, through your prayers, I shall be given unto you " (ver. 22). That these hopes were realised, appear from passages in the First Epistle to Timothy and the Epistle to Titus. In the former are the words, " As I besought thee to abide still at Ephesus, when I went into Macedonia " (i. 3). When Paul formerly left Ephesus to go to Macedonia is recorded Acts xx. i. It was when here, at that time, that he wrote the Second Epistle to the Corinthians; but Timothy had not then been left at Ephesus, for he was joined with Paul in the address of that epistle. For this reason, following Bishop Pearson, Dr Paley places the date of the First Epistle to Timothy, and the journey represented in it, at a period subsequent to Paul's first imprisonment, and consequently subsequent to the era up to which the Acts of the Apostles is brought. Concerning the Epistle to Titus Dr Paley says, " There exists a visible affinity between it and the First Epistle to Timothy." And after quoting some examples hereof, he continues, " The most natural account which can be given of these resemblances is to suppose that the two epistles were written nearly at the same time, and while the same ideas and phrases dwelt in the writer's mind." For the same reason that Timothy had been left at Ephesus, Titus was left at Crete (i. 5). And as Paul was in

Macedonia when he wrote the First Epistle to Timothy, so likewise that he was there when he wrote the Epistle to Titus is rendered probable by the direction given to Titus, " When I shall send Artemas unto thee, or Tychichus, be diligent to come unto me to Nicopolis, for I have determined there to winter " (iii. 12). Naturally connected with that journey are the following passages in the Second Epistle to Timothy, written after Paul's return to Rome :— " The cloak that I left at Troas with Carpus, when thou comest bring, and the books " (iv. 13). This must refer to a later occasion than the visit to Troas mentioned in the twentieth chapter of Acts, which was five years before the date of this epistle. " Erastus abode at Corinth " (when I recently left that city), " but Trophimus have I left at Miletus sick " (iv. 20). Trophimus was not left at Miletus upon Paul's former journey, but accompanied him to Jerusalem (Acts xx.)

" Upon the whole," concludes Dr Paley, " if we may be allowed to suppose that St Paul, after his liberation at Rome, sailed into Asia, taking Crete in his way; that from Asia and from Ephesus, the capital of that country, he proceeded to Macedonia, and crossing the peninsula in his progress, came into the neighbourhood of Nicopolis, we have a route which falls in with everything. It executes the intention expressed by the Apostle of visiting Colosse and Philippi as soon as he should be set at liberty at Rome. It allows him to leave Titus at Crete and Timothy at Ephesus, as he went to Macedonia; and to write to both not long after from the peninsula of Greece, and probably the neighbourhood of Nicopolis; thus bringing together the dates of these two letters, and thereby accounting for that affinity between them, both in subject and language, which our remarks have pointed out."

In this exposition each chain in the evidence is derived from an authentic source. But, because in his Epistle to the Romans, written before his last journey to Jerusalem, Paul had intimated an intention, upon his way to Italy, to visit Spain, it is generally thought that, upon the occasion of his respite from prison, he accomplished a journey to that country. From Spain, limping tradition pretends to have conducted him through France to Britain, and here to have landed him on the coast of Hampshire, at a place since called 'Paul's Grove.' But it is not reported whether the old Paul's cross was subsequently erected to commemorate his visit to London. Probability is greatly against such a visit. In traversing France there were many more important cities to invite his attention than any existing in Britain. And then, can it be supposed that " Paul the aged " would have been competent to undertake the fatigues of the journey hither, and the toil of the ministry attending the planting of the gospel there and here ? *

How long Paul remained at liberty, where and under what circumstances he was again apprehended, are points altogether unknown. His absence from Rome must have been of a much shorter period than the traditional accounts of his journey imply.

The second committal of Paul to prison would not have arisen, it may be thought, from the instigation of Jews, but from an opposition to the doctrines of the gospel raised by the heathen. His case now, therefore, stood upon another ground; it bare the character of a prosecution promoted by the prejudices of Gentiles.

Paul's situation was now different to what it had been formerly, when a prisoner in his own hired house; and this Second Epistle to Timothy reflects the change. It commences with a note of sadness, " Mindful of thy tears "

---

* In " An Argument on the Evidence in Favour of St Paul's having Visited Britain," by Ben. Saville, 1861, 12mo, there are adduced seventeen authorities, as they are called, all of which are regarded as furnishing the soundest premises for the writer's positive conclusions.

(i. 4).   Timothy would seem to have been acquainted with the fact of Paul's second imprisonment.   It speaks mournfully of having been forsaken by former companions. With Paul's altered situation was likewise changed the conduct towards him of some of those who had formerly been his associates.   While he might receive visitors, no man forbidding him the privilege, the shame of repairing to his teaching might be endured, and companionship with him might be maintained by some who had been enlightened by the gospel.   But as prison doors now enclosed him, and permission of access to him had to be obtained from his keepers, and as thereby the applicant exposed himself to their observation, he had few visitors, and was forsaken by many that had formerly resorted to him.   Of those who now forsook him, one is named, and the reason impelling his apostacy : " Demas hath forsaken me, having loved this present world, and has gone [*returned*] to Thessalonica."   As Demas was coupled with Luke in the Epistle to Philemon, and is here said to have gone to Thessalonica, from whence Aristarchus had been deputed, it is to be inferred that he had succeeded that faithful minister in the capacity of Paul's companion.   The sorrow occasioned to Paul by this defection was heightened by the fact that a denial was hereby made by Demas of the efficacy of that grace which Paul in his ministry had declared to be sufficient to enable the believer to overcome every temptation.   Against this instance of defection, two examples of fidelity are set down in grateful terms.   One of these faithful friends of the dear prisoner was Onesiphorus of Colosse.   " The Lord give mercy to the house of Onesiphorus, for he hath oft refreshed me, and was not ashamed of my chain ; but when he was in Rome he sought me out very diligently, and found me."   The imprisoned seclusion of Paul is here plainly intimated, and the active sympathy of this friend is declared for an enduring memorial of him.

The other example of fidelity to the imprisoned Apostle is that of his companion Luke. The Lord had appointed the apostles in couples : and the evangelists were sent forth two and two. Paul and Barnabas had laboured in company at Antioch, and upon their first missionary tour. By a gracious ordination, Paul had afterwards always companions, two or more, in fulfilling his wide-spread ministry. And when no longer an itinerant, but a prisoner, he still had his companions. But after this, his final imprisonment, they became reduced in number, until he had but one only. By the reservation of this one was the Lord's ordination fulfilled in Paul's case to the last.

How consistent with all his previous conduct is the situation in which the Evangelist is found upon the occasion of this, the last, notice of him in the sacred records ! These five words express the Apostle's mind : " *Only Luke is with me.*" As Luke was intimately known to Timothy, nothing is said concerning him but what represents his constancy in the present exigence. These words seem to be an expression of mixed feelings. They seem to speak mournfully. The painful feeling of being forsaken by former friends, and by a companion that had been deputed for the writer's solace by a Church justly devoted to him, had come upon him with fuller force from what he had just written concerning their defection. But having turned from his tablet, and glanced upon the benignant countenance of his friend, when resuming his pen, the words next written took the expression suggested by that glance, " Only Luke is with me." Moreover, these words, " only Luke is with me ! " seem also to utter the writer's grateful feeling towards this friend. They declare an appreciation of the fidelity of this companion. Here by his side was the friend who had grown venerable during his acquaintance with him ; who had forsaken every other connexion and pursuit, that he might devote himself to the solace of the writer; a friend who, since he had joined him in his last journey to Jerusalem, and during the whole of the writer's prison life, had stood fast by him; who had accompanied him from Jerusalem to Cæsarea, and from Cæsarea to Rome; and who had promptly returned to his post upon the Apostle's renewed imprisonment.

But the epistle reveals another piece of intelligence, whilst expressing another complaint. "At my first appearance no man stood with me," or "assisted me" (as it is rendered in the Genevan version of 1557). So Paul had been brought before the imperial tribunal, where he had been left without the benefit of a legal witness or friend. Aristarchus had left Rome, Demas having succeeded him as the Apostle's companion. Yet as Luke was in Rome at the time, it may be asked, Why did he not stand by the Apostle? Upon this dilemma Charles Taylor observes, "No answer can be given to this question,'so rational or so effectual as the recollection that Luke was then eighty years old (more or less)—a time of life when many infirmities become innocent causes of absence in such a case, and when the person can afford but little assistance at best." Moreover, perhaps, in tender consideration for the feelings of his venerable companion, Paul had himself prohibited his attendance with him upon the occasion. But the loss of human aid was above measure compensated by his Master's presence: "Notwithstanding, the Lord stood by me, and strengthened me." The Divine Advocate prompted the arguments of Paul's defence, which, like his defence before Festus and Agrippa, was conducted so that the Apostle's "preaching might be fully known, and that the Gentiles might hear." "And I was delivered," he adds, "from the mouth of the lion"—that is, from an instant condemnation. It is impossible to conceive what were the reasons which prevailed upon the inhuman judge to grant this respite.

In the salutations of friends in Rome which are delivered to Timothy at the close of the epistle, four names are added to the list of those who would have been known to Luke. These are Eubulus, Pudens, Linus (the last being represented by tradition as the first Bishop of Rome after St Peter), and Claudia. It may be amusing to argue, as is done in Dr Smith's large "Dictionary of the Bible," that the Pudens and Claudia here mentioned are the same whose nuptials the poet Martial has celebrated in his verse (iv. 13). The article reads pleasantly in the Dictionary. But surely the incongruity is inconceivable of the disciples of St Paul figuring in the page of a heathen poet, whose writings, unexpurgated, are not fit for perusal. Happily for the grace of consistency, the probability that the Pudens and Claudia mentioned here were identical with those persons bearing these names celebrated by Martial is subverted by the circumstance that the nuptial lines of the latter would have been composed some twenty, or perhaps thirty, years after the salutations were delivered by Paul, the poet having been only a youth when Paul wrote these names.

At the commencement of the epistle, Paul expressed himself as being "greatly desirous to see" Timothy (i. 4). And at its close he urges, "Do thy diligence to come shortly" (iv. 9). And repeating the request, he writes, "Do thy diligence to come *before winter*," for the reason that he might otherwise be delayed by the interruption of navigation. And having now another opinion of Mark than he had upon his first trial of him, for he had recently proved him as his minister in Rome, he directs, "Bring Mark with thee, for he is profitable to me for the ministry." So, notwithstanding his seclusion, the Apostle maintained a special ministry in Rome. Luke's inability for further active service, as well as a desire for their company, would make him anticipate with pleasure the arrival of those beloved Evangelists.

As this might prove the last opportunity of addressing his son in the gospel, the Apostle adds to his other advices a solemn charge. By Christians of the temper of those that had forsaken him in his extremity, a proper advice at this time would seem, " I warn you, my son, to be prudent ; avoid, as much as possible, exposing yourself to persecution." Whereas, adopting the figure of a warfare conducted under the eye of Him who should judge him at His glorious appearing, he charges him, " But watch thou in all things, endure hardness, do the work of an evangelist, make full proof of thy ministry." Timothy was not now a cadet in this service, he had already had a share in the battle, and he had suffered imprisonment likewise (Heb. xiii.)

Hereupon the Apostle describes to Timothy his own attitude. He anticipates being added to the list of the cloud of witnesses for Christ, who through faith overcame. In the gaol at Philippi, with Silas for a companion, he had triumphed, singing psalms of prayer. And now, in a gaol at Rome, with Luke beside him, the great prompter of a realising faith awaits a different deliverance from the one then obtained. He announces, " For I am now ready to be offered, and the time of my departure is at hand ;" and with this prospect before him he dictates his own epicedium, in the divine words—

> " I have fought a good fight,
> I have finished my course,
> I have kept the faith :
> Henceforth there is laid up for me
> A crown of righteousness,
> Which the Lord, the righteous Judge,
> Shall give me at that day ;
> And not to me only,
> But to all them also
> That love His appearing."
>
> —(2 Tim. iv. 6-8).

In the benediction with which the epistle is concluded,

" *The Lord Jesus Christ be with thy spirit. Grace be with you. Amen*," Paul desires for Timothy that which had been the inspiration of all his own great activities formerly, and which was the source of his consolation at the present solemn interval. These are Paul's *last written words ;* and beautifully do they show how the principles of love and confidence towards his divine Master were maintained in him, and with undiminished vitality, to the threshold of the kingdom, a preparation for which had been the object of his converted life to urge upon all within his sphere.

The six epistles whose historical particulars have now been reviewed, furnished (as it has already been observed) the only means whereby Luke's biography could have been followed during his residence in Rome, after the date of his postscript to the Acts of the Apostles. Of Paul's other epistles, six were written during his public ministry, and two during the interval of liberty obtained before his second imprisonment. So, having been present when the Epistle to the Romans was written in the house of Gaius, at Corinth, Luke had been associated with him upon the occasions of the composition of exactly half of his entire correspondence. Moreover, the paucity of information conveyed in these letters concerning this friend, serves further to illustrate his character. This reticence is in keeping with Luke's own productions, so scanty in allusions to himself. What must have been the influence of so close an intimacy with the Evangelist upon the mind of the writer of these epistles, and in what degree that mind was directed to its expression by this intimacy, can be but partially conceived; but this is an interesting consideration here. It could not have been otherwise than that, in some measure, that mind was sustained by the presence, and took a hue from the fellowship, of the friend who was at once the writer's fellow-labourer, his domestic physician, and his constant—and, when the last of these letters was written—his *only* attendant. By this review the thought is suggested, What an unutterable claim has this series of letters upon the reverential regard of every faithful heart! This blessed prisoner had declared that his "bonds had turned out for the furtherance of the gospel;" and this fact is attested besides by his preaching then, and by these letters now, whereby, "being dead, he yet speaketh."

Descending from the date of this epistle, the importance of the sacred records for historical truth is again forced upon the student's observation. All that henceforth befel the Apostle is shrouded in uncertainty. Beyond the fulfilment of his expectation of being "offered up," no authentic particulars are known relating to the close of his life. And very perplexing is the diversity of dates quoted for the year of his death. By Eusebius it is set down as having occurred in the fourteenth year of Nero's reign, that is, A.D. 67.

Towards an elucidation of the date of the Apostle's death, the first step consists of a consideration of certain prophetic declarations that were uttered concerning his ministry. To Ananias it was said, "He is chosen to bear my name before kings" (Acts ix. 15). In the prison at Jerusalem, it was said to himself by the divine Master, "Thou hast testified of me in Jerusalem, so must thou bear witness also at Rome" (xxiii. 11). And upon the voyage to Italy, during the tempest, the same voice declared, "Fear not, Paul: thou must be brought before Cæsar" (xxvii. 24). There is no ambiguity in either of these declarations. And that they were severally and literally fulfilled *must* be admitted. Before the occurrence of the events, there appeared no probability that either of them would have happened. Every step of Paul's intended journey to Italy seemed adverse to his design. But that design being agreeable with the divine purpose also, all agencies were overruled for its accomplishment. His rescue from the murderous intentions of the Jews at Jerusalem, the protection afforded to him from their persevering machinations against him by the conduct of the governors at Cæsarea, his transmission to Italy, his preservation from shipwreck, the good will of the officer by whom he was conducted, the report which that officer presented to the prefect of Rome, and the consequent favourable view which the magistrate took of his case, and the respect which he showed for his personal comfort, were all links in the chain leading to a fulfilment of the last particular of those predictions,—namely, that the chief Apostle of the Gentiles should declare a testimony for Christ before CÆSAR, the chief of Gentile monarchs.

The next step towards the elucidation sought, conducts to the pages of the historian which describe the situation of Cæsar at the period of Paul's residence in Rome. From the relation of Tacitus, it appears that Nero was absent from Rome during the entire period of Paul's two years' imprisonment; that to hide himself from observation he retired to the small island of Caprera, in the Bay of Naples, and that there, and with occasional visits to the continent, old as he was, he continued his diversions and the pursuit of "feats of blood." But that, at length, revisiting Rome, he betook himself in devotion to the Capitol. "Here," relates the historian, "while he was paying his oblations to the several deities, as he entered into the temple of Vesta, he was seized with a sudden horror, which shook him in all his joints, either from an awe of the goddess, or from the remembrance of his foulness and crimes." And the historian further relates, "To gain a reputation for delighting above all places in Rome, he banqueted frequently in public places and great squares, and used the whole city as his domicile." This, then, might have been the season in which Paul appeared before Cæsar, and when he was "delivered from the mouth of the lion." And, although history fails, the imagination may properly conceive how, upon the occasion of the fulfilment of his Master's word, Paul rose to the majesty of his situation, and that he delivered a testimony for Christ, at the hearing of which Nero was once more "seized with a sudden horror."

Another clue to the discovery of the year of Paul's death is found in the next event recorded by Tacitus. He relates, " There followed a dreadful calamity, but whether merely fortuitous, or by the execrable contrivance of the prince, is not determined, for both are asserted; but of all the evils that ever befel the city by the rage of fire, this was the most destructive and tragical." After telling that the fire was not stayed until the sixth day, and describing its effects, and the provision that was made for the people rendered houseless, and the devotions rendered to the gods, the historian concludes, " But not all the relief that could come from man, not all the bounties the prince could bestow, nor all the atonements which could be presented to the gods, availed to acquit Nero from the hideous charge, which was universally believed, that by him the conflagration was authorised. Hence, to suppress the prevailing rumour, he transferred the guilt upon fictitious criminals, and subjected to most exquisite tortures, and doomed to executions singularly cruel, those people who, for their detestable crimes, were already in truth universally abhorred, and known to the vulgar by the name of *Christians* " (Book xv.)

It cannot be thought that Paul survived that persecution. From the several pictures furnished by the historian, it is easy to perceive, that although Paul had escaped condemnation at his appearance before Cæsar, Nero now, maddened by malignity, was hurried for his private convenience to offer him a sacrifice to propitiate popular resentment. The language used by Tacitus concerning the *Christians* was the voice of the people. He says, " The founder of this name was *Christ*, who, in the reign of Tiberius, suffered

death as a criminal under Pontius Pilate, and for a while
the pestilent superstition was quelled, but revived again
and spread, not only over Judea, where it was first preached,
but even through Rome, the great gulph into which, from
every quarter of the earth, there are torrents for ever flowing of all that is hideous and abominable." Nero, a proverb of vice, had withal his fits of devotion towards the
gods. The virtue of the Christians availed nothing against
the charge of pestilent superstition in contemning the vile
idols of the Pantheon. So, the ground for the persecution
of the saints by the "Mystical Babylon" was the same
from the beginning, a pretence of upholding religion.
Paul had wrestled against the principalities and powers of
darkness in the metropolis of the world. His ministry
had been successful. Having preached therein for two
years, a knowledge of his doctrines had spread. He had
become no insignificant person in Rome. The people and
magistrates had awaked up to a sense of the might of this
man and his doctrines. They perceived that those doctrines were as inimical to their tenets as the Jews had
regarded them to theirs. The same spirit animated the
idolators at Rome that had prevailed against Paul at Ephesus, and similar would have been their cry, " Great are the
gods of the Romans!" It would have been observed that
since the spread of Christianity thousands of persons coming
from the provinces to the metropolis failed to visit the Pantheon, and thousands to pass the costly statues of gods and
heroes in public places without observing the accustomed
reverence for them. The Emperor had made a pilgrimage
of the shrines to prove his piety, and thereafter it would
have been little to him to offer the sacrifice of Christian
victims demanded by popular resentment. As the chief
instigator of disaffection to the gods, Paul would have been
the first against whom the executioner's sword would be
turned. There now remained no more any appeal for him

to Cæsar. Stephen had been the first martyr for Jesus Christ at Jerusalem. Between Paul's having witnessed the cruel death of that saint, and this moment, marvellous were the events he had beheld in his own conversion, and the conversion of multitudes by his laborious ministry. And now at length Paul, the Apostle of the Gentiles, became, perhaps, the protomartyr for Jesus Christ in Rome. His Master's word concerning him fulfilled, and his work done, he fell asleep. The great fire of Rome happened in the twelfth year of the reign of Nero, or A.D. 64. And if the persecution ensued in the same year, or at the commencement of the following year, it follows that the date of Paul's death was either at the close of A.D. 64, or in A.D. 65. There are only fanciful portraits of St Paul; but of the Cæsar before whom he had been confronted the student may look upon the veritable likeness in the coins and medals executed in his reign, and in the marble bust in the Roman Gallery of the British Museum. The physiognomist will observe how the countenance of the saint's murderer coincides with his character as drawn by historians.

CHAPTER XXXI.

AFTER the affecting character of the last glimpse obtained
of Luke, it cannot be doubted that he remained in Rome
until after the martyrdom of Paul. As far as literature
avails, there is only a step between that event and the death
of Luke. Dim and contradictory are the notes of tradition
concerning his situation in the interval. A consideration
of the circumstances of the case might direct to the probable course which he pursued. It is very unlikely, after
his friend's martyrdom, and the object of his mission in
Rome had thereby come to an end, that he would remain
in a place that must have become a dangerous residence for
him. He had quitted Jerusalem upon the occasion of the
persecution that arose upon the martyrdom of Stephen, and
he would now leave Rome upon the persecution that was raised
against the saints in that city. A necessity for flight was as
pressing now as then. The language of Tacitus, in speaking of
the Christians, shows the light in which they were regarded
by the heathen of whatever class. The prejudices of these
were based on similar grounds with those which inspired
the hatred of the Jews against them. Both alike disdained
the lowly appearance of the Messiah, and for this reason,
and for concomitant reasons, both persecuted His followers.
Paul had said in his last letter to Timothy, " Wherein "
(that is, in preaching the gospel) " I suffer as an evil-
doer, even unto bonds ; but the Word of God is not bound."

His imprisonment had rather subserved to spread the knowledge of the gospel. He that sitteth in the heavens knows how to make the wrath of man to praise Him ; and like as the persecution at Jerusalem sent forth missionaries for Christ on all sides, so also the persecution in Rome was followed by the same result. Both were ultimate triumphs for Christ. By the dispersion of the Christians from Rome, the knowledge of the gospel was conveyed to the provinces : forasmuch as from Rome likewise the disciples went everywhere preaching the Word.

It would be interesting to know who were the friends that accompanied the venerable confessor upon his retiring from the scene of his last ministry and companionship with his beloved fellow-labourer, and that conducted him to his proposed destination. Perhaps, being perilous times, they were afterwards of the number of those who obtained a martyr's crown. That upon quitting Rome, Luke returned to the East, would be supposed ; and with this agrees every early note concerning him. But accounts differ in representing to which country he repaired. Some report that he returned to Greece. By some writers it is said that Luke retired to Bithynia. And Sixtus Senensis writes, " that having preached in all the regions of Alexandria and the Pentapolis, he died at Alexandria" (" Bibliotheca Sancta," p. 17). But that at the age of about eighty Luke should have gone to Egypt, is quite improbable, nor that he went to Bithynia are there any grounds to suppose. It is not seen that he had ever been there before, or that he had been nearer to that province than Troas. Achaia, on the contrary, has reasonable claims for the belief that it might have been the country to which he retired, and which became the last place of his residence. That peninsula was the nearest place to Italy with which he had been personally connected. And besides this, it had for him other advantages. At Corinth resided Christians to whose re-

gards he had been passionately recommended by Paul in
the letter, which, along with fellow-delegates, he bare upon
the subject of the alms-gathering for the poor saints of
Judea. Here, after the arrival of the Apostle upon his last
visit to Corinth, he had resided for some months. Here he
had enjoyed fellowship with the members of that Church,
and of other brethren who joined the Apostle's company
upon that occasion, some of whose names appear at the
close of the epistle which he addressed to the Romans from
thence. Here, as it transpires in the Epistle to Timothy,
recently written, Erastus still abode. It is refreshing to
linger amidst these, the last associations of the Evangelist ;
to think how he would have been received with open arms
by a former companion who had been joined in the glowing
commendations contained in the letter which they conveyed
from Philippi. Here, too, perhaps, still abode Gaius, " the
host of the whole Church." With sentiments similar to
those with which the Christians regarded, as long as he
survived, " the disciple whom Jesus loved," would the
Christians of Corinth have regarded him who had been the
constant companion of the Apostle of the Gentiles during
his bonds, suffering for their sake. It is consistent with the
principle of Christian love to conclude that he who had bestowed so much solicitude for the solace of Christ's prisoner
in Rome, should receive for a recompense the solace, in his
retirement, of the Christians at Corinth. It pleased the
divine Master that this companion of His servant should
survive awhile, to exhibit in his person the example of the
most aged disciple and teacher of His Word to be found in
Greece. The advantage hereof is manifest. An aged saint
is a monument of the divine faithfulness. The friends of
this venerable confessor, who included all that had bene-
fited by his publications and teaching, were by his presence
and counsel confirmed in the truths which it had been the
employment of his life to declare ; they were refreshed by

the manifestation of his unwavering confidence in the evidence and value of those truths, and by his profession of the sufficiency of the grace whereby he had been sustained throughout all his labours, and was still sustained.

Regrets are sometimes expressed that there are no authentic accounts of the closing scenes in the lives of the apostles and evangelists. Only the martyrdom of one apostle (James) is related in Scripture, and only an account of the martyrdom of one other saint, namely, Stephen the Deacon. May not the divine compassion for the frailty of human nature, in its regards towards benefactors and worthies deceased, account for the fewness of notices of this kind that are found in Holy Scripture? And does not this paucity of intelligence concerning the death of the saints, whether under the old or the new covenant, serve to prompt a lesson? As the only object of worship, it is infinitely proper that God should be jealous of His own glory. That God is thus jealous is, likewise, for the honour and happiness of man. And, therefore, the advantage is great of shutting out occasions for an undue exaltation of human agents, holy and excellent though they may have been. Apostles and evangelists *lived* for our benefit, but they did not *die* for us. Only One both lived and died for us. Of the life and death of this One, memoirs are given in four sacred documents. Attention is to be fixed on these. Accordingly, the subject of them, especially as it relates to the death and resurrection of Jesus Christ, formed the text of all the discourses of the apostles. And, as any preference given to Paul, or to Peter, or to Apollos, or to any of the saints, was repudiated by themselves when living, in jealousy for the honour of the Divine Dispenser of gifts to His servants, how great a wrong is done to their memory, when, being departed, any measure of duliation is bestowed upon them !

The legends which represent that Luke suffered a

martyr's death may certainly be rejected, their accounts being alike contradictory one to another, and opposed to the earliest and most reliable authorities. But, that he died a natural death may be supposed upon the considerations of the quiet character of his ministry, the respect in which he would have been held as a physician, and the benefits of his professional skill to his neighbours. Each of these circumstances would have been conducive to his security. Also, that his was a peaceable death is alike a thought pleasant to entertain, and conformable with his long-life sympathies with the many lovely characters and happy scenes depicted by his pen. Surely, there, in the chamber where lay that servant of Jesus, surrounded by the dimmed eyes of the friends of himself and of his divine Master, those angels were again present concerning whose visits to earth he had told the sweet stories in his books.

That in his retirement Luke had pursued to the end of his life what had been his prime occupation since he was chosen into the service of his Lord, is represented in the following stanza, found written in the front of an ancient Latin copy of his Gospel :—

> " LAMP OF THE CHURCH is the sacred name of Luke,
>   An apostolic man, full of holy zeal.
>   This Gospel, a sacred offering to God,
>   He wrote, and spread throughout the Gentile world.
>   Himself, through many bonds followed Paul :
>   And after teaching in *Achaia*, he passed to high heaven."*
>
>   [*Achaia* is here substituted for Bithynia.]

If, as it has been represented, Luke survived Paul two years, the time of his death was about A.D. 67 or 68.   By

* " Ecclesiæ Lampas sacer, hic est nomine Lucas,
    Qui vir Apostolicus divine flamine plenus.
    Hoc Evangelium Domino tribuente sacratum
    Scripsit, et in totum sparsit Latinissime mundum.
    Ipse sequens, per plurima vincula Paulum ;
    Bithnyaque docens, migravit ad arduum cœlum."

the Western Churches his anniversary is observed October 18, and by the Orientals April 23. April 22 is marked in Latin necrologies as the anniversary of *Lucius of Cyrene.* Is not the contiguity of these two dates an indication of some confusion among the traditionists? For the benefit of his credulous readers, Alban Butler, in his "Lives of Saints," relates, with a solemnity proper to real history, "Luke's bones were translated from Patras in Achaia, in 357, by order of Constantius" (so it was known where to find them more than two hundred and eighty years after their burial), "and deposited, together with those of St Andrew and Timothy, in a gold chest in the porch of St Sophia at Constantinople." He adds that "On the occasion of this translation, some distribution was made of the relics of Saint Luke. St Gaudentius procured part for his church at Brescia. St Paulinus possessed a portion in St Felix Church at Nola, and with a part enriched a church at Fondi. Baronius mentions that the head of St Luke was brought by St Gregory from Constantinople to Rome, and put in the church of his monastery of St Andrew. Some of his relics are kept in the Greek monastery on Mount Athos in Greece." [*Saint Luke's Day.*]

CHAPTER XXXII.

HAVING found that Lucius the Cyrenian, a teacher at Antioch, mentioned in Acts xiii. 1, was the Evangelist himself, we have traced Luke from his native city to Jerusalem. We have seen him occupied there in fellowship with the infant Church, and in procuring materials for his Gospel. We have seen that, having by reason of persecution been driven from Jerusalem, he travelled to Antioch; that he was there engaged in the important ministry of establishing the first Christian Church, derived directly from pagan ranks, and in furnishing the Churches raised throughout Syria and Asia Minor with a written Gospel. We have seen that, after having spent several years in Antioch, he went to Troas; that he was one of the company of four missionaries who first brought the gospel to Europe; that in Philippi he was occupied for several years in a ministry similar to that in which he had been engaged at Antioch, and in promoting the circulation of his Gospel in Greece; that from Philippi he proceeded on a mission from the Churches of Macedonia to Corinth; that after his visit to that city he returned to Philippi, from whence, by appointment of the Churches of Macedonia and Achaia, he was united with St Paul in a deputation to Jerusalem. We have seen that St Paul, having been apprehended at Jerusalem, and sent to Cæsarea, Luke accompanied him thither, and remained in that city during the two years of the Apostle's detention there. We have seen that, with

St Paul, he suffered shipwreck at Malta; that he became a confessor by accepting companionship with him during the period of his imprisonment in Rome until the Apostle's death; and that afterwards, returning from thence, he died in Greece.

Although the character of Luke has been discovered in the several situations of his life as thus treated, it will be profitable to cast together a few of its prominent lineaments; for by the extended view of his history which has been taken, the means are now at length afforded to obtain a commensurate knowledge thereof. It is character by which individuals are chiefly distinguished; and it is the expression thereof, unfolded in their conduct, which alone attracts and interests the sympathies of the observer. Instructive to the biographer is the observation by S. T. Coleridge, where he says: "The great end of biography is to fix the attention and interest the feelings on those qualities which have made a particular life worthy of being recorded" ("The Friend"). And by Stanfield it is observed: "The effects produced by a life are exactly according to the nature and efficiency of the individual character" ("Essay," p. 275).

1. In this glance attention is primarily directed to Luke's character as *a writer of Holy Scripture*. Cicero advises, "In every undertaking, the first thing to be done is to obtain the ability for its performance by a *diligent preparation*" ("De Officiis," 21). How Luke possessed this pre-requisite is manifest by the note prefixed to his Gospel, the several particulars of which have been reviewed in the sixth chapter while describing his Researches, and is also observable in the coincidences of the several situations in which he was found with the events of the Acts of the Apostles, which were evidently described from concurrent and preparatory notes. Another requisite for profitable writing is *vividness of intellectual perception*, described by Stanfield as "a pro-

pensity innate or acquired—a faculty of seizing upon and receiving into the mind with efficacy and enjoyment everything that has relation to the favourite subject" ("Essay," p. 21). In what measure Luke possessed this faculty finds illustrations in every page of his writings. Of him it may be truly said, as it was of a celebrated Roman, in the words of an author of transcendent powers of perception—

> "He was a great observer, and he looked
> Quite through the deeds of men."

Besides these qualifications for literary undertakings, there must be possessed *an ability to convey intelligence in a lucid and interesting manner.* "Men of keen sensibility do not think differently from others; but contemplating more ardently, they receive deeper impressions, and therefore are able, with more distinctness and animation, to delineate the objects which they present." It is by the measure of this realising ability that classes of writers are graduated. Luke's favourite pursuit was the knowledge of the facts relating to human redemption. The delight found in what he acquired of that knowledge impelled him to seek for an increase of it. And the joy at his discoveries both prompted him to communicate those discoveries, and enabled him to do so with commensurate vividness. Ideas obtain expression by words and sentences; the words being chosen, and the sentences arranged, in a manner which shall most appropriately expound the writer's mind. This power does not consist in an affluence of words, but in a proper choice and happy combination of them. Words and sentences are to an emphatic writer what soldiers and battalions are to a skilful general. Here, as elsewhere, compactness of parts gives strength to the whole. Speaking of certain compositions, Charles Lamb said, "There is a *New Testament plainness* in them which affected me very much." Impressiveness consists with simplicity. Simple are the signs by which intellect may commune with intellect, especially by the Holy Spirit's promptings. Luke's writings speak to the student with the simplicity that his witnesses spake to him, and with the impressiveness.

Whether he reports facts received from them, or those he had observed himself, his narratives partake the same realising distinctness by which the subjects of them had been first conceived. He sets the incidents and scenes of the gospel history and the Acts of the Apostles before us as he perceived them ; he introduces us to his acquaintances ; he conducts us with him on his journeys ; he causes us to see what he saw ; to hear what he heard ; to feel what he felt. To such a writer are the emphatic words applicable, "To be communicative of good is a royalty and a beam of glory" (Worthington's Life of Joseph Mede, prefixed to his Works, 1672).

To account for this excellence in Luke's writings, it may be said that he was indebted for it to inspiration. But it must be observed that inspiration does not exempt the agent from the ordinary requirements of composition. As genius elevates to conceptions of the grand or the beautiful, so divine inspiration directs to what is truthful. It directs, sanctifies, and governs, but it does not change the constitutional powers and educational abilities of its subjects. It does not set aside their characteristics and endowments, natural or acquired. The prophets of the Old Testament, whether princes or shepherds, were by nature poets. In the case of the Apostle Paul, how conspicuously was observed in him his natural temperament, both in his conduct and writings. And in Peter, John, James, and each of the other writers of the New Testament Scriptures, the character of their writings is as distinctive as were their person-ages and conduct. Yet they were all equally inspired to an utterance of what was infallible in argument or divine in instruction, and the Evangelists into a relation of what was essentially true as historians.

By a certain class of writers, endeavours are made to dislodge Luke from his place in the sacred records. They allege that he has nowhere claimed to have been inspired. But neither does Mark, who, like him, was not an apostle, make that claim. Yet Luke includes himself in a list of prophets and teachers, and professes to have acted under inspiration upon an important occasion (Acts xiii. 1). Nor need the clamour raised against the authenticity of his books disturb the pious reader's conclusions concerning the evidence they perceive of their divine inspiration. Those conclusions are confirmed by their essential conformity with the writings of the other Evangelists, and with those of the apostles. It has been seen how that by St Paul he was recognised as a writer of a Gospel (2 Cor. viii. 18). His writings have been accepted with affectionate confidence by the faithful through successive ages, and as divine documents they have been conducive to the conversion of multitudes of readers, and to the edification of the Church, equally with the other writings of the New Testament. Only those who will accept no evidence will demand more than this.

2. *Luke's character was simple.* Character is read in the conduct of the individual, in the various situations and circumstances of his daily life, and prominently in those which are eventful, when the soul is exhibited through action. It has been said, "Man pursuing his objects, employed in acts of magnanimity and benevolence, glowing with elevated sentiments or encountering dangers and overcoming difficulties—a man thus highly engaged cannot be contemplated without communicating to the observer a sense of that spirit which influences him" (Stanfield's "Essay," p. 109). A leading quality observed in Luke's conduct is *simplicity.* Christian simplicity is the reverse of

weakness. It is a power. It sustains application, and it guides to the shortest and surest methods of attaining success in the object of its aim. It is contented with few objects, but upon these it concentrates its attention and care. It is called " singleness of heart," because it is an inward principle, its outward developments being candour and truthfulness. It is confiding towards those possessing its own character : these it is ready to believe, and to these to reveal. It is placid as a shaded streamlet, which no wind can reach, no storm can ruffle. It is steady in its course ; it is always progressive, always persevering. That in Luke was observed this character appears in every page of his biography. In him simplicity was a reigning principle. Jesus was his copy. The person of Jesus was his religion (1 Pet. ii. 7) ; and his writings are both the proof and the fruits of the entireness of his accord with His meek disciples, being the result of an intercourse with them for nearly forty years.

3. *Luke's character was spiritual.* It has been seen that Luke was an example of a convert at the eventful Pentecostal season. Although a Gentile, Luke had not been an idolator ; nor yet as a proselyte had he been a Pharisee. No traces are detected in his writings of an inclination towards the carnality that belonged to these. His delight had been in studying the character and attributes of the Supreme Being, as they are unfolded in the Sacred Scriptures, and also in the relation therein recorded of the divine providence towards the Church, in its beginnings and progress throughout all its preceding history. No wonder, then, with a temper so simple and habits so studious, that when the facts of human redemption by Jesus Christ were presented to his mind, their simplicity, along with the spirituality of the doctrines thereto belonging, commended the intelligence at once to his judgment and affections. And whereas the descriptions which he

received concerning the intellectual character of Jesus, and the grace of His teaching, won his admiration, his conversion to Christ as the Saviour, amidst scenes of mysterious influence, compulsory beyond any process of reasoning, would have confirmed and heightened his sympathies with the spiritual character of the new dispensation, of which he now witnessed the dawn. His disposition, and sympathy with the new dispensation, may be read in the circumstance that, of the eighty-six instances wherein mention is made of the HOLY GHOST or SPIRIT in the New Testament, fifty-five of them are found in his two books.

4. *Luke's character was amiable.* In Solomon's investiture of wisdom with personality, he represents that grace as " Rejoicing in the habitable parts of the earth, and saying, My delights are with the sons of men " (Prov. viii. 31). Like wisdom, an amiable character has an aspect towards those that are near, and its sympathies are towards all. By the amiable person a radiance is shed upon all within his sphere. But beyond the common walk of this uncommon grace, this quality was enhanced in the person of Luke by a divine endowment. Having been baptized by the first outpouring of the Holy Ghost upon believers, he became possessed of a double share of this divine grace. His amiable disposition is seen in the choice which he made for the subject of his pen—that subject being no other than the Antitype of Solomon's prophetic personification—a subject than which no writer except his co-evangelists ever had or will have its equal.

The spirit and manner in which Luke accomplished his object, manifests the fellowship of his sympathies with its excellences; and that fellowship was equally shown in his account of the Acts of the Apostles—the ministry exercised by these being Christ's own cause. Luke's character, in its amiable aspect, is witnessed in the *design* contemplated by him in both his books, as it is declared in his letter to his friend Theophilus; and it is shown in the manner in which that design is *executed.* Here the character of Luke is discovered as if portrayed by his own hand. It seems impossible to separate his own character from that of his work.

This aspect of his character is seen in the *delight* that he takes in pleasing incidents, or in investing his incidents with some pleasing point or happy conclusion, even as a flower in a graceful hand seems the more beautiful.

Predominant in an amiable disposition is *cheerfulness.* Upon the rejection of St Paul's testimony by the Jews at Rome, he declared that he would turn to the Gentiles, and that they would receive it. And a bright example of a gladsome reception of the Gospel appears in Luke. This pleasing characteristic reigns throughout his writings. His first book opens with a scene tinted by the heraldic light of the morning star. It opens with the melody of angels beginning a new song upon earth, singing of "peace and good-will to men." It thereafter depicts the Royal Babe sanctifying the straw bed by its tender pressure. It exhibits the greeting given to the Infant by an aged saint who had waited for this "consolation," his hoary locks overshadowing the lovely Face as he stoops to welcome its advent with a holy kiss. Proceeding from Bethlehem, scene after scene, and incident after incident, are redolent with cheerfulness, and discover the amiable disposition of him who selected them, having received them from the lips of his witnesses, and arranged them in the order in which they are read. Upon the amiable character of Luke's Gospel, Oosterzee says, "In studying it, we are more attracted by the loveliness than even by the dignity of the Lord; and the Holy One born of Mary appears before our eyes as the fairest of the children of men. Does it not even seem as if Luke had felt the necessity of transferring to his Master (the Lord) the very calling to which his own life had been hitherto devoted, while depicting to us far oftener than the other Evangelists the great *Iatros*, the Physician who came not only to minister, but who also went about doing good and healing (Acts x. 38), who felt compassion for all diseases, both of mind and body, and whose power was present to heal (Luke v. 17)."

Disposition is affected by the individual's professional vocation. The physician is habitually devoted to an amelioration of the sufferings of humanity by disease. Partaking the same nature, and liable to disease alike with their patients, they are schooled in benevolence. His biography has shown how, with a physician's eye, Luke studied the life and miracles of Jesus, and how with a heart wherein the love of God was shed abroad, he delighted to record acts of the Saviour's compassion, whether exercised in removing the pains of the body, or the sorrows of the mind. That it should have been objected by the misanthropic detractor, that "Luke took pleasure in setting forth the conversion of sinners and the exaltation of the humble" (*Renan*), shows more clearly in what measure Luke possessed that tenderness of feeling which deepens the fountain of friendship.

But beyond the characteristics of the physician, Luke's Gospel also conveys sentiments of health and buoyancy. How many are its pages which seem to ring with cheerfulness, and how many are its notes expressing joy and joyfulness, glad and gladness (his favourite words), whether in the communicator or the receiver! In concluding the book, even the last adieus of the disciples with their Lord are represented, not as those with tears, but as "returning to Jerusalem with great joy" (xxiv. 52).

And surely Luke described his own experience when he reports from the lips of Philip how the Eunuch went on his way *rejoicing*. Moreover, when subsequently seen in the exercise of his own ministry, conjoined with his company at Antioch, Barnabas, having gone thither and witnessed its fruits. was *glad ;* and when by the Church there raised, sharing the grace of the Holy Spirit's presence and power, Antioch became at once an eminent station, from whence went forth the feet of them that conveyed the *glad* tidings of peace to the world. Gladsome, likewise, were the results which attended Luke's residence at Philippi, happy evidence of which is found in St Paul's commendations of the Philippians in his epistle addressed to that Church, the most cheerful of all that Apostle's letters, and wherein he makes *joy* the key-note of the Christian life (iv. 4).

And then as *benevolence* appertains to the amiable character, the stamp of this grace also is set upon all Luke's writings. Of the expressions and deeds of compassion related of Jesus in the Gospels, many of the most affecting of them are reported alone by his pen ! How like his Lord's was his own ministry in this respect ! The first instance of a public collection by a Church in Europe was that made by the Church at Antioch. And how zealously he had been engaged in promoting a similar object in Philippi, is witnessed by his having been chosen by the Churches of Macedonia and Achaia as a deputy to accompany St Paul with their alms to Jerusalem.

5. *Luke an example of a friend.* Simple, spiritual, amiable, the individual possessing these attributes is susceptible of friendship in the highest degree and of the sublimest kind.

Such a friendship is *attractive.* Cicero says, " Virtue," (by which he means every moral excellence), " wins and preserves friendship." The friend of high mark will possess merits indigenous to the individual, whereby a charm peculiar to himself will pervade his demeanour, vivifying every excellence with which he is endowed, and intensifying the appreciation of his character. What was Luke's outward appearance is not in the least known. But that his character was in this manner attractive is certain by an abundance of evidence. His associates were allured and edified by his devotion towards God, by his love of wisdom in its divinest relations, by his communication of the knowledge he had acquired, by a simplicity that chastens every excellence, a spirituality that improves every opportunity of intercourse, and an affability that invites to confidence.

A friend is self-denying. The highest of all examples of friendship " pleased not Himself." Selfishness is dislodged by friendship. The wills of two friends become one will in whatever relates to the circumstances of friendship. Indeed, there is often more pleasure in concurring in the wish of a friend than in accomplishing one's own wish, which had otherwise gone in another direction. Of this self-sacrificing devotion to the claims of friendship, Luke's devotion of himself to the constraints endured during several years' companionship with the Lord's prisoner in bonds is perhaps an unparalleled example of self-denying friendship. In him was found a friend distinguished for a modesty that delighted in self-obscuration.

Friendship is responsive. His praise having been in all the Churches, Luke is everywhere seen to be surrounded with friends. There had been in the beginning the Apostles and brethren with whom he was associated in Christian communion in Jerusalem. Afterwards it is seen, when occupying a more prominent station in the Church, how strongly Barnabas commended himself to his affections. Then there has been observed his friendship with Mark the Evangelist. Then there was Timothy, to whom Luke was first introduced at Troas, a young man loved and honoured as Paul's son in the gospel, who became his faithful fellow-labourer. At Philippi were added to the number of Luke's friends Lydia and her converted household, the first-fruits of the preaching of the gospel in Europe. At Corinth, Luke had for his friends Gaius and Erastus, men of renown in the Church and of standing in the city, with others whose names occur in his history. At Cæsarea he obtained a renewal of his fellowship with Philip the Deacon. On his voyage to Italy, his friendship with Aristarchus, commenced in Macedonia, was cemented by their mutual peril, and by their joint-engagement as companions of the Apostle Paul. In Rome, the persons whose names occur in Paul's epistles written there as his fellow-labourers, or as messengers from different Churches, were all in the list of Luke's friends; and above all was the friendship enjoyed by our Evangelist with the Apostle Paul himself, the character of which, as it has been previously described, is resplendent in all their intercourse.

How charming is the consideration that, under the Holy Spirit's providence, every reader of Luke's books is indebted for the pleasure and instruction derived from their perusal to FRIENDSHIP!

Describing from an impression made upon him by a physiognomical scrutiny of a portrait of a person he had never seen, Lavater sketched his character in these words: "He loves tranquillity, order, and simple eloquence; he takes a clear view of the subject he examines; he thinks accurately; his mind rejects all that is false or obscure; he gives with a liberal hand; he forgives with a generous heart, and takes delight in serving his fellow-creatures. You may safely depend upon what he says or what he promises. His sensibility never degenerates into weakness. He esteems worth, find it where he may. He is the honour of humanity, and of his station in life. Respected personage! I know you not, but you shall not escape me in the great day which shall collect us all together; and your form, disengaged and purified from all earthly imperfection, shall appear to me, and catch my ravished eye in the midst of the myriads in the realms of light." How singularly appropriate are these words to represent in miniature the reader's friend, St Luke, and also to express the sentiment of the responsive heart towards him!

6. *The influence of Luke's character.* That involuntary and little thought of concomitant of human conduct, the influence exerted by individuals upon others, is an important feature of every person's life. For good or for evil, this mysterious principle silently and surely works in and by every intelligent being. Renowned warriors, celebrated philosophers, eminent painters, and skilful craftsmen, of however remote a period, have all exerted a definite influence upon successive aspirants in the several fields of emulation. It was this principle, in its moral potency, that our Lord touched when He declared concerning His disciples, " Ye are the salt of the earth." In the Church, God has all sorts of saints. They are of different constitutional dispositions; they are in different spheres, and have different associates. In some the capacity is small, and the individual may be unconscious of possessing any influence, and therefore insensible of its obligations. As a pebble cast into the stream produces its little emotion of circles, so no intelligence, however tiny, is without its relative measure of influence in society. A little child was the favourite example set before His disciples by the Head of all influence in the Church; and a recognition of this principle, in its minutest measure, was beautifully made when, upon the death of two of his children, the Reverend Samuel Reynolds, father of Sir Joshua, wrote, "I think with pleasure upon some of their actions, which our Saviour points out in children, and which it is always good to have before our eyes. They are little preachers of righteousness, which grown persons may listen to with pleasure. Actions are more powerful than words; and I cannot but thank God, sometimes, *for the benefit of their example.*"

In its higher manifestations, the impress of a permanently salubrious influence upon other minds is the prerogative of superior intelligence and completeness of character. A person glowing with elevated sentiments, habitually developed by word and conduct, cannot live without communicating corresponding impressions. Luke's influence corresponded with his situation in the Church. In Jerusalem, the aversion of the Jewish mind to any foreign contact occasioned it to be limited while he resided in Jerusalem. But when from thence he repaired to Antioch, his influence was soon perceptible. It was seen in the success that attended the preaching of the gospel to the heathen by himself and his company. It was seen in the confirmation given, by their example, to the word spoken. It was seen in the "great number that believed and turned unto the Lord," where such a result had not been anticipated: Luke and his company having been the first to witness the fulfilment of that word, "I am found of them that sought me not" (Isa. lxv. 1).

But Luke's influence chiefly flows through his *writings*. Our Lord taught, saying, "So is the kingdom of God, as if a man should cast seed into the ground, and should sleep and wake night and day, and the seed should spring and grow up, he knoweth not how." Even so, Luke being absent from his readers, and personally unknown to most of them, yet by his narrative embued the Churches with a knowledge of those facts in detail which were proposed in the discourses of the Apostles. How great was felt to have been the influence of the Evangelist through that publication is denoted by a testimony of St Paul. But when to that boon was added a second book, declaring the progress of a reception of the facts and doctrines of the gospel for nearly thirty years, by one familiar with the preachers, and who himself had had a share in the work of evangelisation, where are the words which had then expressed the sense of the Churches' obligations to Luke as a writer of Holy Scripture? And the influence upon those who, through faith in the facts of his Gospel, became members of Christ's mystical body, is to be traced throughout the Church's history. Pleasing evidence remains in the pages of Irenæus, one of the earliest ecclesiastical writers, of the influence of Luke's unique book, the Acts of the Apostles, whose testimony may be regarded as the voice of the Churches in general in the second century. Irenæus was a pupil of Polycarp, a disciple of the Evangelist St John, and who suffered a martyr's death in the reign of Marcus Antoninus, *the philosopher*. Regarding Luke's Gospel and Acts as statute-books, Irenæus says, " Possibly God has so ordered that many parts of the gospel should be declared to us by Luke ; *which all are under a necessity of receiving:* that so it might be received. And so likewise of his subsequent testimony, which he hath given concerning the acts and doctrines of the Apostles ; that by both they might possess a sincere and uncorrupted relation of truth, and be saved. Therefore his testimony is true, and the doctrine of the Apostles is manifest and uniform ; without any deceit ; hiding nothing from men ; nor teaching one thing in private and another in public."

Speaking of the traces of the Acts of the Apostles in the pages of Irenæus, Dr George Benson writes :—" I have, upon examination, found above thirty places in the works of that Father where the Book of Acts is quoted : in several of which Luke is named as the author, and the credit of the Evangelist and the usefulness of his writings is asserted and defended." And hereupon Dr Benson proffers these appropriate observations :—" We may, I think, very fairly and with great justness conclude, that if any history of former times deserves credit, the Acts of the Apostles ought to be received and credited. And if the history of the Acts be true, Christianity cannot be false. For a doctrine so good in itself, and attended with so many miraculous and divine testimonies, has all the possible marks of a divine revelation " (" First Planting of Christianity ").

As an evidence of the estimation in which this book was held by the faithful of subsequent ages, the remark of Erasmus may be quoted, where he says, " he found more various readings in the Acts of the Apostles than in any other of the sacred books of the New Testament,"—a certain proof of the frequency with which it was copied to supply demands for it. And, since the earlier ages, how inconceivably great has been the influence of Luke's books upon the minds of readers throughout successive generations, and among the peoples speaking the one hundred and eighty tongues into which the New Testament has been translated !

> " The force of Luke's unwearied zeal
> The saints still in his Gospel feel ;
> There Jesu's wonders brightly stand
> Recorded by his graphic hand."
>
> *Bishop Ken*, A.D. 1700.

There is felt the influence, with which every Christian congregation is familiar, by the celebration of the Advent of Christ, in lessons obtained from Luke's pages ; and there is the influence which is felt by the devout worshipper, in churches wherein, Sabbath after Sabbath, are chanted the hymns of Zacharias, Mary, and Simeon, and which inspired the bard of the " Christian Year " when he addressed the Evangelist in the verse—

> " Thou hast an ear for angels' songs,
> A breath the gospel trump to fill ;
> And taught by thee, the Church prolongs
> Her hymns of high thanksgiving still."

Works by the same Author.

Works by the same Author.

"We announce this publication with lively satisfaction ; and recommend it to all who study our religious history. The Appendix consists of an alphabetical catalogue of books, and some manuscripts collected by the author, interspersed with numerous notes full of interesting citations, and recondite and useful information."—(*C. Coquerel in*) *le Lien, Journal des Eglises Reformées de France : Paris, August* 1852.

II.

Foolscap 8vo, price 5s.,

THE LIFE OF CLAUDE BROUSSON,

DOCTOR OF LAWS AND ADVOCATE OF PARLIAMENT, AFTERWARDS EVANGELIST OF THE DESERT AND MARTYR, A.D. 1698.

" This volume is one of the most deeply-interesting publications of our day. Claude Brousson was a principal leader of that heroic band which, amidst incredible sufferings, and in the daily prospect of martyrdom, upheld the doctrines of evangelical truth in France. Mr Baynes has been long engaged in tracing the career of Brousson, and the result of his inquiries is eminently adapted to raise our admiration of a man who combined intelligence with great legal knowledge, fearless honesty, intense devotion, and the mildest charity. We cordially commend the memoir to the early acquaintance and confidence of our readers."—*Eclectic Review, Jan.* 1854.

" The work is not merely a biography, however interesting, but embraces, on an extensive scale, a history of transactions most nearly and feelingly connected with the records of purified Christianity in France. The Revocation of the Edict of Nantes, in 1685, is generally regarded as a great event, reflecting extreme infamy upon the guilty authors, the Gallican clergy of Rome in France. But with the continuation of the career of savage and hypocritical persecution, onward to the beginning of the next century, almost universal ignorance prevails. This is remedied by the life of Brousson, which, founded as it is upon the most unquestionable and original authority, gives the work peculiar value."—*The Rev. Joseph Mendham, A.M., Author of " The History of the Council of Trent," "Literary Policy of the Church of Rome," &c.*

"The two volumes, sequent in subject as they are in appearance, constitute a trustworthy and popular guide for the English reader to the secret annals of the Protestant Church of France—one of the most romantic, and at the same time neglected episodes in European history."—*Athenæum, August* 1853.

A NOTE BY THE AUTHOR.

In a Periodical boasting an immense circulation, it is related concerning Brousson, "*the heroic pastor was condemned and hung;*" and, illustrating the text, appears a fancy figure, at full length, of rueful features and hideous mien, as of a veritable malefactor. The figure is drawn with a rope round the neck, standing midway upon a ladder, and under it is inscribed "CLAUDE BROUSSON!" (*See Good Words, Jan.* 1868.) But the case was otherwise than there represented. Brousson *was not hung.* He was condemned to the rack, and afterwards to be broken on the wheel. He was bound to the rack, but its pains were remitted. The method of execution by the wheel consisted of the body being fastened on beams in the form of a St Andrew cross, let into grooves of a large wheel; the wheel laying horizontally upon a scaffold, the limbs were broken by an iron bar. There is an instance of a martyr having received forty strokes in forty hours, before he received what was called the *coup de grace* (*Witnesses in Sackcloth, p.* 83). When Brousson had been bound to the wheel, orders were received to mitigate his sufferings by the substitution of death by garrotting. Accordingly, as he lay bound, he was strangled, and after death his bones were broken by the bar. The scene and the martyr's conduct are described in his Life, pages 335-7.

4

By the same Author—continued.

18mo, price 6d.,

THE PROPHETIC SITE OF CALVARY SURVEYED.

A BIBLICAL EXERCISE FOUNDED ON LEVITICUS i. 10, 11, iv. 12, xiv. 1–7, xvi. 8–11, and 21.

"Let him, then, who searches the Holy Scriptures only fairly make known his best apprehensions; and let him be heard with patience; and let Truth, that charming offspring of Eternal light, come forth, and be produced by those slow degrees, and by that process of inquiry, which the Divine Author hath ordained "—*Edward King's* "*Morsels of Criticism.*"

"Mr Baynes considers that he finds in the prophecies of the Old Testament, and the typical rites of the Jews, as well as in the words of the Evangelists, and in other sources, cogent reasons for concluding that Calvary was in an open place (not a mount) to the *north* of the city. . . . We do not mean to say that we see any very weighty or decisive reasons against such an opinion."—*The Builder, Jan.* 1858.

"A painstaking attempt to decide, *on Scripture data*, a question which has much perplexed travellers and archæologists."—*Journal of Biblical Literature.*

"This little tract contains more than is promised by its title. It is a practical and suggestive discussion of the several points to be kept in view, and sets forth the main question at least lucidly and calmly."—*Athenæum.*